D1204776

The Twilight Men

THE TWILIGHT MEN *A Novel*

BY OTTO BASIL

Translated by Thomas Weyr

Meredith Press New York

No character in this story is intended to represent any actual person; all the incidents of the story are entirely fictional in nature.

First U.S. edition

Library of Congress Catalog Card Number: 68-9517

MANUFACTURED IN THE UNITED STATES OF AMERICA FOR MEREDITH PRESS

CONTENTS

In a completely mundane world
such as described here,
through which, however,
the outlines of today's real world can be glanced,
the author cannot pardon anyone,
only negative characters can occur.
The author considers himself to be
one of them.

The Twilight Men

When the Twilight of the Gods begins,
the Twilight Men appear . . .

OF THE AMAZONS

November 9, was a Saturday. A wet and cold wind swept sluggishly through the streets of Heydrich—Heydrich in the Kyffhäuser Mountains—and stripped the last leaves from the trees. Snow lay in the air, and a feeling of waterlogged decay. The light of late morning had swallowed all color; the scenery turned pale and unreal in the sticky and milkily flowing dusk.

November 9, 10, and 11 ranked among the most strictly observed national days of mourning. But the memory of the great infamy of 1918 had begun to fade even within the ranks of the party, and so the mood of this fog-shrouded autumn morning was no different from other days. A day began, a day like all others.

After a cold shower had tuned his body, Höllriegl stepped as if walking on springs; he almost skipped down the stairs to his consulting room. Freshly waxed military boots creaked on the wooden steps. As so often recently, he was angry with Burjak for not polishing the brass plate on the door. Of late his serf had become increasingly slovenly. (He treated his serfs too well—an old mistake.) The plate said in Gothic script:

ALBIN TOTILA HÖLLRIEGL
Radiation Tracker
Heydrich Office of the National Socialist Guild for Oscillation
Removal of Radiation Damage of All Kinds
Protective Electrodes, Radium Jewelry, Oscillation Belts

Deradiation Chains According to the VDI Rules for Sidereal Equipment
Guidance on Northern Aryan Living
Office Hours: from 9 to 11 except Saturday
Closed Sundays and Holidays
DEATH TO EARTH RADIATION

The gyromant crossed the soberly furnished waiting room with its twelve chairs grouped around the table in star formation and entered his office, which doubled as laboratory and was used for relaxation and meditation exercises. A picture of the aged Führer Adolf Hitler covered almost the whole of the narrow far wall. Höllriegl pulled back his shoulders, let his heels slam together, and lifted his arm in the German salute. Over the years, the picture of the Führer—life-sized and in color—had taken on a reddish hue as if immersed in twilight. The man's features, which bespoke fanatic determination and unbending will for victory, thus had become softer and milder, almost paternal. But at the same time—and this impression grew stronger and stronger—the pink darkness spreading across the picture seemed to resemble the flickering light of some far-off fire. Höllriegl almost thought he could smell the burning, and every time he reluctantly looked at it such observations, which were probably no more than his own delusions, filled him with melancholy. The Führer was very ill; despite tight censorship, the whole country knew it, and half the world whispered it.

Depressed, Höllriegl pulled up to his desk. His good mood had disappeared, as had the feeling of well-being and safety. Letters, brochures, newspaper clippings, and forms covered the table; amid the sea of paper Burjak had placed a tin breakfast tray. The serf was a former substitute teacher from the Warthegau region, who had been assigned to Höllriegl from Subhuman Camp Heydrich (SHC 1238). The gyromant ate faster than usual, although he wasn't very hungry, and absentmindedly leafed through the latest issue of *Odin's Fire*—the trade paper of the German Oscillation Guild. His eyes wandered over to an open book, Schultze-Rüssing's *Textbook of Cruelty*. The chapter he had begun last night, and which he knew almost by heart, dealt with the spiritual toughening of Asian races, and more specifically with the treatment of serfs. Just before going to sleep, Höllriegl had read bits and pieces of the richly illustrated but ponderous tome; not so much to improve his spiritual outlook but, as he admitted to himself, to indulge his fantasies.

The mail would come soon. Höllriegl quickly glanced through his appointment calendar. It was Saturday, the only weekday without regular office hours. Getting up late had been a blessing, even if he had slept through the "Great Awakening of the Nation" program carried by every broadcasting system in the world. (He'd been a weakling again!) Guiltily, Höllriegl pushed down the button to start his radio, and soon a viscous, pastoral voice gushed from the loudspeaker: ". . . All life is grace. German Christendom is—and wants nothing but—the sanctity of all earthly things. The nobility of labor, Eden on Earth, efficient and God-child-like, without thought of life after death, which is only a cowardly escape. So we Germans must grasp . . ."

The Edification Hour of the German Christian Movement from Osnabrück. Höllriegl's mind wandered . . . to certain well-shaped female bodies . . . but quickly returned to the tedious and boring voice. ". . . and if some remain who still do not wish to realize that their role as priestly middlemen has been played out, and who reproach us with a messianic leadership cult or even a vain self-glorification of party and nation, we must answer with determination . . ."

The local party headquarters held the customary weekend courses for officials of Subsection C-Two, beginning at ten that morning. A required course on the new party structure in the Tschandal regions with special consideration of Russian labor camps. Höllriegl knew the teacher slightly. He came from the ranks of the Waräger: the new name for the old SD and the German Self-Protection Service, two groups that had been merged in the east. He didn't like the teacher. But that didn't matter. He'd have to go anyhow. He read on in his calendar. Eleven o'clock: lecture for a group of Transylvanian *Pimpfe*—the junior Hitler Youth—who had pitched camp not far away in Sachsen Castle near Heldrungen. The subject was "Compiègne: November 11, 1918—June 21, 1940; a comparison." He would have to do the reporting on it for the *Kyffhäuser Messenger;* a boring job, but Kummernuss was down with the flu. Afterward he wanted to go up to the newspaper office to dictate some letters and look over the galleys for his Sunday column entitled "Nordic Meditation."

He switched over to short wave. "This is the Wehrmacht Broadcasting System in Johannesburg with the stations Bloemfontein and Vereeniging. We're broadcasting directly from the Convention of the Afrikaner Broederbond in Krügersdorp." On down the dial. A hollow, foggy voice: "He whom we should hold holy, we have cut down. It is not fitting for us to follow the example of wolves as do the greyhounds of the goddess Norn, who live voraciously in the desolate forests. The underworld demands its sacrifice." The Asgard station was on, with German lessons for the youth of Norseland. He flicked the dial again. ". . . you stupid hick. Did somebody rub you down with a wet towel today? You rubber ape. You deserve two years in an old ladies' home."

"Shut your mouth, or I'll close it for you with a rifle butt. You talk too much, you gutterpisser. We don't go for all this crap around here, see. Shut up now, or I'll kick your ass in."

Ankara with a program for the soldiers stationed in the Osman protectorate. Höllriegl had heard the series so often, it sickened him. He changed stations again. The crystalline chirping sounds of a faraway cembalo—probably one of the powerful Volga-German stations—soared through the room with its bookshelves and glass-enclosed cases in which magical objects shimmered: pendulums made of mountain crystal, gold-shining stars to be worn round the neck, silver plates dangling from necklaces to provide immunity against earth radiation; lightning-emitting antennas, high-frequency jewelry, rods, deradiation chains, antique pendulums. Oh, there were the good old Goldberg Variations! Höllriegl turned down the volume of his People's Radio and strolled toward the window, completely given over to the music. As Bach had once built the cathedral of German music, Adolf Hitler had constructed the cathedral of the Germanic world empire. A cathedral that had become an impregnable castle and would remain one: a defiant vessel of the Holy Grail, indestructible to the end of time. But the Führer lay gravely ill—there were terrible rumors. Höllriegl shuddered fearfully. Outside in the fog he saw men standing together in small groups, and on the branches crows sat immobile. At one thirty he had an appointment to pendulate an office on Richthofen Street. And then . . . then he would drive out to the Eyckes'.

The doorbell rang. The mailman. Höllriegl greeted him in the lazy dialect of his Ostmark (Austria) home: "Heitla." The man handed him a few letters and a pack of printed matter. "Heil to the

Führer," he said cheerfully but with some emphasis. "Heil to the Führer," Höllriegl replied with trembling voice. Frowning, he looked over the small amount of mail.

Höllriegl had not been there for long. To be precise, he had been transferred from Göringstadt on the Upper Danube (formerly Linz) a year ago, a forced transfer. Certain agitators in his guild had intrigued against him in Stadl-Paura, the seat of government for the Ostmark provinces ever since the Führer had solemnly excommunicated Vienna. Höllriegl felt young and ambitious. He'd show them! His practice had grown steadily, but again and again he had to fight and defeat underground resistance. The local authorities never missed a chance of tripping up the Ostmarker, something made all the easier by the open aversion certain party organizations, such as the Social Welfare Office and the German National Socialist Doctors' Federation, had shown toward dowsers engaged in therapeutic work. It was a leftover prejudice from prewar days. Originally the aversion had been general. Only after the "metaphysical movement" had triumphed in the party and SS, and Alfred Rosenberg had accepted the protectorate of German gyromantics (just before the historic Toledo war-crimes trials, where thirty-four Allied statesmen were sentenced to death by garrote), had attacks on divining-rod science ceased. For the gyromants had been accused of nothing less than practicing Eastern semantics, of links to secret societies, deviation from the Nordic line, and even of opposition to the party, state, and army. Rosenberg, the apostle of racial dogma, whom the Führer had named after the Toledo trials as paladin of the worldwide Indo-Germanic movement—headquartered at various times in Reykjavik, Delphi, and Banaras—had long admired Eastern wisdom. Höllriegl had always sensed that it, too, was rooted in holy Nordic soil. But Rosenberg, who had remained the great state philosopher until the end, was dead. A new movement, officially proscribed but silently tolerated, which indicated that certain preliminary areas had already been conquered by the new party ideologues, had pushed forward. Opponents had called it NATMAT—National Materialism. Gyromants, branded with the label of Rosenberg's support, faced a new enemy.

Angrily, Höllriegl tossed the printed matter—educational and leadership trash—to the side. Those letters! A canteen owner in a neighboring village has become afraid of cancer after a prostate operation; he suffers from dizzy spells, spasms, nervous diarrhea.

The fruit trees in his garden show typical cancerous growths, he wrote Höllriegl. Were they irritants? The widow of a high school principal from Pforta, whose husband had been killed in action during operation "Sea Lion II" at Folkestone, forty-eight years old and confined to her room by severe arthritis, complains of insomnia, pressure on the brain, petit-mal attacks, and disrupted vision. Change of life or earth radiation? Third case: a railway engineer in early middle age, married, suffers from claustrophobia, impotence, feelings of inferiority, and heavy depressions. Of course the letter writer only hinted at his condition, being most cautious in his choice of words. (Feelings of inferiority were judged a crime against the state.) A laboratory assistant, twenty-three years old, who for the last year and a half had worked enthusiastically with cobalt and cesium cannon at the research center of the SHC Neuengamme and had radiated a hundred cases—mostly eastern material—seemed about finished. He was suffering from nausea, delusions, allergic reactions, total insomnia. Sleeping-pill poisoning? Radiation syndrome? Or earth impact? Probably the latter. The man asked for pertinent printed matter and dispatch of sidereal equipment.

Always the same complaints, Höllriegl thought. Disrupted sleep, mental illnesses, delusions of persecution, disgust with life. A suicide epidemic, kept quiet by the authorities (even use of the euphemistic words "free death" was forbidden), had recently swept not only Germany but the whole Western world the Führer had united. The elite had been hit hardest of all. Unsuccessful suicides were punished with prison terms, and in some cases with forced labor in the Tschandal areas or in subhuman camps. It had to be admitted that the German people slept badly since the greatest victory in their history.

Newspapers and magazines were heaped on the armchair usually reserved for visitors. On top lay the "Strength Through Joy" periodical *The Thousand-Year Reich.* Others included *The Flamethrower, The Black Corps,* and *The Stürmer* (which now battled the yellow apelings, specifically the Soka Gakkai and the Tenno family), and *The Soldier, Racial Somatology, The Master Race, The Armored Bear* and the woman's magazine *Kriemhilde.* With a sure hand, Höllriegl pulled a copy of *Love* from the stack, with a cover picture of a seminude woman standing on a southern shore.

The youth of the Reich enjoyed reading *Love*. The magazine was designed to prepare young Germans and their countrywomen of Teuton blood for those exalted goals which would be achieved later in the breeding monasteries and troth castles. *Love* vented its greatest anger on what it called "uncontrolled" love and individual partner choice. It was a radical publication, devoted to the rearing of the blue-blond race and at the same time, rumor had it, a mouthpiece for NATMAT, but with an aristocratic touch. The editors of this slick magazine, published in Berlin by Hansjörg Fenrewolf Stoffregen, had a knack for tickling the senses behind a pseudo-scientific facade of racial and eugenic articles, thus opening the doors to a new kind of erotica rooted in the "handmaiden" labor camps of prewar days.

The colored reproduction on the cover, provocative in its sharpness of detail, showed a voluptuous woman of about forty-five, her body bent into the required aggressive pose. The fanatic expression on her face came as a surprise. Her long, thick braids were wheat-blond, the dark-gray eyes flashed victoriously, the large, brutal mouth was slightly open in what could only be contemptuous laughter, the teeth were those of an animal. What made this woman so exciting was the almost depraved mixture of Nordic and eastern traits and the way the serpentine in her smothered the heroic. She was clothed in a brief bathing tunic which, because it was sopping wet, not only gave a plastic reproduction of all bodily details, but made them half visible. The nipples of the full, high breasts shimmered brown and pink under the thin white cloth. The shirt was loosely held together by hands that were dainty without being too aristocratic. The picture even reproduced the goose-pimples on the bronze-brown thighs, dusted with sea-salt. It pointed up every drop of water and even the shadowy fuzz on her upper lips and arms. The caption said: "This, German boys and girls, is Ulla Frigg von Eycke, the former commander of the women's concentration camp Dora, and now wife of SS Obersturmbannführer and Inspector for Economics in the Upper Section Fulda-Werra, Erik Meinolf von Eycke, on the beach of the SS Guard Regiment Adolf Hitler rest home at Sochi on the Black Sea." The next line read: "Custodian of the Race."

The Custodian of the Race, as Höllriegl knew from excellent sources, had had four miscarriages. Only the first children were alive: Manfred and Erda, the twins. This vigorous and powerful Baltic German, the ideal of the blue-blond race, resembled a beautiful but worm-eaten apple. For some time now, Frau von Eycke had suffered from inexplicable nervous tensions, delusions of persecution, abrupt changes of mood, attacks of insensate fury, insomnia, and overstimulation of some parts of her skin. Doctors believed that these phenomena were linked to the beginning of menopause, but other signs seemed to contradict this diagnosis. Despite varied therapy, a final cure seemed hopeless. Höllriegl had met the Eyckes by chance at a meeting of the NS Nature Healers in Radebeul. After learning Ulla's medical history, he had offered his services and tried to convince the Eyckes to have their house near Heydrich, where Ulla and the twins spent most of their time, protected against earth radiation. Eycke, a giant with a small, dark, leathern vulture's head and bright evil eyes in his weathered, duel-scarred face (horrible, Höllriegl thought), had only looked hatefully ironic at first. Ulla and he had heard quite a bit about Höllriegl's gyromantics and of his successes—his clients, dating back to his Ostmark years, included high party members and the wives of politically influential industrialists. But Eycke's sickly sister Anselma finally tipped the scale. She had lived long in the tropics and was a strangely slack creature, all eyes, with slow, plantlike movements and pale, liver-spotted skin. A greater contrast to Ulla would have been hard to find. Smiling skeptically and always rather reserved, the Eyckes had agreed. The first séance was to take place this afternoon.

Höllriegl was still of two minds about Ulla, but there was no denying her impact had been magnetic. The aristocratic, domineering and fanatic qualities of the woman had attracted him from the first; the vulgar and brutal repelled him. Her cruelty and moodiness as well as her daring horsemanship had long been the subject of gossip. When Frau von Eycke was still Ulrike Mlakar, she had been one of the strictest of concentration-camp commanders; her administration of Stutthof and Gross-Rosen had quickly become as notorious within the party as her fanaticism among the top figures of the political hierarchy. She had early made a reputation through certain educational methods (which did not always have good results for women prisoners). TV viewers saw her often as an exemplary wife and mother as well as horsewoman. Her name still appeared frequently in the press.

The cover picture had aroused Höllriegl's lust for this woman's body, which held the excitement of mature intercourse. But he suspected, with some pain, that his desires would never be fulfilled. It was strange: The brutality mirrored in Ulla's face roused in him a powerful feeling of inordinate desire for her; but he could no longer admire her victorious and heroic qualities. Perhaps it was all just a mask. The sweaty smell of mares and dirty underclothes seemed to fit the high cheekbones with their slanting eyes and the betraying brown shadows beneath them. And suddenly—Höllriegl hastily shoved the magazine back into the stack—he had a feeling of imminent physical menace. This woman not only aroused in him the lust to beat her and draw blood, but also a desire to be beaten.

The telephone rang. Höllriegl turned off the radio and lifted the receiver. "Heil; Damaschke here," a gruff voice announced. SA man Damaschke. Old fighter from the days of the Krummen Lanke in Berlin, member of the blood brotherhood and badly wounded in the war. Now a telephone operator at party headquarters. "Herr von Schwerdtfeger from Vienna wants to talk to you. You know who that is, don't you? What? The famous novelist. He read his works here once. I'll connect you. . . ."

Höllriegl remembered at once. Years ago in Vienna he had dowsed Arbogast von Schwerdtfeger's study and also ordered the furniture shifted, placing special emphasis on the position of the desk (Schwerdtfeger wrote standing up). The writer, well known even then, later had told him that the rearrangement had helped remove a "bad block." He was able to work with renewed vigor afterward.

"Do you remember your visit with me?" he heard Schwerdtfeger say. It sounded smooth, sonorous, polite, somehow "old Austrian." "Could you drop by the parliament for a moment? I'm staying here. I would have come over myself, but I'm expecting an important long-distance call at any moment, so I can't leave. I have an interesting job for you. Something highly official. Secret business for the Reich . . ."

Höllriegl agreed to come, quickly scratched a few words for Burjak on a piece of paper, and put on his coat. While he took his car out of the garage, he wondered how Schwerdtfeger could have learned that he now worked in Heydrich. Secret Reich business! How did this scribbler come to transmit it? And something else. Schwerdtfeger had used the word "parliament"—one of those terms of derision occasionally applied to party headquarter buildings among trusted friends. How could this fellow presume to use such an intimate tone?

"I've only had business dealings with him, and that was years ago," Höllriegl said to himself half aloud, lost in thought. Could it have been just carelessness? Hardly. More likely he had said it because he didn't care a damn. Or had he said it on purpose? In any case, Schwerdtfeger lived at party headquarters, which usually accommodated only higher officials. Secret Reich business? Hmm.

A light rain began to fall as he drove down the Hindenburg Avenue, and it soon turned into a steady drizzle. Even so, he thought that more people than usual were out in the street. He stopped outside headquarters, a former tank barracks painted dark brown. Rebuilding and additions in the standard Reich style had given it the requisite monumental character. Not a parking spot in sight: The cars of party officials and secretaries straddled the sidewalk as the Wehrmacht's used to. Höllriegl left his VW in a side street and, somewhat chilled, hurried back to the "parliament."

Damaschke was sitting in the concierge's loge with its many portholes resembling firing slits, a telephone around his neck, busily fiddling with his switchboard. ("Heil! Yes, I'll connect you.") While he was doing this automatically with his right hand, which consisted of a cleverly designed pair of steel tongs, he signed Höllriegl's pass with his left. His assistant sat next to him, spreading margarine on a slice of bread. The loge was decorated with many little flags and streamers, a Führer bust, and yellowed photographs showing a grinning Damaschke in the old uniform of the SA taking part in parades outside Jewish-owned stores, or with a winter-relief-aid collection box in one hand.

"Room fifteen, second floor, private wing," he said jovially in his hoarse voice. He limped out of the room on his creaking artificial leg and pointed to the barracks yard with his forked right hand.

The long corridors were overheated and smelled of bad cigarettes, urine, lysoform and red tape. Even the official smell had been fitted to Reich standards. People waited for admission to offices from which sounded the quiet rattle of typewriters. Pictures of the Führer or faded schematic drawings of ancient Wehrmacht weapons hung on the walls. The slogan "Common good before private gain" had long since been painted over, but could still be read. Yet the corridors of the private wing with their red coconut-fiber carpets and mangy vines contrasted pleasantly with the Spartan appearance of the other wings.

As Höllriegl entered the darkened room, Schwerdtfeger walked toward him with outspread arms. The novelist shook both his visitor's hands. Schwerdtfeger, recipient of three honorary doctorates bestowed by famous German universities, looked more like a Hun than a German; he would have made a fine Attila in a Nibelungen film: close-cropped hair and round skull marked by the chiseled fullness of his forehead, handlebar ears, slanting yellow eyes, a pointed, cleanly shaved little mouth, pouting, always pursed, lips, teeth obviously false. The mighty, square-shaped chest, which creaked as it rose and fell, made the man resemble an athletically built waxwork figure. Schwerdtfeger's hands were as delicate and noble as his manners (a prewar cavalier). His latest novel, *The Demons of the Ostmark,* a blockbuster in which he had painted a broad social canvas of an earlier era, had been such a rousing best seller that even Höllriegl, who as a rule hated novels, had not been able to avoid exposure to some of its highlights. In any case: the famous man was from the Ostmark, and that fact alone served to create a pleasant and familiar atmosphere.

Their conversation was short. "I'm on a lecture tour," Schwerdtfeger began, after having offered his guest a drink and cigar. After Höllriegl declined, he fussily lit one himself. "In Berlin," he went on, "I enjoyed the honor of being allowed to read before the highest authorities of the Reich—unfortunately the Führer was not present. You know . . ." Schwerdtfeger at once pasted a sorrowful expression on his face, as if he had kept it in storage for the occasion. "To get to the point: A very important and highly placed person is involved, whose working and living quarters are to be checked out for earth radiation. I talked about you and the successes you've had, especially that time you came to see me in Vienna. The gentlemen were most interested, and thus the assignment came about almost by itself—my initiative, of course. I found out where you had gone, and since my tour brought me into the Heydrich vicinity anyway, I took it upon myself to inform you personally. I gave a lecture here two years ago—very dull public. No real understanding. Well, provincial."

"That's very kind of you. But I would have to know more about the circumstances under which I am to conduct the investigation," Höllriegl said, cutting off the flow of the writer's conversation. "Personal contact would be important, and I should know the medical history in case there is one. Could you tell me anything about it?"

"I'd love to if I were allowed to talk. And really I know too little about it. All I can tell you is that the man involved is very ill. Everything else, whatever the expert needs to know, you'll learn on the spot. Report to T-Four"—Höllriegl suddenly shivered—"to Obersturmführer Hirnchristl—he's a countryman of yours, a very nice fellow and of course an ardent National Socialist. He'll know what to do. You'll get instructions from him. Possibly"—Schwerdtfeger puffed hard on his cigar, which did not draw well—"astrology will be used as well. Perhaps even"—an ironic blinking of the yellow eyes—"the highest astrologer may be called in. You don't object, do you? Or do you?"

"No, surely not, although . . . my investigations aren't worth much without some contact. Of course the impact of the earth on an organism can be determined on an objectively scientific basis. But just how it can influence a specific organism under specific circumstances is a separate and delicate matter. A question of feeling. Call it empathy if you like, intuition, the right touch, black magic. . . . When should I go to Berlin?"

"Let's see." Schwerdtfeger took out his notebook, flipping the pages. "Day after tomorrow—Monday. Hirnchristl expects you at four P.M. You have only to tell the guard your name. You travel tomorrow."

Höllriegl got up. The abrupt, commanding tone in which the last few sentences had been spoken disturbed him. It just didn't fit with Schwerdtfeger's usual manner. The man was hard to figure out—in any case, caution was the order of the day, he realized.

Their parting was on the surface extremely friendly. Ostmarkian, even old Austrian. But Höllriegl walked out feeling very uneasy. The required lecture was due to begin any minute. He was honored by Schwerdtfeger's commission, of course. But what was behind it? And then that oily way of talking—it made you want to vomit. A man anointed and consecrated in the faith without a doubt. Presumably his use of the word "parliament" had been a trap, one among many. He just hadn't noticed the others. Should he have reacted? And what about the circumstances surrounding the T4 offices? Everyone knew it was the former seat of the office for population policy and hereditary health—in other words, the center for euthanasia: Tiergartenstrasse No. 4. Action "Special Treatment 14F13." In 1959 it had still involved about 748,000 people in all of Europe (what a goddamned memory for figures!), but soon thereafter the number had been drastically reduced because all the hereditary defectives halfway able to work had been put into the subhuman camps, where they were kept in special cages resembling pigsties and used for experiments in neurosurgery or for the lowest type of labor. Even debilitated persons who had undergone successful lobotomies were pushed back into the economy. In the meantime, the euthanasia authorities had been moved—Höllriegl couldn't remember just where. But the notoriety had remained. What was T4's name now? Reich boneyard? Who had offices there now?

Höllriegl looked about him. He had been so immersed in his fears that his mind had wandered and he found he had lost his way in the long, empty corridors, one as monotonous and uniform as the other. He had probably turned in the wrong direction right after leaving Schwerdtfeger's quarters. His boots echoed on the stones. The private wing seemed to end here, with the offices in another block in the opposite direction. Outside the bleakness of the barracks courtyard was dipped in foggy light. Höllriegl rushed nervously through a maze of half-dark, crooked passages that narrowed unexpectedly in places. Sometimes he thought that burning stares shot over crooked backs were pursuing him from behind closed doors. Could it be some serfs cleaning up? There wouldn't be any point talking to half-animals. After Höllriegl had mounted a short, curved stone staircase, he suddenly reached a wide vestibule in pale rococo colors with soaring windows on one side and high narrow doors on the other. He no longer felt pursued. He could breathe freely.

Höllriegl had never been in the *Residenz* before—the name people gave to the small palace so badly damaged during the war. The property of an aristocratic family that had died out during the reign of William II, it had changed hands several times during the last decades. After World War I, according to Kummernuss' story, a rich factory owner from the Rhineland had bought it, restored the dilapidated little court theater, and arranged performances in it. When the Führer came to power, that too ended. The *Residenz* became in rapid succession a training school for nurses, a sanatorium for men maimed in World War I, a rest home for Death's Head units in 1940, and later a production plant for one of the many secret arms programs. Kummernuss thought the Ariel Program might have been involved. During Allied terror attacks on the Reich the architectural jewel had been bombed and partly destroyed. The armaments industry vanished underground into a shaft and the ruins of the palace again stood ownerless. After the victory, a member of the blood brotherhood, the highest local intelligence officer, bought the remnants of the building for a song, but he died before restoration could be completed. Again the *Residenz* passed into party ownership, which expanded the building to connect it to the barracks and the parliament.

One event, as fleeting and veiled as all others on that pregnant fall day, would retain a special weight of its own. Höllriegl saw a balustrade at the far end of the hall which seemed to mark the end of the vestibule. Surely he could get out quickly that way—he dare not miss the lecture on the Tschandal regions; attendance was checked. He walked faster. Hurrying past one of those strange narrow doors, he heard coming from behind it a monotonous murmur like a chorus chanting a litany. He stopped, compulsively, and opened the door, which turned creakingly on its hinges. He found himself in the choir of a high, narrow, vapor-filled church, apparently the palace chapel. On the far wall of the empty apse hung a mighty Christian cross (without a crucified Christ) that had an equally large black swastika nailed on it. There were no pictures or other ritual decorations. People jammed the galleries and the nave below. The faithful, most of them old women in mourning clothes, turned ecstatic faces towards an apple-cheeked blackbeard who stood at the foot of the altar, a bird on each shoulder. The man's heavy frame—he could have been a preacher or a popular orator—was wrapped completely within a dark coat. He was one-eyed, and wore a small black patch so ill-fitting the empty red socket could be clearly seen. A large-brimmed hat was pulled down deeply over his face. From where he stood, Höllriegl could not observe the man very well because those kneeling in the pews blocked his view and thin columns of smoke rose from below, darkening the room. It smelled of burning flesh.

The congregation swung rythmically in their pews, continuing the monotonous chant. "The Füh-rer! The Füh-rer!" It sounded drawn out, fervent, and somehow choked in tears. "He sits to the right hand of Odin, the Almighty Father," the skald said in pleading tones, his eyes blazing drunkenly. "The Füh-rer! The Füh-rer!" The choir responded obediently. Höllriegl saw gaping eyes turned toward him, spittle-bedecked mouths in yellow, wrinkled faces. The intruder had been noticed. Soft hands groped after him. The women shoved together to make room for him. Their faded bodies smelled sweetish, a few carried wreaths in their hands. Somewhere outside a horse neighed sharply—it was a cry of death. With gentle force they tried to pull him down onto a seat. "The Füh-rer! The Füh-rer!" the congregation sighed again.

Höllriegl shook off grasping hands which now seemed iron hard. A man as tall as a tree—he had leaned against the wall behind the door—blocked his exit. Höllriegl, giddy and dazed, pushed him aside. They almost came to blows. The door had been reached and, ignoring the uproar, Höllriegl slammed it shut behind him with a loud bang. The brightness of the hall received him.

It was about twenty to three. Höllriegl was due at the Eyckes' at three. He felt feverish without being sick and drove his car nervously through the crooked little streets of the old city, a shortcut that allowed him to avoid the spa with its many cars backed up in front. Right behind the rock, crowned by the ruins of Oberburg Castle, he turned into Guderian Avenue, a major artery leading out of town, where at this time on a Saturday afternoon traffic had become lighter. He stepped on the gas and raced along, a nervous pressing pain in his neck. The destination tempted him, but at the same time he felt as if he should delay the meeting with Frau von Eycke. Now that the fulfillment of his long-cherished desires neared, he became frightened. How unmanly! Still, he could not shake a feeling of foreboding.

A light snow had fallen at midday, a little too early in the year, but now strips had been torn from the cloud cover: a greenish blue

—the blue of an autumn sky playing at summer—appeared unexpectedly, and a watery sun poured its mocking light on the wooded slopes of the Schlachtberg Mountain as he flitted by. Höllriegl drove through an enervatingly warm zone where the air had dried the asphalt. But now and again, maliciously, a wet and icy wind struck his back.

The lecture about the Tschandal areas, which had been integrated into the Reich up to the Ural Mountains—that east wall of the Occident spiked with atomic mines and nuclear weapons—had once again stirred him mightily and made him happy, even though he already knew most of what had been said. The northern and middle regions of the old Soviet Union, settled by the German-blooded armed peasants, were surrounded by a garland of states dependent on the Reich. These stretched from the Baltic protectorate and Finland in the West—the Baltic Sea had become a German water—to the former Reich commissariats, now confederacies, of Caucasia, Transcaucasia, and Rusj (the Ukraine), to which the Führer had granted their own constitutions as Estates of the Realm, patterned on medieval examples. This was their reward for having been the first to rise against the apocalyptic animal of bolshevism. Even Tibet belonged to the German sphere of influence; Mongolia to that of Japan. A deep echelon system of fortifications and settlements secured the lands of the East. Enlightened men had been at work everywhere. Where once extermination camps had stood, the fortresses of the SS *Schwurmänner* and the Valhallas of the ariosophs rose atop artificial hills which, legend had it, were really heaps of skulls. The lecturer had screened a most impressive color film about life in these border fortresses, whose uniform and monumental Gothic architecture had been designed by the Führer himself. Scattered across the vast Slavic land were thousands of racial breeding stables, in which the future elite of the master race was growing up. Right after the final victory, blond Germans and blond Slavs (the Waräger tribe) had been crossed with some success, and these bastards had later proved especially fanatic battlers against the remnants of the subhuman Mongoloids east of the Yenisei River. They had marched out into the steppes, the forests, and icy deserts in order to proclaim with fire and sword the salvation of the ancient Aryan creed, the swastika, to crush underfoot the Tschandal worms, and to clear the depopulated areas for future pure-breed colonies. All this had only been started, but the results were already so tremendous it took your breath away. Heil to the Führer who had created such greatness!

These impressions did not arise in Höllriegl's mind in the same order as here presented, but shredded and overlaid by pictures of a strong blond woman in lustful, lazy surrender—weak and humiliated. He had put the trip to Berlin out of his mind. Was the entire Eycke house built above bad radiation, or were only Frau von Eycke's chambers under the influence of a pathological disorder zone caused by subterranean streams or ore veins? Probably the latter, since Ulla alone had been afflicted.

In addition to the usual control apparatus, Höllriegl had taken along one of the simplest divining rods gyromants use: the hair pendulum with an amber top. He had chosen amber because the fossil resin most closely corresponded to the wheat-blond of Ulla's mane (in secret he called her his amber witch); the hair because it is a living human substance, and because he always had to think of Ulla's hair . . . all of it. His personal reaction to Frau von Eycke's emanations, the total impact exuding from her, would be most important, however. Hopefully she would not be home, for her bodily presence wasn't needed; the essence remained in the house. He would have to do a special job. Much depended on this first inspection, commercially and socially, especially as far as the Eyckes and their evaluation of his person were concerned. To be more specific—Ulla's evaluation.

The pendulum was only a tool. Success or failure depended entirely on his biomotor, on his "electromagicon," as Paracelsus had called it. Would he be able to concentrate enough to exclude all his desires and push out of his mind the secret and oh-so-personal things binding him to the amber witch?

Right on time he stopped the car in front of the broad, trellised gate with the twisted baroque ornaments hinting at a coat of arms. A straight, overgrown pathway led to the mansion. The spacious property, enclosed by high, crumbling walls, lay hidden in wooded country near a branch of the road to Rottleberode, not far from the autobahn. (He'd drive down that highway to Berlin the day after tomorrow; not on Sunday, as that novel-scribbler had said. What a goddamned thing—Schwerdtfeger, T4—what did it all mean?)

Höllriegl had been out here once before at a reception the

Eyckes had given for a group of industrial big shots. He rang the bell and gave his name in answer to a cackling on the intercom. Apparently he was expected, for one of the side gates opened with a distinct click. The gloom of the old pathway swallowed him up as he stepped briskly down the gravel path, while leaves fell from the closely planted maple trees. Nothing stirred in the run-down gatekeeper's house with its closed gray shutters. Somewhere deep in the estate, dogs barked. Otherwise everything had fallen silent.

He did not feel particularly dashing. Anticipation, that enervating fever, made his head hot and heavy. His stomach felt stretched and his knees empty so that his legs, ensconced in highly polished cavalry boots, seemed to move by themselves. He grew angry at himself when he noted that his right arm, under which he carried a briefcase with his pendulum equipment, began to tremble—perhaps because he had the case pressed too tightly against his side. His cramps increased the closer he came to the mansion.

At noon Höllriegl had put on his high-collared blouse matching his uniform trousers and brown shirt. The blouse emphasized his good build. Its apple-green facings were embossed with the tree of life in silver. As a dowser, Höllriegl belonged to the "uninvested healers"; but since he had served in the medical units of both Wehrmacht and SS and been awarded a party diploma for gyromantics, he had been confirmed as a *Hauptstellenleiter* or RAD troop leader—a rank due him as secretary of his professional society.

The wide, windy esplanade opened up in front of him. Crunching gravel. The geometrically laid out lawns had turned graybrown and unsightly. Left and right were sheds and stables overgrown with ivy. He walked past the gaping mouth of a coach house. He could see the glint of the nickel nose on Eycke's limousine. Naturally the master of this manor drove the same model and color car as the SS *Reichsführer*. Next to it stood—a wave of awful tension pulsed through him—the sea-green Opel-Kapitän so well known in town: Frau von Eycke's car, decorated with the tactical insignia of the Black Corps. Ulla was home.

Ancient oak trees helped frame a very German setting. The Eycke house sat on top of a hill with stairs on either side. It had been built in the pretentious style of Kaiser Wilhelm's times (imitation Renaissance) with little towers, fake gables, battlements, bay windows, and similar ornamentation. The whole complex had originally belonged to a fearfully rich member of the sparkling-wine dynasty of Springorum, but the previous owner had been the Reich Labor Trustee for the Saar-Palatinate, Herr Will Fette, who for some years had returned every summer in order to take the cure at the local spa.

A black pennant with the white Reich eagle on it hung from the flagpole in front of the main building: the flag of the youth movement. It fluttered lazily in the wind. Höllriegl remembered having heard that Ulla's daughter, Erda, served as a platoon leader with the young maidens.

A footman clothed in black and pale yellow bowed to the gyromant who, having pulled himself together, strode onto the terrace with a firm step. The servant was a bony, flax-blond, almost white-haired man with eagle nose and prominent Adam's apple, albino-like appearance and aristocratic bearing. Apparently a member of the old aristocracy who had been allowed to enter the service of the new masters. The hall was half dark, and eyes used to daylight could not see much at first. Two men with hats on sat at a table in a far corner and drank tankards of beer. They fell silent but paid no attention to the man who had just entered. Höllriegl thought their faces fleshy, red, and brutal.

The albino said in a pleasant, lisping voice, "Frau von Eycke is not at home. Would the gentleman come upstairs." And with a gesture indicating that Höllriegl should follow him, he led the way.

The hall, paneled in dark wood, was high and as roomy as a plane hangar. Höllriegl remembered it from his first visit. Huge family portraits, blurred with age, hung one next to the other as if the walls were pages of a stamp collection. Man-high Japanese vases and awkward second Renaissance cupboards, their panels covered with Chinese landscapes painted on pale silk, stood in the niches. Everything in the room had a museum quality, gathered together like so much plunder; and was full of a theatrical excess and arrogance. The stained-glass windows, framed in lead, featured battle scenes (one could recognize Krupp's giant howitzer "Big Bertha"), which allowed the autumn light to bleed into the room. The wooden staircase that led to an open hall above them was wide enough for ten abreast to march up. The passages, balconies, and galleries of the labyrinth were crammed from top to bottom with pale busts and bronze hermae, antlers, stuffed elk heads, and bear skins. On the fireplace mantels stood models of old ships. Everything reflected a heavy, subdued splendor; an unmistakable effort to exude tradition and wealth. The furnishings resembled a Wagner opera transposed into architectural terms.

The footman left Höllriegl in the semicircular hall leading to Frau von Eycke's private chambers. He could begin his work, the man said; no one would disturb him. If he should need anything, he had only to ring. "Frau von Eycke won't be back for some time; she went riding after lunch."

The furniture in Ulla's chambers, through which Höllriegl strode quickly, closing the one open window he found, was marked by the same thick coating of romanticism as the other rooms in the house. Nevertheless it seemed much more comfortable. Perhaps because here, very much in contrast to the exhibitionlike order outside, everything had been thrown together in helter-skelter fashion, giving the whole scene a feeling of wild improvisation, slovenliness, even female abandon. Drawers had been torn open and not closed again. Wardrobes gaped lewdly, shamelessly displaying the disorderly interior like entrails. Clothing was strewn over the armchairs, including, as Höllriegl suddenly realized, very personal items. A salmon-colored garter with silk stockings still attached lay in a heap on the floor of the middle and largest room, dominated by an imposing Führer portrait. Paperback novels, Kleenex, and letters had been scattered over the tiger skin stretched across the couch. An enchanting confusion of cosmetics lay jumbled at the bottom of a full-sized oval mirror that was turned so it exactly faced the bed. A pair of riding boots had been hurled into one corner.

Höllriegl grasped these details with one drunken look; he was a quick and sharp observer. He stood in his amber witch's bedroom and for several heartbeats closed his eyes, lost in the sweet dizziness of her flesh's radiation, feeling as if she already lay in his arms. That she had left such disorder behind could have a special significance. Or had she forgotten him and his commission? Was it her temperament? Abandon? Or simply disdain of his person? That too would fit Ulla's "stableboy manners," as people thereabouts expressed it. But Höllriegl, shuddering, thought of Amazonian things.

Although he tried not to look at it, he felt a secret power dragging him to the garter belt, which was no longer quite clean and therefore, for him at least, so very enticing. With an excitement he could no longer control, Höllriegl picked up the elastic thing and buried his face in it. The tart and sour odor of skin, sweat, and Russian Leather clung to it. Höllriegl pressed the garment to his lips, bit into the fabric, and sucked on it. Then he tossed it down quickly, hearing small, quick steps coming close.

A Latin-looking maid, small and delicate, appeared, expressed her horror at Höllriegl's presence in a squall of words (her language sounded vaguely Italian), wrung her hands at the disorder around her, and hastily began to tidy up.

Höllriegl explained the purpose of his visit in the simplest words—the girl obviously didn't understand any of them, she just kept giggling—and asked her with some emphasis to leave him alone. Whereupon she disappeared. It needed no further proof: Ulla's servants had not been informed of his visit. And presumably the footman had been told by the castellan, who had telephoned Höllriegl about the job. Frau von Eycke had forgotten him.

Sobered and thus deflected from his desires, he could more easily muster the needed concentration. He removed his coat and took the amber top from his briefcase. It would take a few minutes before the instrument found its oscillation level. At the end of the hair strand (red-golden in color, a woman's) he made a loop through which he put his right forefinger. Then he adopted a relaxed but straight body posture, placing his free hand, fingers spread out wide, onto his sacroiliac. At the head of the couch stood a silver-framed photograph of the bird-headed Herr von Eycke in uniform. Höllriegl held the top high above the picture, and after a while the amber began swinging, first in tiny flights, then in much larger ones. The tool moved quickly into full sinistral circles, as he expected. However, the pendulum monogram did not emerge fully at once, but seemed confused in its linear development: the number of oscillations varied and took place in different directions, until at last a pure circular configuration was obtained. Above the pictures of Erda and Manfred, which stood next to their father's on the bedside table, the pendulum showed a similar behavior. However, the childish emanations finally forced the apparatus to swing into beautifully shaped sinistral ellipses.

The room was filled with Ulla's enormous radiation. The longer he conducted the oscillation, the stronger he found her incandescence, until he felt faint from the force emitted by her large, strong sex. Suddenly that special fear he always felt when his desires flowed toward Ulla's elixir flooded over him. The feeling of imminent danger merged in that moment with the shivering sensation he had experienced earlier in the day in the chapel of the *Residenz,* and everything that had happened there came alive. He had experienced something ancient, dangerous, and soiled, and the image of the archaic cult he had witnessed become intermingled with that of a domineering beauty who rode horses into the ground and demeaned men in disgusting ways.

Höllriegl gripped the loop of the hair strand more firmly between thumb and forefinger and moved the pendulum closer to the couch. Seconds later the major oscillations described the form of the squeezed circle, the ellipse—the female sign. Shortly thereafter the pendulum began to move in a straight line, perhaps because of the tiger skin, then swung in several directions against the meridian, then finally into clearly formed dextral circles: proof of the presence of water, perhaps stagnant water, deep in the earth under the house. In order to be sure, Höllriegl repeated the experiment with his left hand; again the same results. Now he changed instruments, taking the control pendulum made of nickel and copper to continue his investigation. This showed the early oscillations much more clearly in the shape of an entwined monogram, but soon changed into unmistakably dextral revolutions. Höllriegl tired quickly; the new pendulum gave him a headache. He broke off the investigation. The couch would have to be moved into another room, preferably into another wing of the building. Or should he try to install antiradiation equipment? Nor could he exclude the presence of similar radiation emitting substances underneath the manor house—possibly coal or ores.

Thoughtfully, even reverently, he walked through Ulla's six rooms, groping for earth radiation. He no longer had any doubts. This part of the castle was under the influence of evil water or perhaps some mineral emanation, which was engaged in bitter struggle with that of the domineering female power. For Ulla's nature exuded a witch's fluid, a magic breath, that not only exercised its deviltry on men, but also resisted the forces of her natural surroundings. The resultant currents and tensions (which Höllriegl felt even when he only looked at her picture in the newspapers) could well produce Ulla's attacks of hysteria. Before writing his report, today's investigation would have to be checked with a specially sensitive emanation meter. More precise conclusions were needed here.

He would have to make a drawing. Removal into another tract of the building might have to be carefully considered. Again and again Höllriegl wandered through the suite of rooms, stopping now and again, head bent forward and eyes half closed, in order to allow earth radiation to act on him through the intermediary of the pendulum. More and more he fell under Ulla's influence. Her counterradiation proved so dominating that Höllriegl was flooded with a prickly, wanton excitement which pushed all sensible thoughts from his mind as he sat down to do his sketching. Submission! Oh, sweet submission! He began to draw with a trembling hand, dropped his pencil to run disturbed through the room, dug like a thief among Ulla's clothes and pressed—feeling foolish—an undergarment (one of the warm and wintry kind) against his beating heart. Once he happened upon a hidden door. Turning the glass knob, he suddenly found himself in a luxurious black bathroom with rose-shaped decorations on the walls and large movable mirrors. An old woodcut had been fixed on the inside door showing torture scenes: the Spanish strangling iron, the Pomeranian cap, and other instruments, all on nude, muscular men. A calendar hung next to the picture: Some days were marked in pencil, others had zeros written on them. In front of his amber witch's bidet, Höllriegl fell to his knees to embrace the cool oval and cover the seat with wild kisses.

A thought flashed through his fog-shrouded brain, a thought of such absurdity that he trembled. What if he could measure the radiation power of the Führer's wisdom pitted against Ulla's sex! A metaphysical test, a magic operation. The epitome of male and female against each other. Sun Teutons in a wrestling match with the primeval earth powers of eastern origin. Zio-Zeus against Hel-Calypso. What boldness, what madness! The experiment was the temptation of the gods! While his mind churned with these images, he thought he could hear the Midgard serpent of Norse legend whip her tail against the floor. The most dangerous experiment anyone could ever dare—quite aside from personal and political consequences. But nobody would see him nor learn of it. It would have to take place at once. Right now.

He ran into the adjoining bedroom and stepped onto the couch, whose pillows were of debauching softness. His whole body trembled as he took the picture of the Führer from the wall and placed it across the pillow and on the tiger skin where the imprint of Ulla's body could be clearly seen. Then he took the nickel-and-copper pendulum from his coat pocket and let it dance above the picture. Seconds, minutes of panting tension—then a strong stimulative zone appeared in the oscillation picture the pendulum had drawn. The sidereal perpendicular quickly entered into the revolution of the ions circling above the Führer's picture, for photographs are not dead reproductions but electromagnetic reflexes of personal essence, as the pendular sciences had proved long ago. Adolf Hitler's interest in gyromantics was an added factor. The Führer himself had once received a pendulum from a popular delegation and with genial empathy had done successful gyromantic work. As a result, no disruptive influence need be feared.

After each round, Höllriegl placed the top for a moment upright on the inside of his left hand, a fast, almost mechanical procedure designed to remove any disorganizing collections of od (magnetism) from the pendulum. This time he would have to go ahead very carefully. A great deal was at stake.

The pendulum reacted strangely. As an indicator of soul and spirit, the sensitive instrument could provide an answer to any questions asked of it. Höllriegl now wanted to see how the most powerful man the world had ever seen would force his will upon the most marvelous woman on earth. The Führer's titanic will would have to make the Amazon's flesh do his bidding.

The gyros shuddered under the impact of contending forces. Circles whirled first clockwise then, briefly, the vertical appeared, directed at Höllriegl's heart. After several revolutions came the horizontal—negation. And again the circle, this time running counterclockwise. Höllriegl should have been satisfied with the outcome, for the oscillatory field had been completed harmoniously and the sign of the cross been clearly visible. The strong horizontal element in the final figure signified negation, renunciation and—interdiction! How weak in contrast were the perpendicular oscillations: apparently Höllriegl's eroticism had become intermingled and battled—what a ridiculous enterprise—the forces emanating from the picture. As for the meaning, it could be this: Ulla was denied him; she stood in the crossfire of powers much greater than his own. He had seen very clearly the sign of prohibition announcing danger.

A feeling of paralysis came over him, but he allowed the experiment to continue. Repeatedly the pendulum swung along the same path, and always more clearly, somehow cleansed, the shape of the cross emerged, finally to change quickly into a multiplication sign. If this were interpreted as the "other cross," the Andrew cross, it would mean that the vibration source, in this case the Führer, was a creature of highest wisdom already in contact with eternity. The cross and multiplication sign taken together meant death. Had the Führer been marked by death—would he sweep Ulla with him?

Now Höllriegl saw everything with frightening clarity. The configuration of death clearly involved the Führer; Ulla only played a catalyst role. The sign of death hovered over the Führer—when would he enter the eternal shadows? He must be dying or was already dead; but even in death he still exercised power over life—the life which in Höllriegl's experiment was symbolized by the female, by Ulla.

He put the picture back in its place, seized by a coldness in which he could only recognize the chill of the grave. He jumped down from the couch. The blood beat heavily against his throbbing and painful temples. His body was drenched in sweat, teeth rattled from nervous hypertension. He heard steps—hard, manly steps—coming closer. Outside dogs played, howled and barked. Höllriegl ran to the window and once again he had that feeling of emptiness, of automation, in his legs. Down in the courtyard two grooms were leading a horse swathed in blankets toward the stable. As he stepped back, he faced Frau von Eycke.

She seemed hot and a little out of breath. She tossed her riding hat behind her and shook her unruly hair off her forehead. Then she stepped in front of the mirror and as she did so her slanted eyes shot a look at Höllriegl. He could not fathom her expression. He just stood there, the wave of blood that poured over his face chased the ice from his veins.

"Oooh, Hauptstellenleiter Dürriegl," Ulla said, drawing out her words. The *r* sounded almost foreign, rolling mockingly. "Heil Hitler!" (This in reply to Höllriegl's heel-crashing German salute.) "I remember—you're our gyromant. Have you found anything?" Again the strange undercurrent—or was it only his imagination? Not a trace of embarrassment because of her forgetfulness or the disorder. Abruptly she turned and stretched out her hand.

Höllriegl bent over it in order to kiss her thin fingers. But with a sudden jerk Ulla withdrew her hand, so that his bow ended up more servile than chivalrous. A warm cloud of perfume enveloped him.

"My dear lady," he said in his sonorous, charming Ostmarkian way, which at once seemed to him enormously stupid and wretched, "I received the order . . . I was called yesterday and told to be here at two. Forgive my . . . just walking in."

"Oooh, that's all right, Mr. ——"

"Höllriegl!"

"Oh, yes, Höllriegl." She took off her jacket, quite indifferent to his presence. Underneath the shirt, cut in male fashion and wide open at the collar, her breast arched forward, elastic and quivering. Wet splotches stained her shirt under the armpits.

Then something terrible happened that could never be set right again. With a suffocating scream in which a whole sentence, a confession, gasped for air, Höllriegl fell to his knees in front of Frau von Eycke. He grabbed the suddenly rigid woman with all his strength and embraced her, boldly fondling her belly (he would never forget how elastic, tight, and full her behind had been), kissed the *Mons Venus* arching out underneath the skintight riding pants, and bit, groaning, into something that was cloth and flesh at once: blood-warm, soft, flowing, and smelling pungently of horses and leather.

At that moment, Höllriegl felt a burning pain run across forehead and cheek. Ulla had broken from his embrace and hit him silently, vehemently, with deadly aim. The riding crop slipped from her hand, but not before a second blow, this one from the whip's handle, cut across his right eye. Half blinded, he staggered out of the room; panting, he felt his way through endless passages and down staircases. Later he could not have said how he had managed to escape the labyrinth and return to his car, or if anyone had seen his disgraceful retreat. Tears came as he switched on the ignition. He let the motor warm up and shifted into gear. His brief-case? It was upstairs, together with his pendulums. He had only grabbed his coat. Would Ulla talk?

His memory of the drive home was hazy. He could only remember later that while he sobbed with fury, shame, or sorrow (no one should have seen him like this!) he sang a battle hymn learned in the days when he had been an illegal member of the banned Hitler Youth in Austria; sang it, babbled it, over and over. "We were born to battle—battle for the Fatherland—we have sworn to Adolf Hitler—to Adolf Hitler we give our hand." Numbed, he allowed Burjak to take his coat and pull off his boots. Since everything had gone to hell anyway, he didn't even bother playing a member of the master race before this dog of a serf. He was dead-tired, crushed, torn inside. Would Ulla talk? Would Ulla talk? Would Ulla talk?

He stepped to the window as was his custom, and looked out without seeing a thing. His forehead burned fiercely. Suddenly, on the roof across the way, he saw the blinking of a familiar neon sign, which brought him back to reality. "The Party thinks for you," he read, and the slogan, which the Berlin radio tower used for station identification, filled him with satisfaction and solace.

Burjak came into the room bringing two letters delivered from party headquarters. It was embarrassing the way the subhuman looked past Höllriegl's scarred forehead. The orders for his trip to Berlin were in one envelope. He was to report to Ostuf Hirnchristl, Tiergartenstrasse 4, and place himself at his disposal. The usual passes for driving through the "small" restricted zones B and D had been included. (What a stupid formality.) He was to leave on Sunday: There might be trouble if he waited a day before starting out. His lodging orders were limited to a week. He would live in the Pension Zweenemann on Uhland Corner. His address was hand-written on the second envelope, a private letter. Stiff paper in heli-otrope and a clinging sweet smell. Letters drawn too long and mixed with old German and Latin script. Dated in Berlin, the letter said:

Dear Party Member Höllriegl!

Quite by accident I've heard (don't ask from whom) that you are to spend some time here. Please be sure to call FREIsslerhorst 82-57; mornings until eight is the best time. Or call GNEIsenau 69-11, extension 272, until 5 P.M. Would love to see you.

With German Greetings!

Anselma Geldens, née von Eycke.

P.S. I hope you won't bet on the wrong horse again!"

Herr von Eycke's strange sister. The letter confused him. Should he interpret the "wrong horse" politically or privately? In any case a very gross hint. Did the remark refer to Ulla? The tone of the letter was pointedly personal.

Höllriegl spent the evening hours of that catastrophic day—they seemed to last an eternity—only half conscious, lying stretched out on the couch, his eyes poking holes into the sky. After an inner struggle he had swallowed a few tranquilizers which, although officially banned, were widely used. Once or twice he sat down at the piano to play out his romantic fantasies as he used to do in his Linz days, leaning heavily on the pedal and indulging in virtuoso flights of fancy with the tears bright in his eyes. In between he made cold compresses for himself. The whole room smelled of Epsom salts. From time to time he heard the sound of muffled drums. Did it come from the street or through the walls? The weals on his forehead were blood-red, one eye swollen and black. He would have to continue the compresses all day tomorrow without a break if he wanted to look halfway decent on Monday. Would Ulla talk?

Again the sound of drums and right after them the roar of the lures, long and drawn out, terrible, as if the end of the world had come, the Ragnarok, the great eclipse of the gods. What was all that? He finally realized that it had to be more than just a special message to the nation. His heartbeat stopped, he felt his neck stiffen, the pressure on the back of his head grew unbearable, the floor under his feet swayed and seemed to rear up in front of him. He had an urge to vomit.

He turned on the TV set. It was 10 P.M. exactly. The Reich Minister for Public Enlightenment and Propaganda appeared on the screen. His picture was distorted, the contours seemed unnaturally sharp. Hollow-cheeked, exhausted, the small, chiseled head bent forward, enormous concentration and exertion of will reflected in his features; he seemed to look deeply into Höllriegl's and indeed everyone's heart—and spoke in a voice full of sadness this one sentence:

"German people! The Führer has entered the eternal Valhalla."

The picture disappeared like a phantom. And again drums and the call of the lures. And then a voice spoke a Nordic litany. Höllriegl sank to his knees. He could hear his heart hammer in the stillness.

THE ARCH JEW OF THE THIRD REICH

It had poured all day Sunday, and now, Monday noon, it was still drizzling. Never had the world seemed as funereal and ominous. The catastrophe, overpowering as no other in the history of the West, had convulsed the globe. A state of paralysis, strange and unexpected, Höllriegl thought, had come over the world. At the same time this universal numbness might reflect a state of extreme tension. No one had yet dared to ask what would happen now—but the question hovered on everyone's lips. One of Höllriegl's Heydrich neighbors, a certain Dr. Senkpiehl, a psychiatrist, had been more specific on the telephone. (Höllriegl had not set foot outside the door.) He spoke of catatonic conditions, spastic paralysis, stupor, and similar things. So others felt it too, only everyone explained it in his own way. "Something is in the air," the man had said, and it wasn't clear if he meant the threatening situation in the Far East.

In spite of everything, and as much as it hurt and annoyed him, Höllriegl was unable to feel real sorrow. He lusted for pain. He had idolized the Führer till the end—idolized him as he had so long ago when he had been a young, nameless, illegal fighter in the Ostmark against the regime of Jews, Freemasons, and priests. But Adolf Hitler was no more. Odin had summoned his messenger to Valhalla. Further than that Höllriegl did not want to think; indeed could not think. And how strange, in hours as decisive for the fate of the world as these, he felt something akin to relief. Now the amber witch would not talk. The great event which touched the heart of every German, which had plunged the most powerful nation on earth into deep sorrow, would leave that ugly little incident forgotten.

The dampness chilled him to the marrow of his bones. Höllriegl had not turned on the heater. He hated that lazy warmth in his car. The electronically controlled street barriers around the zoo slowed him to a crawl. The capital of the Reich was drowned in black cloth. Sopping-wet flags of mourning, twisted into rope strands by the wind, hung from every window. Every party and army office in the world had received orders to show the flag. Black crape hung from the half-masted standards, flags, and storm banners. It all looked tattered, undignified, a macabre joke. The flags swung from their poles like men who had been hanged. Many of the people on the streets wore black clothing, and some of the women were deeply veiled. In this weather few pedestrians were in the streets, but many cars. Otherwise there was nothing out of the ordinary; except perhaps for the fact that police patrolled in pairs and that units of the National Socialist Power Drivers Corps (NSKK) controlled traffic at major intersections.

Höllriegl had driven half the night, enjoying travel after dark. He loved the quiet, lonely wayside inns along the autobahns, with their sleepy waitresses (whom he called "enchanted princesses," he did not exactly know why) and the warm smell of coffee. He met only truck drivers and guards at the security zones, uncommunicative and peevish folk. This time—he had stopped twice—depressed silence predominated. Everyone seemed busy with his own thoughts. Near Eichmannstadt—the inn was shaped like a windmill and extremely comfortable—the waitress, a faded, flax-blond goat with red eyelids and goiterous bulging eyeballs, seemed to pursue him with importunate glances. Sometimes she would interrupt her knitting and steal a look at his forehead. (The Mark of Cain!) He was the only guest. When he went to the men's room, she followed, pretending she had business in the narrow passage, and pressed past him—a silent scene—so that, whether he wanted to or not, he had to feel her thinness but also her very large and spongy bosom. While he took care of his business in the lavatory, he thought she listened outside the door. But it proved an illusion. When he reentered the dining room, the "enchanted princess" sat once again in front of her espresso machine and stared at her knitting. When he left, he said good-bye in his slovenly way: "Heitla." The girl pushed the coins he had given her into a heap and murmured absently, "Good day."

Anyway, the tranquilizers had made him doze half of Sunday away. He had only done a little work for the *Kyffhäuser Messenger* and answered a few queries. Before going on to the pension on Uhland Eck, he wanted to take a quick look at the house on Tiergartenstrasse.

The broken tower of the Memorial Church—it, too, a victory monument to the great night of fire—poked into an endless and empty sky. The weather had turned so dreary and dark that fog lights gleamed from auto hoods. Slow-moving traffic took Höllriegl's car across the Landwehr Canal, whose waters pushed soot-black and oily underneath the bridge. At the end of Graf Spee Strasse, the first trees of the Tiergarten loomed out of the fog. Höllriegl drove past a closed cinema, decorated with insignia and black drapes, which only on Saturday had featured the Karl May film *In the Empire of the Silver Lion.* An almost physical pain went through him. Every schoolchild knew how much the Führer had loved that book.

Happy to realize that he could still experience sadness, he turned the corner into Tiergartenstrasse, where traffic was less dense. In the Tiergarten section of town, only high-ranking officials were allowed to park their cars and then only with special permits which were strictly controlled. His orders, which he had had to show a number of times, would, he was sure, do.

Tiergartenstrasse 4. A large box eight stories high, whose facade had been strikingly renovated to stress simple lines, yet with a hint of monumentality. Brown paint indicated its official character. A single flag at half-mast and hung in black crape—the flag of the NS space program.

His practiced eye quickly moved down the housefront. The great gate, flanked by Doric columns that resembled a temple door, was shut. Not a guard in sight. Behind most of the windows neon lights burned the day out of one's eyes. In a park clearing on the other side of the street, a brigade of subhumans was busily erecting a banner depicting the Führer making a speech.

Höllriegl got out of his car in order to read the signs on the entrance more easily. Office for Physical Training, Greater Berlin

. . . Keough and Sons, Pearl Cultivators and Exporters, Hong Kong/Kobe . . . Leodegar Schwemmle, Machinery . . . German Space Front: Commissioner for the Dissemination of National Socialist Thought in the Universe . . . German Reich Bank East, Administration of the Volga Gau . . . Reich School for Atmosphere Control and Radiation Protection (obviously "his" office) . . . Madame de Saint-Punt, Predictions.

Some of the plaques were new; the wet bronze had a rosy gleam. Others appeared older. The building housed private businesses as well.

Behind the wheel again, his thoughts returned to Schwerdtfeger's "secret Reich business." And what had been his other remark? The highest astrologer would be involved too. That could only mean the former deputy of the Führer (his office and five suboffices no longer existed—Reichsleiter Martin Bormann himself had dissolved them), who, after his liberation from a British prison and an embarrassing trial before the highest party court, had suddenly disappeared. Schizophrenia? Something like that had been talked about. In any case a living corpse . . . though perhaps allowed to practice his hobby, astrology. Had he been rehabilitated? Incredible. Or had that scribbler merely used one of those symbolic phrases that indicate membership in the "inner" circle? A simple party member just couldn't know.

And something else. From whom and through what channels had Frau Anselma (what was her married name?) learned that he would be in Berlin? Perhaps she knew more—for example where and for whom he would work.

Höllriegl had made a date with Anselma Geldens for one thirty that afternoon in a little Danish restaurant on the upper Kurfürstendamm. The place would not be too crowded then. He liked it on sight: the dim atmosphere, the small tables with gleaming white tablecloths set in a long funnel-shaped room, the amber lighting. He found a snug little corner for two and stared expectantly at the entrance. Latin-looking waiters scurried about silently; the muted voices of the guests, the sound of cutlery and dishes, the popping of bottle corks, everything seemed as it always had. A healthy, peaceful, and enormously secure world! It was marvelous! He felt wonderful. Softly he began whistling through his teeth. In the pseudo-antique mirror opposite, his head appeared framed in sluggish tobacco smoke. (Not bad-looking, really . . .)

Suddenly he felt a hand on his shoulder. Turning around, he saw Frau Geldens in front of him, small and delicate. "I sneaked in," she said, smiling at Höllriegl, who jumped up to greet her. "I couldn't find a parking place on the street and had to enter by way of the courtyard. How are you?"

He kissed her delicate hand and helped her out of her fur coat. (Something special—monkey fur?) The childish neck shimmered like ivory. Underneath the boyishly short, dark hair, Höllriegl noted with sudden delight Anselma's small, nobly formed ears. A sultry fragrance clung to her clothes: very astringent, somehow musty. Dying flowers smelled like that. Mrs. Geldens naturally wore mourning.

Höllriegl had seen Herr von Eycke's sister only two or three times and then very briefly: once in Radebeul, later at receptions. She had remained in his memory as a doll-like, sickly person, always feeling cold. She must have suffered from a touch of tuberculosis or liver trouble. She had lived for many years in Indonesia as wife of a steel representative of Dutch descent. Mijnheer Geldens was no longer alive.

"Let's agree on two things right away," she said. "You won't ask me how I know that you'd come to Berlin, and I won't ask you where you got that cut and the pretty eye. Agreed?"

He answered her conventional chatter mechanically, but never stopped observing her even while he ordered two vegetarian plates and fruit juice. Anselma had fine bones, her complexion was pale, spotted and transparent as if the skin stretched around her joints had been a shade too light and too shiny. Nervous, elegant gestures. A low, intelligent forehead. Strange—the face looked different in profile than it did from the front. Anselma was really two-faced. Her voice had a soft, sensuous tone, but not warmly so; rather it was cold, even glassily cold. It was inconceivable that this voice could ever be loud. The woman had something of a child about her; undeveloped, yet at the same time a little old. (The gently crumpled mouth.) She was probably younger than Ulla, but her bloom had begun to fade. And she did not try to hide the fact. On the contrary, she stressed it through her perfume, through some perhaps involuntary hints in her clothing.

Anselma's eyes! Yet it wasn't the eyes, he decided, which were so captivating. The iris was spotted brown-green. A stinging, sucking sheen glowed in the pupils. But her immediate and chief fascination came, he thought, from her penetrating, rigid, knowing, "old" look. The eyes seemed overly large in that narrow face with the slightly withered cheeks.

They talked about all sorts of things while they ate. Both were supporters of German nature healing, founded by Bilz in Radebeul. In talking about the Nature Healers' Congress, Anselma spoke briefly about her sister-in-law. She did not seem on particularly good terms with her.

"Ulla is a poster beauty done in Nordic style and for all that more a Slav than a Teuton. She is enormously alive and ego-possessed, did you know that? I wonder if Erik is happy with her. I have no idea. My brother is very close-mouthed, just interested in politics."

She left the discussion of her family quickly, but not before glancing mistrustfully at Höllriegl a moment. The pendular sciences interested her. He'd have to come and dowse her house too. Funny, without really noticing it, they had slipped into a bantering kind of verbal skirmish replete with double meanings. It was as if they undressed each other—in all chastity, of course. Höllriegl began to exhibit his mythological knowledge, reciting verses from the *Völsunga Saga,* from "Helgakvidha Hundingsbana" ("In ancient days, when eagles sang . . .") and from "Sigrdîfumâl." Then he moved to a frontal attack.

"I'm sure you have a charming Asiatic honorary name from the years you spent there," he said, a twinkle in his eye. "Or an erotic one?"

He looked at her brazenly. Perhaps too brazenly. Quickly he glanced away.

"My name is Kostbe̲ra, the treasured one, but I would much rather be called Knêfrōdh, the kneeling one." Her eyes, gliding across his shoulders, had something humble about them and at the same time lascivious. She looked at him from below, straight in the eyes. He met her gaze and held it. A pause arose, which the angel of silence—a most unholy silence—crossed slowly.

"You *are* a treasured one. The name fits. But Hyrr, the flame, would be even better, or Ridhill," he added, reeling off more mythological incense. "For me you are Sinfiötli, the Chain of the Senses."

"You're confusing everything, just tossing things together." Anselma's derision was gentle and well modulated. "Ridhill is

Reginn's sword and therefore—fie upon you—something neuter. I could only be the sheath. And Sinfiötli is a man, Siegmund's son and the grandson of Völsung from the 'Sinfiötlalok' —you know, the lost heroic epic, which Herms Niel has turned into such a stupid opera." And suddenly she sang in her soft voice: "Son, leave the beard be . . ."

She knew her mythology. He was a neophyte in comparison.

"Nevertheless, I shall call you Chain of the Senses."

A pleasant shudder went through him, prickly in his veins like champagne. Anselma was magic. Warm waves flowed from her body with its swollen little bosom. His nerves vibrated under the onslaught.

The conversation turned back toward more harmless things. Frau Geldens worked in the economic-policy section of the Foreign Ministry. She was employed in the Office for the Reich Protectorate Indonesia which, as an enclave in the Jap-controlled part of the world, was threatened terrain. Anselma's knowledge of local conditions made her a valued employee; in addition to Dutch she spoke fluent Malay, a little Chinese, Japanese, and pidgin English. She lived near her office on Wilhelmstrasse, on the top floor of a renovated house in a very elegant and apparently quite large three-room apartment with a roof garden. She showed him photographs which revealed her bizarre and exotic taste in furnishings. Her Chinese cook, a serf she had brought with her from the South Seas, completed the ménage.

Höllriegl kept trying to feel his way back to a more intimate sphere. Above all else he wanted to find out if she had any good connections in the Reich's capital. At first Anselma's answers were ironic and evasive, but then she let slip that she did have influential friends and well-wishers. Thus she knew the nephew of the former Reichsportsführer for Tschammer and the East, who held a leading position with the Reich film-censorship office. She talked of her friendship—a flexible concept—with Lieutenant General Hansjoachim von Geyl-Aufsesser, at the time a section chief with the Army High Command in charge of educating new leadership cadres. She dropped Bonhoeffer's name, which meant big business. Finally she mentioned a source in the Führer's presidium. That was all Höllriegl needed. He was speechless with awe.

Only once did they touch very briefly on the problem of death.

Anselma, in contrast to Höllriegl, did not believe in an existence after death, or in the afterlife of the Führer's soul. Man came from nothing and would have to return there. Höllriegl was amazed at her mentioning such heretical ideas to a semistranger. However, extreme racists, Werewolves, and NATMAT supporters did deny the possibility of afterlife. For Anselma the German people as a whole would become carriers of the Führer's soul; the Master Race would turn into the "mystic body" of Adolf Hitler. She did not venture any further than that, perhaps out of consideration for Höllriegl's romantic ways. For he still loved the world of the Nordic gods—not that he believed in their metaphysical existence, but rather in the idea they embodied. Thus he was convinced that the eternal German people had sprung from the holy seed of the mystical ash tree Yggdrasil, but this conventional article of faith, taught in every school, could not withstand Anselma's mocking eyes.

As if by mutual consent, nothing more was said about the Führer's death, much to Höllriegl's relief. Anselma only mentioned the rumor that on his deathbed the Führer had put his political testament on tape but that it had disappeared. The prime suspect was the "Forest Devil," the most feared man in Germany. This Ivo Köpfler, a German Croat who took his title from his wartime guerilla operations against the Titoists, had managed to build up his two key roles within the party into an impregnable position. He had been staff leader in the office of the late Martin Bormann, who had died under mysterious circumstances. After his death (or disappearance), the Forest Devil took over the orphaned office and pushed Bormann's chief assistant aside. At the same time the Führer named him Chief of the Reich Chancellery, even though Ivo Köpfler—his political name—was anything but a diplomat. Köpfler, party boss of the NSDAP, Chief of the Reich Chancellery and Minister without portfolio was, next to Adolf Hitler, the most powerful man in the state. The Führer had trusted him as no one else.

And Frau Geldens told him something else, something pretty awful. Right after the news of Hitler's death had spread around the globe, bloody unrest erupted in the United Vassal States of America (UVSA), mostly in the Apemen Reservations (AMR) and the Apemen Camps (AMC) of the south. How the subhumans had learned the news remained a mystery because ever since the three-man council of the KKK seized power and reintroduced slavery, just as it had existed before the notorious Emancipation Proclamation, the already rigorous measures separating the races had been made much harsher. But in Neosho, Missouri, and Wickliffe, Kentucky, open revolts had begun. Political criminals and colored apelings had killed the camp guards and—hard to believe—broken into a cache of laser guns. In Wickliffe a former Negro priest had led the uprising.

"The Minutemen grabbed that bastard, hung him upside down on a branch, and roasted him. The guy is supposed to have yowled Jewish psalms while they were doing it." Radio and newspapers had not carried the stories. They had been mentioned only in internal party reports which she occasionally saw.

"Speaking of roasting," she said smiling, "I'm taking an advanced Spartacism course, and just a little while ago they showed a marvelous new film series. You should have seen it—new educational material, all done by amateurs. One of them I found very impressive: decapitation of rebellious subhumans with the hand ax, in all phases and close-ups. That kind of execution is only used for terrorization. One steer-necked Bulgarian's head—he'd tried to make love to a German-blooded girl—just wouldn't come off. The hangman, obviously one of those drafted idiots, had to hack three times before the fellow died. And another film: punishment of female material on the pyre—with sound. Sensational! You should have heard them scream when their feet began to broil. It's incredible how soft some people are!"

Anselma's eyes shone, she seemed all eyes. "I mean the ladies from my office when I say 'soft.' First they can't wait to take part, then they collapse. One got deathly ill, she threw up big lumps and peed all over herself during the performance. Another one rolled her eyes, as if she had an epileptic attack and fussed on and on, even though she had already taken a special course. It's all hysteria, of course; all they need is . . ."

Again she looked at him, her eyes at once lascivious and lazy. Höllriegl held her gaze, but it took some effort. It was like a long, secret touching. "What are they going to do when the next series is shown? Interrogation and lethal injections for the disobedient. Slow-motion pictures of strangulation with a wire loop draped over a meat hook, the work with the garrote, or—perhaps best of all—our experiments in the closed sections, LSD 25 and such."

With such conversation they passed the time. Höllriegl felt they were coming closer, touching one another. Anselma was not his type—he yearned for the Nordic light figures, for heroic women with big buttocks (suddenly he thought of Ulla—oh, how that hurt), but Anselma's charm, a mixture of tropical intelligence and that new, sharp, and matter-of-fact manner he admired so because he could never adopt it (I'm too old-fashioned) had fascinated him. Undoubtedly she was a woman of rare breeding, a real von Eycke. And he? What was he? A mixed breed.

When they parted he promised to call her soon. "I'm busy tonight, but tomorrow, perhaps . . ." Her eyes again ran over his body, leaving delicious imprints. "As a good Ostmarker you had to choose the name of an Ostrogoth king . . . only sometimes you can't conquer Rome without suffering a black eye. Totila is really a student's nickname. My father—his student corps was the Wormser Black Teutons—called himself that on the fencing floor." And then, her voice full of meaning, she said, "Your name ought to be Moldwerf—Mole. . . ."

The manicured child's hand with its fine bones lay in his big paw and quivered as he kissed it.

A dark November day, as dreary as before lunch. Across the street from the house on Tiergartenstrasse the gray-uniformed subhumans were still putting up the banner. Höllriegl looked at his watch and walked to the building, his steps as light as ever.

The concierge's loge had been turned into a guardroom and resembled a small army encampment. He gave his name and that of his contact man and was handed a timed pass. The house swarmed with uniforms. Guards stood on every staircase landing like black statues, tall men whose empty eyes stared into a vacuum.

Ostuf Hirnchristl, a cheese-faced, thin man with receding hair, a blond little moustache, and jutting chin, glanced at the pass and then greeted his countryman effusively. "Great that you're here," he said in the soft and lazy tones of the Ostmark. He knew right away what it was all about.

"You're to work tonight. We'll pick you up about six. You live"

—again a quick glance at his pass—"at Frau Zweenemann's pension on Uhland Corner? Hope you won't mind riding in a Black Maria. You're not supposed to know where you're going. Orders."

Hirnchristl jumped up and down like a rubber ball behind his fortress of a desk and gestured with his arms as if directing traffic at a busy intersection. Three telephones had been planted on the table in front of him: one red, one black, one white. They rang in turn. Conversation with this "countryman" was possible only telegram-style in bits and pieces.

The office contained a round table, two leather arm chairs, and a couch. Across from Hirnchristl sat an elderly woman at the typewriter, her hair braided around her head. An office like a thousand others: cold neon light, a Führer portrait hung with mourning crape, and a few potted plants (the result of a recent German Labor Front order "to create sunny working spaces"). On the wall in awkward Gothic script was the slogan "The Party thinks for you," which had long ago supplanted "The Party cares for you."

"When you're through, don't bother coming back here—just call me before going home and I'll pass the word to the higher-ups." After another telephone interruption he continued, "We have another patient for you. Do you know who Gundlfinger is? I mean the philosopher or whatever he is . . . oh, kiss my ass!" The oath, murmured under his breath, came in response to a ring on the red telephone. Nevertheless the Obersturmführer was all business at once, shaking off his easygoing casualness to bark: "Yes, sir, we'll do it . . . a dirty trip . . . ha-ha-ha-ha . . . yes, sir!" And so on.

Turning back to Höllriegl, he asked again, "Do you know Gundlfinger?"

Höllriegl nodded. Of course he knew the name. Just a little while ago he had read one of the great man's essays in a manual for party functionaries. He remembered it well. What was the title? *On the Humanity of Concentration Camp Punishment,* or something like that.

"You're supposed to do a little dowsing at this Professor Gundlfinger's house. A Herr"—Hirnchristl consulted his calendar—"Schwerdtfeger, a big cheese in the Reich's Writers' Union, recommended you. My compliments. Your contacts aren't bad." Another pause, while Hirnchristl answered the phone. Then: "How'll you get there? The professor lives pretty much alone. Wait a minute, it's in"—again he flipped through the calendar—"Sauckelruh near Rundstedt, Villa Walpurgis in the Harz Mountains. You can take the autobahn to Magdeburg and from there through Halberstadt and Wernigerode, a state road. Of course the Harz isn't exactly on your way . . . but you can do it somehow. It doesn't matter when you get there—on your way home. Here's the professor's telephone number and the area code. Oh, he's got a telex too. Pretty good, eh?"

How smoothly everything was fitted together. Höllriegl felt like a chess figure pushed from one square to another by an invisible player. The thought calmed him. It was good that way. Everything was good. Sometimes it was nice not to have to think. Others—the mighty—did it for you. A sane world.

The secretary wrote the time on his pass, and Ostuf Hirnchristl scribbled his signature. Höllriegl said good-bye, slammed his heels together, and shot up his right arm. The man opposite did likewise, thrusting forward his chin. As he did so, his pale eyes took on a steely luster.

As Höllriegl walked down the steps past the guard, he suddenly felt terribly tired, as if liquid lead flowed in his veins. He needed time to rest. Back to the hotel, and quickly.

Once in his room—overheated, narrow, and impersonal—he threw himself fully dressed on the couch and quickly fell asleep. It was not exactly a refreshing slumber. He was haunted by one dream which kept recurring. A black-bearded, one-eyed man, dressed in an overcoat and broad-brimmed hat, a slaughtering ax in hand and surrounded by butcher apprentices with blood-spattered aprons, was trying to kill a tethered horse. Höllriegl somehow knew it was a mare. But if you looked closely, the mare turned out to be a naked woman, light-skinned with wheat-blond tresses and full-bosomed. The fetters cut deeply into her flesh. Höllriegl wanted to rush over and free the victim, but the butchers grabbed him and tied him to another stake. The man with the empty eye socket had disappeared, and in his stead the naked blond woman, now unfettered, swung a knife which she was sharpening on an old-fashioned grinding stone, as Höllriegl remembered them from traveling knife-grinders in his childhood. Now the woman was not the beautiful Amazon of a minute ago, but a pale, bony, fake-blond creature with red-rimmed, bulging eyes and balloonlike breasts. She approached him with an inquisitive expression on her face and slowly slit his throat. Höllriegl wanted to scream but could only gurgle and cluck. A stream of blood tore from his mouth. . . .

He woke up. It was a quarter to six. He felt heavy pressure and pain in the back of his head. He let some water run into the sink and washed his hot, dry face. Then he took two pendulums and a rod from his suitcase. Carefully and with complete inner concentration he checked out the instruments. When he was finished, the bell rang.

Two men in civilian clothes stood in the vestibule. What do guards look like? They don't look like anything, and that sums them up. Silently they accompanied Höllriegl to the car waiting at the corner. A wind had sprung up and dusted a thin rain into his face. Horrible weather! The brightly lit street was empty.

A dark-green police car with blue lights waited. One of the men opened the door at the back and helped Höllriegl get in. There were no windows; only small, covered openings that did not afford a view of the outside. A pillow had been put on the wooden bench. How touching, he was to be treated as a special prisoner. The door slammed shut; he was left alone in the dimly lit compartment.

When the vehicle began to move, Höllriegl automatically put his hand under the seat. Had an exhaust pipe been built into the inside? He found nothing. This was not a death car.

The trip lasted about half an hour. Perhaps a Berliner with practiced ears could have figured out the direction they were taking. But Höllriegl didn't know the city well enough to orient himself by the street noises. Twice he heard elevated trains thunder over a viaduct. Then it became more quiet, with only the occasional noise of a motor breaking the stillness. Fresh, cold air flowed in through the slits.

The car drove slowly along what he could feel was a curving road. Then it stopped. The door flew open and a guard entered. "I've been ordered to blindfold you," the man said. He helped Höllriegl step out, then led him slowly away. Some light filtered through the blind.

"Careful—steps."

They walked thus for a while, with the man giving directions in short, sharp sentences. A dry, desertlike heat beat against him. Once again light filtered through the blind, a little weaker this time. After they had climbed up a creaking wooden staircase and walked through several rooms—or halls—the guard stopped.

"You'll stay here," he said roughly and took the blindfold from Höllriegl's eyes. "You'll be picked up for the trip back." And the man disappeared.

Höllriegl found himself in a high-ceilinged chamber whose windows were covered with thick yellowish curtains made of some heavy, waxlike material. The room gleamed darkly in yellow and gold. A candelabrum (was it ebony?) spread a diffuse light. The contours of baroque and obviously expensive furniture took shape out of the darkness. A strange radiance glowed from the pictures on the walls.

Höllriegl remained where the guard had left him. He looked at every corner of the room with extreme care, sensing danger. Where was he? It would be easy to observe him here from behind the curtains or through slits in the pictures. Relaxing his face muscles, he adopted a careless stance and placed rod and pendulum on a small table. He walked about the room, ready to take cover at any moment. Had he fallen into a trap?

Strange, the pictures in their ornamental frames even glowed in dark corners. He stepped closer and his astonishment grew. They were illuminated from within, and every one depicted reptiles, animals of fantastic shapes and unique ugliness. Some stood half upright on their hind legs, others ran about on all fours. Their claws and teeth resembled long daggers, the toadlike heads armed with quills were an agony to behold. The lizards appeared to be prehistoric. In the glimmering light they seemed to crawl, their heads to move. The pictures, or rather slides, had captions. "*Varanosaurus, Permian—Texas*" was written under one. "*Seymouria, Carboniferous* under another. A salamanderlike creature with spiteful, gaping eyes and sharply fanged jaws was called "*Baphetes*" and described as "*Stegocephalitic amphibian, Canada.*" There were also crocodilelike animals with winged flaps of skin that seemed to circle above foreign vegetation. Höllriegl went from picture to picture —all delicately framed as if they were amorous scenes from the rococo—and examined the collection with some distaste. Was he in a zoological circus? Was the owner, whoever he might be, a lover of extinct beasts or an explorer of the primeval world?

Höllriegl became agitated. Where was he? He jumped to the

nearest window and pulled the curtains aside. Terrified, he recoiled from the glittering blue light that stung his eyes. The building seemed bathed in the glare of searchlights. Blinded, he groped back to the little table on which he had put his instruments. He thought he had seen the silhouettes of trees.

Still dazed, he did not notice that someone else had entered the room. The man did not move. Only after Höllriegl almost bumped into him did he bow ceremoniously; then he shoved aside the heavy curtains behind him and opened a hidden door. Höllriegl, picking up his rod and pendulums, followed.

The same tropical heat he had found bothersome earlier fell against him like heavy surf. The air was very dry and smelled of ozone. The moment Höllriegl crossed the threshold, he felt the proximity of illness and death. This was obviously a death chamber.

Not much could be seen in the room, but what was visible suggested a woman's touch. Here, too, the dominating color was a dull and gloomy yellow. White transparent curtains at the windows. A man—a gentleman, rather—lay with closed eyes on a low, curved bed that resembled a flat black shell with a canopy. A silver candelabrum shed a pale light. The candles—Höllriegl counted seven of them—had already burned low.

The man's head rested gracefully on a pillow. His hand, showing below lace cuffs, moved quiveringly across the sheet. Notwithstanding the heat, a heavy blanket had been spread across the bottom half of the patient's body. His breath came fast.

Höllriegl marveled at the dying man's beauty. A sallow countenance of Roman features and gemlike sharpness with dark-green shadows around eyes and mouth. The hands were lovely. Except for an indefinably oriental cast, one might have thought of a Roman emperor facing his last hour. Black, smooth hair framed the high, narrow forehead. Nevertheless this was an old man.

Höllriegl's art—anyone's art—was too late. Why had he been called here? What good would it do if he could determine the impact of earth radiation? Obviously the bed stood in a bad zone. The smell of death filled the room. Höllriegl wondered why the candlelight did not flicker.

The majestic gentleman slowly opened his eyes and looked at Höllriegl for a long time; a sad look. Then he motioned for him to come closer. Höllriegl sat on a stool, and at once the sick man began to speak, quickly and lispingly. But the movements of his mouth at once destroyed the harmony of his noble face, as one grimace after another passed across it. Suddenly Höllriegl realized that it had become apish. The dying man was not a member of the master race, but an apeling, a Tschandal.

He spoke in such low tones that Höllriegl had to bend down to hear. The articulation was sharp and hissing, as that of a talking parrot. The man's face was turned a little to one side, as if he were afraid his breath would offend.

". . . his name was Hersch Glasel and he was a Thora writer," Höllriegl heard him say. "I went to school in . . . (it sounded like Rustschuk) and even today I shake with disgust when I think of my brethren in the faith who shared my classroom bench. They all stank of garlic and sweaty feet, and of garlicky and sweaty learning. All that stinking study from Zeraim and Nezikin. Careful, I think I'll throw up. Even the daughters of Israel whose asses we pinched stank of garlic. The Talmud says that garlic is a healthy food, good for the Yids. Later I knew: It wasn't garlic that stank so much but the smell of the racially inferior . . ."

Höllriegl froze. The apeling was—a Jew! How long had it been since he had last seen a Jew? Neither white nor black Jews existed anymore. They had been exterminated long ago. The "Jew" had become a concept of ontology, a historically abstract word. Jews existed only in museums of natural history, where they had been stuffed and put on display as a strange fruit of hominoid split off from the human race, an animal-demonic type mankind had expelled in reaching for physical and spiritual emancipation and the Apollonian fulfillment that lay beyond. Again and again the "animal" in man has been extirpated in order to realize the Nordic man, heroic and bathed in light. Individual Jews who had escaped the Final Solution, the so-called Günther Enterprise, may have found refuge somewhere in the Tschandal regions at the edge of civilization. But news of SD actions against a Jew—smoking the man out of a cave and the like—was rare. Not even Jewish mixtures existed anymore because after the victory of the Pan-Aryan movement within the party, selection for the subhuman camps was carried out on the basis of the stricter regulations imposed by the Reich Law for the Protection of German Blood and German

Honor. Jewish mixtures of the first and second degree (two and one Jewish grandparents respectively) had been slotted for extermination categories V and VI after Gypsies, Freemasons, Bible scholars, and those condemned by genetic courts. They had also been used in the famous experiments on racial odors which will forever be linked to the name of Traugott von Globke-Lynar.

And now this Jew—right in the middle of the capital and obviously in an important post! "A very important person—secret Reich business." Was he dreaming? Could all this still be real? Wasn't it already madness?

Höllriegl again noted the sickly sweet smell in the room, which he had first thought was ozone. Instead it was the racial smell of the Jew, even of the washed ones, whose chemical formula Baron von Globke-Lynar had discovered.

". . . I started out in a bank. The manager, a certain Dowidl Aufwerber, a bachelor, took to me. I was pretty good-looking and Dowidl was queer. Once Dowidl's secretary—she was nuts about him—caught us in the toilet. We'd forgotten to lock the door. You should have heard all the noise! And the scandal! Just because she went and blabbed it all. Aufwerber was transferred to the head office in Bucharest. As for me, they moved me first to Ploeşti and then to Hermannstadt, Sibiu in Romanian. Young as I was, I soon made head cashier. Everyone bought and sold in those days. The war hadn't been over for long. In Hungary Béla Kun had just come to power. Money wasn't worth a damn; the lei fell way down, the Austrian crown, the Czech crown. The first shiksa I got into was the daughter of an industrialist from Kronstadt—steel, I think—German, of course; a girl with forget-me-not eyes, thick blond tresses, Gretl hairdo, long legs, and big breasts. Nineteen—and so appetizing! *She* didn't stink of garlic."

Voluptuous shapes arose spontaneously in Höllriegl's mind, diverting him from the apeling's babbling. And the pain he felt then continued as he stared blindly into the sick man's face, which never stopped talking in a sharp sibilant voice.

". . . the second scandal was even worse. I lent the goy money to play the market and her old man had to pay me back, lei on lei, even though he kicked the Jew boy out of the house. The Germans in Romania risk friendship and marriage only among themselves —God help a German who ever has a little affair with a Romanian or a Gypsy or a Yid. They kick him out of the family fast. So the shiksa, her name was Christa, first wanted to kill herself because of the disgrace and the money she lost, but then she managed to land a guy, a first-rate Aryan with lots of dough, and she forgot all about the Jew boy. So I had to figure out another way of getting into high society, and I thought of the Masons, and, you know, I made it. Aufwerber, that miserable bastard, was a big cheese at Humanitas in Bucharest, and he wrote to his lodge brothers in Sibiu and even found two witnesses for me. So what with one thing and another, I got into the lodge of the Three Crowned Stars. I really was a seeker, though of course not in their way. The day of my induction was my birthday, the twenty-fifth. I'll never forget the festivities . . . burning candles . . . the many flowers . . . the speeches. Neither clothed nor naked, neither shod nor barefoot, stripped of all metal, and eyes blindfolded, I was led to the door of the lodge. Oh, when I think back on my apprentice's days, everything seems joy and laughter. The tests for a first-degree Mason, the swearing-in ceremony, the Feast of Light, the old duties, everything . . . everything. What is the time? High twelve. Do you have the key to the secrets? Yes. Where do you keep it? In a box of bones that can be opened and closed only with an ivory key. Is the key hanging or lying? It is hanging. On what does it hang? On a band nine inches long. What is it made of? It is not made of metal; it is a tongue of good repute, as good behind a brother's back as it is to his face. Fifteen years later I was Heydrich's right hand in setting up the lodge museums. . . ."

The dying man seemed delirious, his hands moved restlessly across the blanket as if he wanted to smooth it down. Had he swallowed a drug? His face glowed. Why had he, Höllriegl, been selected to hear this apeling's confession? For the man confessed in the face of death. Höllriegl wouldn't say a word. A tape recorder must be running somewhere to take everything down.

The Jew's life poured out of his mouth to become a tapestry of the world between the great wars. He had gone from Bucharest to Vienna and moved very quickly into the world of high finance: from the stock exchanges of central Europe to the commodity markets of the world. He had taken a hand in mineral exploitation, been a pioneer in uranium prospecting, traded in diamonds, machine tools, religious articles, and white slavery. And done it under a hundred names: from Ferry Westphal in New York to Mijnheer Jochen Schuller tot Peursum in Amsterdam. After the great Wall Street crash in 1929, he looked for more permanent investments not subject to fluctuations and decided on mining and politics. Soon he had all the riches of central Europe in his hands and began pumping money into the Führer's political movement.

"In those days I used to meet Heydrich all the time to talk about turning synagogues and lodges into museums, teaching museums for the German people. I organized the traveling exhibit "The Eternal Jew." I was everywhere and I was nowhere. Of course I had my doubles, in the Reich and abroad. My favorite was a countryman of mine, a certain Dr. Demeter Barbu from Cluj, a former doctor and psychosyphilitic; Freud pupil and so on. He worked for me even before 1933. Good old Barbu. I used him as my alter ego mostly in negotiations where you had to depend on psychological tricks. A good head, Barbu, just terrific. Like a bee. He looked just like me, down to copying my way of talking, my gestures, and two cosmetic operations made the likeness more startling yet. I liked him, I really did. And he made a lot of money off me. Unfortunately, with time he knew too much. Much too much. And he wanted to know more. That's always bad. Thank God he was a big man with the women, just as I was. In Athens I got him involved with a Eurasian—sweet seventeen—after all, why else would you have contacts in the most important love markets in the world? A broad! I tell you, she'd crucified many a bull! Two years of making love with that little bitch and the good doctor was finished, and I mean finished. He only stayed alive by going from one sanatorium to another. Then suddenly I took the girl away. From one day to the next. He couldn't stand that, so he pumped a bullet through his little head. The stupid jerk. I felt sorry for him, my dear good Dr. Barbu. His lousy nerves are responsible for it all. When we stood around his grave, I almost had the feeling they were putting me down. After all, he was my other ego, down to all that business with women. And anyway, he was an Aryan. And I never did Aryans any harm unless I absolutely had to. But Barbu dug his own grave."

The apeling's face had turned ashen; his strength was ebbing fast. He grabbed Höllriegl's hands and pulled him abruptly down. Hoarsely he whispered:

"What did I want to do? Make the Rhine into the Jordan . . .

There is one much stronger than the God of the garlic stinkers —Odin. And Hitler is the true Messiah. He was the true messenger of the gods—the true, strong gods. And I, Egmond Thor (the last of my names), I had always dreamed of putting a hammer in my Führer's fist that would make lightning fly, and put it there I did. . . . The bomb fell on London, the capital of the Masons and Jews, the whore of Babylon that sits on the waters. . . . I gave the Führer the big atom hammer that smashed them to bits, the garlic stinkers who wanted to take over the world. . . . The Messiah defeated the enemies of the Chosen People, the Germans . . . and Odin was the big bomb who killed the little Jehovah. . . . And I was allowed to help—yes, me, little Naftali Stern . . . a grain of salt in the ocean . . . I was allowed to help. . . ."

Terrible cramps again seized the dying man, and this time the pain did not let go. The body jerked convulsively, the hands moved fitfully across the blanket—like windshield wipers, Höllriegl thought. The face was wet with perspiration. The lips moved mechanically, but his words choked in a guttural *chchchchchchchchch.*

What should he do? Höllriegl got up and stood undecided for a moment. Death might be close. Call a servant, a doctor; do something. Suddenly the feeling of anxiety which had accompanied him as he listened to the Jew's confession thickened into a clear realization of his own danger.

Why had he been selected to listen to a dying man's confession? Could it be an accident, or had everything been calculated and planned in advance? That he had been told to dowse this place had to be a bureaucratic error based on wrong or outdated reports. That sort of thing did happen. But suppose it had not been a mistake but a pretext? Or something else that would be fatal for him? Did they want to test him? *They?* Who? Did he have enemies, secret opponents? Had he fallen into the hands of the guild's secret court?

Again he feared a trap. But in heaven's name, who could be interested in baiting a trap for a small, loyal, unknown party member? Who could it be—the Eyckes? Did they want to ruin him for reasons he did not know and would never know? His orders to come to Berlin had been issued before his fateful meeting with Mrs. von Eycke. Or had that experiment only been arranged to lead him into temptation? Had someone foreseen the embarrassing outcome? Were the authorities all-knowing? And Anselma? What about her? She seemed to know more than he gave her credit for. . . .

As one question chased another through his mind, he looked about him. Had he been locked in? The villa was heavily guarded; he had seen that himself. How could he get out? Obviously flight would be futile. And anyway, where could he flee to? There was nothing for it but to wait—to ring for the servant.

The sick man groaned loudly and tossed on his bed. Again he seemed to want to draw Höllriegl to his side, but he paid no attention.

The servant who had brought Höllriegl to this room suddenly materialized out of nowhere. Silence seemed law here. He bent over the patient, disappeared as quickly as he had come, and returned with a hypodermic needle. Morphine? Höllriegl thought he was forgotten. Where was the door? He found it, grabbed his tools, and pushed it open. His guard stood outside.

"Are you finished?" the man asked.

"Yes." What else could he have said.

The guard tied the black blindfold around his head and walked slowly ahead of him. Höllriegl, one hand placed on the other man's shoulder, followed with small, uncertain steps. It took much longer this time . . . or did it only seem so? Höllriegl, alone with his wild thoughts, moved like an obedient robot. Downstairs, someone helped him into the car.

Where would they take him? They zoomed along at a good clip, but the trip seemed endless. His thoughts kept turning in circles . . . the Eyckes . . . Hirnchristl . . . Anselma . . . the apeling . . . Ulla . . . Schwerdtfeger . . . Anselma . . . the apeling . . . Ulla. When he was told to get out, he saw to his vast relief that the car had halted outside Zweenemann's pension.

It was eight thirty. Perhaps Hirnchristl was still at the office. Höllriegl couldn't unwind. He wanted to make his report at once and, while he was at it, demand an explanation. Of course Hirnchristl would pretend he didn't know anything. Reich School for Atmosphere Control and Radiation Protection—that was it. He found the number, dialed.

"This is the doorkeeper of Tiergartenstrasse 4."

"Heil Hitler. Please connect me with Ostuf Hirnchristl, if he is still in the building." No answer. Höllriegl heard a babble of voices and laughter.

"What was the name?"

"Obersturmführer Hirnchristl. I'll spell it. . . ."

"Fantastic name. Never heard of him. In what office is the Herr Obersturmführer supposed to work?"

"Atmosphere Control and Radiation Protection."

"Just a minute." The distant laughter turned into a roar that ebbed and flowed. The voice returned.

"Obersturmführer Hirnchristl absolutely unknown here. A gentleman of that name never worked here, doesn't exist. Must be a mistake. Heil."

Höllriegl put the receiver back. He felt discombobulated, and furious. What game were they playing? Did they want to make a fool of him? He would have no choice but to check into this more closely the next day at the radiation office itself. Could this Hirnchristl have been a figment of someone's imagination?

Höllriegl sat down at the desk and began to write his report. He had not got beyond the first few lines when the house phone rang. A thick, husky voice—Frau Zweenemann. "Please come into the dining room. A special message to the nation from the Reich Council will be broadcast in just a few minutes."

The dining room was a desolate, badly lit room, its tables covered with oilcloth. Each table crowned with identical cheap vases holding artificial flowers. A few guests had already arrived, others bustled in with frosty glances. The men all resembled country bumpkins, the women looked like employees for some maternity advisory office. They all had a worried and distant air about them. Most wore mourning. Höllriegl was in uniform and provided the only splash of color amid the black and gray.

On the blue-flickering screen—the TV stood on a pedestal underneath a picture of the Führer draped in black—appeared pictures of the Reich Council. A commentator talked ceaselessly in a whisper. The eye of the camera roamed around the giant auditorium. Shaped like an old German beer hall, it was decorated with shields, horns, and the historic standards of the national uprising. Over the last few years some of the greatest decisions in history had been made here. The hall itself was the model for thousands of community auditoriums in the worldwide Greater German Reich. The sight always inspired Höllriegl anew. The past of a great nation came alive in this hall: its nobility, traditions, spirit, and the greatness of its ancestors.

The seating arrangement in the Reich Council was a strict one. Rank and name determined a man's place. As tradition demanded, the lower echelons sat near the door, the higher-ups closer to the tribunal. The camera swung boldly to focus on one or the other of the Reich's nobles. The tribunal was still empty. Mounted above it was the portrait of the Führer, covered with national emblems; above it the gold Reich eagle. Two guards stood at attention, immobile as cast iron, holding the Führer's orphaned standards. The many SS men provided an unusual sight: They packed laser pistols that resembled optical instruments.

The only sound on screen besides the commentator's voice was an occasional clearing of throats or creaking of benches. No one dared say a word; they waited with bated breath for what was to come. The blood aristocracy of the Germanic World Empire had assembled. The Reich Councillors took their seats on benches near the Führer's tribunal as the commentator explained in a hushed voice that they had gathered to hear a message of decisive import for the future of mankind. All the world's great networks had hooked into the broadcast. Special relay stations would transmit sound and image to the remotest regions. Pictures of similar gatherings in Rome, Paris, Madrid, New London, Corpus Christi, Buenos Aires, and Pretoria flashed across the screen—a demonstration of the session's global significance.

Giants of history appeared: Marcel Déat, leader of the Breton Free State; old Pierre Laval; Vidkun Quisling; General Vlassow and Sir Oswald Mosley; the Chancellor of Burgundy, Léon Degrelle; the Caudillo; Mussolini's successor, Vinciguerra; and the chairman of the Ku Klux triumvirate, Senator Brad "Gusto" Fazlollah.

When the lures sounded, every eye turned toward the great gate opposite the tribunal. Klieg lights flamed up. At that moment a slender man of indeterminate age entered the hall. He did not have a retinue. He was beardless and hollow-cheeked, the small mouth collapsed as if toothless. The skin of his face was yellowish, leathery, artificially brown; the hair thin, colorless, and receding from the forehead. He wore boots and a simple black, ill-cut SS uniform without insignia of rank. His bearing was military but without the usual snap. A forest of raised arms greeted him. The heads of the dignitaries turned as he stepped quickly through the crowd toward the tribunal, his right arm raised in the German salute. He carried a briefcase. Höllriegl noted with some misgivings and dread that the black warriors had brought their laser guns into firing position.

Suddenly a young voice exploded in a ringing, exultant yell that broke against the vaults of the hall: "Heil Köpfler!" The retainers of the Reich Council joined in to roar and shout without end: "Heil! Heil! Heil! Heil!" The hall shuddered to its foundations, and from the chaos of wild ecstatic shrieks emerged a mass chorus shouting rhythmically: "Köpf-ler! Köpf-ler! "Köpf-ler!" The slender man seemed impervious to the uproar. For a long time he stood in silent sorrow before the Führer's black-draped standards. Then he took his seat on the tribunal, and the big crane spiked with TV cameras dollied in to flash onto the screen a series of long and close-up shots of the man (and of his cheap, worn, plastic briefcase). Köpfler's posture on the tribunal seemed somehow unnatural, as if he were ready to leap to his feet at a moment's notice.

Who was the man? Everyone knew the high rank he held in the party and that he had been one of the Führer's most trusted paladins. But no one could say for sure whence he came. Some claimed he was a Croat—a theory his Christian name, Ivo, tended to support —and that he had joined the movement while an unemployed bookkeeper in the "years of dishonor"—the time after Versailles. As a colonel in the Brownshirts, he took an active part in the Röhm revolt, but had not been shot at once. Instead, a special SA court martial sentenced him and other conspirators to death. In prison he had adopted the name Köpfler, an epithet given guillotine candidates. Deliverance came at the last minute: For unknown and undiscoverable reasons the then SA Chief of Staff, Lutze, set him free and put him at the Führer's disposal. Little was known of Ivo Köpfler's life after that except that he had switched to the SS. Only during the war, when he organized "Operation Forest Devil" against the Yugoslav guerrillas did he reenter the limelight. He conducted that small war with such fanatic determination and exemplary cruelty that his name soon became a legend, especially among the Werewolves. But a short time later Köpfler again disappeared from view. It was said he was one of the "quiet men" of the country, and in the party leadership he was known as "the Trackless One." In the vernacular, however, he remained the "Forest Devil," and people treasured his Nordic name "the Terror Helmet" (the "Oegishialmn" of the *Edda* songs). He had helped liquidate the office of the Führer's deputy, working closely with Martin Bormann, whose chief of staff he was, and, as we've mentioned, after Bormann's death advanced to the all-powerful post of Reichsleiter, Chief of the Reich Chancellery, and Reich Minister. It was the fastest and steepest career to date in the Thousand-Year Reich.

Höllriegl thought of all this as he stood, together with the other guests, right arm raised, in front of the screen. Slowly the uproar died down, although some shouting still echoed through the auditorium. Köpfler took a tape recording from his briefcase and, still seated, gave it to the Reich Minister for Education and Propaganda, who reverently inserted the reel into the machine. After the tumult the sudden silence, descending on the hall as if on command, seemed more awesome, more sinister. The Führer's voice now filled the hall and the world beyond the borders of the Reich; it sounded as vigorous and pithy as ever, and his followers listened with gaping mouths.

"German People! I feel the approach of my last hours. Soon I will report to Valhalla about my deeds and those of the glorious German nation. A half century has passed since I first placed my strength at the disposal of my country as a volunteer in the First War imposed on the Reich. In these five decades, love and trust for my people have guided my every thought and action, and indeed my life itself. They gave me the strength to make the most difficult decisions and to solve the hardest problems a man has ever been faced with. The crowning achievement of my efforts to restore Germany to her rightful place in the sun was the most glorious victory in our history, a victory unlike any other. It has eradicated once and for all the rule of those international statesmen who were either of Jewish descent or who worked for Jewish interests. I have given orders to wipe international Jewry from the face of the earth and I have also given orders that those nations which made themselves the handmaidens of the Jewish world conspiracy, together with all racially inferior peoples—coloreds, Tschandals, and apelings

—be subject forever to their German masters, the blue-blond race called on to dominate the world, and to all those who fought on our side and made immeasurable sacrifices for our victory.

"I die gladly, remembering our soldiers' great deeds in the last war, and the enormous task of reconstruction our party completed in peacetime. I die gladly in view of the heart-warming achievements of our women and mothers, the accomplishments of our peasants and workers, and the unique contribution made by the youth that bears my name. To all of them my deepest thanks, and my wish that they continue to battle the enemy in peacetime wherever and whenever he shows himself—even if it be within their own ranks—and to wage that battle with the same fanatic determination and devotion which have become symbolic of our movement. I order the leaders of our army in the Reich, in the occupied territories and overseas, of the navy, air force, and our astronauts—already crowned with so much glory—to strengthen the National Socialist spirit of our troops with all the means at their disposal. I command the members of the party, from Reich Minister to the youngest *Pimpf,* to give our troops a shining example and to be ready, day and night, should a new test of our resolve come upon us. Be on your guard, German men and women! Already I see a threatening thunderstorm brewing in the Far East. A clique of traitors appears to have been at work, trying to rip the heroic Japanese people from our side—that people with whom we stood shoulder to shoulder in winning the victory, and who now rule China and Mongolia, the Pacific, and the sixth continent, the Magna Japonica. Although we won the greatest victory in German history and, indeed, in all history, we must strive to maintain the fruits of that glorious deed and to bring about a millenium which later historians will have cause to call heroic.

"In order to secure internally the continuation of the German nation and of the Western world, I am expelling from the party, before my death, former Reich Marshal Tycho Unseld, the unworthy successor of my late comrade Hermann Göring. Unseld has been stripped of all rights he could derive from the Decree of June 29, 1951, as well as from my declaration before the Reich Council of September 1, 1953. Reichsleiter Ivo Köpfler will take his place and become after my death the Führer of party and state. In addition, he will at once assume command of all German forces on land, water, in the air, and in space.

"Before I die, moreover, I am expelling from the party and from all his offices the former Reichsführer of the SS and Reich Minister of the Interior, Manfred Diebold. In his place I have nominated Gauleiter Gernot Firbas as SS Reichsführer and Chief of the German Police, and Gauleiter Uwe Heckroth as Reich Minister of the Interior. Unseld and Diebold have committed treason against the nation by repeated attempts to undermine my authority, to destroy the direction of party and armed forces, to sow the seeds of discord, and, contrary to the law, to seize power in the state. They have thus done incalculable harm to our whole people, especially to its political representatives, the National Socialist German Workers' Party, not to mention their perfidy toward my person.

"I have proscribed both traitors, ordered the arrest of their families, and confiscation of their property. In order to give the German people a government made up of energetic men able to meet their obligations to guard the German Empire and the nations under its protection against foreign and domestic enemies, I have appointed, effective today, the following men to serve as members of the new Cabinet: my successor, Reich Marshal Ivo Köpfler as party chief with the authority of Reich President, Chancellor, and Minister of War; State Secretary Gandolf Henke as Minister of Foreign Affairs; Gauleiter Uwe Heckroth as Reich Minister of the Interior; the President of the People's Court of Justice, Dr. Dr. Dr. Dieter Loeffelholz, as Reich Minister of Justice; Gauleiter Gernot Firbas as Reichsführer of the SS and Chief of the German police . . ."

The list rolled on until the Führer reached the appointment of Gotthold Auffahrt as Minister for Church Affairs. "The appointments take effect the day Party Member Köpfler announces them. I express my thanks and the thanks of the nation to the departing ministers for whom other worthy posts will be found.

"May the new men be hard but never unjust. Let them make boldness and courage the counselors of their action, and place the honor of the nation above all other things on earth. May they always be aware that our task of securing, for all time, Western culture under German leadership is the work of centuries to come and that it commits each individual to serve the common weal first, even at the expense of his own advantage. I ask that all National

Socialists, men and women, and all the soldiers of the Wehrmacht remain loyal to the new Führer, my successor, and his government, unto death. Above all I command the leadership of the nation and the entire community of our people to obey carefully the racial laws and to resist fiercely all those unwilling to accept the blessings of the new order and those who try to undermine it, thus putting into jeopardy the existence and growth of Western culture. . . . Given at the Berghof in Berchtesgaden, November 3, 196——"

In their soundproof cabins the interpreters had broadcast excerpts of the Führer's speech into all the world's languages, with the original text faded under from time to time. Hitler's message had hardly ended before Köpfler leaped to his feet and said in a high cutting voice (the close-up showed his magnetic eyes):

"My fellow party members and countrymen! The former members of the Reich Council, Unseld and Diebold, expelled by Adolf Hitler from the party and their offices, have fled, and their whereabouts at present are unknown. As the guardian of security and order, I command all members of the party and Wehrmacht, and all Germans, to be on the lookout for the fleeing traitors and either to turn them over to the jurisdiction of Reich authorities or, if necessary, execute them at once.

"In order to make sure that my orders are carried out quickly, I hereby release Gauleiter Gernot Firbas from his duties as SS Reichsführer and Chief of the German Police, and until further notice will take over these duties myself.

"In addition, all the Werewolf units are to come under my direct command.

"The immortal Führer and founder of the World Empire will find his last resting place in the Kyffhäuser Mountains. The exact time of the funeral has not yet been determined; it will be announced later. Until that none-too-distant day, the national mourning I have decreed will remain in full effect within the borders of Greater Germany and all its protectorates.

"Heil Germany!"

Again the thunder of endless calls of "Heil!" "Heil Köpfler!" "Heil to the new Führer!" "Heil Germany!" The broadcast to the networks of the non-German world had cut off when Köpfler began speaking. There the leaders and subleaders addressed their own people.

Only in the early days of the great victories had the songs of the nation been sung with such enthusiasm. Höllriegl returned to his room drunk with pride and happiness. He didn't bother watching the great banquet that took place in the Reich Council after each session—in memory of the evenings at the Bürgerbräu it belonged to the great awakening ritual. The other hotel guests too departed. No one said a word. He was so excited he couldn't sleep for a long time. And only later did he realize that there was much about the demonstration he had witnessed that filled him with a secret disgust, perhaps even fear and horror.

MOTHBALLS

Strange things began to happen. Early in the morning Anselma telephoned while Höllriegl was rewriting his report. At first he was happy she had reached him before he had managed to call her. Her voice sounded strained; she stuttered several times as she talked, apparently from sheer nervousness. Could he have lunch with her? Tonight was uncertain. And she didn't have much time, so she would expect him at the Foreign Office cafeteria.

"If I can swing it with the office, we'll see each other tonight—at my house for a Chinese supper. In that case, don't forget to bring your divining rod . . ." Höllriegl felt jumpy—the adventure continued. It probably wouldn't amount to much more than a passing affair.

He wrote a few cheerful lines to Kummernuss and to his Heydrich girl friend, a beautician. But he did not feel particularly cheery. Then he got into his car and drove to Tiergartenstrasse 4. It was still dreary, but the rain had slackened. Traffic appeared less heavy. A cold wind blew through the streets—Berlin weather as he liked it.

He told the gatekeeper at T4 that he wanted to see the officer on duty at the Reich School for Radiation Protection. Even as he walked up the stairs past the frozen guards, he was convinced he would find Hirnchristl. After a long wait, he was allowed to enter the anteroom. A young, resolute-looking man in civilian clothes sat at the desk with the three telephones, and blandly denied ever having known an Obersturmführer "Hirn-kristell." "I've been here since yesterday. My predecessor's name was Pribilla."

There was no point fighting such deliberate obstinacy. The typist was the same as yesterday—or was she? They all looked alike. The woman stared past him with so apathetic an expression that he didn't bother talking to her. He kept his report in his pocket, muttered an excuse, and had the secretary stamp his pass. He left without saying good-bye, feeling lost. And again he sensed that nebulous, impending threat, this time more imminent than ever before. He walked faster. The piece of paper with Gundlfinger's address remained in his pocket—that at least was real.

In the hall of the pension he met Mrs. Zweenemann. Her eyes were inflamed, and she avoided looking him in the face. Höllriegl drew her out. Her brother, she whispered haltingly, had been missing since noon yesterday. A man as punctual as the clock, and so exact. (Since the death of her husband she had managed the pension with him.) Her brother had planned to take some money from his account at a nearby branch of the Reich Bank—since then not a trace. People in the bank claimed not to have seen him.

"But they acted so strangely and what they said was so contradictory that I ran straight to the police. No money had been taken from the account. But at the station house the officer hardly bothered to ask me any questions when I reported him missing. . . . They've arrested Albert; they've arrested him!" The widow's face was wet with fright and excitement; her hands trembled, and Höllriegl noticed how again and again she dug her fingernails into her palms.

"Since Saturday people have been disappearing every hour," she whispered. "They've been taken from their jobs, and others just don't come back. Mostly it's little people—laborers, white-collar people . . . the Werewolf is at work. . . ." She looked all about her, even though her voice was barely audible. "Poor, poor Albert! I'll never see him again!" Now she really began to cry.

People disappearing without a trace! And another thing worried Höllriegl, even though it seemed completely irrelevant: a water shortage. Water had been short all over the whole Reich and the rest of Europe all summer long, as if the sources had suddenly evaporated. It had been the hottest summer in memory, and in the fall news had filtered through of catastrophically bad harvests. The authorities ordered strict water-conservation measures, which were not eased even after heavy rains fell in October. In the pension Höllriegl found signs with the party command: "Brothers: Save German Water!" And when he entered his room after meeting Frau Zweenemann, he saw a little placard hanging above the washbasin: There would be no water at all from 10 A.M. to 4 P.M. and from 8 P.M. to 4 A.M. He found a basin half filled with water—clay-tinged—and two bottles of mineral water on the shelf.

Once again he carefully reread his report. For whom had he written it? The question kept returning to shake his confidence. Where was the system, the safe world? Had leadership failed? Orders were issued and left dangling somewhere in midair, in empty space. What was it all about, for God's sake? Höllriegl remembered every word of his conversation with Schwerdtfeger. His traveling orders too were real. And Anselma's letter: "I hope you won't always bet on the wrong horse." Anselma could have heard from Schwerdtfeger that he would be coming to Berlin. That scribbler of fiction found open doors everywhere—certainly in the Foreign Office. And Anselma was an attractive woman. Hirnchristl knew at once what it was all about. Whoever gave the orders, they had to have gone through official channels. That much was clear. And the Jew's confession! Höllriegl had not supressed it completely in his report, but only touched upon it as the product of a sick imagination. Certainly he had been sent there too late. A pastor would have been more suitable. The simplest thing would be to put his report in an envelope and address it to the office in T4. Let them handle it. As far as he was concerned, the job was done. Or should he tell Anselma about it? Höllriegl rejected that idea as quickly as it came.

He regarded himself critically in the mirror. His black eye glittered in undiminished glory. Ulla, Ulla! She was lost forever, even before he could dare try and win her. The whole thing had been madness. He would have to rip Ulla out of his heart, no matter how much it hurt. But maybe Anselma would . . . ? She was Ulla's sister-in-law. A von Eycke. It would be sweet revenge on Ulla if he . . . if Anselma . . . His heart beat faster as he thought of Frau Geldens, her slack body, her exotic ways . . .

He wasted the rest of the time. Somehow he was afraid of going out, as if he were safer within his four walls. Or should he ignore his orders and move to another hotel? Change his domicile several times? No, that wouldn't work. If they wanted to pick you up, they picked you up.

After the reconstruction, the Foreign Office had moved back to its old quarters—Wilhelmstrasse 74–76. Höllriegl had to pass through a triple cordon of guards. SS men in ice-gray raincoats were everywhere. He obtained a pass, asked where he would find the cafeteria, and walked across a courtyard filled with police cars and armored reconnaissance vehicles. Soldiers walked around fully armed. He found Anselma, childlike and dark, sitting in a side room. She sat with a young woman, perhaps a colleague, who left as Höllriegl approached.

He greeted her smartly, which drew a responsive smile. But she seemed cold and distant today; or was she inhibited by the uncomfortable, half-official surroundings? There was a constant flow of people pouring in and out. Groups of loudly talking girls, many of them in uniform, sat along long tables. Service was businesslike, but there were only waitresses. Mourning was little in evidence except for dark clothing. Yesterday's session of the Reich Council did not seem to have made much impression.

The many thousands who worked at the Foreign Office had to be fed in four half-hour sessions. Anselma said at once she could not stay much longer. Höllriegl bought a meal ticket. They ate quickly without saying much.

Yet in the end recent events had shaken Höllriegl so much he threw all caution to the winds and even ignored that instinct of self-preservation which had become second nature. He found the noise of eating and talking a protective wall. Was someone watching him? He didn't give a damn. Anselma's aloofness excited him; when she wasn't looking he devoured her with his eyes. He thought her particularly pretty that day, and the prettiness hurt. She had blue shadows under her eyes. What had she done yesterday? He wouldn't get this woman either! Still, her call had made him happy —for a while he could forget Ulla. . . .

When they had finished eating, he touched her hand, pretending he had done it unintentionally. When she did not withdraw it, he covered her hand with his own. The warmth of her blood excited him. "I like you terribly, Anselma, I'd like to . . ." He looked passionately into her eyes, which suddenly, or so it seemed to him, held an expression of surrender. Despite his feeling of not giving a damn, his own boldness frightened him. For the first time he had used her Christian name. Impulsively she moved closer to him for a moment. For her, too, the surroundings seemed to disappear. Their faces were close to one another. Anselma's hand began to quiver in his, but then she pulled it back.

"I thought you loved Ulla." That was frank. A direct attack.

"Yes, . . . I respect Frau von Eycke . . . I respect her a great deal. Like an idol." Höllriegl lied, yet did not lie. "I venerate her." He avoided Anselma's look, which was not without irony. At one end of the hall he could see an inscription, freshly whitewashed but still legible, written in the florid style sometimes found in old German wine cellars: "Think Western, Act German."

"What do you want from me?" A question of glimmering coldness.

"I want you. You please me." Again he grabbed for her hand. "I love you. I love you. I love everything about you: your strength, your breeding, your od—I could be happy with you. I've never been, not since I started thinking. You exude strength, a kind of victorious confidence! You make me strong and confident. You're a wonderful woman! So different from the others . . . so special . . . sovereign!" He felt the triteness of his words, but excitement made his voice deep and painful.

Anselma looked at him carefully. She smiled over so much folly. Her eyes would not let him go. "I'm afraid I'm not a suitable object for your desires. I'm sober, not as romantic as you. You're an old-fashioned type who loves to unpack his emotions. But . . . I like you too. I liked you before, when you only had eyes for Ulla—and at the same time I don't like you. You're too soft. You let yourself go too much. That runs against the grain, doesn't fit into our times. Perhaps you're even 'human'? The devil take it . . . I don't believe in your so-called love. The word should only be used when it's a question of preserving the species. What do you know about it? What you mean by love doesn't exist—and never did in that romantic sense. It's like parading your old clothes: They smell of mothballs. There is only loneliness—that is real. So you look around for someone to take to bed. It's less lonely, and anyway it's fun. But that's all it is. You're looking for a woman to forget yourself, aren't you? Or because your glands are still too young and stormy. Don't you have a girl, poor thing?" She was silent a moment and again his eyes lingered on her body. "You like me, do you?"

The question was a disarming one. (Christ, what a flirt she was!) Höllriegl grabbed Anselma's unyielding hand and kissed the delicate knuckles. He wanted to open that fist, break it open, to kiss her palm. She guessed his intention and whispered: "Be careful; we're not alone." But they both ignored the warning, their eyes eating into each other so deeply, so long and so consumingly that everything about them seemed blurred. They had reached an island together. Anselma's face turned serious, submissive.

"Sinfiötli, I love you! I want you, I want you!" he said quietly.

"My name is Knêfrōdh."

"Oh, no, I'm the one on his knees—before you! I adore you! You can do anything you like with me. Do it, why don't you! I love you!"

"Love? Oh, you mean the business with the glands you call love? You want me . . . and I want you . . . maybe. That's all." Anselma didn't lie. Her eyes didn't lie.

Confused, Höllriegl groped for words. "I feel intoxicated. I'm happy. You make me happy, and yet I'm unhappy. I'm inflamed——by you, Anselma!" He knew it was lust he felt—stupor, escape. He was ashamed and did not bother hiding it. "I could die with you!"

"In bed? And enter Valhalla? But we'd have to part once we got there—you belong in the men's section." Anselma's eyes changed color. Comtemptuous brown-green fire. He began to realize what excited him so much about her: her erratic behavior, her childishness, her intelligence and cruelty. Her breeding.

"To Valhalla or the underworld, to the eternal gods or into the realm of the dead. Anywhere. But only with you, with you, Sinfiötli."

"Do you really believe all this nonsense? Only the *Pimpfe* do. Everything ends with death. Your Nordic gods are fairy tales told by nursemaids. There is nothing beyond the moment in which we live! And there is nothing beyond the nation! In order to live and rule, we must be harsh and hard, as hard as bone, you hear! It's all a question of power. After us the Deluge! I thirst (Anselma's eyes glowed fanatically) for a new time. The Third Reich would have died of old age anyhow. Look at all those weak-kneed SS men, this comfortable Gestapo, these fat, bloated, ancient SD agents! And their routine tortures! Those idyllic subhuman camps! It's all degeneracy! And these guilt feelings everyone has! The eagle isn't the symbol of the Reich anymore: It's the hypodermic needle. We're too well off. We've become fat and lazy. The Germans were only great in their destruction. When I was a little girl, I prayed to Frauja" (Höllriegl understood: Anselma used the Gothic word for Jesus in order not to mouth the hated Jewish name), "but then I crucified him, every day. We children played crucifixion, and I thought up the worst kinds of torture for the traveling preacher from Galilee. Today I'd like to crucify Odin and blow up the whole silly heaven of the gods, where everybody does nothing but drink mead and sleep on bearskins. You're upset, aren't you? You didn't expect me to say that. What else? A new, tough, manly time is approaching. We're all going to have to fight hard instead of running after our little jobs! All these aged party idiots rely on our invincibility, on atomic science, laser, rockets, and these ridiculous satellites. They dream of miraculous new weapons while they turn around in their beds and fart. But I tell you: A time of the jungle and cannibalism is coming, and it's coming fast, when people will fight with jackknives in their hands; man against man and woman against woman, and behind us, the wall."

"Did you know that in some parts of America all hell has broken loose?" she asked after a pause. "In at least two Pacific states of the United Vassals the militia has gone over to the rebels. We didn't know it yesterday, but we know it today. And that's not all. This morning I saw a report that the yellow apelings have been flying continuous reconnaissance missions from Australia all the way into Nevada! And who is going to stop them? Why am I telling you all this? To make you tough, tough for what's ahead. I'm not spilling any state secrets. You'll hear much worse in the evening news. The eternal cover-up, the euphemisms, are over. Köpfler has ordered unsparing frankness. It looks as if the Japs are preparing a major amphibious assault against the American West Coast. They're jumping like toads from one island to the other in the northern Pacific and in the Bering Sea, and the eastern coast of Australia is spiked with launching pads. Banzai! It's going to be great! I wouldn't be surprised if the Soka Gakkai land tomorrow in California, Seattle,

Vancouver, Nome, and Dutch Harbor—without firing a shot. All they'll do in the benighted States is pray to Frauja and quote the Bible. The biggest mistake the old regime made was to reduce our troop strength over there and rely on the rednecks and Ku Kluxers. Now we can watch how the Minutemen will handle the yellow apelings and the revolution in their own country. The Japs won't hesitate opening the subhuman camps. As for Asia—we can forget about Indonesia, and the prayer mills of Tibet turn exclusively for a Japanese victory."

She bent over to him and whispered, while looking at him fixedly: "The time for dreaming is over. Do you know that eleven of the new ministers are members of the Werewolves? Finally! Now we're going whole hog and without mercy. They'll deal a new deck, you'll see. I expect you to bet on the right horse. . . ."

She spoke in an imploring tone. Amid all the noise her words were hard to understand. Such candor had put her at his mercy. Did she mean to do that? Her eyes glowed like wan lights; the look in them had something blind about it, inhuman. He had seen such eyes before, again and again. The look of young Werewolves. The snake look of NATMAT. It was the look of the new heretics, the despisers of death, the death-addicted.

Moved, he said "Anselma, probably you are right in everything you say, but it doesn't belong here. I can't think of anything else but you now! I am your slave—you are my goddess! I wish I could kneel in the dust before you, look at you, worship you. . . ."

"Oh, those are just words; don't make such a fool of yourself! Once you've had me, you'll forget me quickly enough, you romantic! You like me and I like you. That's like a contract, a business deal. I felt it yesterday, that you wanted me. Somehow we're dependent on one another: I sell you my thing, you sell me yours. An exchange of goods, nothing more. We come together in order to do it—a community of interest. What do you want with your funny love? . . . I've got to go, I should be upstairs already."

"Anselma, why do you talk that way? You know it isn't true. Love is something real and noble. I feel so much for you. You are marvelous, wonderful. Love isn't something you trade like goods in a store; if you give yourself to me, you don't sell yourself. Perhaps that's your attitude with other men—you've gone through a lot. But you must believe in my love! Of course I want you! I desire you, your skin, your hair, and all! But I wouldn't want you if I couldn't love you. I honor you, admire you! I don't know why I didn't see that the other time we met—but you were so cool, so matter-of-fact. And your brother . . . the many people . . ."

Anselma had risen. She smiled. It could have been a happy or indulgent smile. "Will we see each other tonight? I'll manage to be free. Only I don't know when I can get away. Please, would you bring your divining rods? If I'm not home when you arrive, make yourself comfortable. Ko Won, my servant, we call him just Ko, will expect you. About seven. Is that all right? Neuburgerstrasse 38, five flights up, subway station Hallesches Tor."

Silently they walked back across the courtyard, and he accompanied her to the elevator. For a moment they were alone in a side passage. Impulsively Anselma clung to him. The buds of her breasts suddenly jutted sharply out from under her black silk blouse. He wanted to kiss her mouth, but she wouldn't let him, so he kissed her hands, and then people came. She jumped into the elevator. Höllriegl stared after her for a long time; his devouring look encircled her figure.

While the Sunday and Monday papers had published almost nothing but photographs on the death of the aged Führer: Adolf Hitler on the peaks of his triumphant life, and, in contrast, pictures of his body covered with the mourning flags of the twenty-third of November, first in his study at the Berghof and later in the Reich Chancellery—that event now receded a little in view of the historic Reich Council session. The black-bordered newspapers were still full of Adolf the Great (as historians had begun calling him), his wars and his founding of empires, but a definite trend had emerged to move the grand old man more into a legendary background while his successor was pushed to the forefront—for example, in the retinue or at the side of the Führer at important state occasions of the past, or arm in arm with him during private walks. Tuesday's continental edition of the *Völkischer Beobachter* frontpaged expressions of faith and trust in the new leadership from all the membership of the German Academy of Poetry and Truth in Weimar, among them a poem—scripted in giant letters resembling one of Pindar's triumphal songs—entitled "To Adolf Hitler in the Stars" from the pen of the triple National Prize winner, Edwin Erwin Zwinger, in which the author sought to single out

Köpfler as the "mighty heir of world empire" (". . . high the daring head awaiting the laurel crown of fame . . .").

Next to events of such magnitude it seemed almost unimportant that on Saturday morning, even before Hitler's death, a group of astronauts had blasted off from the space port at Peenemünde on the thirty-sixth multiple-person space flight. Once again, subhumans manned the space craft, which indicated an especially risky experiment. At first "WvB Baldur XXXVI"—the insignia of the space capsule—had been on schedule, carrying out promptly and without a hitch all the orders radioed from the ground station. But suddenly the spaceship had left its predetermined orbit and started moving with increasing speed away from the earth. It began, according to somewhat vague reports in the Tuesday papers, to shake and then to turn faster and faster around its own axis. The signals became weaker and weaker. On Tuesday morning the radio had broadcast for an hour the orders sent upstairs from Peenemünde and the gasping replies of the astronauts. It was forbidden on pain of death to turn off such "toughening" broadcasts.

Now Köpfler's fanatic eyes pursued all citizens of the Reich from wall posters. Overnight pictures of the Reich Council session and the banquet that followed it had been plastered everywhere, as had the red wanted lists of the Gestapo about Unseld and Diebold. Höllriegl didn't feel like going home to the pension just yet, and so he strolled on, lost in seductive thought. Absentmindedly he glanced at the flaring headlines of the newspapers; he was too full of Anselma to pay much attention. A pale sun, like the moon by daylight, peeked briefly from behind winter clouds; it was cold, the air smelled of snow. At the corner of Wilhelmstrasse-Leipzigerstrasse, in front of the entrance to an atomic bunker, one of those loudspeaker towers that resembled a menhir poked into the sky. The noon news was just being repeated. A few passersby stopped and looked up aimlessly. But then they looked at one another.

". . . Low-flying planes of unknown nationality have attacked our mine installations in Little America. Nine men of our Antarctic expedition were lost to aerial fire. Damage was slight. . . . In the Weddell Sea, reconnaissance planes flew at high altitudes over a convoy of ore freighters. . . . Coast Guard ships operating in the waters off Kaiser-Wilhelmsland (New Guinea) sighted several midget submarines of the Japanese Nata type and fired on them. . . . Reinforcements for our troops stationed in Ribbentrop Sound were flown into Antarctica from Ushuaia, Punta Arenas, and the Falkland Islands. . . . In the area of Juan Fernández on Sunday, unmarked jet fighters strafed the Mexican motor freighter *Tezcatlipoca,* sailing under the Reich flag. Rockets and napalm bombs set the ship on fire, and it sank within an hour. A small number of crewmen, including three Reich citizens, were able to reach shore at Más Afuera. . . . The Navy High Command South Pacific has ordered air and surface convoy protection for all German-flag shipping. . . . Units of the Fourth Nuclear Missile Submarine Fleet have left their bases to begin operations in the South Pacific. . . . Fast units of our navy have halted the Chilean freighter *Esperanza* near the Galápagos Islands. The crew of the ship, Japanese commando and sabotage groups, was wiped out after fierce fighting. . . . Strong air and land reinforcements have been sent to advanced Reich bases in the South and North Pacific. . . . A large fleet of the Reich Navy, including aircraft carriers, is engaged in operations off the coast of Baja California. . . . Our SD troops have fought several partisan-style engagements with the rebels in the Chocolate Mountains of southern California. . . . Near the city limits of Sacramento, units of the infamous free corps Abe Lincoln and George Washington, supported by Japanese air strikes, managed to smash through Minutemen lines in several places. These breaches have not yet been closed. Loyal Militia and Minutemen are fighting with exemplary contempt of death. Enemy planes have not hesitated to use poison gas. In retaliation, MM General Snedeker has given orders not to take prisoners. Heavy fighting continues. . . . The attempt to destroy the Boulder Dam with ICBM's carrying conventional warheads has failed. Boulder City suffered great destruction with heavy civilian casualties. Military targets were not hit. Our rockets delivered a counterblow at once: Thor and Ausra missiles last night leveled residential districts in Sydney, Newcastle, Brisbane, Christchurch, Wellington, and Auckland. Our reconnaissance planes this morning found wide-scale destruction of military installations; for example to mobile launching pads in Wollongon and Parramatta near Sydney. . . . This is the end of our foreign news at noon. And now several announcements: The two traitors Unseld and Diebold are believed hiding in the surroundings of the Reich capital. Their personal descriptions . . ."

Höllriegl was badly shaken. This was not limited war, but all-out war. After the news and what Anselma had told him, it was obvious that fighting had begun days, perhaps even weeks, ago. Only now did he understand the Führer's warning—he had meant it for this moment; not for some distant future.

Suddenly he felt drunk with pride and joy. Battle! He didn't have a clue what had happened. No one did. Only those on the inside, like Schwerdtfeger, had known. Battle! Now the Valkyrie would hover over the heads of the warriors. Finally battle! Perhaps it was even a reason for the unbelievable fact that an order could go haywire, like his instructions to come to Berlin. People in higher places must have panicked for a while. In his selfish concern with private, all too private things, he had found himself—even if only for a short time—outside the community of his nation. How right Anselma was! There was nothing but the nation! Nothing existed beyond "the moment in which we live." He could do nothing but obey . . . whatever he would be asked to do. Suddenly he was in a hurry to get home. The rocket action in the Pacific was only the beginning. Tomorrow the heart of the Reich could be hit. Every child knew it lay within the reach of Japanese ICBM's and the one-man kamikaze bombers. For the time being, both sides used only conventional weapons, but tomorrow—tomorrow atomic war could erupt! Strange, the thought did not fill him with terror. On the contrary: He felt overjoyed. The great decision was near. Now everything depended on speed—whoever could strike the first decisive blow. But Köpfler would certainly be faster, and thus assure Reich domination of areas now in Japanese hands. That would mean mastery of the whole world. Heil to the new Führer!

One thing was clear. He would have to return to Heydrich at once. But this one night he wanted to keep for himself—for himself and Anselma. Anselma, the magnificent and strong. And Ulla? Where was she, what could she be doing? Why did he always get so involved with these women? The amber witch was unreachable and would remain so. But Anselma . . . she was real, earthy, you could touch her, hold her in your arms, kiss, perhaps possess her. What rapture! Wild excitement seized him when he thought of her body.

Should the war approach the borders of the Reich—and that could happen with lightning speed—he would be better off in Heydrich. Perhaps his draft call already awaited him; the party would need him too. In this hour of trial everyone would have to do his part.

He'd certainly take the route home over the Harz Mountains. Sauckelruh near Rundstedt, Villa Walpurgis. He had written everything down, even the professor's telephone number. The small detour couldn't do any harm. However, his orders were most specific about the route he should follow. Höllriegl hesitated, then stopped the car. Slowly he did something he would often remember in the coming days with misgiving. Checking a road map, he changed the typewritten entries and scratched some illegible markings below them. He knew the restricted zones exactly; he'd simply drive around them. Anyway, he was allowed to pass through B and D, and probably C as well, even though that zone—perhaps by mistake—had not been included.

Back in the pension he looked over his report quickly. A decent job, that. In the middle of his reading someone knocked on the door. Frau Zweenemann, who had avoided his look when he greeted her at the door, said, "Total blackout tonight. Flashlights for the guests are in the hall."

Höllriegl dug out Hirnchristl's note and dialed the professor's number. He was curious and a little nervous. Gundlfinger, that famous man, his client! It happened that he couldn't dial directly any farther than Sauckelruh; the operator, who talked with a foreign accent (probably an overseas German), said something about circuit trouble but that a connection to Villa Walpurgis would be established quickly. Höllriegl waited for the click which signaled that the DHW (the German Telephone Listening Guard) had hooked into the line. He listened very hard. Nothing. Many Germans, he included, put the DHW on voluntarily in accordance with the party slogan "A Friend Listens in"—or, in its popular version, "The Party Has Long Ears." No click. Luck? Or had the warning noise been removed? After a while he heard the usual dial tone and the connection was established.

"Who is on the phone?" a high voice asked.

Höllriegl gave his rank and name and briefly described the purpose of his call.

"Oh, yes, wait a minute please, stay on the *Pörneit.*"

Oh Lord, he thought. They talked Mother German. He'd really have to watch out.

After a few moments again the clear voice: "The *Inarteram* wants me to tell you that the whole thing is *gänsixer*. He never gave any such orders. Would you just wait a second, please?"

Höllriegl was delighted by the voice, which could belong to a child or to a very young woman. His earlier anxiety had disappeared.

Gänsixer—he remembered the word well. He had come across it repeatedly in "Odin's Fire," which had a special section on Mother German, a language formed from German and dialect roots. Its supporters were true fanatics in battling the growingly anemic and dry administrative tongue of the Third Reich, the so-called "sad German." But chances for a breakthrough were slim: Influential party circles merely smiled at their efforts. *Gänsixer* meant mysterious, and the word had a slightly sarcastic tinge to it.

". . . The *Inarteram* says he has no objections to your coming. Do you drive a *Brufart?* If you do, then leave it in Sauckelruh and walk up to our place or take a bicycle. You can rent one at Eigenulf Schicketanz; I repeat: Schicketanz, An der Pfordten 3. The *Pörnamt* says you're calling from Berlin? When do you leave?"

"I'll start out tomorrow and should reach Sauckelruh in the afternoon. If it's agreeable, I would come by to see the Professor on Thursday morning."

"The *Inarteram* is working on some new problems and lives very quietly. But his interest in what's happening outside is very lively, so do come. Thursday is a good day because the *Inarteram* talks to visitors from near and far. . . ."

Höllriegl decided to leave his car at the pension because of the blackout and used the subway. Only a few people waited in the cold at the Uhland Street U-bahn station. Traffic had been curtailed. Höllriegl was told that this was the first blackout exercise in a long time. Was it just an "exercise"? Those who didn't have to go out stayed home.

A civilian patrol stopped him. He showed his papers: draft card, lineage passport, identity card with finger and palm prints, party identification, his travel orders—the whole collection. When the three gloved, suspicious-looking men had finished—his heart almost stopped when they inspected his travel orders—the train arrived. He felt humiliated, somehow ridiculous with his arms full of chrysanthemums. A romantic gesture which did not suit Anselma. What had she said? Mothballs . . .

He sat brooding in a corner of the almost empty car and mechanically read the advertising posters or touched the hair pendulum he carried in his pocket. Funny, the joy he had taken in Anselma decreased the closer he came to her home. What was wrong?

Wittenberger Platz . . . Nollendorf Platz . . . Gleisdreieck . . . Hallesches Tor. He had to get off. There was little difference between the subway tunnel and the street above, whose deep black was illuminated only by the glow of a few flashlights. Slowly and uncertainly he went his way. A loudspeaker at the Hallesches Tor blared the finale of the "Peer Gynt Suite" into the empty night. A few people glided past. Blind houses rose like mausoleums into a sky without end.

The few cars with their darkened headlights moved slowly and uncertainly through the streets. As he crossed Lindenstrasse to turn into Nauenburgerstrasse, he noticed another patrol, whose blue lights blinked menacingly. Instinctively he dodged them, yet felt disgusted and upset without knowing why. A Wehrmacht patrol this time. Groping streams of light, like drooling saliva, appeared in the night-dark sky. In the south they formed an intricate lacework.

He greeted the warm, dim lighting in the lobby of Anselma's apartment building with a sigh of relief. Outside the night seemed threatening, but it was safe inside. He didn't take the elevator but walked up the stairs (good leg training) and tried to concentrate on Anselma. A fashionable, obviously quite new building. The light trap in the hall and the blackout blinds disrupted the homey impression somewhat. Two youngsters with some kind of armband, still boys really, came toward him, accompanying an elderly man. The man did not have hat or coat on and was tieless. Höllriegl greeted them; no reply.

He rang at Anselma's door, whereupon scuffing steps became audible inside and someone looked through the peephole. Höllriegl identified himself. A white-haired Chinese with nickel-framed glasses and a thin little chin beard opened the door, bowing profusely. The delicate man in his blouselike suit of semiEuropean cut smiled incessantly, showing dark-yellow, clublike teeth set wide apart. He kept his hands hidden in his sleeves. Ko Won looked more like a scholar than a servant.

The only thing Höllriegl could gather from the flow of words in German, pidgin English, and what he presumed to be Chinese, was that the "Missie" was not home yet but would come soon. Ko led him into the adjoining living room, which was bathed in dim light coming from several bizarrely formed lamps. Höllriegl recognized the rooms from the pictures Anselma had shown him. They were furnished in Far Eastern taste and appeared cool, almost bare, with sliding wooden walls. The only furniture in the living room was a broad couch and a low table with stools. A single, obviously old *kakemono* with a woodcut print and several grim-looking war masks of red-brown lacquered wood hung on the walls. In one corner stood a vase with large, sand-colored thistles. No pictures—no Führer picture!—no books, nothing.

Ko Won motioned Höllriegl to make himself comfortable on the couch while he waited. The servant had made a small ceremony out of arranging the pale-violet crysanthemums Höllriegl handed him. Then, giggling, he carefully smoothed out the pillows and said, "Missie here, gentleman there," and *"Kabu-wake, kabu-wake"* in Japanese flower language. His behavior was amusingly suggestive. He pointed several times toward a certain place on the couch, stroked it, and said again and again, "Missie" and *"Hon-kate,"* and "Flower there, good position," and "Gentleman there, side of Missie, oh, good position, lovie-lovie, Missie like that," and, "Lie on side there and Missie this way, flower there, much lovie-lovie . . ."

Ko left the room after offering him a dish of sweets. His words and even more his gestures aroused Höllriegl. How much he longed for Anselma to come! His pulse roared, he rolled around the couch, sniffed at the pillows and the blanket, which exuded Anselma's old-fashioned perfume: a sweetish smell of decaying flowers.

He stood up and paced the room. It was hard to master this nervous excitement. Why wasn't she here? Where was she? At lunch today she had had shadows under her eyes, last night she had gone out. Sinfiötli. Chain of the senses. He fought down a surge of jealousy (how stupid!) and gazed at the picture on the *kakemono:* a scene in faded colors of a little pond with grass, dragonflies, snails, and water bugs. When he lifted it a little, he found a television set hidden in a niche behind it. The masks, perhaps of Malayan origin, had open eye slits and broad, flat noses. They were fixed to the wall.

He tried the sweets. They tasted vaguely of pistachio, but much sweeter and left a sharp, burning aftertaste like pepper.

The pendulum. He sat down, closed his eyes in order to relax, and took the knotted hair—it was Ingrid's, his Heydrich girl's—between forefinger and thumb. But he found it impossible to clear his mind even for a second of the thumping desire that filled him like the sea whenever he thought of Sinfiötli. He called her picture to mind: It stood before him clear and painful in outline, and yet strangely insubstantial. Only Anselma's body lived in him. He could think of nothing but her sex and all the possible ways of making love to her. Again and again he tried to empty himself of thought and only to observe. The longer he thought of her, the more his hands trembled, and the lightweight, ring-shaped pendulum shot about giddily; and when he tried to keep his hand quiet in order to take Anselma's od into himself, the mantic oscillations became more convulsed and blurred. No winged figures became visible, only a kind of paralysis.

With Ulla he had felt as if he were dealing with a phenomenon of nature. It was submission—abstract submission—to a power so strong he was only a breath of air before it. But here, during this pendulum exercise, nothing but naked desire emerged, desire to rape the woman whose equal, if not superior, he was because, as he sensed, he pleased her. Höllriegl felt that his masculinity, even his "romantic" manner, could make an impression on Anselma, and this gave him confidence. But at the same time he knew his self-confidence was deceptive—with her coldness, her intelligence, her breeding, her sarcasm (especially her sarcasm!) she could easily play games with him. Secretly he was afraid of her, but the fear, too, put him under her spell. In some things she was vaguely like the amber witch; only Anselma had old blood and noble lineage and, in addition, her sick nervosity. Deep down he was convinced he could wreak his will upon her, but he shuddered at the thought of falling prey to a woman who was so cruel a sexual animal. He stood up and put the pendulum in his pocket. After all, he had come here to exploit Anselma's weakness. Only for an evening. Tomorrow he would leave.

He looked down the long, narrow corridor. At the end of the hall he heard Ko bustle in the kitchen. It was, as he had seen, very tiny, more like a closet—the real kitchenette of a bachelor girl. Finally —steps in the hallway, steps that seemed to come closer. He thought he heard someone whisper outside or smother a laugh. But he must have imagined it because nothing moved. It was not Anselma.

Silently he moved back into the room and pushed aside the heavy winter curtains that covered the whole front wall, carefully extinguishing the light first. The broad glass door that appeared behind the curtains led out to a terrace that might serve as a roof garden in summer. It was pitch-black, only the light cones of the air-defense command fingered the low sky. Suddenly he heard steps again, light steps, this time in the entry hall. Anselma's voice!

The blood shot into his heart. Hastily he drew the curtains, turned on the light, and glanced through the door. Nothing. Apparently Anselma had gone into the bathroom. Höllriegl listened intently, even holding his breath because the sound of his breathing seemed to crash in his ears. And then he heard how she let her urine flow in the stillness, tore off a piece of paper, and flushed the toilet. With greatly sharpened senses he heard how she took off her clothes. The walls seemed to let through every sound. Then water rushed into the tub—just a little. Showering was forbidden. She washed herself.

Höllriegl still stood at the door as Anselma entered, wearing a dark kimono flamed in orange. Moaning, she slipped, a tiny salamander of fire, into his arms. He felt her childlike, water-cool body arch toward him, savored her searching hands which took posession of him, her wide-open, tongue-playing mouth. Underneath her kimono Anselma was naked down to garter belt and stockings. The robe fell to the floor as he tossed her onto the couch. Oh! Her shoulders and armpits, the breasts with their stiff black nipples, her brown, opening sex. In his drunkenness he wanted to fall on his knees, but he was afraid of making a fool of himself. (Anselma's submission demanded strategy!) He sucked in the smell of her sex, took possession of everything about her with wild, grasping desire and a naïve joy of discovery, which aroused her wantonness. They didn't talk. The noise of sucking kisses and unarticulated sounds filled the room. Höllriegl's mouth searched out all the openings of her body. His kisses soon turned into bites. He felt her firm, elastic flesh between his teeth and enjoyed her soft screams like nothing else. In the moments of highest pleasure Anselma's face had the expression of someone undergoing bitter torture. He told her and she replied with melting eyes, "Torture me . . . go on, go on." They reached their first climax together, and sank almost at once into a new wave of lust.

Anselma also loved the little tendernesses which, aping Ko Won, she called "little lovie-lovie." One in particular tickled his senses. She told him to kiss her eyes and when he did she opened her lids slowly so Höllriegl's tongue slid across her cold, smooth, wet eyeballs. Even the inside of her nose, the finely fluted nostrils, had a secret love meaning.

"Little lovie-lovie."

When they were sated, they dressed scantily. Anselma rang. Ko Won appeared, smirking with satisfaction, and brought in one after the other of the trays on which, in little dishes and cups, supper had been prepared. Anselma told Höllriegl that she did not always eat a vegetarian diet, but had ordered the meatless meal only to please him. (He was smart enough, anticipating her ridicule, not to tell her that as a young Nazi he had become a vegetarian, nonsmoker, and nondrinker in order to imitate the Führer and had so remained until the present.)

First Ko brought in unsweetened fresh pineapple slices, then preserved Tientsin cabbage. Next came Cantonese noodles like Italian pasta, with dried mushrooms soaked in warm water and young onions. (Höllriegl wanted all the dishes explained.) Soy sauce accompanied each course. The cook served fried rice and lichee nuts as dessert. They drank warm rice wine in little sips which Anselma—another little lovie-lovie—let pour from her mouth into Höllriegl's.

She saw his flowers, or acted as if she did, only after they were eating dessert. An ironic expression rolled across the smoothness of her face like a fleeing wave, the laugh wrinkles around her mouth grew a shade sharper. Höllriegl had not expected her to thank him for this attention. To his great satisfaction, however, she did—with even an expression in her eyes which was at once thoughtful and sensual. ". . . that you thought of it. Do you love me?"

"Yes, Anselma, completely."

"Please let's do it again, and again, and again. Lots of times. I have such desire! Come on!"

She had risen and slipped off her kimono without waiting for his answer. She stepped very close to the sitting man. He embraced her with all his strength and again and again kissed the secret treasure of her body. Ah, Anselma's smell and taste, that fine old-maidish aroma of withering garlands. The odor of her secretion. She pulled him to her onto the bed.

Their caresses were no longer as wild as they had been earlier. They did everything with some deliberation and whispered to each other how they would do it. Höllriegl feared nothing—nothing that Anselma wanted him to do or that he thought up himself. Slowly they became exhausted. They were satiated, worn out, and the tiredness, too, pleased them. Gratefully she snuggled close to him and licked him like a satisfied animal. (She didn't behave any differently from most of the others!) And so they slid into a state of half-sleep.

"I needed it so," Anselma said after a while.

"No, it is love," he contradicted her. A long pause. She seemed asleep.

"It's desire, lust, a tickling, nothing else. I invited a few of my colleagues to watch us. . . ."

Höllriegl jumped up. Everything in him tensed into knots, every muscle vibrated. An icy shower ran through him. She was mad!

"What did you say?"

"I invited some friends from my office. To watch," she repeated quietly and without irony. "Over there, the masks on the wall. You can watch from the next room through the eye slits. This time was my turn. Yesterday somebody else's. We pick strong fellows, who know how."

He didn't move. Horror paralyzed his every reaction. The expression on his face made her laugh. "Don't take it so to heart. Don't you do that sort of thing out in the sticks?" Now she was making fun of him.

"Whore!"

When she touched him, he pulled back. Disgust! Paradise just a few moments ago and now the abyss. He wanted to vomit. A prickly cold crept from his toes into his legs. Suddenly he froze and trembled with cold. Without saying a word he got up and put on his clothes. He avoided looking at her. He had been made ridiculous. Everything was ridiculous. For a heartbeat he thought of Ingrid —that was the retreat, perhaps even his salvation. The last thing he had left. Ingrid . . .

"Don't make a tragedy out of it! Let's stay friends. You were only thinking of Ulla the whole time, isn't that true? Ulla turned you down, that's not hard to guess. Perhaps she just didn't feel like it, or you went about it wrong. Otherwise my dear sister-in-law isn't that way at all."

He didn't answer. Disgust, paralysis, disgust. Suddenly the sirens howled outside. Alarm! Alarm One, the signal to go down to the deep bunkers. Without prior warning—the real thing, not an exercise. Atomic danger. A sneak attack.

The monotonous, high-pitched howling ripped through the air. Höllriegl looked down at Anselma, who still lay on the couch in her horrible nudity. They traded terrified looks. Anselma jumped up, grabbed her kimono, and disappeared.

Incredible things had happened. Since Saturday everything had changed. Humiliation had followed humiliation. The blow Anselma had dealt him was much worse than the beating he had taken from Ulla. Now he didn't give a damn. Let a bomb destroy them all. He was finished.

Numbed, he remained standing where he was for . . . seconds? minutes? hours? Time wasted away, ran into the sand. The howl of the sirens ebbed into a hideous meowing, and died.

In the weird silence that followed he heard an announcement over the loudspeaker in the hall. Anselma stood in the corridor in a radiation suit and fur coat. Ko carried the prescribed air-raid-protection suitcase and his mistress' helmet.

"Come quickly."

The announcement was repeated. "All residents of Neuenburgerstrasse 38 are to go into the deep bunker. Bring radiation suits. Serfs will assemble in the laundry room downstairs. Further orders at ten-o-five. End of announcement."

Only then did Höllriegl become aware of four persons, more shadows than persons really, who were waiting for him and Anselma. They were already outside in the corridor: a man and three women, one of them almost a dwarf. In the dim blue lights of the staircase, like light at the bottom of the sea, everything appeared unreal: the faces were chalky with deep shadows, mouths distorted and without speech. Anselma's cutting voice dominated the group.

"You'll put on your radiation suits in the bunker," she said to them, presumably her friends from the office. Silently they went downstairs, the ladies swinging their elegant hips. They all avoided each other's eyes. When they had reached the ground floor, Anselma again interrupted the silence. "Ko, you come with Missie to the bunker, not the cellar." Frau Geldens could obviously afford to ignore orders.

After they had put on their radiation suits (Ko didn't get one) and been given helmets which lent them the appearance of an elephant crossed with a griffin, they passed through hermetically sealed security cells—or rather, were pushed through them. In the hall-like, vaulted sitting room of the bunker, which, considering the place, was quite comfortably furnished (Höllriegl noted with glee that they had forgotten to take down the large Hitler portrait), they found themselves faced with a strange company. Some tried on the bird masks and cackled as they did, or sniffed loudly through their trunks; others admired themselves in their ash-colored suits, figure-fitted for the ladies. Armed air-raid wardens equipped with Geiger counters scurried about busily. Here too the light was dimmed, but it was bright enough to read by. Generally people talked in whispers. From time to time orders to auxiliary personnel and serfs came over the loudspeaker. Höllriegl was so numb from the shock upstairs, so filled with an "I don't give a damn" feeling that he could barely register what was going on around him. He simply ignored Anselma, who had sat down next to him as if nothing had happened. The thought of her body, her submissiveness, made him freeze. He listened to the quiet conversation about the sneak attack on the Reich capital, the apparent failure of the radar warning system, and the political and military world situation as it had developed since the Führer's death and Köpfler's accession. Every word expressed confidence, the will to victory and trust in the new party and army leadership. The Greater German Empire was a world power which could no longer be destroyed. Another viewpoint simply didn't exist, and if it did, no one would have dared mention it.

Höllriegl did not fail to notice that the three ladies eyed him with open sympathy and desire. Especially the dwarf, a deformed woman of indeterminate age with a beautiful face and glowing eyes, devoured him with her glances when the others weren't watching. In order to avoid making the already embarrassing situation unbearable, he pretended to be entirely at ease and took part in their conversation, although he didn't say much. The dead Führer had to be left out of the game—that tendency was now general—and the new leadership, Köpfler and his Werewolf retinue, was praised to the skies. He gathered from the conversation that the man and one of the ladies were married, and were a television announcer team, who used to do multilingual commercials from the beach at Sylt. She was honey-blond and had a sweet, motherly personality, just what the German TV and other Reich-controlled broadcasting systems had ordained down to the inch. He was a broad-shouldered man who spoke guttural German, had dark skin, an energetic face, and gray temples: a ski-champion type, as featured so often in the pages of sports magazines. He wore black sunglasses even in the bunker despite the dim light. Höllriegl learned his name: Monnikendam. He was Dutch but had long been a Reich citizen, a friend of Anselma's late husband. The Monnikendams moonlighted in Frau Gelden's section. The dwarf had some kind of key position in the personnel department of the Foreign Office, and the fourth person, a young girl—Höllriegl now remembered having seen her at Anselma's lunch table—also worked in the Foreign Office: a thin, brunette Swede whose good figure and bearing recalled a fashion model. Her name was Helle. Ko Won cowered on the concrete floor and smilingly busied himself playing a solitary Mah-Jongg.

They all seemed to have reached a silent agreement not to allude to the goings-on the four had witnessed in Anselma's apartment. But their glances spoke loudly enough. Höllriegl's imagination conjured up visions of an orgy, mostly Lesbian in nature (three women against one man) the four of them had held in the adjoining room after watching him in action. Theoretically every erotic activity which did not serve procreation was forbidden, and deviation from sexual norms, if brought to the attention of the party or the NSGZS (National Socialist Community for Breeding and Morals) were heavily punished. But despite all the precautions, now and again the authorities did uncover orgies. People called such amusements "songs," and discovery of them was a welcome pretext for holding a show trial at which all the dirty laundry was washed in public in gratifying detail. In practice, however, especially if influential people were involved, the authorities overlooked such failings even in cases where the female lust objects were of inferior race or serfs. Well, the four of them must have had their "song." Höllriegl didn't have to care—he had already grown used to their complicity.

Little news came in from the outside. The air-raid warden for the block obviously didn't want to say too much in order to prevent panic among the entombed. But the general nervousness increased as rumors flew that ICBM's had plastered not only Greater Berlin but other parts of the Reich and done great property damage and killed a large number of people. No detonations had rocked the bunker, only once had the earth trembled a little. In between announcements from the air-raid warden's office, the loudspeaker played marches, including Köpfler's favorite: "We Wolves Howl at Night." Finally the warden tuned in the radio and the house residents heard this laconic report:

"Two ICBM's of the Banzai type with conventional warheads exploded over the territory of Greater Berlin, a third fell into the Wannsee. Property damage is extensive. The elevated line from Spandau-West to Staaken has been interrupted in several places and the subway tunnels between Alexanderplatz and Schönhauser Avenue and between Spittelmarket and the Central Station have been partially destroyed. Reports of other attacks have come from Kassel, Paderborn, and Bielefeld, as well as from the Middle Rhine and the eastern Pomeranian region. No details are as yet available. Two missiles fell into the sea in Lübeck Bay near Haffkrug-Scharbeutz. The sneak attack on the Reich was carried out by weapons equipped with conventional, not atomic or chemical, warheads. No radioactivity was found in any of the attacked areas. Massive retaliation on a worldwide scale is underway."

When the announcer had finished, the warden said: "The all clear for Greater Berlin will be sounded shortly. House residents will leave the bunker in ordered discipline and with exemplary cheerfulness. Radiation suits and masks are to be taken upstairs. End of announcement."

Höllriegl took advantage of the exemplary good mood—and in fact a kind of wretched jollity had spread at once among the people who lived in the house because the announcement had mentioned only conventional warheads—and disappeared amid the small uproar at the exits into the darkness without saying good-bye. It was flight. Anselma, perhaps unintentionally, had not bothered introducing him to her friends. What was he, a footman, a serf? Her body had been his property just as his had been hers. They were even. He never wanted to see her again, nor Ulla either. He'd had bad luck with the proud von Eyckes—yes, he belonged to the lower classes. But as he thought about it all, he felt a dull pain as from some incomprehensible wound.

The dark streets under a fire-flecked sky, the color reminding him of the darkened Führer picture at home, gradually became lighter with emerging flashlights. A strange, sweet, stuffy smell lay in the air. He heard a distant howl that came quickly closer until it deafened his ears. As he walked across a large square—it must have been Blücher Platz—truck after truck tore past him with headlights turned up. The vehicles were filled with young soldiers who shouted a single word over and over: "Ausra! Ausra! Ausra!" Höllriegl understood: Ausra was one of the most terrible weapons of destruction in the Reich arsenal, a missle named for the old Baltic Goddess of Dawn, and at the same time the word was a military abbreviation for "eradication."

He found the subways had closed down, so he had to walk. It was tough going; several times he was stopped by patrols and barricades. The more he tried to flush Anselma out of his thoughts, the greater, more painful and more cutting did the wish become to see her again, to possess her, to avenge the shame done him. How ridiculous! He was taking the whole thing much too seriously. Such games were part of the amusements practiced in certain circles, whose members were always bored. Anselma moved in such society and had to adapt to it if she wanted to stay in it. Perhaps she had been forced to do it. But why should he still try to find reasons for her actions? Wasn't that already half forgiving and forgetting?

"Let us remain friends," she had said.

"Ausra . . . Ausra . . . Ausra . . ." the cry went on.

IN THE CATACOMBS

It happened behind Schicklgrube, a little village on the road from Schlewecke to Bad Harzburg. Overnight the "special" restricted zone designations had been changed, and Hörriegl, whose pass was limited to them, had to make a long detour. There had been little traffic on the autobahn—he could have safely parked in the passing lane—and the absence of long-distance trucks was most striking. Many had been requisitioned. Only the most urgent trips were being made in private cars. High up in the sky he heard a low, incessant roar.

After the weather of the last few weeks, it had turned into a surprisingly warm day for this time of year. The sun blinked through the clouds and the foothills of the Upper Harz gleamed wet and brown. The air was luminous, like mother-of-pearl. After Höllriegl had passed the village, which nestled in a hollow, he saw a huge building towering on top of a hill that fell in terraces down to an almost waterless pond. He screeched to a halt and looked at the edifice, obviously one of those memorial castles the Führer had built after the victory. A chain of such memorials for the Reich's fallen heroes stretched from Spain to Ytemest, the former Hammerfest, in Norway, and from Archangel down the Urals and Caucasus to the south of Greece. The memorial castles were all the same. They were impressive because of their mammoth and somber majesty. Their surroundings—small oak groves, moss-covered stone steps, pedestals of square-hewn stone with panlike bronze vessels to hold the eternal flame, the reflecting pool—were always identical. The building had the shape of an immense archway, of gray, crude cement, like a bunker.

Höllriegl felt solemn. Whenever he came in contact with death, in conversation or at cemeteries, this unmanly, sentimental mood overcame him; his eyes misted and he had to swallow hard. The memorial reminded him of Böcklin's painting "Isle of the Dead" that had hung at home in the living room. Sorrowfully he thought of his parents, especially of his mother. They had been dead a long time.

But then Ulla's white body flamed in his thoughts, and at once he thought of Anselma. How often he had already that day! A lady had telephoned this morning as he was getting in his car, ready to leave. Frau Zweenemann had tried to call him back, but he drove off. Let Anselma know there were no bridges left. He felt a childish stubborness.

During the long drive that followed, with its many stops and controls—only Werewolves in civilian clothes patrolled the highways; the NSKK, whose regular job it was, was nowhere to be seen—he had mentally castigated Anselma again and again. He placed his words like whiplashes. An Anselma of thin air, an Anselma who didn't answer. And still, now and again he breathed the warm smell of her skin, heard her soft, hard voice, felt a fine-boned hand placed on his when he took a curve too sharply.

Anselma! The more his fury and contempt grew, the more he felt his own impotence. She was a creature with the instincts of an intelligent animal, unassailable because incredibly she lived only in the present. Did she have any memory at all? Brains for history? Anselma's reactions were always right, always sure, simply because she was an animal. An animal with the cutting mind of a . . . surgeon, but with the temperament of a whore. She was—yes, that was the right word—she was a strumpet. Why hadn't he thrown that word in her face? "Whore" was so common. Anselma could open things, lay them bare, show their anatomy, making you sick, like undergoing an operation while fully conscious. She must be as cruel as a child. And as dangerous. (Höllriegl didn't like children; sometimes they had played rough tricks on him.) She probably tore off spiders' legs when she was bored, and wings from flies. She'd wanted to try that on him.

He turned the radio on; somewhere he would surely find serious music, the kind that would fit the memorial. Briefly he was angry with himself: in face of the heroes who had died for Führer and Reich he had nothing in his head but women.

No music except marches, and on every station the same news and announcements. It had been that way since morning, with the announcements often coded so that only higher party authorities could understand them. A certain vulgarity had cropped up in news broadcasts: military objectivity had given way to crude propaganda. The announcers were obviously under orders to read the text with as much hatred in their voices as they could muster.

". . . the early-warning system in Thule reported this morning the approach of several Wakaihito missiles. They were pushed off course and exploded in the Arctic desert. The despicable enemy parachuted guerillas and kamikaze commands in the area between the former cities of Omsk and Semipalatinsk. Supported by eastern subhumans, they attacked our advanced outpost villages east of the Irtysh. Merciless hand-to-hand combat is underway. The enemy is flying in reinforcements. The border fortress at Ragnar Lodbrok was lost after glorious resistance. Wherever the slit-eyed jackals have gained a foothold they have opened the camps. As a result the Army High Command in Transural has ordered the liquidation of the SHC camps and prohibited taking of prisoners. Step on the Tschandal worms wherever they appear! . . . Attention, attention. Uncle Theodore calls Annemariechen . . . Edelweiss two, Edelweiss two . . . to all posts. . . . Heads or Tails . . . tails or heads . . . heads or tails. . . . The Reich's Pacific Air Force last night carried out continuous annihilation attacks on the Japanese home islands and the Chinese mainland, against Indonesia and Australia, now occupied by the yellow apes. Singapore is a sea of flames. Osaka and Kobe no longer exist. Sino-Japanese paratroopers have been dropped on the Reich protectorate of Hong Kong. Our brave troops have made contact at several points with a numerically superior enemy who fight like common murderers. The Japs managed to secure their positions on the Kaulung Peninsula and the Bay of Siwan. After a heroic battle Siwan fell into the hands of the enemy. . . . Defense commandos of the Second and Eighth air fleets have repulsed numerous enemy amphibious operations directed against the American West Coast. However, in Estero Bay, near San Diego and Agua Caliente, the enemy managed to expand its bridgeheads thanks to the help of traitorous American forces. . . . The situation in central California and on the Nevada front is unclear at the moment. . . . The Dalai Lama, who has been undergoing treatment for the past year in a Cologne neurological clinic, died today of a brain embolism. The Living God of the Tibetans, whose schizophrenia had been diagnosed as incurable, was forty years old. . . . Bitter fighting between Boer farmers and black apes is reported from several parts of the Boer Free State. The black beasts committed unspeakable horrors on defenseless whites, especially women and children. Fast units of our protection troops and V-Brigades of the Afrikaner Broederbond and the Boer SS are en route to rebel territory. . . . Yesterday evening one of our U-boats operating in the Alenuihaha Canal shot down an enemy bomber with a resultant nuclear explosion. Hawaii and Maui have been declared radiation zones. It has thus been proved that the Soka Gakkai clique of war criminals is about to attack the German World Empire and her allies with nuclear weapons, a historical challenge the German people cannot leave unavenged. Since midnight German time we have retaliated in kind. Our Führer Ivo Köpfler has ordered the Strategic Air Command North to fly toward enemy territory and drop atomic bombs at a specified time over specified targets. . . . Heidehopsassa, heidehopsassa . . . what's Aunt Ute doing in the Bohemian Forest? . . . Birthday present arrived, cake still edible. . . . Preparations for the ceremonies attendant upon the funeral of Adolf Hitler in the Kyffhäuser Mountains necessitate designation of the region Kelbra-Hackpfüffel-Rottleberode-Heydrich in Gau Goldene Aue as a major restricted zone. Only permanent residents and possessors of WW-12,000 and RAD-III identity cards as well as army and party members stationed there may enter the zone. Ivo Köpfler has decreed that the area will become the future national shrine of the German people. . . . Arrest of the traitors Unseld and Diebold is expected momentarily. They have been encircled and their final disposition is only a matter of hours away. . . ."

The radio babbled on. The most important news obviously was the fact that the enemy had begun atomic war after all. It did not shake Höllriegl unduly—like many others, he had secretly expected it. (Those yellow devils!) Nevertheless Reich territory might be hit if the electronic shield did not hold fast. And England was a good example of what that meant. It had not staged an economic recovery since London's eradication in the spring of 1945.

But for the moment and for the near future the fact that his home was part of the national restricted zone was more important to him. Although it would have no immediate impact on his life, since he worked in the party health office, it would have a long-range one. His laboriously built-up group of clients would be lost for sure.

Höllriegl got out of his car and took a deep breath of the fine country air. Not a soul far and near—how peaceful the world was! Only high above him that quiet droning. He stepped to the side of the road and began doing breathing exercises according to nature-healing methods. After a few minutes he felt relaxed and strengthened. While immersed in concentration, he had not noticed how much louder the droning had become: It seemed to come crashing down right on top of him. Looking up, he saw a fighter dive straight at him like one of those prehistoric Stukas, whip close to the ground, and then rise up vertically, the whole maneuver carried out with lightning precision. Knowledgeable about aircraft types as a party functionary had to be, he recognized the new Nih-156-D, of German-American manufacture, "The most up-to-date multipurpose fighter with all-weather capability." Höllriegl remembered the exact wording in the Defense Manual for German Officers: "Able to perform with equal brilliance in aerial combat, ground-support missions, dive bombing, and reconnaissance." As the plane disappeared, screaming from all its jets, and suddenly shrank to mosquito size in the distance, Höllriegl's lips mechanically mouthed the memorized sentence: "This most reliable plane, which can start at once and from almost any point, has fulfilled and exceeded all previous calculations. Armed with lasers, the Nih(il)-156-D (Death!) is the most effective assault weapon in the hands of the new world order. . . ." He smiled happily. The little episode had strengthened him and renewed his confidence.

He hastened up the broad flagstones that led to the lowest terrace of the memorial castle. Up close the buildings made a rather dilapidated impression. The reflecting pool was nothing more than a stagnant pond. Dry thistles stood about everywhere, and man-high, dirty brown burdocks grew around the cracked pillars and walls. Here and there steel showed through the concrete. Some of the stone benches that invited meditation and prayer had collapsed and not been repaired. On the front of the highest terrace wall, Höllriegl found a weathered inscription:

MAY MILLENIUMS PASS
ONE WILL NEVER SPEAK OF HEROISM
WITHOUT THINKING OF THE GERMAN ARMIES
THEN THE IRON FRONT OF THE GRAY STEEL
HELMET

NOT YIELDING AND NOT RETREATING
A REMINDER OF IMMORTALITY
BUT AS LONG AS GERMANS LIVE
THEY WILL THINK
THAT THESE WERE ONCE SONS OF THEIR PEOPLE.
ADOLF HITLER, *MEIN KAMPF.*

Fresh black paint had been smeared over the Führer's name. Somebody had stenciled on the wall: HEIL TO THE GERMAN WW—and painted an open wolf's jaw underneath.

That bit of blasphemy disgusted him. Pride and joy vanished at once. Deep in thought and haunted by somber premonitions—even the sun had hidden behind clouds—he wandered around the memorial. As he could now see, the artificial mound continued into a natural tree-covered shelf of land behind the castle.

He sat down in order to catch his breath and then lay on his back, massaging the back of his head with his hands. Again that awful, nervous pain in his neck, that stiffness in the vertebrae. Höllriegl was aware that something enormous and erratic was happening inside the German people, in the depths and deeper depths of the popular soul which pushed toward a new beginning as it had long ago, as it did in 1933! Discord—in this historic moment! These were days of terrible decision, of decision for him, for every single citizen. Where did he belong, where did he want to belong? To the old guard trooping around the dead Führer and his inheritance, or to the new men? "I hope you won't always back the wrong horse. . . ." Should he, like Anselma, howl with the Werewolves?

Sitting up, he saw that the dell before him had come alive. A gray mass in the winter grass moved slowly toward the place where he lay. What was it? A herd of pigs? It would have been easy to believe. He listened intently to hear if they grunted. It sounded more like a hoarse murmur. No, they were humans, but humans who walked on all fours.

Höllriegl had heard and read that biologists and neurosurgeons in the SHC's had begun sensational experiments to reduce certain types of human beings into animals. It was part of the grand scheme of existence: a highly bred master race, made up of nobles and freemen, a holy, Nordic-blooded aristocracy to rule the world, their power supported by specially trained vassal peoples; while below the lords and their servants only animals—of every kind of intelligence and developmental stage—would be allowed to exist. This human cattle would at first be developed from very inferior or criminal Tschandal material. They were destined for robotlike herd existence, and from a sociological point of view they would rank between domestic animals and machines. Machines would solve the most difficult mental problems and do the heavy work while the human animal would be assigned the lowest form of drudgery, completion of which nevertheless involved something like comprehension. Lobotomies would crack the human ego, change thought into primitive instinct, make him faceless and let primeval drives take over. The whole concept had arisen in part out of fear that the more highly developed and hard-to-control machines might some day withdraw from the oligarchy's control and think and act independently. This danger did not exist with genetically changed subhumans. In everything they did they would be much more automatic than machines and therefore less dangerous. Slaves were cheaper too; they could be exterminated more easily en masse, even brought to the point of exterminating each other. The life reformers of NATMAT already dreamed of the day when civilization would consist only of human cattle reservations and highly developed machine parks—all of them of course subject to an elite already being created in the pure-breeding colonies, in the strongholds of the SS and in the Valhallas of the ariosophists. Everyone knew that breeding human animals was still in a very early stage of development, and it was generally regretted that the Jews had been eradicated so quickly and so completely; probably they would have been ideal test material.

Höllriegl remembered a sentence he had once learned by heart in preparation for one of his exams and which had become permanently embedded in his mind.

"The subhuman, that biologically apparently identical creation of nature with hands, feet and a kind of brain, with eyes and mouth, is in reality a quite different, terrible creature, merely a draft of man with apparently human facial expressions. Spiritually and mentally, however, it is lower than any animal." He had also heard that before skull operations were performed, test groups of subhumans had been imprisoned for years in very low-ceilinged cages, like pigs, suffocating in their excrement, even eating it, until the survivors began to crawl on all fours or slide along the ground. A stiffness or deformation of the spine had set in during the confinement, while the muscles adapted to the new form of movement. As a result the creatures found it difficult to get up on their hind legs and walk. At the same time these four-footers gradually assumed the appearance and manner of animals. However, the final product of the experiments, which were under way all over the Western world under such code names as "Hippopotamus," "Thutmosis," and "Ka" (Ka was lethal for those involved), was still far distant, although individual results, according to the *Kyffhäuser Messenger,* gave hope for excellent future achievements.

Höllriegl had never seen these artificial animals. And deep inside he did not want to believe in the possibility or success of the experiments, even though they were an open secret, vaguely and euphemistically discussed in the racial-theoretical newsletters available to party functionaries and healing assistants. He could not reject them from an ideological point of view—something he told himself over and over—because in his concept of a heroic hierarchy and an idealized world of gods existed rulers and the ruled; a killing and a being killed; a higher development of the species at the expense of its lower form. But as the human animals slowly crawled up the hill toward him, he felt sick and faint from the horror of their stench, and by the disgusting sight of their unkempt crooked bodies. He realized that a biosurgical dream had become reality.

Frozen, he stayed where he was and involuntarily groped for his dagger, the only weapon he had on him. (As a functionary he was under orders to carry a gun while traveling, but he had left it in the car.) Coated with dirt and dressed in asbestos-colored smocks (or what was left of them), the beasts seemed peaceful. Nothing human remained. Snouts on the ground—or were these still noses and mouths?—they went their way, nodding their heads in a hoarse singsong. When one of the animals began to sniff at him, he made as if to hit it, his whole body trembling. The creature—had it once had a human face?—retreated screeching, its voice a woman's voice. It showed its foul teeth, but in a kind of smile. The rest of the herd hardly noticed him.

Suddenly Höllriegl became aware of something that jolted his nerves like a shrill alarm. He jumped up with a single bound. Where were the keepers, the guards? Not a man in uniform to be seen. The herd seemed left to itself; if it were a labor battalion on assignment, guards would be present. No, the human animals were voluntarily following a creature indistinguishable in appearance and action from themselves, with the sole exception that it walked half erect, as if under a heavy burden. It seemed to be a trusty or a sort of group leader. The creature—it was grotesquely ugly—chanted something like a litany in which his gruesome retinue joined from time to time, half mumbling and half singing.

The sound of some of the words seemed familiar to Höllriegl; he listened more closely—yes, it was Czech. During the resettlement of the Czechs from the former protectorate, now the Reich Gau of Bohemia and Moravia, only a few native groups, selected on the basis of intelligence, had remained behind. Occasionally these had been shipped to the SHC's, biological laboratories, and the experimental stations of the space ports of Peenemünde and Beydritten for defense projects. The Czech people as such, like the population of former Poland, had been distributed among the four Russian Waräger provinces, where they had to do serf work for the German frontier farmers and were subject to the orders of the SS Reich Governor for the Eastern Territories.

Czech! As a child, Höllriegl had spent several summers in southern Bohemia on a dairy farm in the Budweis region. He'd been a sickly child, and his German-Bohemian mother, afraid he would catch tuberculosis, had sent him to a relative for a "cure" so that he would grow stronger and healthier through the warm cow's milk and invigorating air of the pine trees. And, in fact, it had worked. The boy had learned the local language very quickly. His devout relatives sent him into the neighboring village church to serve Mass every Sunday because he remembered the half-Latin and half-Czech prayers so easily. And he had retained some knowledge of Czech over the years.

"... *duše má Boha,*" Höllriegl heard the trusty chant. In singing the psalms, the leader repeatedly threw his arms into the air. "*Skoro-liž* ..."

Hoarse-voiced and forming the words with difficulty, the chorus joined in "*Slzy mé jsou* ..."

Again the choir leader called out, the saliva spurting from his lips: "*Sud' mne* ..."

And again the crawling animals replied with nodding heads.

Höllriegl understood every word despite the rough, broken sounds. It was like a summons, a stream of light from the distant past. It must be the psalms or something like it. He was more surprised than shaken. So the light had not extinguished in these creatures, the human light! Perhaps they could not communicate among themselves, but they could still pray together.

"*Abych přistoupil k* ..." the litany drifted away as the herd passed the hill. Lost in his memories, Höllriegl stood where he was, his jaw gaping. He saw himself, small and weak, stand in the church of Bukovsko, dressed in the white collar and red smock of an altar boy. His carefully parted hair smelled of burdock root oil. He saw the pale-pink nave, the shining, painted plaster saints and angels, the fuchsias in their pots. The Eye of the Almighty, terrible and gaping, looked down from the ceiling; it was triangular. He saw the gray-brown rotted wood of the choir and benches, the tin pipes of the organ, whose bellows he was sometimes allowed to tread. Always it smelled of cold incense and tepid rainwater in the tubs underneath the stations of the Cross. He heard the buzz of wasps, the crunch of peasant shoes on sandy flagstones. The Eternal Light glowed ruby-red. He saw the small, bulging confessionals with their whiff of venial sin. How obese they were, those velvetlike closets with their dark violet, wornout curtains hiding the heated face of the priest. And he would remember forever those horrible sentences written on a slip of paper fixed above the latticed windows inside the confessional. *Casus Ordinario reservati:* 1. *Perjurium solemniter emissum.* 2. *Homicidium voluntarium et procuratio abortus effectu secuto.* 3. *Copula incestuosa cum consanguineis vel affinibus primi gradus.* 4. *Incendiarii crimen effectu secuto.*

He no longer understood the sentences, but they must have

meant something awful. How could he have forgotten it all? It had all happened only yesterday! He had even seen Božena kneeling on the women's side, among the other villagers all dressed up in their Sunday best. Božena, she could have been his mother, who sometimes showed him her nude, fat, milk-white behind and, in front, the dark triangular fleece. An Eye of God turned on its point and no less terrible. There she sat now and turned her pious eyes toward heaven—she who always waited for him in the dark, fondled him, and led his hand to a certain place on her body.

Abruptly something tore him out of his reverie. He felt someone stare at him. Yes . . . there . . . a human figure down on the terrace of the building, looking steadily up at him. A woman, a young woman. In her hands she held bulging heavy bundles. The lid of a kettle peeked out of the knapsack she carried on her back. A girl, a villager judging from her clothes, not half bad-looking, only unkempt. Finally a creature who walked upright. The animal screams of the herd shrilled in the distance.

Apparently the village woman had observed him for some time. When he looked at her, she smiled as if she had expected him, nodded, and came up the steps with her baggage. She pushed a few sounds out of her mouth the way dumb people do, and indicated through a movement of her body that he should follow her. They went, the girl ahead, Höllriegl, stunned by what he had seen, somewhat hesitantly behind. He followed her around the memorial castle and they left the enclosure.

At the edge of the forest the dumb girl stopped to rest. When Höllriegl offered to carry one of her bundles, she pushed him back with all her strength. She had a wild, shy manner, and her blue eyes, her best feature, flashed at him. She shook her light hair as she did, and again the incomprehensible sounds came from her mouth.

A small overgrown path led deep into the woods. It was a young mixed forest, not at all well kept, with the underbrush so thick in places that they made only slow progress. Wet leaves covered the ground; the sweet smell of fall reminded Höllriegl of Anselma's perspiration.

They walked on and on. From time to time the girl rested without looking around. In the middle of this solitude they passed a dilapidated hut around which scrub grew thickly. A half-broken fence surrounded a small clearing, and Höllriegl noticed high heaps covered with weeds and leaves. On closer inspection he suddenly saw white teeth gape in the wide open mouth of a horse's skull: a boneyard, a knacker's workshop. (What had T4's name been in earlier days? The Reich Knackery!) The association brought Höllriegl back to himself. His senses were strained to the utmost. He smelled a trap. And again that distant roar high above the trees.

Why in the devil's name had he followed this dumb woman? He could have been on his way a long time ago. Still, he had plenty of time—despite the detour he had been forced to make.

The forest fell gently to a valley grown wild. The ground became sandy, the underbrush less dense; pine trees swayed in the wind. They crossed rusted rails where weeds grew and finally followed a small-gauge track whose rotted sleepers kept disappearing in the sand. Here they found footprints on the wet ground, impressions of men's shoes, two pairs of boots with metal heels running next to the tracks of a woman's shoes. The valley, still almost an impassable thicket, broadened into a gorge which resembled an abandoned quarry. The walls were high and steep and crowned on top with thick bushes. Overturned mining carts and the remnants of a barracks blocked their path, and they had to climb over a spoil bank before reaching the hillside. All about Höllriegl saw small openings into the interior of the mountain, nailed over with planks or blocked by slag. His guide stopped in front of one such entrance, which they had reached by pushing through thorny bushes. The wall turned out to be a door: with certain planks pushed aside, a mine shaft opened up. The girl turned on a light. They had to walk bent over and breathe deeply. It smelled of mildew and congested air. The shaft had timberwork of heavy pitprops. Later, as it grew wider and sloped downward, Höllriegl noted that steel frames replaced the wood. The passage ran into a roomy concrete tunnel, sparsely lighted with electric bulbs, that led farther into the interior of the mountain. A sharp breeze—a wind from hell—drifted toward them. There seemed to be an artificial ventilation system down here.

Höllriegl realized that he was in one of those subterranean factories which had manufactured armaments before the war and during the air battles over the Reich. A thick net of such plants had covered half of Europe, with each unit designated by a number or call letter. These "tunnel factories" had produced important or delicate parts—often only a single part—of a certain weapon on an assembly-line basis and shipped their output on to the next plant. Only top management and supervising engineers and, of course, Intelligence, knew what weapon was involved, where and how it would be put together, and the overall production plans. After the final victory most of these tunnel factories had been shut down. Some were dynamited, others turned into vocational schools or museums, a very few found use as SHC's. Very likely one or two had been forgotten in the process.

The tunnel opened into a low, domelike room from which several shafts exited. Again they had to climb over a narrow-gauge track and several switches and turntables. A train, made up of a dozen little cars, stood here—and probably had for many years now, ready for any passengers from hell who might pass by.

A man stepped out of one of the shafts. He had obviously been waiting. He was dressed like a mechanic and wore a lined leather jacket and fur cap, which made Höllriegl, who had been lost in his own thoughts, suddenly realize how cold it was and that he had started shivering. The man greeted the dumb woman in a friendly way and took her bundle, giving her in return a paper and some money. "Thank you, Paule," he said, "and come back tomorrow." At the same time he gestured to her in sign language and made several funny faces. The girl grinned and lifted her skirts, shouting more incomprehensible words. "You're crazy," the man called out in his throaty drawl, but the woman had already disappeared in the darkness.

"You must come from Professor Gundlfinger," the mechanic said, more as a statement than a question. He shouldered the bundles. "You're expected. The gentlemen have assembled and the thing is ready." His pronunciation was pure for a worker.

Now the mechanic acted as guide. Again they walked down a long shaft, crossed a factory hall, empty except for a few machines, and dived into a tunnel, which this time sloped upward. A true labyrinth! Several times the man put his bundles down and fingered a wire or guide rope by holding a kind of slide rule to it. Electric signals? Since the path had become steep, Höllriegl helped with the bags.

When they reached the top, Höllriegl found himself in a comfortably warmed ogival chamber with bookcases reaching up to door height. Five men sat at a long table covered with papers and books. In the middle an elderly man was enthroned on a raised chair with armrests. He was a head taller than the others. All glared at Höllriegl from behind their glasses.

"This is Gundlfinger's messenger—a new one," the mechanic said and turned around, dragging the bundle behind him.

The chairman looked at Höllriegl with a kindly smile. The garland of white hair surrounding his gleaming bald pate had been combed into ringlets. His face and hands, like those of his colleagues, were pallid and sallow, like cave plants. He appeared tired, sleepy, ancient, and exuded a slack paternalism. Höllriegl had the feeling of facing a slightly deaf chief surgeon or university professor, who looked on him as a patient or candidate for a degree.

"So . . . so . . . you are one of Gundlfinger's people. That is identification enough," the man said thoughtfully. He seemed friendly. "Your uniform is a good cover. Usually he sends a young man to us, a perfectly charming young man. The work which Gundlfinger asked us to do is finished. It wasn't always easy to follow the thoughts of our friend and patron. We have tried to give our commentary the character of a faculty opinion. Do you know what it's all about?"

Höllriegl, who knew nothing, having slid into this situation like Pontius Pilate into the Credo, pulled himself together. "No . . . the Herr Professor did not inform me, not yet. I'm new in his service. Perhaps he'll do so later."

That was bold. Had it been smart as well? Traps lay all about him. Shouldn't he show his real color, tell the truth, confess the whole thing was a misunderstanding? But it was much too late for that now. Was he mixed up in a conspiracy? It looked like it. It would be best to let the chairman go on talking, and keep quiet.

The four others looked a lot less friendly than the speaker. Their faces remained ironic and stony. They, too, had that certain "clinical" look: cold, objective, weighing him, deprecatory. For them he was a thing, a number, a case. Höllriegl hated that—and to make matters worse, they seemed to stare steadily at his black eye and his scar. He felt like a student taking an exam in an anatomy lecture hall.

The hall was high and resembled a chapel. Above the books on the middle wall hung, framed in glass, *not* the Führer but a white-bearded gentleman with bent head and brooding face, his expression indicating deepest thoughtfulness. A barely legible inscription interspersed by wet splotches ran around the walls below the ceiling. Astonished, Höllriegl spelled out the words: *Co ito ergo sum.* And below that: *Flectere s equeo su eros Acheronta movebo.* Höllriegl had never been very good at Latin, and he'd forgotten most of it. He read the inscription several times but couldn't supply the missing letters, and for that reason alone the meaning escaped him.

"I see you're reading the inscription and are surprised by it, my friend," the chairman said in that patronizing and at the same time probing manner of his. "Hm . . . couch situation . . . infantile . . . hm. The milieu is new for you, has to be. But perhaps Gundlfinger will again make use of your services as a messenger to the underworld. That we are psychoanalysts you know. The last, or, if you will, the first—the first, again. The last shall be first. We are psychoanalysts who hide for well-known reasons, but remain in very close contact with science aboveground, with scholars in all countries and all disciplines. That we live underground—must live that way—even has a deeply symbolic significance. Our science, of which today's youth knows nothing because they are not allowed to, deals with the underground, the hidden, invisible, but always evident powers of the human soul. . . ."

Höllriegl froze to ice, disgusted. He vividly remembered how as a boy, back in March thirty-eight, when the Führer had marched into Linz to bring the Ostmark home into the Reich, the streets and squares had seen fires of joy: fires of joy that had soon become burning stakes—a repetition of that historic May 10, 1933, before the University of Berlin. The illegal Student SA of Upper Danube had tossed all books by Jews, Freemasons, and representatives of the old order into the flames. He too had helped clean out bookstores. Works of a certain Freud had been among them. How had the fire slogan of the SA gone? "Against the swinishness of the Jew Sigmund Freud! For the aristocracy of the German soul!" He remembered it so well, just as he still knew all the other slogans. And the Black Corps had attacked the "psychosyphilitics." Later, when he had worked in the healing section of the SS in order to prepare for his present profession, he had heard again and again about the unparalleled shamelessness of this destructive Jewish teaching. As a gyromant he also had to have the official "German Soul Science" at his fingertips. In the two volumns elucidating the science, author Bruno Marbod Wammse, Professor of Spiritual Depth Sounding and Factory Morality at the Technical University in Hanover, devoted two whole sentences to Freud's obscenities. Höllriegl had learned them by heart: "At the time of the German peoples' deepest shame the false teachings of the Viennese Jew Sigi Freud grew exuberantly, like poisoned mushrooms. When he took power, the Führer cleaned up that pigsty together with other garbage and smut, much to the sorrow of Yids the world over, who did a great deal of wailing about it."

This was a devil's conspiracy, no doubt about it. And he had fallen into the trap! How would he ever get out in one piece? Impossible without outside help. The chairman resembled an amoeba, but the four others seemed to be strong, bony fellows despite their years: the husky one on the far left could have been champion of a wrestling club. Then the mechanic, and the labyrinth! Who knew what other surprises were hidden in the underworld? Höllriegl regretted for the second time that day having left his gun in the car.

"In case you should come again and I cannot be here," the chairman continued in a fatherly tone, "one of my co-workers will represent me. They all speak very good German, although they are not Germans. That gentleman"—he pointed to the man on his right—"is Professor Guy de Saint-Phalle—a pseudonym, of course; the gentleman next to him is Dr. Géza Fekete-Bino, formerly of Burghölzli; and the man over there"—he turned to his left—"is called Tootlewasher, Irving S. Tootlewasher, formerly of Oxford. The fourth in our union is Señor José Otón Artega y Gaudemiché, a pseudonym, former holder of a Chair for Experimental Psychology at the University of Madrid. You see you are dealing with top-ranking specialists."

The specialists did not move, no one smiled or even acknowledged the introduction with as much as a nod. They sat there like pale, petrified judges of an Inquisition court, their eyeglasses glaring at him as before—malicious and hostile, he thought.

"Every one of these gentlemen has written some well-known work . . . I mean, well known in the underground world of experts. Just to give you an example, Professor Tootlewasher has written a paper called *On the Theory of Human Aggression,* which —you'll laugh—no less a man than Schultze-Rüssing used for his textbook of cruelty. Of course, we're quite satisfied when our theories and research find some echo "up there." One of his other essays, *The Power of Thought and Political Leadership,* was detoured into the Reich Chancellery and used by important officials. You may think me a megalomaniac, but we've been able to discover several of our arguments in the Führer's speeches! Some of Professor Tootlewasher's other papers include *A Devil's Neurosis in the Concentration Camp Natzweiler, Ejaculatory Fantasies of a Man Castrated for Racial Shame, Animism in Modern Mass Society,* etc. etc. Dr. Fekete-Bino, before the war one of our greatest experts in the field of analytical myth research, has written in the past year *Genius and Genitals,* and *Fiction in Old Norse Poetry.* And so on. Our friend and co-worker Guy de Saint-Phalle too has done significant research. His fundamental treatise *Thoughts about the Taboo on Female Genitals* once again is much discussed in underground analytical circles, as well as his other important essays: *Bed Wetting and Dry Humor,* and *An Attempt at a Structural Analysis of Cruelty,*—a work we plan to bring to the attention of Professor Schultze-Rüssing and Harry Styles Lynn of the University at Suwannee—*Anticipations des principes de psychanalyse dans l'oeuvre d'un poète naziste.* At present, Saint-Phalle is working on a very important matter, a commission from Professors Pitigrilli, Kapauner, and Hodenbruch of the Leyden Museum of Sexology. The work is entitled *The Placenta as a Ritual Meal with the Cora Indians.* Finally our friend over there, the flower of Spanish blood and spiritual aristocracy, is working on a number of timely subjects, among them *Ejaculation as the Victory of the Urethral over the Anal, Analogies in German and Jewish Clan History, Psycho-*pathology of the Soldier's Language (a commission from the German Academy for Truth and Poetry in Weimar), *Pinchas' Spear as Penis Symbol,*—there are many such titles. We may boast of having permanent secret collaborators in the highest ranks of the Roman Church, for example a very high cleric, whom we call Pater Praputius—this fiery Augustinian spirit recently finished a particularly brilliant study: *Annotations to the Psychology of the Black Mass.* I myself am writing an eagerly awaited essay entitled

Some Contradictions in the "Old-Mexican War Hieroglyphics Atl-tlachinolli" of Alice de Tribade. Naturally, we are all overworked. Not only do universities and academies present us with the most interesting problems, we also exchange our experiences with other underground centers, which results in a plethora of fruitful discussion and polemics and, unfortunately, many personal quarrels. I don't want to hide the fact from you that at present we are engaged in bitter strife with a powerful group hidden in the ruins of Old London and directed by a Frau Professor Nebenzahl. You will understand this more easily when I tell you that she has dared to represent Freud's teachings *in nuce* and today attempts to develop them anew from the source while at the same time accusing all the other centers of the gravest deviations from the general line, branding them as apostates, charlatans, and hypocrites. Of course we, who belong to the old guard, could not sit idly by. Above all, we and two other centers, disguised as groups of novitiates attached to the monasteries at Megisti Lawra and Argesi, are leading the battle against a petrified orthodoxy which no longer fits into our world. Without doubt such internal conflicts result in the loss of much time and energy, but on the other hand such competition among individual groups contributes to the strengthening of our scientific authority, keeps our methods elastic, cleans up dogmas, and leads them toward a final Apollonian form. You know what Gundlfinger is working on now?"

"No," Höllriegl replied, confused, "I'm new at the job."

"Excuse me, you said that already." The verbose chairman obviously enjoyed listening only to himself, and continued unswervingly. "Gundlfinger has nothing less in mind than a new proof for the existence of God; this emerges quite clearly from the problems he has given us to solve. To the extent that we know his plan of work, he has made this quotation from Pascal the basis of his speculation: *Nous ne vivons jamais, nous espérons toujours seulement de vivre*—— What is it? What is it?"

The exasperated question referred to the behavior of the four others, who flashed their eyeglasses not only at Höllriegl but at the chairman as well and simultaneously scratched their feet across the floor.

"The gentlemen find that I talk too much. Moreover they're hungry—it's almost lunchtime. This thought of Pascal's, consistently developed, inevitably leads us into a quasi-schizoid situation such as the masses today do in fact experience. For in the final analysis the difference between mental ills and so-called normalcy is slight. The schizophrenic person accepts the horrible lot of estrangement from the world of perception as his fate, whereas today's healthy individual more or less consciously becomes detached from the world of appearances, indeed must become detached under the impact of a traumatic and enormously dangerous era ruled by arbitrary power and violence. Recognition and decision are the wellsprings of action here. And thus symptoms of disease emerge in the average man of today—perhaps in you as well, if you'll forgive me—without his being able to resist them. You might say he slides into an artificial schizophrenia; waking turns to dreams and vice versa, the dream becomes trauma. . . ."

"Hunger, hunger," the choir of colleagues muttered, and they scratched loudly with their feet.

"Patience, my friends; I'll ring." The chairman pressed a bell. "It is quite understandable that our average citizen, exposed and defenseless against the aggressive drives of those in power and robbed of his right of self-determination, yes, even of all his human rights, is searching for a new metaphysical support, a new God, whose existence, however, he must first prove to himself. Man has hallucinations, but do they help him? In the idea of God, in the ideal of the father image, we do at least see the effort to break the vicious circle of autism in which today's so-called sane person sits imprisoned as if in a cage, trying to achieve in his dreamworld the character of reality. The idea of God provides consolation in a merciless and hostile world, and consolation means security or its illusion, a feeling of pleasure therefore—an increment of pleasure—and thus the hallucination of God brings desire and reality together, dissolving both in each other. Magic, as Freud, Rank, Ferenczi, and others have proved, demonstrates a similar attempt to lend an objective cloak to the world of our desires. These are last resorts. The true schizophrenic has withdrawn from reality all its real characteristics —this of course goes beyond the concept of God—to as far as his illness can reach. On the other hand the so-called sane person can, with the help of the idea of God, break out of his autistic prison into which he has fled from a much more terrible world. And because actual revolution is impossible given today's conditions, we consider Gundlfinger's metaphysics a politically revolutionary act. Unfortunately, if our latest information is correct, the proponents of NATMAT know it too——"

The mechanic came in from a side door and interrupted the chairman's flow of speech. "It's noon exactly. Lunch is served. I've set the table for nine."

"That means," the chairman said to Höllriegl, "that a place has been reserved for you." And before Höllriegl could object, the gentlemen had risen from their chairs and pushed toward the exit. The chairman took Höllriegl's arm. "Whoever comes from Gundlfinger belongs to the family . . . my name is Kofut, Professor Kofut-Eisenach, pseudonym Cunnilingus," he said softly, with that overpowering fatherliness which is peculiar to all directors of psychiatric clinics, and led him into a side room.

A frugal but plentiful meal was ready. In the middle of the long table, decorated with pine boughs, a stew steamed in an earthen dish. In addition to the five scholars, Höllriegl, and the mechanic, two other men were present: middle-aged, dirty, unkempt, and unshaven, whose terribly hollow faces Höllriegl immediately realized were familiar, although he could not place them. Both wore brown uniforms and boots.

The luncheon guests helped themselves to the food. The water was fresh and had a pleasant, metallic taste. "We discovered acidulated water in one of the shafts," the chairman, who had asked Höllriegl to sit at his side, explained. They ate silently. The four colleagues ate ravenously.

The uniformed men looked uneasy; their hunted manner was conspicuous, as was their exhaustion. When everyone had eaten his fill and they had started on their "dessert"—pieces of a soft, black peasant's bread—the chairman said half aloud to Höllriegl: "They are refugees. We've granted them political asylum and are trying to put them back on their feet."

"We're Unseld and Diebold," one of them said abruptly, turning his hollow-eyed look on Höllriegl. The other man stared down at his empty plate, not lifting his head. The words shattered Höllriegl like hammer blows. "The police were close on our heels, but these people here helped us."

"We're hiding them because they are Werewolf opponents," the chairman continued softly. "Of course they're not criminals. If the

Werewolf came to power, we'd all be finished—we and our friends up above. We're in contact with the anti-Werewolf forces in the party and the Wehrmacht to the extent our isolation permits. What's happening now is a repetition of history: Jacobins against the Gironde. We're Girondists, if for no other reason than for self-preservation. Only our scholarship is filled with a Jacobin spirit." Not even in this situation could the professor leave aside his didactic manner; he simply could not be sidetracked.

"Whoever you are," the man who had spoken before broke in again, looking critically at Höllriegl's uniform, "listen to what I am going to tell you and tell others. Köpfler and his henchmen murdered the Führer, they poisoned him bit by bit, in small doses. The last will and testament which Köpfler flaunted to the Reichstag is a stinking lie from first to last—a clumsy forgery and piece of political skulduggery. Either the Führer was on drugs when he put his last will on tape, or a voice forger who has often found employment in the Reich Chancellery, a plumber called Möldagl from Ried on the Inn, Gau Upper Danube, who can imitate the Führer's voice down to the smallest detail, read the testament. It's certainly strange that Hitler's body was only shown twice on television and then very briefly, and was photographed from some distance away. He was laid out in his study flanked by a guard of honor, every one of them proven Werewolves. Since then the Führer has lain in a closed coffin, and the coffin is guarded day and night. Köpfler wants nothing but to put himself and the Werewolves in power. He's kept a few harmless yes-men from the old Reich body, but that's just a front. Some at the top of the party hierarchy know it but don't have the guts or the will to speak out. The truth would mean civil war. The conflict with the Tenno, which erupted against the Führer's will, has forced the party to gloss over its internal quarrel, and Köpfler knows how to use this weakness and hesitation. But the reckoning will come as surely as the last judgment."

The man spoke slowly with an unmistakably Rhineland accent, forming sentences with difficulty as if he had a heavy tongue. No doubt about it, the man who had spoken was Manfred Diebold. Höllriegl had seen his picture occasionally, although it was precisely Diebold who was known as the foe of political publicity. Diebold the SS Reich Leader, successor of the late Heinrich Himmler, the great "Heini" Diebold who had been Reich Minister of the Interior and Chief of the German police, until his purge one of the most powerful men of the world empire, perhaps the most powerful after the Führer; now wanted dead or alive.

"We'll end the meal," the chairman said and rose, giving the signal for the others to comply. Höllriegl was so dumbfounded by all he had heard that he swayed as if drunk. The professor had to help him up. The four colleagues disappeared without saying good-bye. Only Diebold shook Höllriegl's hand and looked away as he did so. "God protect Germany," he murmured.

In the library the chairman handed Höllriegl a thick binder full of typescript. "Our treatise," he explained, twirling his curls. "A collective labor. I think you'd better tie it to your back with these cords, yes, under your shirt—oh, by the way, your bump is turning a beautiful brown—party color—ha-ha-ha." He pointed with a patronizing air to Höllriegl's stigma. "Wherever you got it, as a member of the master race you shouldn't just let this insult lie. Still—you carry your trauma quite openly. Say hello to Gundlfinger from his devoted friend Kofut. And: I warn him! He should go underground as soon as possible, disappear underground. It's getting to be high time for him, too."

Höllriegl hid the typescript as instructed. When he had rearranged his clothes, the mechanic approached. "I'll take you outside," he said and led the way. Again they came to the central tunnel, where the cold wind blew. Höllriegl heard the distant thumping of a machine. A pump, a generator, an air-conditioning plant?

The whole thing was monstrous! Köpfler a murderer? The Führer's closest confidant his murderer? Could one trust those two—Unseld and Diebold—even for a second? They had been proscribed before the entire nation. Everyone had the right to kill them on the spot. It was his duty to burst the foul bubble. And at once, in the next village!

In the next village? Would it have a police station? And the villagers? At least some of them must have connections with the "labyrinth," might supply it with the necessities of life. All the surrounding villages must have known about the hideout of these traitors, otherwise it wouldn't have been possible to maintain. But nobody had let out the secret. It was horrible, as horrible as the thing itself. And if no one had taken any action it just proved that the conspiracy had a very broad base and already a certain amount of power, not to mention a network of underground centers that apparently spanned the globe (if the chairman wasn't just bragging) and cooperated with recognized, loyal scientists "upstairs." No, these weren't harmless idiots but dangerous criminals intent on destroying the security and existence of the Reich and the Nordic race.

But a report could not be made too quickly, because of the risk of being done in. Who knew if and to what extent the authorities, in this case the local police, were involved? The slightest suspicion and he might simply disappear! On the other hand, speed was of the essence if Diebold and Unseld were not to escape again. There was no doubt that the two criminals would soon be ferried on to other underground groups outside the Reich.

Incredible how safe these gentlemen believed themselves. Not for a moment had anyone thought to ask where he came from or where he was going. The fact that he had come with the dumb guide had been identification enough. And Professor Gundlfinger? That was the worst of it—an important philosopher with solid party reputation, a light of the Western spirit, as the *Kyffhäuser Messenger* had called him recently, he too in the same boat with these plotters, these atheists and crap-intellectuals, secret supporters of a false Jewish teaching supposedly eradicated long ago! Gundlfinger a conspirator, perhaps one of the leading conspirators!

Wait a minute now, how was that? He, Höllriegl, had been given the official task of pendulating the famous man's house. The same office which had sent him quite senselessly to the dying Jew had sent him to Gundlfinger. Obersturmführer Hirnchristl . . . ! Why had they denied ever having seen Hirnchristl or heard his name at T4?

Höllriegl's brain whirled. He followed the mechanic automatically. The guide stopped from time to time to signal by the wires.

Was Hirnchristl the key figure in this whole mess? Or somebody else? Schwerdtfeger? He had sent him to Hirnchristl in the first place. ("Nice guy, Ostmarker, passionate National Socialist.") And his travel orders had been issued by the "parliament" in Heydrich.

But the most awful thing was that the two traitors had made such an honest impression. Had the man spoken the truth, the gruesome truth? When a man has been that close to death—and what a death it would have been—he doesn't lie. The Führer murdered? Poisoned like a rat? The whole thing a plot by the Werewolf and its backers?

Now they were walking uphill in one of the shafts. When the mechanic pushed open a barricade, they were still not outside but in a low, dim cave. Höllriegl took a deep breath, waiting till his eyes got used to the greenish daylight. He saw half-ruined concrete walls with slits covered by tangled plants and rusted iron rods blocking most of the light. It was a small air-raid shelter in the middle of the forest. Obviously an attempt had been made to blow it up. How many other exits were there?

The mechanic described the route he should follow to get out of the woods. Höllriegl memorized the instructions and repeated them. Then he said good-bye with a routine "Heitla."

"God be with you," the mechanic said and dived into his shaft.

Although Höllriegl thought he had remembered the directions, he was soon lost in the dense underbrush. He oriented himself instinctively, left the valley with the high-trunked pine trees behind him, and walked as fast he could through the neglected young forest. More by chance than anything else he came to the clearing where he had seen the boneyard. He hurried past this Golgotha without turning around. From here on the path he had followed with the dumb woman was easy to recognize, the trees became less dense and, almost running, he reached the edge of the wood. Perspiration stood on his cheeks and forehead. He listened—there it was again, that distant thunder above the clouds.

He walked around the memorial castle in a wide circle. His car was still parked below. Once he sat behind the wheel he breathed the fresh air deeply and greedily. He was now determined to deliver the notebook to Gundlfinger and under the guise of pendulating look around the philosopher's home before denouncing the conspirators. If Unseld and Diebold managed to escape the police net—that was all right too. They were the old guard of National Socialists. Like him, despite everything! Despite Anselma and the devil! But those "soul searchers," those devil's intellectuals! Those gnawing rats! In their arrogance they had thought him an idiot, a milksop. He'd show them.

A painful surprise—his pistol and reserve ammunition were gone. The gun had been hidden behind a polishing cloth in the glove compartment. And the street map on which he had marked down the latest extensions of the restricted zones was gone too. A bad thing, that. Now whether he wanted to or not, he'd have to go to the authorities, and at once. But . . . wait a minute. He'd have to think about that too. He had been negligent in leaving the car unlocked. A party functionary should be more careful—he was supposed to be a shining example to the others. His forgetfulness could be punished, especially in times such as these.

He jumped out of the car and checked the trunk. Nothing missing there. He could see that at a glance. He opened his suitcase, hastily making sure. Even his money was intact. The thieves had only gone through the glove compartment. Furiously he warmed the motor up. This had never happened to him, in this country, in his own car. (On a vacation in Italy once he had been robbed.) Music! He had to calm his nerves. He turned the knob. The radio remained silent. Somebody had cut the connection to the battery.

For a moment he thought of a patrol. Ridiculous! They'd have left a ticket or something in writing. Who had done it then? What a goddam mess. Involuntarily he thought that the human animals might have had something to do with it—or perhaps the dumb woman. Paule was her name. Should he go back to Schicklgrube and play the informer? And again that icy terror went through him: The human animals had not had guards!

Peace and quiet. No cars anywhere in sight. Overnight the world had been emptied of men. In the next village, Belzehude, he counted exactly two people in the streets. And everywhere the same scene: on the walls blood-red wanted signs with the faces of the two traitors ("Whoever you are . . . listen to what I am telling you . . . and tell it to others . . ."); here and there a mourning flag, banners torn by wind and rain. And always the sign of the Werewolf and Köpfler's eyes.

He drove slowly, so slowly that anyone watching would have known he was lost in thought. Before Bad Harzburg the street joined, as he remembered, Route 6, which he would have taken if the change in the restricted zones had not made the detour necessary. But then he would not have made the acquaintance of those rats. What was it all to him? He was a simple party member, not a politician. But as a party member it was his duty to turn them in.

He stopped for gas in Bad Harzburg, and while his eyes followed the pump indicator he began conversation with the attendant, a plump girl from the Mansfeld region, judging by her accent. She had fantastic news: "The Japs are supposed to have landed this morning in—wait a second, where was it now?—oh, yes, in Ireland, Portugal, and the Crimea. Landed from the air in large numbers, masses of them." Where had she heard that? They'd talked about it at party headquarters when she went there to deliver gas-ration stamps. By the way, did the gentleman know that gas and oil rations had again been reduced? The quotas for every type of car and all three emergency categories had been cut sharply. Very tight rationing! First water, now gas. Höllriegl paid and the girl stamped his orders, recording the amount he had bought. "If things go on like this, we'll have to close," she said as she wiped his windshield.

Strong fog descended behind Bad Harzburg—he had really been worried when he drove by an open police station there—and he could barely see the patches of forest that moved past him on the road. The scenery turned unreal. The windshield glistened in the dimmed headlights; the fog was a pale elastic wall. The route Hirnchristl had suggested lay on the other side of the mountain. In order to reach the connecting road, he would have to drive as far as Wohlstand. The damned fog! He knew the way by heart, and he wouldn't have to report the theft of his road map because it was only a survey map on a scale of 1:1,000,000. He owned more detailed maps, but they were in Heydrich. The party had begun confiscating them and the party knew what it was doing, but as a *Hauptstellenleiter* and healer they wouldn't be taken from him.

And he could hide the fact that his "personal firearm" had been stolen. It was a self-loading pistol used by the Wehrmacht before the war, a 6.35 mm. He'd been meaning to ask for a newer and more modern one. That would have to be done at once now. Kummernuss' brother-in-law was in charge of such matters in the "parliament"—he'd buy an explanation that it had been lost.

Between Schierke and Wohlstand he met only a single vehicle, a darkened postal bus. Only a few people sat inside, like dolls. But in Wohlstand a car with blue lights lurked where the road turned off to Rundstedt. Höllriegl drove slowly, as if traveling over eggs, inviting the patrol to stop him. But nobody bothered.

The way led gradually uphill, the road squeezing through the mountain valley in many curves, and despite fog and darkness he could see that it narrowed several times into picturesque ravines. Where waterfalls once had roared, a trickle now dripped over the rocks. Höllriegl rolled down the window and with flaring nostrils sucked in the air, which smelled of rain and freshly cut pines. The mountain road ahead of him gleamed black and scaly like a snake. After a while he passed a sawmill, blacked out in accordance with air-raid protection rules; the machines pounded and the saws screeched, but not a single workman was to be seen.

The whole region was famous for its association with Walpurgis Night, and Höllriegl took delight in the verses from Goethe's *Faust,* which, mixed with hotel ads, were written on street posters. The signs had obviously been mounted when the Harz Mountains were still a tourist center and a source of classical associations. Since then Goethe, that arch Freemason, Francophile, and servant of plutocrats, had been pushed into deep disfavor. True, the party had not yet eradicated Goethe's existence from the cultural conscience of the nation, but he was suppressed wherever possible and hardly mentioned in school. No doubt the day was not too far distant when Goethe's works would be burned in the fires of a new and healing purge.

The sea of fog remained behind in the valley; the rain let up. Höllriegl could see clearly again and drove more quickly. When he turned into the road to Sauckelruh, he heard the familiar wail of air-raid sirens. This was a missile alarm, not an early warning. Bright-orange lightning flashed on the western horizon. Höllriegl braked the car, his heart in his throat. A short time later he saw red flecks spread across the clouds. They seemed to shimmer as if at sunset.

As far as he could judge in the darkness, Sauckelruh lay at the end of a wooded valley. The road came to a dead end here. The main square was pitch-black, cars stood crowded next to one another, and he had trouble finding a parking spot. No one was in the street. An epidemic seemed to have struck the village.

Höllriegl thought—not for the first time that day—of the clear voice he had heard on the telephone, an eternity ago, it seemed. Secretly he looked forward to the meeting, but not only out of curiosity. Did the voice belong to a woman? If it did, she would have to be young and beautiful—and pure. Purity! How he longed for it!

From what he had understood of the Mother German, the village had several good hotels. But it would have made little sense to look for any one place in this empty darkness. He had passed a gas station on entering the village, and it probably had a motel. No, he didn't want to turn around—he'd go to the next inn he could find and get something to eat. He was hungry. Perhaps they'd have a free room.

He looked around and switched on his flashlight. The houses, mostly villas built in the style of Kaiser Wilhelm's day (they reminded him of the Eycke's castle), had been carefully blacked out. Apparently they now provided lodgings for summer tourists.

Höllriegl got out of the car, his steps resounding on the cobblestones. The beam from his flashlight groped across walls, along closed window shutters, latticed fences. He picked out an inn with bull's-eye windowpanes, like those in a stage set, and knocked on the door. After knocking several times—each blow thudding through the stillness—he heard shuffling steps. A fat, slovenly woman looked him over suspiciously.

"I'd like a room for the night. Do you have one free?"

The woman banged the door shut and locked it. After a while, by the time Höllriegl was already angry and ready to leave, the door opened again, this time by a man, a shabby waiter, to judge by his clothes. Again a once-over from head to toe, the man's eyes stopping at Höllriegl's boots and uniform blouse.

"We only have a garret free, out in back. Everything's taken," he said.

"Good, I'll take it. And can I have something to eat?" After the frosty reception he did not have much hope. Höllriegl sat down in the dingy café, which might have looked quite pretty in a better light.

"The cook can make scrambled eggs," the man said, pointing to the bloated woman leaning against the bar, her back to Höllriegl. "Our kitchen is closed for the day."

"All right. Please fix the eggs quickly and bring me something to drink—fruit juice, anything." He went back out to his car for his suitcase. Good thing he wouldn't have to spend the night in the car.

When he came back, he heard the maid bustling about in the

kitchen. Fat sizzled. The fruit juice, some kind of lemonade with a stale taste, didn't refresh him. He went into the kitchen and asked for some fresh water, but no more drinking water was available that day—only rainwater to wash in.

"Where are the other guests?" he asked, trying to start a conversation with the woman. He hoped to learn what had been happening.

"In the cellar," the woman answered curtly, rattling her pots. He wasn't going to get very far here.

"Any news?" Höllriegl yelled above the clatter. No answer.

The waiter, who served as night clerk as well, brought the registration form, and Höllriegl filled it out. The man too was closed-mouthed, obviously on purpose. A dull, stupid bunch. He answered Höllriegl's question with a gesture to indicate that it would be superfluous to say anything. He sighed as he did so and raised his eyes to the sky.

Then they went up to the attic. A surprise—the garret was pleasantly furnished. A slanting wall, simple furniture, a bright, stiff linen curtain at the window. No running water, but an enormous, inviting bed. Another surprise: After the man had turned out the light and rolled up the blackout blinds, he became talkative. "From up here the gentleman will enjoy a fine view when the weather is clear, all the way to the Schnarcherklippen and the Feuersteine, with nobody across the way. But now you'll have to go down to the cellar. I'll be punished if we're found up here. The place is checked." Again a meaningful look at Höllriegl's uniform. "I can't tell you when they'll sound the all clear. Yesterday we sat in the cellar for four and a half hours." And when they were out on the stairs he whispered, "The cook and waitress, a couple from Hungary, have been missing since lunch. I'll bet they've fled. The authorities are after them. The two of us, Katrin and I, have to run the place by ourselves."

Someone had pointlessly dimmed the lights in the cellar. The guests sat listlessly on their suitcases or on stools. Except for a young woman in uniform, they were all older people, mostly single, and they stared ahead with expressionless faces or tried to read despite the dim light. A gray-haired lady scribbled on a letter, others whispered together—mood and voices are identical in all air-raid shelters. Something boring and at the same time tense lay in the atmosphere, as if they were in the waiting room of a cancer specialist. The cellar didn't have a loudspeaker, and consequently no outside announcements could be made, which annoyed Höllriegl. And no one had a portable radio. He was still anxious to hear the news.

The waiter went upstairs again after he had put on a white-and-yellow steel helmet resembling a chamber pot, indicating he was an air-raid warden. Now he'd have to man the listening post on the radio. The uniformed woman, tolerably pretty and impudent-looking, read some trashy novel, a conceited expression on her face. She had only given Höllriegl a fleeting glance, but that didn't bother him. The girl attracted and yet repelled him. He couldn't have said why.

The two men who sat next to him whispered animatedly. At first he tried to listen; then he simply joined the conversation. One of them came from the nearby town of Aschersleben, a sales representative of washing machines and soap flakes. He did not introduce himself, but the other, a Berliner by his dialect, pulled out his card at once. His name was Clemens Südekum, a composer—Höllriegl had heard the name. The man had been very successful after the war with a romantic soldier's opera, *Lilli Marleen,* and had written popular film music, his latest being for a picture called *Girl on the Heath.* (All this was printed on the card.) He was also prominent in the record business. Both wanted to see Gundlfinger—tomorrow the Villa Walpurgis held open house. Herr Südekum hinted that he planned to make Gundlfinger the central character of a "symphonic film poem," which would depict in striking episodes the history of German thought.

The two men seemed to have good connections to higher-ups in the party. The washing-machine salesman worked as a volunteer in the county administration of the German Labor Front and had, as he mentioned with some pride, organized this year's "Production Battle of German Enterprises" in his hometown. He was obviously a fanatical party member, but he seemed—Höllriegl had a sixth sense about such things—still devoted to the old party cadres. The musician, whose smooth manners, eternal grin, and dapper appearance recalled the majordomo of a tourist hotel, did not express any direct opinion. His basic political color seemed to be colorlessness. Otherwise, however, the two gentlemen resembled each other like matching party insignias; one could have been exchanged for the other without any difficulty: the well-fed, ruddy, bespectacled faces, the ball-shaped heads (though the composer's was bald with a carefully trimmed halo of hair and the salesman's topped by the military brush cut with its part on the right), altogether a uniformity that reminded Höllriegl of the crowds at Nuremberg. It filled him with confidence, even gratification, every time he encountered it. A sane world indeed, whose strength found expression in such similarity.

After the two men had explored the newcomer's ideological outlook, the salesman opened up. The latest news, which he had heard in Aschersleben—he knew some of the lower party codes and thus could figure out certain radio reports—confirmed what Höllriegl already knew but had believed to be only a horrible rumor: Strong Sino-Japanese paratroops were operating in the middle of Europe. Heavy stratospheric transports had dropped them over five points on the continent and established a well-functioning air lift. Enemy troops were in action in the Crimea, near the Spanish-Portuguese border, in Armagh, Northern Ireland, at Oulu in Finland, and between Verona and Mantua. The enemy had received support and reinforcements from the local population which made possible creation of bases and hedgehog positions as well as mobile operations. Counterattacks, blockades, and other similar measures had been attempted at once, but no one knew just what had happened to the Wehrmacht and SS forces stationed in those areas. It was almost certain, however, that in the Crimea the Stuba I (Upper Bavaria) of the SS Death Head Formations East and several Waräger units had been utterly destroyed. A Dublin mob, egged on by Catholic priests, had burned down the Race and Settlement Office for the Irish Free State and brutally murdered all those trying to flee from the building. Japanese armored columns had reached the outskirts of Milan and in a northward thrust had reached the southern shore of Lake Garda, after capturing the entire staff of the commander in chief of Army Group South in Caserna Passalacqua. The First Missile Commando group, a tough and very mobile unit, had also been destroyed. The "Brown Houses" in many towns of Venice, Friuli, and Lombardy had been set on fire, their inmates lynched by the mob, and all German-blooded women raped to death in public. Auxiliary fascist militia had taken part in the plundering and executions. The "Land of the

Confederates," the German-Swiss region, which the Führer had always mistrusted, was also in revolutionary ferment. However, news of that development had been given in a more difficult code and thus been incomprehensible to the washing-machine man.

Höllriegl listened with stoic equanimity, even complete indifference, as if these events were taking place on the moon or Mars. He hadn't the slightest doubt that the Reich leadership would know exactly what needed to be done, and in the one right moment unleash a globally destructive blow. After all, the Reich disposed of manned and unmanned spaceships able to drop nuclear bombs on any spot on earth. The enemies of the Reich's world domination would then have drawn their last breath. Tyr, the powerful one-armed god, had already raised his sword, Höllriegl felt, to deliver the deadly blow. . . .

But later there was worse news. In the early hours of November 13, several units of the Strategic Air Command North had refused to obey orders. Squadrons of the 16th and 17th air fleets had sabotaged Köpfler's orders to attack air bases, missile plants, and centers of arms production on Sakhalin, Hokkaido, and Honshu with thermonuclear weapons. More was not known.

Höllriegl later learned from reliable sources that the commander of the bomber group "Fegelein"—supposedly the same Knight's Cross recipient who, as a simple Air Force sergeant-major in the early summer of 1945 had unleashed the historic bomb over London and since then had lived in voluntary anonymity—in agreement with most of his comrades had radioed to Air Force Headquarters in Smithersland (the former British Columbia) and asked that he and his crew be relieved from carrying out these "suicidal" orders of "unforseeable magnitude." The request pointed to the worldwide consequences which would result from unleashing "unlimited thermonuclear war"—as if limited nuclear war were possible—not only for the Reich, the master race and its allies, but for all the peoples of the earth. (This, of course, being of lesser importance.) The commanders of six other air squadrons quickly declared they agreed with this decision, and the ground crews and fighter units of the XXII SS Flying Corps, a Death Head elite troop, joined the mutiny, undoubtedly because it was directed against Köpfler. His personal orders, therefore, were never carried out, for other, loyal, units had been forced back by the enemy's air defenses. Massive deployment of Soka Gakkai suicide fighters claimed heavy German losses. Allegedly, a smaller H-bomb had detonated when the plane carrying it was shot down over Tigil' on the Kamchatka Peninsula. The blast had flattened the town, turning wide stretches of the peninsula into a fiery desert and making the air above it unbreathable. Radiation Alarm I was in effect at present for all Northeast Asia.

As Höllriegl also learned later in Heydrich, the mutiny in the northern Pacific was the immediate cause for Köpfler's decision to withdraw nuclear weapons from the Reich's entire air power. He expelled the mutineers from the Luftwaffe and proscribed them. The Fegelein group commander committed suicide. Subsequently the new Führer issued that fateful order to consolidate all nuclear firepower under home-based missile and logistic units that were already subject to strong Werewolf influence. Only missile-carrying submarines were permitted to continue waging total thermonuclear war on their own, and missiles with atomic warheads could be fired from specific naval bases against "any place on any continent." This move had aroused the Luftwaffe's bitter anger.

As far as the man from Aschersleben knew, to whose tale we now return, the military situation in the Western Hemisphere had deteriorated because fighting on the Pacific Coast, with its heavy losses on both sides, had spread over nearly all the territory of the United Vassal States. The bitterest engagements took place in the Middle West, a Minutemen stronghold, but the war had exploded with incredible fury in the south and southeast, in Mexico and the Caribbean area. The insurgents had been able to open the SHC's almost everywhere, moving with lightning speed before the inmates could be liquidated. The fighting, in many places a guerilla campaign, resulted in unparalleled cruelty. There were no survivors. Reports told of hour- and day-long tortures. Although the Ku Kluxers were obviously in deep trouble (their dilemma was illustrated by the fact that their closest allies, the Minutemen, had installed a fascist countergovernment in Duluth which proposed a softer policy and volunteered its services to mediate the "conflict" between the two world blocs), a government delegation from Corpus Christi, the new seat of the regime, had started out for Germany in order to take part in the funeral ceremonies for the immortal founder of the Germanic World Empire. This nine-man group had now arrived in Berlin.

As far as Australia was concerned, the white population of several parts of the continent had risen against Japanese rule. The air and U-boat arm of the Reich operating in the South Pacific had supplied the insurgents with laser weapons. This was a development which might help the Reich and its allies, although according to encoded messages, the Australian rebels had interfered with the amphibious operations of German submarines. It was hard to distinguish clear lines. Everything was still in flux and depended on the further development of the situation in Europe and America.

Höllriegl's eyes moved around the bunker, groping from one face to another while he listened intently to the whispering. It was enough to make one despair! A war was supposed to be won with people like these! He looked again at the woman in uniform, still reading her cheap novel with a stiff, determined, haughty expression on her face. Suddenly he realized why that face had touched him so unpleasantly.

Zézette! The woman, although made up in the required German-Aryan-Nordic style, reminded him of Zézette! Zézette from Martinique—a dark, no, *the* darkest episode of his life, a shameful dark-skinned episode which he had eradicated thoroughly and purposefully from his memory and about which he dared let no one know or even suspect. What he had done was punishable by disenfranchisement and death! Zézette from Martinique . . . Six years ago he had gone to Paris to serve a short tour of duty in the healing section of the SS. Every day he had to travel in the *métro* from his hotel, a run-down dump in the rue St. Denis, where he lived in a two-bed garret, to the barracks and back. Oh, the stale warmth in the *métro* tunnels, the oily smell, the hissing, the distant rolling noise. He could still see how the bolts slipped from their hiding place outside the carriage window, driven by compressed air to lock the door; and then, when the train stopped, how they slid back, and like the sexual act the process was always repeated. The snakelike hissing of the compressed air, the distant rolling, the wilting heat! As a member of the master race he rode first class, of course, and the French were not allowed inside. But chocolate-brown Zézette stood in the jammed green carriage behind, pressed against the window, looking him over. An enchantress, a voodoo witch! He could not resist the scorching blaze of those eyes—he could still feel them deep down in his spine. It was all as real as if it had happened yesterday, and a shudder ran through him when he thought of the woman. Between the stations (how would he ever forget their names?—Barbe Bleue, Lune Perdue, Le-Chien-Qui-Pisse, Brouhaha, Schlageter, and Père Pervers) he had fallen in love with Zézette. It had been love at first sight, or rather, the look of that dark-skinned witch had hypnotized and hexed him. There could be no other explanation for his having forgotten his race. A demonic, poisonous spell! He, a member of the master race, and this colored person. She got out at Frédéric-le-Grand and he had run after her like a little dog through the long passages of the Correspondance and she had waited for him on the platform where the trains went to Carthage and Napoléon-le-Petit, squeezed in a corner, smiling—victorious! Later they met in secret again and again and in all kinds of places, although they could barely talk to one another. What else did he know of Paris? He really only remembered the paper sack which had hung under the sink in his hotel room with the inscription *"Hygiène Feminine."* And he still recalled exactly the sentence: *"Glissez votre garniture périodique dans ce sachet. Ne jetez rien dans les W.C.—Merci."*

Suddenly a word tore him out of his reverie. He listened closely to the man from Aschersleben, who was saying, "The Bundschuh . . ." The Bundschuh had started out as the ideological branch of the Reich Ministry of Food and Agriculture, created in order to soak the German farmers with newly developed National Socialist thought. Later the association, whose membership was limited to active farmers, made itself more or less independent of the Ministry and appeared in the framework of the party as a separate movement with its own press, labor offices, and functionaries. The Bundschuh, tightly organized and regionally grouped, received orders from the Reich Leader for Farming, whereas earlier it had been subject to Section VII of the Food and Agriculture Ministry. It enjoyed special prerogatives, had a permanent representative at the Reich-controlled Farm Court, and a decisive voice in all questions of farming and soil legislation.

As Höllriegl now learned, the Bundschuh was in ferment. The peasantry seemed about to split: a part, the smaller one, leaned toward the Werewolf; another, which had lately begun publication of a mass-circulation paper, *Der Arme Konrad,* condemned Köpfler's policy in the most caustic language and demanded a revolutionary renewal. That group must enjoy immense support even within the government, otherwise it would never have dared utter such criticism. A test of strength was in the offing; anyone could tell that. A test of strength that might well shake the world empire to its foundations. The latest issue, published as a leaflet (the man from Aschersleben furtively showed Höllriegl a copy), called on the peasants to attend a mass meeting at Stolberg in the Harz Mountains, the birthplace of Thomas Münzer, not far from here. The call was in open defiance of the strict ban on public meetings that the party had decreed for the duration of the war. *Der Arme Konrad* demanded formation of a peasant government and proclaimed its slogan: "The pressing need of the German nation." In an editorial —and this was tantamount to treason—the paper demanded "people's rights before the nation's," and said that "weeds must be uprooted in time, before the wheat ripens." It also asked for "a strict nonparty investigation of the circumstances surrounding Adolf Hitler's death." The Bundschuh was obviously willing to risk everything: It ended the appeal with a quote from the days of the Peasants' War: "Stab, beat, kill, whoever can."

Most of the opposition seemed directed against SS Brigadeführer Sausele, a notorious Werewolf adherent who had been named Minister of Food and Agriculture in the Führer's so-called last will and testament. The washing-machine salesman only hinted at all this with great caution, while Südekum added that he knew from reliable sources that Gauleiter Gernot Firbas, who had been named Reichsführer of the SS and then stripped of power by Köpfler against the Führer's wishes, had close contacts with the anonymous editors of *Der Arme Konrad.* Firbas supposedly said that he would know how to protect the meeting of the peasantry at Stolberg against any Werewolf attack. Without doubt the *Gauleiter* counted on the support of certain police units, especially the gendarmes in the countryside, but also on SS reserve troops and the disgruntled Luftwaffe, disciplined by Köpfler. The position of the armed peasants in the eastern prefectures was still unclear. They had all been grouped into the so-called Asgard Ring, which was ideologically close to NATMAT and the Werewolf. In view of the present situation—enemy landings far in the rear of the East Wall and the belt of settlements in central Russia—they would, however, be cut off, and the coming contest within the Reich itself, his two informants agreed, would be limited to the radical wings of the Bundschuh and the Werewolf groups.

That was about the worst and most threatening thing that could happen. Höllriegl felt hot and cold chills when he thought about it. His own people in ferment, particularly the peasants, who had always been the Führer's most faithful followers! Hard to believe. The others, however, acted as if all this had been going on for some time.

"Now we've talked so much," Südekum said to Höllriegl, "that I've gotten really hungry. The doctors have put me on a diet because of my heart, but pigs' knuckles and beer—that would really hit the spot. Or a lean goulash, or herring with onions. And a tall, light beer. Oh . . . I just don't understand why a man with heart trouble can't eat pigs' knuckles——"

At that moment the door to the bunker was flung open and all eyes at once turned to the night clerk-waiter-air-raid-warden who, steel helmet tipped to one side, seemed to be in the grip of great excitement. With a hoarse voice he stuttered into the stillness: "The first atom bomb has fallen on the Reich . . . in the region of Lemgo–Bad Salzuflen . . . radiation alarm!" A moment of paralysis; heartbeats stopped. But then everyone was on his feet, shouting and running about. The women screamed with terror, only the lady writing a letter remained seated and looked at the uproar with kind and stupid eyes. Apparently she was deaf and hadn't understood a thing. The young woman in uniform behaved most hysterically, pressing her hands against her ears and screaming in the highest register. The panic could not have been worse in a plane about to crash.

Höllriegl maintained a calm that he himself found uncanny. Somehow he had lost all feeling in the last few days. He just didn't give a shit. Everything he had experienced had the quality of a dream—it had to be dreamed to the end, whether you wanted to or not. Instinctively he had moved through the uproar toward the young woman who was still screaming at the top of her voice and stamping her feet as if she had lost her senses. Her haughty expression had changed into a grimace of fear.

But the girl was devilishly pretty, and he had already noticed her slim and rather hairy legs. Under pretext of calming her, he squeezed her close to him, noticed by no one. He felt her trembling body, her thin arms. He grabbed furtively for her hard, elastic breast. Weeping, she threw herself into his arms, into the arms of an utter stranger, whom she had scarcely noticed before.

Nobody could make himself understood in all the commotion. The air-raid warden tried several times to shout orders, then quit. Höllriegl kept the trembling girl pressed close to him and stammered soothing words; in the whole terrible and lamentable scene this young creature was the only living thing it made any sense to protect. He saw Südekum and the man from Aschersleben talking to the air-raid warden, then they left the bunker as if fleeing. Somebody, an elderly woman, suddenly called out: "The party thinks for you!" and at once people picked up the slogan and shouted: "The party thinks for us, the party thinks for us, the party thinks for us, the party thinks for us!" Whereupon others answered: "That's why we thank the party, that's why we thank the party, that's why we thank the party!" And suddenly one man shouted: "Heil Köpfler, hail to our Führer," but no one picked it up.

The air-raid warden returned, accompanied by the men Höllriegl had talked to. He swung a cowbell with a loud, tinny sound, and gradually the people calmed down.

"I must ask all present to behave themselves like Germans," the washing-machine salesman said in his big announcer's voice that held the balance between persuasion and command—a real selling voice, worth many a commission. The crowd grew quiet at once, only one small voice whimpering like an echo, "The party thinks for us."

"Of course the party thinks for us, what else? But every German must know how to act, and act sensibly! The orders of the air-raid warden are to be obeyed at once. Every one of you has gone through enough radiation alerts to know that keeping calm is the most important thing you can do. So take it easy. Cold blood and warm underpants. And the second-most-important thing: Grab your radiation suits! There's no imminent danger of radioactivity, but nevertheless we'll have to find some suits."

"There are twelve suits in the house," the warden said. "And there are"—he counted quickly—"nineteen of us, with the cook. Those who want suits raise their hands, ladies first."

Eleven women, including Katrin, the cook, were at the inn. An old man received the twelfth suit. "I'll get yours," Höllriegl told the young girl, giving his words a jaunty, gallant tone. The girl sat down on a stool and clutched her knees. She sat there staring numbly in front of her, obviously worn out by her seizure.

When he went out with the men to get the suits, he remembered the incredibly bright flashes of lightning he had seen flame on the western sky. So that had been the bomb! Radiation must have reached the Harz Mountains a long time ago. If the bomb was a small one, the dose was not lethal at that distance—not immediately lethal. Anyway, he didn't care, he didn't give a damn. Ulla, Anselma, and his Heydrich girl—how far away they all seemed! Only the moment counted now. And in a moment the Reich would strike back. Now! Perhaps the enemy no longer existed. But why had the explosion been kept secret for so long? Höllriegl thought back; he had seen the flashes when he had turned into Sauckelruh. And now it was—incredible! The party thinks for you, the party thinks for you, the party thinks for you!

He heard the warden saying, "The SS took the Pope out of the Vatican at noon today. He's already in Germany behind bars." (That, Höllriegl learned later, was exaggerated. The Pope had indeed been taken into custody and flown under SS escort to the Reich. But he was not in jail and not a hair on his head had been touched. On the contrary: He had been brought to a luxurious sanatorium, the same one in which the Dalai Lama had been treated, where he would undergo insulin shocks under supervision of his personal physician and several eminent German specialists. At that time Höllriegl learned also that the Patriarch of the Orthodox Church had been a candidate for party membership but that his application had been rejected a short time before.)

When Höllriegl handed the young woman her radiation suit, she looked at him as if he were a stranger. She still trembled, her hands shook constantly. "I'll take you up to your room; there's no point staying down here. The cellar provides protection only against conventional explosives." He helped her get up and took her arm.

"The all clear hasn't sounded yet," said the washing-machine salesman. He seemed to have taken command. But the warden let the couple pass and followed them, muttering something unintelligible. He had to go back to his radio. Höllriegl's flashlight, its battery almost dead, lit the steps with a weak reddish sheen.

They walked upstairs silently, their shadows swaying up and down. The girl had not said a word. Höllriegl squeezed her closer to him. When he wanted to knead her breast, she said in a high voice, "Lay off!"

But in front of the girl's door their lips found each other. She pulled him into the dark room. "Stay with me," she whispered, and again he felt her teeth, the warm wetness of her mouth. Then she escaped him and he heard her take off the uniform. She smelled unmistakably of the Wehrmacht, of sweat, Lysol, lockers, barracks.

"Get undressed," she said, "and spend the night with me—I'm scared. Perhaps it'll be the last time." Höllriegl watched her flit to and fro like a pale shadow. She lighted a cigarette and stepped out of her underwear. Slowly he too took off his clothes. Silence. As she bent over the washbasin, he pulled her to him. She felt cool, her skin rough. Perhaps she was twenty.

"What's your name?" he asked, just to say something. She had a slender, sinewy body and hard, strong breasts. (Zézette had been quite different in that department!) She still trembled as if freezing. He let her go and she began to rub certain parts of her body with cologne.

"My name is Elke Franken, Elke Angurboda Franken. Angurboda is the bearer of fear." She laughed. "A bearer of fear who is afraid . . . I come from Lower Silesia," she added. Again she offered him her lips, blew smoke into his mouth (which made him want to cough), and made very bold with his body. "You won't catch anything from me—if that's what worries you. I had a checkup the other day, and since then no one has had me."

Now she had become a human being for him, not just a creature of skin, hair, entrails, and warmth. She became bolder, her touch coarse. "Quick into bed, I'm cold," she said in her brittle, childish voice.

GUNDLFINGER WORKS ON A PROOF OF THE EXISTENCE OF GOD

He left Elke during the night. She had fallen asleep in his arms and he went without waking her. As he climbed up to his garret, he heard a distant howling and the screech of a woman's voice that cut to the marrow. He didn't care. He was dead-tired. Again that feeling of paralysis, of just not giving one good goddamn about anything, of realizing that when all was said and done, he was a nonentity. The party thinks for you indeed! His own unimportance and the illusory quality of everything around him thickened into a terrifying sense of alienation. The shock of it stopped him cold. Suddenly everything changed. He too was a different person, as if he carried someone else's head on his shoulders, used a stranger's eyes, thought with another's brain. The painful pressure on his neck and the back of his head grew worse. Everything seemed agonizingly unreal. He shook himself and with quick strokes massaged his head. The main thing now was to survive, somehow to survive.

It was pitch-black outside. He opened the window of his room and listened. In the distance he still heard the woman screeching in a high treble, ceaselessly, agonizing to listen to and depressing to boot; the screams of a man and the dull roar of a mob were interspersed through the dim sound of someone making a speech. Could they be holding a rally? In the middle of the night and during an air-raid alarm? He closed the window to shut out the woman's voice and pulled down the blackout shade before turning on the light. How comfortable the room was, despite the pale-blue light.

Only now he saw the large sheaf of paper lying just inside the door. He had not noticed it in the dark. It must have been shoved through the crack while he was still with Elke. He unfolded it: a kind of poster, framed in black, like a death announcement. The stenciled text was arranged in the form of streamer slogans. With growing dismay he read:

THE COMMUNITY MUST THINK EXCLUSIVELY IN TERMS OF THIS LIFE
IT MUST RECOGNIZE ITS OWN LIMITATIONS
IT SHOULD STRIVE FOR CLARITY AND PRACTICE SCIENCE
IT SHOULD SMASH GOD
AFTER THE TOTAL DESTRUCTION MUST COME A REALM OF DECENT STANDARDS
ONLY WHAT THE COMMUNITY HAD PLANNED MAY BE LAWFUL
OUT OF THE GREAT COLLAPSE SAVE FIRST THE RECOGNITION
THAT NO BARRIERS CAN HOLD MAN'S SPIRIT
AND THAT NO DESPOTISM CAN BE ALLOWED IN ADMINISTRATION
NO ONE A FÜHRER
YOU ARE THE ESSENCE OF EVERYTHING
BECOMES SIMPLER AGAIN IN LIVING
STRICT AND SIMPLE
BECOME MORAL AGAIN IN YOUR THINKING
STRICT AND MORAL
BECOME HUMAN AGAIN IN YOUR ACTIONS
ALL TOO HUMAN
THIS WE EXPECT FROM THE FUTURE SOCIETY
AND THAT THERE BE AMONG MEN NO MASTERS AND SLAVES

The text contained spelling mistakes. It bore the signature *Der Arme Konrad,* flanked by two crossed black flags.

Höllriegl read it over several times. He was petrified. No doubt about it, every word violated the highest ideals of the master race, undermined the foundations of Western civilization and the New

Order, denigrated the Führer-Cult, Führer-State, and Racial Selection, and every other article of faith of the party. This was open rebellion! To make matters worse, he had read much the same thing in the releases of the NATMAT people—the extremes touched each other in the most alarming way. No one a Führer! No masters and slaves! Madness. It was all madness! This was simply the abyss—the abyss of all abysses. Who had pushed the leaflet his way? And why to him of all people? Had the other guests received one too? It could be a trap. . . . What should he do? Take the leaflet to the gendarmes or to the political officer at the nearest party office? He would have to make a formal report.

And then his conscience troubled him: He had already failed to make an official report—at least failed to do it so far. He had been together with dangerous conspirators, he had sat at the same table with two outlaws and traitors. Who would believe that it had been an accident? Nevertheless, he'd have to report everything, and at once. But no—he'd do that after his visit to Gundlfinger. If he still had time. The bomb! Atomic war had broken out, no doubt about it! But he was not afraid. . . .

He slept three or four hours, haunted by nightmares. He had set the alarm for seven o'clock. He woke up just before eight with a pounding, drilling headache. He had slept through the bell. He washed quickly; the cold water refreshing him. Some deep knee bends and his arm exercises as usual. The party thinks for you! The party thinks for you! He slipped on his clothes.

Great activity in the halls. Most of the guests were up; apparently a number of them planned to attend Gundlfinger's open house. He didn't see Elke. He scratched his name, address, and a greeting ("And thank you for a beautiful night") on a piece of paper and shoved it under her door. Then he hurried down to the dining room.

The others were already seated, looking taciturn, listless, and tired as they ate. Even the gentleman from Aschersleben seemed to have lost his big selling voice. It was like trying to enjoy a banquet before a prearranged stomach-pumping session. The waiter was not to be seen, only the cook shuffled through the room, bringing Höllriegl his food. He paid for his room and breakfast, but got only a dirty look for his pains. What a fleabag! This hick town would never see him again.

Before he left he checked his suitcase. Divining rod and pendulum lay ready, and he still had the report from the underground. It would provide him with a good entry to Gundlfinger's house —now he could cite the "underground" as well as Schwerdtfeger and Hirnchristl. One of these recommendations would surely identify him as trustworthy.

Fog enveloped him as he stepped outside. The air was leaden. No one anywhere. Truly, the world had emptied of men. The marketplace stank like a butcher's shop. Here and there red-brown puddles. A dog, too ancient to bark, sniffed about him. On a wooden frame hung two badly mutilated cadavers, creatures barely resembling men. Without any feeling of horror, more curious than anything else, Höllriegl came closer, careful not to step into the puddles. A man and a woman hung there; although naked, their sex was hard to determine. (Aha, the screaming at night!) In place of breasts one of the bodies had plate-size flesh wounds. The blue-tinged entrails hung down from the cut-open abdomen. The second victim's genitals had been burned and his legs roasted. Both cadavers were eyeless. Höllriegl recalled a childhood memory—it had happened in a fish market. The fishmongers would hack the fish's heads off with a cudgel and cut them up. But the dissected bodies still jerked pitifully about, even in the shopping bags of the women. (This slaughterhouse would have been a feast for Anselma!)

Blood-drenched pasteboards with barely legible inscriptions hung around the necks of the corpses. Höllriegl thought he could make out the name István. He remembered the waiter's tale. The couple from Hungary. Caught . . . Presumably the other serfs had been forced to watch. A wild night!

He felt nauseated from the smell of blood, but otherwise the whole thing didn't make much of an impression. He climbed into his car and wondered where he should garage it in the village. What had the creature with the chimelike voice said? It would be better to leave the car in Sauckelruh and rent a bike or walk to Walpurgis. The chime voice had recommended an *Eigenulf*, a mechanic. He'd forgotten the name, but he still knew the address: An der Pfordten. He'd go there, leave his car, and have the radio repaired. He felt stranded without news.

Mourning flags hung from the houses around the square. They

resembled black ropes. And everywhere the red wanted lists with Unseld and Diebold's faces on them. He stopped outside the party office—this hick village didn't have a proper party headquarters building—to deliver the leaflet. Here, too, a yawning emptiness, most of the rooms were locked. On the bulletin board he saw a poster:

> Contrary to the widespread current practice of distributing radiation suits first to the old and infirm, it is hereby ordered that in case of scarcity, suits be given exclusively to those who are in full possession of their faculties. Men and women up to 35 take precedence. Then in the order of their importance for Führer and Reich come the older generations. Men and women above 60 come last, as do the sick or crippled. The following persons are excluded from this order . . ." Then lists of members of blood orders, decorated and wounded war veterans, wearers of the Motherhood Cross, the golden party insignia, and so on.

Finally he found a white-haired bull of a man dressed in a radiation suit dozing at his desk. He explained to him how he had found the leaflet.

"Yes, we know all about it," the man murmured. "Let me see it. Every day people come and bring us such stuff. We can't handle the large number of reports—anyway, it isn't all that important. It's much more important that we catch all the serfs who have run away. My colleagues, the younger ones, are helping the police. There's a lot to do. I've been retired a long time, but they called me again. I live in Hasselfeld and I just help out here. The others are all gone. Were you out there last night? Crazy, eh? You weren't there? Well, you missed something. The circus reminded me of the best times I had in Poland back in nineteen forty, when I was still with the SD."

Höllriegl let the man babble on. He'd find the repair shop without him.

Now and again townsfolk pressed past him in the narrow, foggy streets. On the main square all the stores had been closed, but here he found some still open. Women had formed long queues, and the local police, dressed in radiation suits, patrolled in groups of three, machine pistols around their necks. (You rarely saw laser guns in the provinces.) All at once VGN-Ia—necessary consumer goods—had been rationed on a wartime level. It was going smoothly because in recent years rationing had often been imposed on a test basis, sometimes remaining in effect for weeks. Each of these tests had had a special name. The last one had been called "Landgrave, Get Tough!"

Höllriegl always carried a IIb rationing card with him in case of sudden crisis. Kummernuss had managed to sneak him out of the IIIa classification into the next-higher category. Such a crisis had now arisen, but Höllriegl doubted if he would get anything on presenting his card; he remembered his experience at the pension. Südekum had explained that all food distribution in the Reich was handled by air and computer-planned to the point where even if wide areas or large cities were completely devastated, supplies for ninety million Germans would move on schedule. The steady roar in the skies did not come from bombers flying against the enemy but from stratotransports on supply missions. The Reich's entire civil aviation had been put on emergency footing Monday to deal with the distribution problem.

Höllriegl drove slowly past the picturesque old houses. Everywhere he saw posters announcing rationing, but also ads for "radiation-safe vegetables" or baked goods—all emergency packing regulations had gone into effect automatically. The Reich fetched its daily bread from bunkers and underground warehouses as large as whole villages. No radiation could penetrate that deeply, and food had been stored there for years, "atomically" packed and hoarded for the time of need. How edifying! Heil!

Schicketanz, the owner of the garage, lived at the edge of the village, and An der Pfordten was one of the major roads leading out of Sauckelruh to the northeast. Höllriegl found him working under a truck with a man suspiciously eastern in type, just as if there were no atomic war and as if the Reich had not been hit the night before. Höllriegl explained the business with his car radio as innocently as possible—you never knew. Fixing it wasn't too difficult. And he'd pick up the car tonight or tomorrow morning at the latest.

"Any news?"

"Only bad," Schicketanz said and wiped the sweat from his blue-red forehead. "Several atomic missiles were destroyed on their approach—but who knows what the next few hours will bring. We don't bother going down to the cellar anymore; there's no point to it. We've all suffered radiation damage. But Köpfler will make it, as Adolf did. The Japs are going to get it so hard they'll vomit bones —that's for sure. But now you'll have to excuse me, I'm in the middle of work. Take the shortcut over there to the professor's house. Lots of people have been going up."

Höllriegl continued to walk, freezing in the cold, foggy air. He felt the lack of sleep in all his bones, and the girl had done him in too. (Angurboda—what a strange name.) Briefcase under his arm, he marched at a fast clip and only slowed down when the path mounted steeply. Fog flowed through the high-trunked fir forest and hung in shreds from the branches. What had his grade-school teacher said? The so-called Brocken ghost is a wall of fog. Sometimes special light patterns project shadow pictures on it. . . .

The path snaked around moss-covered granite blocks, and Höllriegl decided he wanted to look down on the countryside. Quickly he climbed up on one. He couldn't see very far, but the sight of the slender yet powerful trunks stretching up from the fog-shrouded depth filled his heart with pride and confidence. (A German, a Nordic, an Aryan forest!) And he felt comfortable and warm. Peace covered everything. What was that thing called war? But the distant, low humming that now broke through the stillness to reach his ear spoke another language.

After a while—signs marked the way and he had passed resting places for people short of breath—he came to a high plateau over which croaking rooks flew. The outlines of a villa emerged from the fog. As he came nearer he saw it was monumentally ugly: a kind of castle with truncated towers, pointed arches, bay windows, ornamental lattices, steep little gables—a giant turn-of-the-century bad dream. Höllriegl was revolted; he thought only the Führer's huge buildings beautiful, or those high-gabled SS settlements with their mighty four-sided tracts and wide courtyards. Gothic was abstruse Christian stuff, and he almost hated the Ostmark's Baroque.

Now people emerged from the fog, more and more of them. They had come up the wider and more comfortable road. He saw bicycles and motor scooters, a paralyzed man manipulated a wheelchair. All of them were moving toward an open door, where a woman greeted the guests in a broad Lower Saxon dialect. She asked for silence, the professor had already begun to preach. From the entry hall steps led up to a gallery decorated with small pillars. The whole display aroused mixed memories in Höllriegl: half aristocratic, half amazonian, in any case memories he was ashamed of. But there was no wasted space at Gundlfinger's—everything was kept to moderate bourgeois dimensions.

The hall was jammed. Höllriegl could just squeeze through the entry. Other latecomers had to stay outside on the driveway. The listeners crowded together, frozen into pious statues. Only a handful had found room on the few stone benches; they must have come very early. (The story went around in Sauckelruh that some people, who kept making the pilgrimage to Gundlfinger's house, often waited all night to be allowed inside, even in the foulest weather.) Others had brought folding chairs or pillows with them or had simply sat down on the plaster floor. Höllriegl, a trained athlete, was able to find a place on the pedestal of a pillar (his briefcase proved quite a hindrance) and from there look out over the multitude. Up front in the first row women kneeled; their arms hung down and they held their heads bent over as if in a trance. The entry to the gallery was blocked off by a red velvet rope.

Despite all precautions, the new arrivals caused something of an uproar, but the listeners took no notice. They concentrated too hard, like congregations Höllriegl had seen at ariosophic meditation exercises which he had visited from time to time for training purposes.

But all these individual impressions he registered only gradually. His attention was riveted on the speaker or preacher who stood behind the balustrade, his hands placed on it, a picture of professorial calm. He was a short, stocky man, perhaps close to seventy, with a high forehead, fleshy face, and sparse, graying hair. A strong nose, thick moustache cut in the English fashion, pink cheeks (as if they had been lacquered), slyly shining little eyes that wandered quickly and with a cool, abstract expression across the heads of the listeners from under fat lids. His mouth was as doughy as that of an old pantomime actor. Gundlfinger wore strangely formed glasses, perhaps "hearing" glasses. This famous thinker could just as easily have worked in a bank, say as a branch manager in the provinces, his exterior was that average, even drab. He exuded patience, mildness, goodness, something like sentiment—or was it only a deception? His words dropped quietly into the silence. These round, shiny, facile words had something all too round, shiny and facile about them, like coins, like small change.

After Höllriegl had listened to the lecture for a quarter of an hour (he had barely understood three sentences), he began to think of the doctor as a salesman of yard goods in a department store, nimbly and glibly measuring his fabrics and urging his customers to buy them. Although the subject was above him, the impression grew stronger with each passing minute that everything—every word, every sentence—had been prefabricated, stenciled, carefully prepared and planned (as planned as Gundlfinger's averageness) and now it all came clattering out of his mouth with the precision of a properly programmed electronic brain.

Gundlfinger's clothes were strange for the region, resembling alpine dress: black, with moss-green facings and trimmings, with horn buttons on the loden jacket. A dark-embroidered velvet cap, once the symbol of Viennese property owners, lay on the parapet. Gundlfinger probably wore thick woolen, mended socks, and slippers instead of shoes.

A sudden interruption drew Höllriegl's attention back to the lecture. One of the women in the front rows had used one of the short pauses which the philosopher built into his artfully baroque sentences—not because he was short of breath, but in order to let the beauty of certain ornamental thoughts glitter and sink in—to ask a question, a question which made everyone listen. The woman spoke with her head down.

"Is God a disease?"

". . . why, certainly, my dear comrade, certainly." Gundlfinger's expression did not betray the slightest embarrassment. "God is a disease. But a disease which is so odd and open to so many interpretations, so many-layered and so deep that we cannot grasp the fullness of its essence. If God is a disease, then every kind of religion is the proper if insufficient cure—not a cure of the cause, but of the symptom. For we do not know the cause, the root of the sickness. It lies somewhere else in each individual case, and therefore we are unlikely ever to find it. If God is thus understood as an incurable disease, as simply evil, a cancer of human thought, then the word 'God' becomes a collective designation for all the suffering that comes from HIM and branches out into our body-soul.

For your question, my dear, can also be answered by saying that this disease is at the same time the highest form of health. What do disease and health mean here? They are only symptoms of tension of one and the same existential condition. Our people, our great, chosen people seem at present quite swamped with it, it lives in this existential condition of a disease called God. I ask: How does our life, the life of our people actually continue? Surely also as tension between health and sickness. . . . God is created inside us like a disease, but also as its cure: health. But at the same time we call the tension which swings between these two conditions of body and soul, like between two poles with different names: God. Indeed it is nothing else but HE. I know of people who perceive God as disease and of others who experience him as health. If I may say it—those closer to God experience HIM as disease. HE reveals himself to them in his whole, terrible power of pain. Why? because the man fallen ill with God—and everyone is—experiences HIM much more strongly in a condition of sickness. And so we may say, simplifyingly: God expresses HIS SELF most strongly, most immediately, in disease; in other words, in a convulsion of body and soul that comes from HIM. To put it yet another way: Our diseases are the doors through which the sickness, God, enters into us. And that is why we experience HIM as disease, because HE lets himself be recognized in it, reveals HIMSELF in the burning thornbush of our pain. . . . God identifies HIMSELF, so to speak, with the diseases of those creatures HE has let go, that are dependent on HIM. Whoever suffers pain, therefore, feels God—God as HE works in him, lives in him—and dies in him. For God can die. HE is mortal! He dies with us! When men have ceased to exist, God will no longer exist. That is our triumph! Is that clear to you, my dear comrade? For us men, God is the disease of death, a misfortune and hardship, a disaster which must light up our soul because from the beginning it has been alight in us. Once again: an incurable disease! God is nothing else but the path into death, and the atom bomb will be the end of the sickness of God. Perhaps all of history should be interpreted as an allegory of an enormous dying, in which at one time the disease, God, appeared, and at whose end man, and with him God, dies of old age. . . ."

Höllriegl's intellectual powers stumbled over the glibly minted ideas of the professor who was chatting along up there. Gundlfinger's sentences made him physically ill: He had trouble swallowing, a headache, and a slightly dizzy feeling; occasionally that annoying "strange head" of his returned, as if everything going on here were not of this world, not a reality that concerned him. All of a sudden he no longer understood his own situation. He seemed unable to grasp where he was and what was happening around him. Was he dreaming? Was he thinking with someone else's brain? Or had he turned, hide and hair, into a different creature? In order to come back to reality he stared harder at the listeners, but the contours of their faces only dug themselves more painfully into his consciousness, without making any more sense than before. The feeling came and went, came and went.

He noted again, as he had done in the air-raid cellar at the pension, the absence of young people. Gundlfinger's public resembled a gathering at a cold-water spa for a cure. These were people drilled in deep breathing exercises and nurtured on diet foods, who sought condolence and tranquillity and a very special kind of self-castigation. Gundlfinger seemed to have a tranquilizing effect on these refugees, for they all were that. He was—like Höllriegl—a therapist, moreover he was a master of stupefaction: a magnetizer, sleep inducer, persuader. What he had said about God was like scratching your right ear with your left hand. And to make matters worse, whenever the man, for whatever reason, had become more comprehensible, his words were politically suspect. Above all, Höllriegl had retained the sentence that at present the German people found themselves in a state of sickness—a condition circumscribed with the word "God," but it also could be read to mean "Führer." Wasn't Gundlfinger afraid the Gestapo monitored his lectures? If he declared in a public assembly that the master race, whose mental and physical health was axiomatic, was sick, even very sick, and thus dared make innuendos which could cost him his neck, he must have very convincing reasons. Höllriegl's mood grew even more somber, sweat poured from all his pores. Where was the safe and sane world, his world? Where were security and order? He knew that the German people were sick and undergoing a heavy crisis. He felt it more strongly than others. But he would never have dared—nor for that matter allowed himself—to take such things into the public domain.

". . . let us say: the atoms, but as far as . . ."

The audience listened entranced, pious, slack expressions on their faces, mouths half open. Some distance away Höllriegl noticed Südekum standing crushed in the crowd. Feeling Höllriegl's eyes on him, Südekum looked back, raised his eyebrows, and rolled his eyes to let Höllriegl know how much he appreciated Gundlfinger and to share his delight. He couldn't spot the washing-machine salesman, but then most of the men here looked like washing-machine salesmen.

". . . as soon as the individual as a whole at the end of his days finds himself in a world which has gone off the track . . . this destruction of the individual in a universal world . . ."

Gundlfinger took his hands from the balustrade and motioned behind him, whereupon a youth who had stayed hidden until then stepped out and handed him an open book. The boy, who might have been about fifteen years old, was beautiful. The face of an angel, pale with a comely, severe expression, was framed by dark-blond curls cut in pageboy style. Höllriegl could not register more; the apparition disappeared at once. Only the light from the steel-blue eyes brightened Höllriegl's gloom-shrouded disposition; he thought the boy had looked at him for just a moment.

The philosopher read something, or cited a passage from the book. The beauty of the boy's face had hit Höllriegl like a bolt of lightning. A messenger from a bright and sane Nordic world! As a child Siegfried might have looked as shining and noble—Siegfried, if he had been a Greek. In this child, Valhalla and Mount Olympus became one. Everything—the speaker, the audience, the present—shriveled away. This was unbelievable! Beauty existed—and paired with purity! An angel on earth!

By contrast with the apparition—Höllriegl thought at once of the chime voice—the crowd around him seemed even more depressing. And threatening! These were terrible faces, he only saw it now. The women in the front rows—had he not seen them in his nightmares? He remembered the little old ladies in the chapel of the *Residenz*. How they had groped for him with their smeary-soft, clumsy hands—ugh! Disgust choked him. Outside! He looked down on a woman who stood in front of him, leaning against a pillar, then looked at her from the side. What a vulgar, wanton, bloated piece of feminine flesh—and those gaping eyes that stared adoringly up at Gundlfinger. With her russet skin and drooping breasts she looked like a rusted battleship of love, like a veteran streetwalker. And how she smelled!

Höllriegl slid down from his post and pushed wildly to the exit. He had to use force, for the people wouldn't budge. Gundlfinger the magician, the smart talker, the hypnotist, had bewitched them. Fury, mixed with nausea, rose up in Höllriegl. The air in here! Outside in the hall the pack grew less dense; he could move ahead more quickly. Finally the exit. The foggy air lapped against him like a sea of ozone. He breathed deeply, his steaming breath hanging in the air.

A weak howling came up from the valley—air-raid sirens down in Sauckelruh. The alarms were never-ending. Höllriegl strolled out into the wet cold chaos and slowly circled the clearing around Gundlfinger's villa, that building of banal imagination which rightly bore the name Walpurgis. The fog-shrouded contours resembled the decorations of an amusement-park horror house. Höllriegl frightened hordes of fat rooks which had already flown their ellipse and now rose heavily into the air for new flights.

This Gundlfinger was a sinister character, a Nibelungen, he was sure. Perhaps he was more—a Fafnir. The speech in the hall was a scene from the empire of the dead. Fafnir preaching to the black elves. But what did this dragon guard? The hoard of wisdom? Or was the treasure he protected a boy—that messenger from Valhalla with the chimelike voice? Had he seen the young Siegfried, the Sigurd of the *Edda* songs? The northern lights had blazed, and for a moment the splendor of the gods had struck him—straight to the heart!

What would Anselma say about all this? Höllriegl saw her arrogant face pull into a grimace. "It smells of mothballs here," she'd say. The romantic belief in the gods from grandmother's day, life a Wagner opera! ("Do you really believe all this nonsense? You can only tell *Pimpfe* such fairy tales . . .") And yet . . . something beautiful and shining *had* to exist! Anselma was hard and cutting, she was a werewolf. It was no accident that his pet name for her was masculine: Sinfiötli, chain of the senses. God knows it fitted. Werewolves, NATMAT—all that was the blackest of the dark powers, monsters from the bowels of the earth like the Nibelungen. But Bundschuh and *Der Arme Konrad* . . . where was the golden mean? Was the party the middle ground, the womb from which the new aristocracy had sprung? The cradle of the master race? Wherever he stepped he felt quagmire. What did he have left to hold on to? What did he himself have left? He recalled a saying from the "Fafnirmâl," a sentence whose deeper meaning he suddenly understood: ". . . everything endangers the fallen." More than ever that was minted for him. And Ulla? Was it she of whom the eagles whispered: "And thus did Wotan stick a thorn through the dress of the maid who lusted after men." Ulla, that marvel of beauty, the golden girl! She had scorned him, the cruel, grisly bitch! Never again! Never again! The scar burned on his forehead like a flickering flame.

He saw people hurry out of the villa and disappear into the woods. Either the reception was over or had been broken off. It seemed as if the earth had swallowed Gundlfinger's visitors. He scurried through the bushes—yes, there were entrances in the forest floor and among the boulders: caves, shrapnel-safe foxholes, entries to bunkers. That might all be fine for boys playing "chase the Jew." But what good was it against deadly radiation?

But now he'd go back and take care of everything. Make his report, as the law required. But against whom? Would anyone believe him? The whole thing seemed like some wild dream. But out of the chaos of that dream he still had something very real: the commentary from the underground.

The villa was empty. In the driveway, where Gundlfinger's disciples had massed, a kitten chased a windblown bit of paper. Höllriegl saw loudspeakers everywhere—Gundlfinger's sermons were transmitted to adjoining rooms too. The gatekeeper's room was open; a woman, the one who had let people in, drank coffee (made from herbs, to judge by the smell). The kitten, the woman, the steaming drink . . . idyllic. The world of war disappeared with the meowing sirens.

On the guest list he found an entry for Thursday, ten thirty, written in a childish hand: a gentleman to dowse, sent from Berlin. Someone had put a question mark at the edge of the page. Farther down was Südekum's name and the comment: "Music maker." It was almost half past ten.

"The professor expects you over there . . . in the small house. I'll ring."

The woman showed Höllriegl through a gray, overgrown park.

In back of it the wood opened into a narrow avenue as neglected as the park. A one-story wooden house surrounded by a wretched bit of grass stood at its end. As he came nearer he saw it was a riot of wood carving, black and weathered.

What a curiosity. The posts flanking the entrance resembled Indian totem poles. Nightmare beasts straight out of Gothic cathedrals poked long necks from the molding. The pillars in front had been so gnawed with painstaking carving that they looked like the air-cooled barrels of machine guns.

In the stuffy, half-dark rooms, the walls too were filled with carving; all sorts of carved junk stood about everywhere. In the dusty light of dusk one could only guess at the symbolic and erotic nature of the ceiling decorations. Every style on view in an anthropological museum seemed to have grown together here into a single horror. A type of Indian ornament appeared to dominate; in addition, there were carvings that recalled Negro sculpture, Byzantium, the idols of Easter Island, old-Slavic icons, and the stonemason art of the Aztecs.

Höllriegl looked with some discomfort at the frilly sculpture. The carvings expressed an ardor which he experienced as unclean lust. This excess, this restlessness, this wantonness of the spirit! Upsetting too, the senselessness of so unbridled an exhibitionism! The psychologist in him was aroused.

"You are Alfred from Berlin."

Frightened, Höllriegl turned around. The professor stood in front of him, dressed in a radiation suit, and with a broad grin stretched out his right hand. A hasty glance at Höllriegl's uniform, a closer one at his collar.

"You're a RAD troop leader?"

"Yes, that's my rank. I'm a healing assistant—a dowser."

"Oh, yes, of course. The tree of life. Our most beautiful rune . . . I see you are engrossed in . . . ah . . . our curiosities. In any case, welcome to Faust's study! Let salamanders glow, Undine uncoil, sylphs disappear, and so forth. Come along!"

They climbed up a creaking ladder and Gundlfinger explained: "You're new here. The concierge of the former owner—he called himself the castellan—carved the whole thing. A dreamer and a castrate. Carving was his hobby. The most beautiful thing he did was a cradle for the child he could never have. He died a little while ago at an advanced age under private care. It took a lot of trouble to prevent his euthanasia. There's his picture."

A yellowed, framed photograph hung on the wall—a revealing portrait with an artist's mane on his head and delicate hands crossed over his chest. A glassy look from under arched eyebrows.

"In here, please." Gundlfinger's study—for that's what it must have been—swarmed with carved monsters too. A roughly hewn table, often found in peasant halls, took up most of the room. No books, but folders and manuscripts lay about everywhere, even on the floor. On one side, near the wall, stood a switched-off Teletype machine. The radio shouted raucously in a corner.

The professor lowered the volume of martial music to a whine and with an ornate gesture motioned his guest to sit opposite him. Höllriegl resolved to say as little as possible and to listen; a resolution which quickly proved superfluous. Gundlfinger was obviously used to doing all the talking.

"Have you heard about the catastrophe? No? How come? Well, early this morning two more banzai missiles hit Reich territory. One exploded in the Allgäu, the second—unfortunately a neutron bomb—smashed into the Ostrau region. The Teletype message was coded in key two-one-jay, but garbled so badly that I couldn't make out the full story. Since then my telex has remained silent. Either the line is down, or . . . hm! They admitted the explosion in the second morning newscast. Permanent radiation alarm . . ."

Schicketanz had not known about that.

Gundlfinger tinkered with the telex. "Still nothing," he murmured.

"The Allgäu blast had great mechanical destructive power, according to the secret report. But the neutron bomb . . . this suit is fine for a masked ball, isn't it? Refugees from the Lippe region are supposed to have passed through Sauckelruh this morning. They reported that after this first atomic night Germany looks as it did at the end of the Thirty Years' War. That surely is an exaggeration. Incidentally, we retaliated hard. If you like, that's some comfort. Everything now depends—and within the next few hours—on our seizing the initiative. The early-morning news, before the enemy attack was made public, said that a second massive attack against the Sino-Japanese area had succeeded. Ausra missiles (there must have been a whole salvo of them) and large-scale thermonuclear attack from the air have extinguished all life on the Japanese islands north of the fortieth parallel as well as in Manchuria. Not even vegetation exists there anymore. A shock for the yellows . . ."

A pause. Gundlfinger sat bent forward and made a face as if hard of hearing. Openly he mustered his visitor from top to bottom; the results of the examination seemed to satisfy him.

"I hope you bring good news: from our Berlin friends and from Professor Kofut. You have their commentary?"

Höllriegl took the folder from his briefcase. "I have no news at all from Tiergartenstrasse. I was merely ordered to undertake a gyromantic investigation at your house. The man who gave me my orders, or rather his middleman, is Obersturmführer Hirnchristl."

"Yes, of course, Hirnchristl! How is he? Always busy. By the way—I note from your German that you're an Ostmarker, a countryman of Hirnchristl, then . . ."

Höllriegl gave a short matter-of-fact description of his strange experience with the Obersturmführer. When he mentioned that Hirnchristl's existence had been denied in his own office, the philosopher blanched. But despite his visible surprise, he said at once with a broad grin: "You know, Alfred, that sort of thing can happen in such an enormous complex. One hand often doesn't know what the other is doing, and the successor knows nothing of his predecessor. It doesn't have to mean anything."

(What a stupid explanation, Höllriegl thought.)

Unconsciously Gundlfinger's speech had taken on an Ostmark coloration. He spoke through his nose in what he obviously felt was properly relaxed Viennese. Perhaps the philosopher adopted the color of his surroundings automatically, but he might also have done it very deliberately. He spoke the Ostmark dialect only allusively, however, like a dilettante imitator.

"What's up with Karl? I wonder. Karl—perhaps you know him under another name—worked as a messenger for Psi, just before you did. . . . You see, right now I'm waiting for another and much more urgent report, this one from Kappa. And Karl had orders to get it before the tenth. But he hasn't come yet. And not another sign, not a word, nothing. Surely nothing's happened to him. . . . As you know, I am currently engaged in working on a proof for the existence of God, and I use the latest work done by our wise men. I badly need Kappa's commentary on the particle picture of radiation to the extent it contradicts the particle theory, as well as information on current research into the quantum theory of wave fields. I hope to deduce my proof for the existence of God directly from the structure of matter—I have the vision, but in certain intricate questions of physics a child can lead me by the nose. My work is thought out as a modern counterpart to Nikolas Chrypffs' *Theological Complements,* only I prove the existence of God from a single formula, you might say, from a mathematical central sun: Heisenberg's matter equation. The thought model of the 'world' as a vague spherical space is abandoned and suddenly, on the basis of a cosmological deduction, transferred into a mystic view of God—I'll get that down, you can depend on that; not a sentence will be flat. I can already say that the secret 'ten to the fortieth power,' the so-called connecting number between atom and cosmos, will play a decisive role. Can you follow what I'm saying?"

"No," Höllriegl admitted. He wished desperately to be allowed to leave, to end this dubious mission.

"That doesn't matter," the imperturbable Gundlfinger said. "Did you hear my speech today?" Höllriegl nodded. "Please don't be surprised that I took advantage of the marvelous prerogative of German philosophers to express myself in such a way that no one else could understand the text. Moreover, my person and my name are bound to a certain style. Nor do I wish to hide the fact that the party looks with growing suspicion on my work. My immediate superior, the philosophy officer at the Friedrich Schiller University in Jena, has already denounced me twice to the higher-ups—something I learned accidentally from someone in our cell up there. Moreover, I reek of fire and brimstone to those university officers who frequent Under den Linden 69 and enjoy the confidence of the Minister; although I don't know if they still do of the newly-appointed Herr Luyken. My most influential opponents are, I know, active in the Ministry of Propaganda and, grotesquely enough, in the Reich Office for Seismographic research in Jena. Now do you see the connection? I would have to be enormously stupid if I didn't sense that the Werewolf hates me like the bubonic plague. The NATMAT people especially would love to kill me or shove me into an SHC camp. What else can I tell you? The

Bundschuh? The ferment there is too great; no one knows if anything will come of it. Of course I've managed to keep my head above water, but for how much longer? I can't tell you how much I welcome this war."

"Professor Kofut believes it is high time that you disappear while you can." The warning slipped out against Höllriegl's best intentions.

"My good Cunnilingus! Do you know my Nordic name? Thiodhvitnîr, which means world-wolf-fish. A good name. I'm going to wait a bit, wait for a definite sign. In any case: Don't fan a fire that won't burn you. My proof for the existence of God, should it ever be finished, can't be published as long as Köpfler is in power, that's clear enough. At least not openly and not in Europe, Eurasia, and the two Americas. I hope to be left undisturbed for a little while, provided the war will give us that time. It doesn't look that way . . . who knows if we'll still be alive tomorrow? Nevertheless: The party does give me official commissions which I fulfill in spite of everything. My proof for the existence of God, at least formally, charts a course approved by the Propaganda Ministry. Officially I base my work on that of the German mystics as well as on party-normed German physics. But no one can even be allowed to guess that I have made thoughts my own that are not entirely racially pure—thoughts you can find in the works of Moseh ben Maimôn, Jehuda ha-Levi, Nachmanides, Levi ben Gerson, and other peripatetics and scholars, not to mention the fact that I fully support the teaching of Freud, Einstein, and Nils Bohr. Did you see my young assistant Axel down in the hall? Isn't he the model of Germanic youth? Well, Axel doesn't have a drop of Aryan blood in his veins. He was given the name Enoch at his circumcision. His father's name was Isidor Angelson. He was a rabbi, university professor in Uppsala, and, incidentally, a renowned coin collector. I saved his only child. What's the matter with you?"

"Please go on," Höllriegl said in a hoarse voice. He began to shake. His "other head" was back.

". . . I saved Axel literally from the talons of the SD. The Angelsons, two exceptionally beautiful people, lived underground in Aberdeen, where they had fled from Haparanda after the annexation of Sweden. At the time I attended a much-discussed congress there on "Ariosophy and Metapolitics." I got to know the couple through a secret contact. A little while later the two were seized and shoved into an SHC. The government needed test material for the first space flights. I adopted the boy, and a Scottish monk baptized him. I never heard anything again from Axel's father. But the mother—shall I tell you what they did with the mother?"

Höllriegl shook his head wildly. (Again he saw the bodies of decapitated carp dance through the air.)

"Please forgive my digression. I only wanted to say this: Isn't Axel, alias Enoch Angelson, the perfect refutation of this whole damned racial theory? And look, that's just how it is in philosophy. Blood means nothing, spirit everything. . . . I use Spinoza, Eliphas Lévy, Weininger, Bergson, Oskar Goldberg, and Cardinal Newman pretty openly. A special chapter will deal with the question of why God gradually disappeared from man's memory: had to disappear, especially from men who live under this global system of supertyranny. An investigation of memory based on quantum physics will round out the section. In the process of developing this phenomenology of forgetting and its biophysical interpretation, I plan to discuss the function of the supermechanical, and naturally the various behavior patterns of those most complicated molecular complexes which we call 'Meme'. . . ."

The professor, lost in his rambling theories, did not notice that something strange had happened to his visitor. Höllriegl had sunk forward, head propped in his hands, his face (which Gundlfinger could not see) twisted. The professor could well believe that "Alfred" was listening with great concentration. But Gundlfinger's voice penetrated to Höllriegl's ear as if from some great distance. The words made no sense, everything turned into a porridge of sounds.

". . . and finally I came to the conclusion that God wanted to be forgotten . . ."

"Yes?" Höllriegl looked up. Yes, God wanted to be forgotten. That was it! Purity? A Jew boy incorporated it, incorporated it to an extent that he had never believed possible. He had found purity only in music, or thought that he had found it. He had never really experienced it. Enoch Angelson—the son of a Swedish rabbi! Someone sent from God, a messenger of the gods, like Hermes, or one of the host of the dead of Asgard, whether from Mount Olympus, from the Jewish or Christian heaven. It didn't matter! And suddenly Höllriegl thought of that dying Apeling—it all happened such ages ago. What had the Apeling said? Odin is the . . . Elohim—or something like that. And Father Rhine and Father Jordan are one and the same thing. Was it really like that? Höllriegl taxed his memory, but the more intensively he thought about it, the more his memories dissolved. He couldn't even remember the face of the dying man or the room in which he had lain. He only knew one thing—the Apeling was Satan, Beelzebub, one of those Jews who had been held up to ridicule by the *Der Stürmer* and *Das Schwarze Korps* during the party's battle era. But Axel-Enoch was his opposite: someone dispatched by God, no matter what that God's name. And then the most staggering thing of all! The Jewish devil had helped party and Führer to victory; he had participated in the extermination of his own race. But Axel, the Nordic angel, had been presecuted by just this party. If it had not been for Gundlfinger, Enoch would have ended in an extermination camp.

All at once he saw Gundlfinger in a different light. He was surely a charlatan, a fellow traveler, an ass kisser, that much was clear—but circumstances had made him that with the constant need to disguise himself, to adapt. But whatever the philosopher had done, Enoch's salvation had atoned for it.

Höllriegl was so confused and lost in his own thoughts that he could not follow his prattling host, nor did he want to. But suddenly he listened. What had Gundlfinger said?

". . . if I did not know for sure that Victoria Regia was already well under way. An open secret—sparrows whistle it from the rooftops. As far as I know, Hirnchristl too was busy with important work; the Reich Radiation School had a special task. When the situation grew tense after the Führer's death, he sent me a telex, I suppose he did to others as well. Wait a minute, I'll find it. . . ."

Gundlfinger dug among his writings and came up with a piece of paper from which he read the following: "I am in a position to supply diamonds to customers of my Amsterdam branch. Today's greatest demand is for faultless stones of one quarter carat, four millimeter diameter, which I can send to you in any desired amount for a price of two hundred fifty-eight Reichsmark each. Other descriptions are unnecessary because I deliver directly to the buyer at absolutely rock-bottom prices and on a very small profit margin. This is an excellent value. You may examine the diamonds for ten days and then pay or return them. The diamond supply decreases day by day because they are a product of nature which need millions of years to form. Therefore prices rise every day. My offer is good for fourteen days. Heil Hitler—Erdmuth Budrasch of Harry Urban, diamond importers, Berlin SW 61, Hasenheide 32. The telex is dated November 11. That was on Monday.

"This means," Gundlfinger said after a pause, "that the big secret weapon flopped—and we only know as much about it as the government leaked for the express purpose of keeping the very stupid in line. In the last war we won the race for the miracle of God by half a length. Enterprise Mjöllnir. But today atom bombs belong in an army museum, for what kind of miracle of God is a weapon others carry in their quiver? And the East has a lot more in its quiver than we suspect. I'll give you that in writing. But the antiparticles . . . well, the antiparticles . . ."

Höllriegl had heard about the miracle weapon on which scientists were said to be working so feverishly. He remembered some time ago having read a long lead article about it in an educational manual, but he had understood very little despite the popular scientific language used. The article had discussed a controlled impact of matter with so-called antimatter, of antiatomic nuclei, antiparticles, and other antithings. As murky as it all was, the conclusion was crystal-clear: The Reich had the lead in atomic physics, and whoever learned to control antimatter, whose explosive power exceeded the London atom bomb by meganumbers, was absolute master of the world and would have to win any future war. Apparently Anselma knew more about this thing than she had dared tell him. The superexplosive was the Werewolf's weapon!

"But that also means," Gundlfinger said as he let Hirnchristl's telex glide once more through his fingers, "that the whole Reich government has packed its trunks, that an airlift of secret archives has started and that evacuation of certain highly placed people and their families has begun. The golden pheasants always go first! No one except the chief pilots know the destination. Some think it's a secret zone on the Amazon, others claim the code 'Victoria Regia' points to the Far North or to Antarctica, the deep freezes of the Reich, where bunkers, even whole underground cities complete with heating plants and all other modern conveniences have been abuilding for years. You know that, don't you, Alfred?"

Dr. Senkpiehl, Kummernuss, and others had indeed discussed that legendary northland fortress and described it as a counterpart to the alpine redoubt of the last war. Even his Ingrid, hairdresser to the Heydrich party officials' wives, had talked about it. But who really knew? One of his Heydrich clients, the managing director of the salt works, had once told him off the record that the famed Northland fortress was the same myth as the castle of the Holy Grail.

Gundlfinger leaned back comfortably in his swivel chair and continued: "It's not a bad time to hide. The master race's elite need not wait long in its radiation-proof shelters before the human race is completely poisoned. The neutron load dumped on Ostrau is only a modest beginning. After the planet is rid of mankind, the master race, or rather the surviving elite, will crawl out of their polar bunkers and again set up an absolute dictatorship. Over whom? Why, over a part of themselves, of course. Because they will—and here I'm following an idea of the Tau-Omikron group whose work I prize highly—at once split into two groups, two classes: into leaders and led, into free and unfree, into masters and slaves, into supermen and subhumans. For it already is quite obvious that this conflict between white and yellow, between swastika and shakubuku, is not only racial or geopolitical but has turned into a glorious apocalyptic muddle. Clear fronts no longer exist. In the midst of a violent heat wave, the Australians are fighting tooth and nail against their Japanese oppressors and are doing it with our support. However, these are the same whites fighting us in Indonesia, where we are or were the oppressors. Tomorrow these same whites will have to defend Indonesia against the Japs . . . Of course in the shadow of a nuclear world war these are really idle details. Atomic war is here and has made itself independent. Given the aspect of planetary death, territorial aggrandizement or loss, even if continents are involved, becomes a laughable proposition. Total war has created political vacuums no one would ever have thought possible, and has done it even in areas where atom bombs have not been used. It almost seems as if this upheaval had tossed the past back into the present, as if, after such absolute tyranny, there could be no future. I heard on the radio this morning (not a German station) that Brazil's Führer Council has been overthrown. And because no one could think of a better alternative, they proclaimed the country an empire once again. *Dom Pedro redivivus!* The whole world would split its side laughing if it did not have other troubles at the moment. Yes, for the past twenty-four hours Brazil has had an empress, the granddaughter of the Countess d'Eu and the great-granddaughter of Dom Pedro the Second. What do you say to that? Perhaps the Hohenzollerns or the Hapsburgs, in case any are still alive, should now mount their orphaned thrones while the Fenris wolves sharpen their fangs in their northern ice holes. Wherever blacks have killed whites in Africa, they are returning directly to the stone age: to their childish amulets, rain voodoo, and human sacrifice. That seems to me to be a very desirable cultural stage, especially for the survivors of the atomic night . . . should there be any. Hirnchristl wrote that I should be ready to travel within fourteen days. That's a long time, if one remembers how fast the horsemen of the Apocalypse ride. However, the telex was written at a time when no one could be sure that atomic war would begin at once. He says he'll let me know through a messenger when and where I should hold myself ready for departure. His offer refers to diamonds; that means ice, and faultless diamonds mean the arctic ice region. Project Bifröst, the greatest airlift ever attempted, has thus begun—I first heard about it a year ago. Hirnchristl was always hard to figure out. Is he the party official chosen to handle this flight into nowhere, or is he an outsider powerful enough to play a role in it? He's proved a hundred times that he's against the Werewolf. We can count on him a hundred percent —if he's still alive. Truthfully, I expected you to be the messenger. . . ."

Höllriegl sat up straight. It was time to put his cards on the table. Axel's savior deserved an honest answer.

"Professor Gundlfinger . . ." He spoke carefully in order to make it easier for a man hard of hearing. For the first time he looked at him with some sympathy. "I only met Obersturmführer Hirnchristl once. I could not tell you anything about him or how reliable he is. I was sent to him on the basis of orders issued in my home town of Heydrich. My name is Höllriegl, Albin Totila Höllriegl. I'm a divining-rod specialist, a healer, gyromant—I've already said that. The Ostmarkian novelist von Schwerdtfeger . . ."

"Oho, Schwerdtfeger," Gundlfinger interrupted. "Henricus Arbogast Edler von Schwerdtfeger. This gets more and more fantastic! Do you realize that I've known that man since World War One? We were comrades in the trenches—Austrian and German regiments were posted alongside each other in Volhynia. We became Russian prisoners on the same day. And by accident we found ourselves in the same prisoner-of-war camp. I got to know him well in the barracks of Novo-Nikolayevka. Typhoid made us all brothers. Brest-Litovsk tore us apart again. An exchange of prisoners brought us back home: He went to Vienna and I to Nördlingen. Later I lost touch with K.K. Ensign von Schwerdtfeger. Only after the foundation of the Greater German Reich did I meet him occasionally at conferences, political rallies, once even at a reception in the Reich Chancellery. As far as I know, Schwerdtfeger served as an officer during World War Two—somewhere on a staff in France. I was not fit to serve, thank Wotan. Is Schwerdtfeger one of our men? He belongs to the laureates of the party. . . ."

"I owe to him my acquaintance with you, Herr Professor. Hirnchristl was only my middleman. On Schwerdtfeger's recommendation he gave me the commission to dowse your premises. I had a similar job to do in Berlin. And now I'm on my way back to Heydrich. I've got to get back quickly—perhaps I'm badly needed there."

"Oh, yes, now I remember. Schwerdtfeger once told me about your . . . magic tricks. The influence of earth radiation seems plausible enough. I'm acquainted with the work of Benedikt, Heermann, and Lakhovsky. If the air raid doesn't disturb you, you can begin your work in the villa. I've suffered from insomnia for months . . . and . . . ah . . . general irritation. Perhaps you can find the causes with your divining rod, if there's still any point to uncovering such trifles as earth radiation."

Gundlfinger and Höllriegl too got up. "Please wait a moment; I'll call Axel. He'll show you my room." After a look at his watch and at the visitor's list: "Good God, five more people to see."

The professor called through the open door: "Axel, Axel, come on up here!" The boy appeared quickly, light-footed, as if on angel soles. His step on the ladder was barely audible. His dark-blue eyes shone. Hermes, the messenger of the gods!

"Axel speaks good German, even though he sometimes gets expressions confused. Mother German is his great passion, but a lot of other people don't understand that."

"I'll understand him," Höllriegl said, staring at the smiling messenger of the gods. "Axel, I'm the man from Berlin with whom you telephoned yesterday. My name . . ."

"The gentleman is called Alfred," Gundlfinger interrupted. "He'll examine the place for radiation. Axel, yesterday we talked about this curious earth radiation . . ."

"Yes, Herr Professor. Yes, Herr Alfred."

At that moment Höllriegl heard a series of dull, rapid explosions, three, four, ten of them: The windowpane pulverized into a glittering rain of glass and a cloud of dust and splintered wood rose on the opposite wall. Gundlfinger staggered and held his head with both hands. Höllriegl and Axel both cried out.

"Quick, get away from here," the professor whispered and took cover. His face was covered with blood. He pressed a handkerchief against his right cheek and ear; at once the red soaked through. Panting: "It's nothing; they didn't hit me."

Höllriegl too had taken cover, instinctively, and pushed Axel to the floor. The boy was chalk-white, but the paleness gave his face even greater beauty. Gundlfinger's cold-blooded calm made an enormous impression. The professor crawled back to the table, switched off the light, opened a drawer, and took out a delicate object of burnished metal. Höllriegl recognized it as a laser gun. How timely: Philosophy was armed.

"Would you give me your handkerchief? Mine is . . ." He staunched the blood as best he could and crept to the door. Icy air flowed through the torn window.

"They were after me . . . I've received threatening letters. Just let them think they hit me. I'll disappear into the cellar. I have bandages down there, and there's an exit into the wood."

He listened for a while and said, "I don't want to endanger Axel. Take care of him for a while, please! You wear a uniform. He'll be safe with you. Take him somewhere where he'll be protected. I'll try to fight my way through to the Psi people, I mean Kofut. You'll find me there—if not, they'll know where I am. But quick, now."

The professor was already on the stairs when he called back softly: "Axel, stick close to our friend Alfred; you can trust him.

You hear me: Trust him blindly! He's a good man, he won't desert you. And we'll see each other again too—of course we will. Be quiet, completely quiet. God be with you both."

Höllriegl put his finger to his lips after Gundlfinger had gone. But Axel could not have uttered a sound. Only once did he sob out. The floor was spattered with blood. The room filled with cold, milky light.

He had to think. It would be difficult to reach the edge of the wood, to cross the empty plain between the little house and the first tree. One made a good target there. But it could be reached in two or three bounds. Anyway, "they" would have fled by now.

Who are "they"? As Höllriegl and Axel climbed down the stairs, Höllriegl in front and anxiously intent on protecting his charge with his body, all kinds of questions whirled through his brain. Could they have been SHC inmates? The train of human animals rose in his excited imagination. Ridiculous. Why should they want to kill the philosopher? Moreover, those who had fired were practiced shots, sharpshooters. They had missed Gundlfinger by a hair. The fog had obstructed their aim. A Vehmic tribunal of the party? Just as unlikely. Those people would have used lasers. Werewolf? Bundschuh? NATMAT? an ideological murder? Or a conspiracy by the university officers of whom Gundlfinger had spoken? But they too would have laser guns: Laser is noiseless, kills with a slight, hissing sound. The rattle had sounded like submachine-gun fire.

Höllriegl reached the door. He opened it a crack and looked outside. Everything was quiet. The rooks again sat importantly on their branches. The fog had grown thicker, the sky looked pale yellow and wintry. Nothing moved. Peace! Peace! Where was the war?

Just a few hours later, Sauckelruh offered quite a different picture. The spearhead of refugees had reached the Harz Mountains that morning, and thousands upon thousands of people followed behind, squeezed into every conceivable kind of vehicle. They poured down from the northwest of the Reich into the Middle German plain in three major columns, in the process engulfing Höllriegl's home region, the Halle-Merseburg Gau. Truly all hell had broken loose everywhere, and even though bloody clashes had already occurred in several places, the police, SS, and SD were incapable of stemming the deluge. Moreover, it looked as if the ark of salvation had burned down in the bargain. Ahead of the panic-stricken columns marched, invisible yet reflected in every face, the fiery cloud of the first atomic night. Terror, at once new and ancient—as if the dinosaurs of old loped behind the hunted—spread far and wide, almost tangible even on those who had no contact with the refugee stream. But that wasn't the worst of it. The real horror lay in the fact that anyone who took the trouble to think realized at once how pointless flight really was.

Nevertheless highways and dirt roads were soon jammed. Trucks, trailers, and private cars stuffed with hastily collected household effects, suitcases, bundles of old clothes, and as often as not with utterly stupid and sometimes quite macabre things, thronged every roadway that offered even half a chance of passage. Overcrowding was especially bad in Sauckelruh. As Höllriegl had correctly surmised, the village lay at the end of a valley, and the junction highway, as it was called up there, ended in town. No one could move forward or backward. Furious, desperate men climbed out of cars locked in the mammoth traffic jam. None of the refugees had any gas left, and gas stations were empty and abandoned. Those who had started out with half-empty tanks and come a fair distance were soon stranded. The wrecks lay heaped on both sides of the road and even on the highways themselves.

There was one bright note amid the chaos: a sudden ample supply of water, even though the government had insisted that a catastrophic drought in late summer and fall had caused the water shortage. Everyone was delighted at the unexpected relief, but it did give rise to rumors that the shortage was part of a snap discipline action invoked under the "Landgrave, Get Tough" program. As one refugee put it, "Now they're shitting in their pants, and while they're at it they made water." You couldn't miss the Bundschuh insignia the man had painted in black on his cooler, right next to an atomic mushroom. The emblem was displayed more and more openly now.

But even the easing of the water shortage proved deceptive. It lasted a day, and then the restrictions were back in force.

Schicketanz gave Höllriegl an extra tank of gas and didn't take ration coupons for it; perhaps because he like Höllriegl, or was impressed by his uniform. Höllriegl didn't need the gas then, but later it turned out to be invaluable. The mechanic had fixed the car radio, and he even told Höllriegl about a dirt road deep in the woods that circumvented the clogged highways. They had to talk surreptitiously, for atomic refugees besieged the shop, outbidding each other to buy gasoline, determined to go to any extreme to get it. Schicketanz and his assistant carried submachine guns, the only thing that prevented an attack on the shop.

Höllriegl planned to take a series of shortcuts to reach the Kyffhäuser Mountains. They would take him through Braunlage, Illfeld, Nordhausen (now called Kesselring), and Kelbra. A funny feeling crept into his stomach—he thought for a moment of the road to Rottleberode and the Eycke castle. Ulla! Suddenly he felt a wild desire to see her again, even if only from a distance. . . .

It was quite a feat, driving down that narrow, furrowed path, which sometimes dipped steeply. Moreover his eyes had watered incessantly since that incident in Gundlfinger's cottage. His nose and throat scratched as if the air were filled with sand. Even his breathing passages were affected. His bronchial tubes hurt, and he had a repulsively sweet taste in his mouth. Was he about to come down with the flu or something? No, it wasn't like that, and besides his trouble had started too suddenly. When he had wandered down into the valley with Axel, he had felt as if his eyes had lost their adaptability; at a certain median distance he saw everything blurred and purple-edged. It was difficult to distinguish moving persons or things within this limited field of vision. The flow of tears increased. Now, driving in wooded terrain, it was especially bothersome.

Axel sat next to him. Even the clumsy, grotesquely ugly radiation suit clung to the youth's body in a special way. The boy had not talked much during the flight to Sauckelruh. He had only said something to the effect that the *Inarteram* should have told the authorities in time. He, Axel, knew that certain groups had been against the *Inarteram*. He took great interest in the *Poricht* (he meant the repair) of the *Idommel*—the car. He and Schicketanz seemed to be good friends; they joked together. It was soothing to listen to the boy's still immature voice. And all those pretty, foreign-sounding words!

Höllriegl had led Axel by the hand like a child as they went through the woods, and this fatherly gesture made the boy happy. An almost physical stream of affection bound the two accidental companions—the man who had grown up in the illegal Hitler Youth, and the rabbi's son whose family had been wiped out. Höllriegl stole furtive glances at Axel from the side. The Nordic attraction of his face disappeared on closer examination; it was a gentle deception, a facade, as with Ulla. The softness of the features, the sensual sweep of the lips and the deep nose-lip fold, the short nose, Grecian in shape with its delicate, flaring nostrils, the finely shaped low forehead, the thick lashes (like a forest!)—all that was un-Germanic. Secretly, Höllriegl carried out the nose-and-ear test he had learned to do in ethnology. It did not provide a clear picture, however, because Axel's features were still youthful. The most one could have said was that Sephardic and Ashkenazic traits had been crossed and that a strong infusion of Nordic-Hellenic, perhaps Baltic, had blurred the primeval Jewish face. Nor did Axel have the typical "Jewish look" as described in such detail in Rasse-Günther's textbook. Who knows how many peoples and races had mixed in his ancestors in order to fashion this creature! (More and more Höllriegl resisted the thought that he had to deal with a full-blooded Jew.)

Occasionally the lad flashed a grateful look at his protector. His eyes were of the purest azure, and on top of it that dun-colored hair! It seemed to Höllriegl that a deep secret lay hidden in human beauty, and he felt this with painful devotion, as he had with Ulla: The creator took a direct hand in the flow of genes, an act of grace. It could not be thought of in any other way. What he admired most in the Nordic figures of light he had been taught to emulate were the toughness, the strength and the courage, the aptitude and the cunning (the proverbial "Nordic cunning" of the scheming Loki) with which they mastered life. These supermen had always been his idols, and even Anselma's derision couldn't change it. Everything Nordic and heroic had always attracted him. He equated it with the masculine element of creation, with the progenitive principle, with conquering manhood. Even the amber witch was a masculine being, despite her brutally sexual female charms. The Aryan being was beautiful by nature—a beauty harsh, hard, and victorious.

Beautiful as battle is beautiful. In contrast, Axel's beauty had a shape that recalled paradise, silence, and innocence. Was that beauty devilish because it was Jewish?

With eyes aswim in tears and pain stabbing limbs and joints, Höllriegl brought the car slowly down into the valley. The radio was turned on; it bawled out marching music or broadcast victory bulletins. Apparently all airborne enemy troops on the continent had been encircled. After initial successes in Upper Italy, Portugal, and Finland, the invaders could look ahead only to destruction. All reinforcements had been cut off and enemy advances halted. Air bridges to the Crimea and central Russia had collapsed. A major air battle did rage above Ireland, which dissident American free-corps units had tried to turn into an "anchored aircraft carrier," but it was the only one. Those who had committed treason against the New Order by supporting the enemy in battlefield areas now faced massive SS and SD retaliation.

One hand on the wheel, the other turning the radio knob, tortured by disrupted vision, Höllriegl could not pay Axel much attention. When he had to stop for a moment, he took a quick look at his companion, and saw with dismay that Axel's features were stricken. Tears gleamed in his tired eyes, and he shaded them with one hand against the gloomy forest light. Silently they drove on; but from time to time Höllriegl stroked Axel's left hand.

Again that unwonted warm feeling boiled up: He was allowed to protect another human being, to be responsible for him. He had never done that before. He didn't have any friends, only comrades, which was more, perhaps, but could not replace true friendship. And he'd had only sexual relations with women. ("No use kidding myself on that score.") What he had sometimes mistaken for love was really naked greed, lechery, no more than a straw fire—it hurt to feel that, but he preferred to deceive himself because he could think of no other escape. Anselma had spat in his face and had been so right. A milksop, a weakling incapable of love, at best a secret romantic.

Snatches of news whirled around in his mind like the snowflakes that had now begun to fall from the blackening sky. ". . . Köpfler has disbanded the Roman Curia. . . . The body of the Dalai Lama has disappeared from a Cologne clinic, no explanation yet. . . . All the activities of the Congregation of the Holy Office have been suspended. . . . The Deutsche Bank and the Credito Italiano have taken over all Vatican participation in banks, especially the Banco di Roma and the Banc del Spirito Santo, in mines, textile factories, oil companies, steelworks, steamship and airlines, and in the pilgrim industry. Shares were exchanged at the rate of three to one. It was determined that the church's share in stock of all these companies amounted to 65 percent. All church-owned real estate in countries under the protection of the Reich has been transferred to state control. Only the so-called Patrimonium Petrae, as defined in the accord of October 9, 1870, is left under Vatican jurisdiction. . . . Unfortunately little Erna fell sick with the mumps yesterday. Her guardian is asked to postpone his planned visit until the Feast of Lights and until then to remain united with the dear sick child in thought. . . . The national synod of bishops in Worms will, in accordance with the wishes of the Reich leadership, select a new father of all Catholics from its midst. As has already been announced, the future Pope may choose the name Suidger I (the name of the German pope Clement II) or Soter II. The new Pope will have to put the universal church under Reich supervision and adapt Catholic doctrine to Bormann's major theses as well as to Rosenberg's teachings on the blood myth. Reichsführer Ivo Köpfler has canceled the so-called Galden Agreement between the Reich and the Lamaistic church concluded on August 21, 1953, because Tibet violated the provisions of the twenty-five-year treaty. In the early morning hours of November 14, fast-moving Wehrmacht units occupied the Forbidden Land. Advance detachments are closing in on Sangnatschosdsong, the headquarters of the criminal Tashi-Lama clique that conspired with the Soka Gakkai. Scattered Tibetan resistance was smashed. The Tashi Lama was court-martialed and shot. Thus the fate of the plutocratic monastery state —a foreign body and powder keg within the new order in Eurasia —has been sealed. The swastika has waved over Lhasa since four o'clock local time this morning. . . . These measures are designed to smash for all time Peter's primacy, to strip power from the Roman community which presumed sole apostolic origin, and to assure the primacy of the Reich as the leading power of the Aryan-Germanic family of peoples over the Roman Church. All Catholics look expectantly toward Worms. . . . The soldiers of the glorious campaigns of thirty-nine–forty-five saw that their officers, the young first and second lieutenants, were always first against enemy lines. . . . The church archive and museum of the Lower German Reformed Church reports a number of interesting new acquisitions, among them . . . the Frankish and Hispanic national synods have been allowed to elect subsidiary popes and to delegate them to Worms . . . The Institute for Indogermanic Intellectual History in Munich has proved beyond doubt that Frauja-Christ was blond and blue-eyed. He was descended from Thracian princes who in the course of the Diadochian disputes were taken as hostages to the East. Several volumes of documentation on this subject will be sent soon to the Reich Genealogical Office, the German Research community, and the Reich Archives. . . . For Christmas Mommy wants a nutria coat with collar and cuffs of Siberian sable. Daddy will have to dip down deep in his wallet. . . . The Reich Ministry of Health in conjunction with the Reich peasantry has worked out the following norms for December for the healthy adult male German: 6¾ hours sleep daily; 2,300 calories daily for sedentary activity as a white-collar worker; 2,700 calories for sedentary physical work; 3,000 for medium labor; 3,500 for medium-heavy labor; 4,000 for heavy labor; and 5,000 for the heaviest-labor category. The daily amount of stool with mixed food intake is set at 131 grams; for vegetarians the figure amounts to 370 grams. . . . In the battle for Ireland the Reich never surrendered control of the air, even for a moment. Parachute units and airborne troops of all the services gave a good account of themselves, as did the Air Force. . . . Officials of the Reich Ministry for All-German Questions, created by executive order on November 12, have been assigned the Civil Service grade 2b, in accordance with the Thirty-Eighth Amendment to the General Wage Law of March 27, 1946. All salaries are subject to the three currently valid regulations covering reduced wage payments in favor of winter relief. . . . The strong influence of mongoloid elements, which leads to evident decrease in skull capacity, brain size, and therefore . . . SS Standartenführer Wolfdietrich Sawade has been named Minister for Atomic Refugees. . . . Wherever Indo-Aryan thought deviated from the symbolic-transcendental ideal of religion and the aristocratic social organization of their ancestors . . . the legal basis of radiation protection from atomic law. . . . man in the situation of panic . . .

leukemia as a result of radiation damage . . . radiation damage and trauma . . . chromosome change in light of . . ."

The intermission sign was tapped out over all stations: "The party thinks for you—the party thinks for you—the party thinks for you—"

Quite enough! Not one of these damned Reich stations had said a single word about the nuclear explosion. As if this monstrous event had not taken place, the most monstrous in memory! Atomic missiles had fallen on Reich territory, the heartland of the world empire; missiles so large they made the historic London bomb—The Bomb of the history books—resemble a firecracker. All the highways were jammed with refugees, chaos had begun. And the radio had nothing more important to report than salary regulations, the advance in Tibet, about which no one gave a damn, or about Indo-Aryan thought. Advance! Blitzkrieg! What madness! Diluvial strategy in a rain of atom bombs!

Höllriegl ground his teeth. In his fury he shifted so hard that the car reared up. And suddenly he beat on the wheel with both fists. Axel looked at him shyly. The blue lightning of his angelic eyes returned Höllriegl to his senses. . . .

For on the other hand, the Reich leadership, and that meant the party, knew what it was doing. The party thinks for you! It thought, planned, and directed the fate and history of the Western world. It did it for everybody, for every single comrade. Köpfler took care even of him, Albin Totila Höllriegl. In just the same way the Führer and Reich founder had once cared for him and for everybody. And suddenly Höllriegl remembered those verses (his lips formed them like a prayer) which had gone so often through his heart and mind in that distant illegal era when he was a nameless Hitler Youth in Austria:

> My Führer, look, we know about the hours
> in which you carry the hard burden,
> in which you place a loving father's
> hand on our deep wounds and do not yet know
> how you will heal us!
>
> In many nights it may have happened thus:
> We sleep and you watch with fearful cares.

How many nights must pass that you will
worry through in order to see the
light of morning with clear eyes?

My Führer, look, we know the sacrifices
that you have made for us:
The burden of loneliness that you must carry
in order to forge our people's fate in sad
and happy days.

That's why our love is so great;
why you are the beginning and the end.
We believe in you, faithfully and unquestioningly,
and our work of mind and hand is formed
only of our thanks.

As it was in the beginning, so be it now! The Führer had created this holy German empire, and the Führer continued to live in the party and all its organizations. He was the beginning and the end. He was immortal, as the party was immortal. What had Anselma said? The Führer had become the mystical body of the German people. Adolf Hitler's great soul lived on in the soul of every single German. In him too! In his breast he carried the Führer's eternal inheritance. How could he have lost faith in the party? The party thinks for you, the party thinks for you—you couldn't repeat that often enough! If the party suppressed news of the bombings, then it knew precisely why. "We believe you, faithfully and unquestioningly." That was it. The narrow-minded, fainthearted man who did not see the large picture and its historic ramifications—could not and dare not see it—might, in his weakness, begin to doubt and despair. But of course that was stupid, even criminal. Simply absurd! Good God, life must have some meaning, at least one meaning! And that meaning was Germany!

They had come out of the wood, and on the road ahead an endless column of cars, bathed in the pale sheen of headlights, crept through the fog. Luckily traffic here was not bumper to bumper, and he had little trouble finding an opening. Schicketanz had been right: Not only was the path a shortcut, it apparently had helped him avoid the worst congestion.

His eyes were tearing less now. Only a sharp burning, a sandy dryness, remained. His vision had improved too—the darkness did his eyes good. But the aching all over, the gently pounding pain in his joints!

Where in heaven's name did the refugees plan to go? Was there any refuge left? From time to time, Höllriegl let some car come up close and asked the driver where he was going. The answer was always the same: someplace in eastern Germany, in the distant underpopulated areas, to Pomerania, into Kulmerland, the Warthegau, the Masurian Lakes, to Kurland. Everybody seemed to have friends or relatives there who had gone ahead and established refuges; they would meet them in Stolp, Cranz, Tilsit, Gotenhafen, Bromberg, Thorn, Marienwerder, Heydekrug, and go to hide in some village. (Höllriegl remembered that Ulla too came from that part of the Reich; perhaps she and her children were already on their way there.) The more distant and remote, the better. Only to get away from big industries and the mammoth cities!

Didn't these people know that fake factories were spread across the east, and that these could as easily be targets of attack? Moreover, subterranean armament plants had been built in the remotest corners of the east, where no one would be likely to suspect their existence; for example, on the Rominten Heath, where the brother of a girl he knew worked as a chemical lab assistant in an underground city built beneath the village of Pemsel.

There was one rumor he encountered again and again, and it almost seemed to him as if it always came from the same source: the Sensai, leader of the Soka Gakkai, had recommended use of missiles and so-called "clean" bombs to depopulate territories of the old Reich and settle groups of Manchurian peasants there, since they had proved most resistant to the "clean" bombs' relatively small amount of radioactive fallout. According to the grapevine, settlers had already been brought in by air.

In order to distract Axel and cheer him up a little, Höllriegl switched on the car radio again. To the hollow-rustling accompaniment of an organ, a man's voice sang an old sentimental song: "Two Red Lips, a Sweet Kiss." For a while they listened to the sprightly chatter of a girl pioneer troop engaged in harvesting potatoes. He fiddled idly with the radio button while he drove the car through a thick snow flurry, right behind the Mercedes of a refugee family from Remagen.

". . . will in some detail go into administrative matters and cite numerous examples to illustrate application of emergency . . . the name Adolf, which many Germans have already added to their own names, has been enshrined among the Nordic hero names. Reichsführer Ivo Köpfler is the first to assume the hero name Adolf in honor of the immortal Führer and founder of the world empire. The Reichsführer's complete name now is . . . massive fighter bomber sorties were flown and for the first time ultra-cold media, a triumph of German cryogenics, were used . . . mausoleum and urnfield on the Kyffhäuser according to plans which the founder of the Germanic World Empire and greatest builder of all time. . . . in this sense the Research Institute of Aryan Languages has suggested replacing the word "war" with the older and holier word "Orleg" . . . whereas her counterpart in the old Reich usually waits and sees if her date will pay for the entertainment. . . . The heaviest German, Frau Edelheide Pschichholz, age thirty, died Tuesday in Merxleben as a result of a kidney ailment. She weighed three hundred sixty-nine kilograms; brain weight: one thousand twenty grams . . . the Reichsminister for Education and Propaganda has ordered effective immediately that the daily early-morning broadcast "German Faith" begin not with the rhythm *tamtamtamtam* but with *tamtam*. . . . And now my dear German ladies and gentlemen, the biggest gun of today's world champion concert: Sex Söguthätt with that certain Nordic something, the great favorite of our missile striking force (loud applause), sings her big hit, "I'm a Ghoul from Thule" (thunderous applause) . . . two years ago won the great Skalden Prize of the nation . . ."

Still nothing about the bomb (didn't matter a damn). Most of the radio stations seemed intact and working, and their programs didn't differ much from the regular fare. It was depressing, though, to have that endless gray column of refugees in front.

Up ahead traffic slowed, cars crawled. In the milky light of dimmed headlights—night had fallen completely in the meantime, and the snow drifted from a blustery sky—they could see many cars parked around a long, one-story roadside inn built in the customary style of a high-gabled farmhouse. Several NSKK men —at least here the Werewolf had not yet taken over—ran about waving their arms in order to unsnarl the traffic tie-up and keep the road clear. The men carried their weapons at the ready: lasers. Despite the threat, many cursed loudly. "Dirty shitheads," Höllriegl heard someone say. And someone else: "Bundschuh awake, down with Köpfler! That was too much. If something drastic wasn't done now, then . . . but most of the refugees drove silently and slowly on.

"A *Labenat,"* Axel said.

"Are you hungry?" Höllriegl was ravenous. He had not eaten since early morning. Salvos of laughter boomed out of the restaurant, and despite the blackout one could see that all the rooms were brightly lit.

"Yes—but the Antjocharde!" Axel pointed to the men in uniform, who waved their dark-blue lights.

"Never fear. I'll try and park."

They found a hole in the chaos of cars behind the garage. A big car followed hesitantly behind, and five figures wrapped in heavy fur coats tumbled out, perhaps two men and three women; it was hard to tell. They all entered the place together.

A regular orgy of eating and drinking was underway in every room of the quite large establishment. Men and women sat jammed together at the tables, here and there a man had a woman on his lap. Children ran about screaming. People drank from mugs and jugs which passed from hand to hand. The drink smelled of wine and schnapps. No sign of waiters or owners. The refugees had apparently plundered the cellars of the abandoned restaurant and taken care of their own needs.

The noise was deafening, the smoke-filled air thick enough to cut. Most of the guests were drunk. They lifted their glasses to propose incessant toasts, bawling and swaying in rhythm. As Höllriegl and Axel pushed their way into the large dining room, a bench collapsed. The swayers rolled on the floor amid laughter and howling; some of the poses they adopted left little to the imagination. Höllriegl pulled Axel away. He was sorry they had stopped here.

But he had no time to think; it was too late. They were surrounded, embraced, kissed, were trapped and pushed forcefully down onto a bench—two girls had swung themselves up on the table in order to make room for them. Glasses fell over, wine poured across the table. A man with an apoplectic face held Höllriegl fast while the woman who sat opposite, an elegant but disheveled-looking matron, put a jug to his mouth and in spite of his protests—in the uproar no one could hear his profession that he was, like the Führer, a teetotaler—he had to drink again and again. The wine ran down his uniform coat. Axel did not fare any better: two women loaded with jewelry pounced on him. Höllriegl yelled to his neighbor: "We're hungry!" At once he was given sausage, cheese, and cold chicken. Two fat, not unpretty blondes fed Axel, who sat sunk into himself, pale and disturbed, as if he were a child, a cherub among demons. He too had to drink from time to time. He lifted his hands defensively, protesting that he had always practiced abstinence, could not tolerate *Brannat* and drank only milk—which made the woman opposite take out one of her fat breasts and stick it under his nose. Höllriegl saw across the table how the hags mustered "his" boy with lecherous eyes, their hands busy under the table. Perhaps Axel was smart enough to simulate drinking—but it was unlikely. Not even he had succeeded in doing that, for the company had noted his resistance and made sure he downed his share.

Despite the animal heat in the room, people had either kept their fur coats on or sat on them. Höllriegl recalled that furs were supposed to offer some protection against radioactivity. Furs with buttoned-in linings of elastic protective cloth—boron and several artificial fibers—had become the latest rage. The ads had stressed that such coats even offered some protection against neutron-bomb radiation (which was surely nonsense).

Nevertheless a veritable fashion show of furs seemed underway in this place. Wherever one looked, nothing but furs, some so precious as to indicate their owners enjoyed fat bank accounts—mink, sable, nutria, chinchilla, tiger, snow leopard, ocelot, seal, platinum fox, down to rabbit, skunks, and pony.

A witch with curls dyed blue, a face lift, artificial lashes, shiny false teeth, and imposingly pendulous breasts was hoisted onto the table, whereupon her ermine coat fell from her shoulders to the floor. She made a speech no one could hear in the din and lifted her skirt up to her panties to show off her remarkably slender legs, adorned with varicose veins. Everyone toasted the old lady, poured wine between her breasts, and snatched her back into the depths. But already another man had climbed onto a chair to gesticulate wildly. The whole thing, it seemed to Höllriegl, had nothing joyful about it, was mere frenzy and desperate stupor.

The red-faced type on Höllriegl's right, whom his drunken girl friend called "fussy Friedrich" (a biscuit manufacturer) suddenly got up and shouted heavily: "I empty my bladder to the welfare of the ladies!" He said it, and disappeared in the crowd. His partner shoved over to Höllriegl and put one arm around his shoulder. "Fussy Friedrich," she said, "is my husband—an ass hole, but still my husband." One of the members of the table round let a knockwurst dangle from his fly, and the biscuit manufacturer's wife began to draw the skin off the sausage and nibble at it. The guests roared their approval.

The wine began to have its effect. All of a sudden everything around him jumped into focus, yet seemed terribly unreal, as if it all took place somewhere else and he was only an innocent bystander. His "other" head was back. Scenes unspooled with lightning speed, only to alternate abruptly with those that moved at a maddeningly slow pace. Yet these too were hard to follow because he lost track of what happened. Clearly and drawn out, as if in slow motion, he saw what the two fat blondes, who had flung their polyp arms around his Axel, were doing with the boy. Höllriegl wanted to protest, get up, but he couldn't, didn't want to; who gave a shit anyway? Axel seemed feverishly excited and let the women do what they willed—of course the two ladies handled him in the most scandalous fashion. One of them, her face was marked by a wild, fixed, ecstatic smile, tried to drag her victim close to her and kept whispering something to the boy. Höllriegl saw with disgust how she dug her tongue into Axel's ear.

From time to time the scene changed without his knowing how or why; he could no longer absorb details or combine events. It was just too much for him. Suddenly he found everything pleasant and even quite marvelous, only his stomach couldn't keep up the pace. All kinds of people talked to him, he sat at other tables or on them —what a damn nice Ostmarker he was. All Ostmarkers are nice and *gemütlich.* He howled and swayed with the rest of them. A good thing there were so many women about, wherever he sat down, he got his hands on female flesh. He talked drivel about Ulla and that other one—what was her name?—and got on a first-name basis with total strangers at once, for example with a hero of the Narvik campaign, who never stopped talking about the naval battle at Jan Mayen. He asked a Catholic priest from Besançon in France (his card said *Monsignore Aloys Barmherzigkeit, Prelate*) if God were a disease, or what the hell is God anyway? At the same time he jingled the insignia which the prelate wore on his cassock. A radio reporter from Bad Tölz kept telling him dirty jokes. He made fast friends with an old fighter from Pirmasens, whose hand he kissed in an outburst of enthusiasm because he too had been at Pirmasens, a great thing that, only unfortunately that too could make you vomit, because now he felt sick as a dog. The old fighter said he was still a romantic but now he looked for the blue flower in the wine list, which of course was funny as hell. And a professor from Strasbourg's skull university explained something very complicated about the pineal gland, and a not too old women's leader from Hörde with a very challenging derriere, who had sat down on his lap, giggled as she explained how she had smashed up her VW on the Ruhr expressway but that sweet guy over there—a pale, bony, worn-out looking youth ("My name is Treffz, Detlev von Treffz")—had taken her along in his Porsche and later taken her on himself ("You must know that I gave Ingold a quite new feeling for undies"), and now the pair wanted to go to the sweet guy's cousin who had married a man in Heiligenbeil on the Frische Haff, close to the Baltic, and that might be the right place to make future flight plans. O.K., why not? And the advertising director of a Rhineland champagne factory—horse breeder, gray receding hair, sinewy and vigorous expression, eagle eyes—who invited him out to the toilet (". . . you must be an onanist, or are you normal? . . .") had been at Auschwitz back in '42. His eyes lighted up. Extra cigarettes and Jamaica rum rations after the "heavy cases." Cigarettes and Jamaica rum had never tasted as good again. And the delicate brunette with the lascivious tadpole mouth and the rubber bosom under her sweater . . . She was a typist at Euratom in Speyer who gabbed on and on about atomic power, fossil fuels, and conventional-heat production. She knew all about the prices for heating coal in account units of the European Payments Union (under Reich Bank control) pro ton (she said "pro to") from the mine, for bituminous slack from the United Vassal States of America c.i.f. European ports; she knew everything by heart, a neat factory brain. He didn't give a good goddamn about anything she said, but he liked it near her. You had something to lean against, her tits to play with, and she smelled so nice and fresh, her shoulders were so thin and childlike, and she kissed so chastely with her depraved lips, which were small and hard and would not open. Höllriegl kissed her often and thoroughly in order to stop all that shop talk. And then there was that strange giant, undoubtedly a personality, in that terribly expensive river-otter coat—he stressed the price right away—who reminded him of someone, but of whom? (Oh yes, his homeroom teacher in high school, old Tartaglia!) A secretive man, white-haired, sunburned, had come directly, so he said, from Switzerland. He had a slightly deranged look and smiled with the corners of his mouth pulled down deeply. Again: a personality! The man explained that he had been director of that Spanish-Moroccan company "Hisma," which in 1936 had arranged the air transport of Franco's troops to the Civil War front. ("I'd just as soon not tell you my name.") Christ, Tartaglia. How far away all that was! Gone and forgotten. Tartaglia, the confirmed bachelor: German, History, and Geography. Born in Trieste, he had been honorary president of the Schnauzer Club in Urfahr. And his fellow students—what had happened to them? Scattered across the world, dead, missing, one or the other killed in battle. He still knew all their names in alphabetic order: from Brill, Calé, Christlieb, to Vaik, Walch, and Zwerenz—and the only girl in the class: Gritti Ledwinka.

Shit, how his head hurt! For several minutes he closed his sand-clogged eyes. Someone began to hammer in his brain. The factory expert had moved away and now talked with some of the others, so he could put his pounding head on the tabletop. Sleep, sleep, not to know anything! He felt absolutely lousy, the noise, the drink, the smoke—it could make you puke.

Where was Axel? With great effort, Höllriegl tried to think clearly, to see clearly. The boy was gone! Where, at what table had he left him behind? He looked about him. Horrible! Nothing but strange animal faces. None of the people were left who had given Axel and him food and drink when they arrived. Desperately he shouted: "Axel!" And again: "Axel!" The Euratom girl moved closer, embraced him; he pushed her away.

Axel—gone.

Dizziness and nausea. Stiff neck. Eye cramp. Despair. As he tried to stand up, his legs failed him, and he felt that they were cold and stiff. Horror shook him, sweat ran down his forehead. He whined "Axel" and fell back onto the bench. Voices, many voices, surged across him.

Prostata the ladies . . . there he is my husband . . . why sure, man . . . I don't want a thing . . . empty your glass, old man . . . well, so what? . . . were you lucky . . . that funeral is going to be a great production . . . look, fatso, a little brandy . . . then we'll just use nerve gas or climate weapons and it'll be all over . . . get your hand out of there . . . that's what you think . . . for fifteen Pfennige? . . . that guy has been a dead ass hole for so long . . . what, the carpet eater? . . . heaven is blue and black is the hole, white is the horse, in it must . . . right in the kisser . . . but Emmi is the Herr Betriebsführer's sperm collector . . . and if the prices for used cars go up strongly . . . and no one thinks a thing about it . . . girl, girl, do I love you . . . it's all shit! Tastes are different . . .

The carpet eater? Somebody had really said that, had the nerve to say a thing like that. Who was the dirty bastard? Höllriegl saw in his mind's eye how a mighty atomic mushroom shot into the sky, lighting it up like a thunderstorm, but then it was more an eruption of muck and mud—a volcano of mud—curse words, the oldest, stinkingest, dirtiest, were whirled up out of the deep and spurted about. Muck! Had not Gundlfinger said something very similar? The oldest, most primitive things returned to the surface? And at once—it was marvelous, wonderful—the apparition broadened and branched into a tree of life. Marvelous, thrice marvelous! This was not a tree of life; it was the Führer's ancestor chart, which hung on his wall at home and which he knew by heart. Hitler Alois, customs official, later farmer, and Klara Pölzl; both died in Leonding. . . . Healthy, German, Ostmarkian peasant blood. And these criminals insulted the greatest of all Germans —had called him a rabble rouser! Who had said that? He'd smash his teeth in and shake his skull. But where was Axel? Axel! Axel!

Höllriegl rose slowly. He swayed and held his head with both hands. Where was he? It was hard to open his eyes and keep them open. Again everything was blurred and purple-edged. A stinging pain pounded against his temples, and he had to turn his hands about constantly because his joints were stiff and lifeless. He was cold.

No one paid any attention to what he did. Once again he watched the others with a feeling of tremendous distance between them. The whole thing was a distortion, a dream, delusion. Over there some woman was being auctioned off, at least it looked that way. She was young and pretty and very drunk, wheat-blond like his amber witch, but much younger. With her slim legs she stood swaying on the table and had to be supported by many hands or she would have fallen off. A man with a blue-red head and leathern neck—but he knew him, surely?—kept shouting something, although he could only see how he tore his mouth open and banged it shut again. No one could understand the auctioneer, but each of his words drew a roar of laughter.

Carpet eater. Quick, he had to slug somebody. Fury boiled high. Or was it his stomach juices? He'd make an example of someone. The Führer was only—how many days had the Führer been dead? Today was the how-manyeth day? Ah, shit. But now something had to happen very quickly, no matter what. Something drastic, a chastisement, that bunch of swine had forgotten who the Führer was. Two ridiculous atom bombs dropped on Reich territory, and those motherfuckers had forgotten who Adolf Hitler was. He'd hold court.

It happened very fast. With clenched fists he stumbled toward the auctioneer. The Euratom brain screamed, he had brushed her off like a flea. Höllriegl got the leatherneck from behind. As he turned, Höllriegl hit him as hard as he could, flush in the face. It was soft and flabby; for a second Höllriegl felt the badly shaved cheek. He hit him again and again (that swine sold biscuits for the last time).

They all dispersed and screamed in confusion. Höllriegl was grabbed by the collar, dragged back, thrown hither and thither; then someone threw him onto the floor and knelt on his belly. A choking grip. He heard his own panting. The cold fury and exertion sobered him. He rolled back and forth. First he tried the follow-me grip he had learned in the SA, then the Heil-to-you-my-Führer grip. Joints cracked, or were they finger bones? Open-hand uppercut against his opponent's chin, karate chop against the elbows, kick in the face. He saw the bloodshot eyes of a stranger. A chop to the kidney—it was like the German drill. Howling, groaning, moaning.

A horrible uproar erupted above the thrashing bodies as people tramped over them. It seemed as if the whole world were beating him, but Höllriegl didn't feel a thing. Axel! Axel!

He tried to crawl under a table, take cover, escape. Axel! Axel!

He had a metallic, sweetish-nauseous taste in his mouth. He still saw how people knocked each other about and tables were overturned. Someone kicked him in the neck, a flash shot through his brain. Abruptly the light went out. It became night—and nothing was left.

THE BURIAL IN THE KYFFHAÜSER

November 17: a wintry, cold Sunday morning. A storm had blustered the whole night through, and the windows on the west side of Höllriegl's house were badly shaken. But by early morning the clouds were gone; a pale, clean-swept sky arched over Heydrich, the sun rose radiantly. Hitler weather, Höllriegl thought ruefully as he looked up. Jet trails hung high in the blue.

He had not slept all night and not just because of the storm: A great clatter had risen from the streets. At three in the morning the first of endless rows of marchers had moved out of barracks, SS bivouacs, and cantonments, to take up carefully selected posts around the Kyffhäuser. All the roads into the area were clogged, and people surged through Heydrich itself. Great mobs of people had made the pilgrimage, the enemy's terror raids notwithstanding. They came from every *Gau* in the Reich—on foot, in cars, by train, often under the most difficult of circumstances and at great personal hardship. The Reich's railways had made a superhuman effort to accommodate everyone despite widespread destruction of track and depot, and had dispatched hundreds of special trains. Some Hitler Youth units reportedly had started out for the Goldene Aue right after the news of the Führer's death was published, even though Köpfler had not announced the burial in the Kyffhäuser until his November 11 speech to the Reich Council.

Moreover, something quite strange had happened: Not a shot had been fired since noon on Saturday. Was the enemy paying tribute to the dead Führer, the great ally in World War II? Or had the Japs simply quit? Höllriegl (and everyone else) knew that heavy retaliatory attacks had hit the Japanese home islands, China, Manchuria, and other parts of the Japanese-controlled mainland. At least four H-bombs had detonated on target—enough to knock the East right out of the war, at least for all practical purposes. Rumors flew. A reliable source in the "parliament" had told Höllriegl the same mutiny story the washing-machine salesman in the air-raid shelter had only hinted at, but this time with full details. The few radio bulletins could not give a clear picture of the situation. So far not a single, comprehensive Wehrmacht report had been published, only scattered dispatches. Unusual, but in a way reassuring. And yet! There was something uncanny in this undeclared armistice—as if a great terror were coming closer and closer.

My nerves are shot, Höllriegl thought, and I'm overtired. He froze. An icy wind blew through the apartment. Burjak had destroyed the electric heating system. Burjak! He had cut out during Höllriegl's absence, had stolen a brown shirt as well as Höllriegl's old SA blouse and cap (Sturm 46/Standarte 107, red-brown collar patch). But apparently he had kept his canvas pants, the hallmark of a forced laborer—hard to believe. In addition were missing a fur-lined windbreaker, a pair of army boots, and Höllriegl's old knapsack from his days in the student SA. The pantry was cleaned out, even the ration cards were gone. Höllriegl had reported everything to the police and Party Headquarters. But good God, was it just his imagination? The officials had seemed disinterested in what he told them and took down the information in routine fashion. He had been issued an emergency ration card.

There was nothing for it but to install a beat-up old stove whose funnel stuck out the window. It didn't give much warmth, and the fire kept going out. But Höllriegl had other reasons for bitterness. He had come home sure of finding his call-up orders. But nothing! Only a mountain of letters from patients awaited him. What was up? Had he been forgotten, or did they want to push him aside? Didn't they trust him? Yes, he was an outsider; he didn't belong. Goddamn! And then Burjak had smashed a tube in the TV set. That hit hardest. Telephone and radio were in working order, and the lights and hot plate were intact too—the hot plate even gave off some heat.

Höllriegl switched on the radio. The "Fehrbelliner March," and right after it "We Wolves Howl at Night." What he had never admitted openly, not even to good friends, could not admit, was that he had treated Burjak decently—like a servant, not a serf. That galled him now. Here too he had failed. The rogue must have seen it as a sign of weakness. He, Albin Totila Höllriegl, would never be a true member of the master race, able to rule over others. Neither Ulla nor Anselma, not even his own Ingrid. True, she was utterly devoted to him, but only because he took her to bed once a week.

How disgusting it all was. He'd lost the VW just outside Berga. For all he knew, the wreck still lay in a ditch there next to other derelicts on the great refugee road to the northeast. A crash—a smashed engine. Some idiot had slammed into his tail. His head still buzzed, but it had buzzed before. Nothing but losses. And Axel! It hurt to think of the boy, almost as much as when he thought of Ulla. . . . Landgrave, Get Tough.

Höllriegl had gone to see Kummernuss right after his return to arrange about the stolen gun. Kummernuss, who had no wife (they were divorced, an infertility divorce), lay in bed with a pain-twisted face; he had suffered an attack of his famous calf cramps and still hadn't recovered ("a complication: pleurisy"). His serf, a half-wit from the Bukovina (in Roumania), was still there. A dog whip hung next to the bed.

They discussed the situation. Kummernuss, who served in a communications unit, said he didn't have an extra car but did know a black-market man who worked as an auto mechanic with the SS Motorstandarte 86 in Sonderhausen. The man would surely have a Volkswagen or perhaps even an Opel Kadett in good shape. As a last resort, Höllriegl could still drive one of the *Kyffhäuser Messenger*'s cars. Given the growing shortage of gas, that might well be the smartest thing to do anyway.

Kummernuss, who kept massaging his calf, suddenly grimaced. Not exactly like a thinker; rather like someone who has trouble with a crossword puzzle. "You remember when the U-Two-Oh-Nine fired on a Japanese bomber and supposedly set off an atomic explosion? That meant the Jap had an A-bomb on board—a small one—and that gave us the pretext to retaliate in kind. A pretext, you understand."

Kummernuss fell to musing and brooded for a while. "No, don't worry about that shitty pistol. I'll have my brother-in-law fix that up, or through the secret police boss in the parliament—Vitzdumm, you know him. In the meantime, take one of my things. . . ." He switched on the radio. ". . . on the basis of an amendment to the conservation decree of March 18, 1936, it is now forbidden to damage or remove the following wild plants . . ."

Höllriegl kept thinking about Kummernuss' remarks. For the third time today he relit the fire in the oven. A lot of smoke and little heat. Then he made himself some camomile tea and gruel. He had to take care of every stupid little thing himself. Whenever Ingrid had any free time, she had to work with the women's organization. But, most disgusting, ever since that stupid drinking bout at the inn he was suffering from diarrhea and therefore didn't dare go out of the house. He had to run to the john every minute.

He glanced over the mail from patients with a distracted and disparaging air—prostate trouble, cancer nodes, impotence, circulatory cramps, disrupted sleep. The holiest thing, the Reich, was in danger, but people only bothered about their own aches and pains. Since his return the letters had lain unattended on the sofa, and piles of printed matter, magazines, and newsletters had accumulated in his office. He didn't feel like doing anything. His constant running even spoiled the comfort he found in listening to the radio.

A rhythmic yelling drifted up from the Hindenburg Avenue. Although the authorities had ordered silent marches, and one of Köpfler's appeals to commemorate the day in dignified fashion had been read on the radio, spontaneous political demonstrations erupted everywhere, especially among the many foreign delegations. This time Höllriegl heard the rhythmic national slogan of the Americans, the battle cry of the Minutemen: "Com-mér-cial, Com-mér-cial! Com-mér-cial!" Equally rythmic shouts of "Siegheil!" rose in reply.

In case the charcoal finally stopped his bowels—as a nature healer he abhorred synthetic drugs—Dr. Senkpiehl would pick him up in his car between four and five. Senkpiehl's specialty was German soul research, but he had received orders to act as a physician on the burial day, and would have to work with the local sanitation corps. Perhaps then they'd be able to see at least part of the festivities. To lie in bed with a hot-water bottle on your belly on this great day was an affliction of God.

Höllriegl listened idly to the radio all day. He couldn't concentrate on reading. Before daybreak it had been announced that all networks not in enemy territory or directly involved in the war were to be hooked into the Reich's network. Worldwide radio and TV coverage thus seemed assured, though not without attendant ironies. Sir William Joyce, the legendary "Lord Haw-Haw" of World-War-II fame, anchored the English broadcast. After the overwhelming triumph of German arms, Joyce had returned to England where he had been knighted but had then dropped from sight.

An announcer was describing Adolf Hitler's funeral garb. According to ancient Nordic tradition, the corpse was swaddled in the *Valhjamr,* and over this was the Führer's customary uniform: brown shirt, long black trousers, the swastika armband—exactly as the world knew him. On his chest lay only two medals of the Kaiser's army: the Iron Cross Second Class, won in December, 1914, and the Iron Cross First Class bestowed on the then-private first class four years later. The Führer's will apparently prohibited embalming him or casting a death mask. (The masks that were promptly distributed to high party officers—and just as promptly appeared in the stores—were made from a bust, appropriately retouched.) Strange: In the newspaper photos, Hitler's hair for the first time looked snow-white!

The tomb had been erected over the remains of Kyffhausen Castle near the Kaiser Wilhelm Memorial, according to plans made secretly by the departed leader. It resembled Theodoric's mausoleum at Ravenna, but on a gigantic scale, in the best tradition of the old Nibelungen film sets. For the moment this monstrous construction had been slapped together as backdrop for the funeral: The real monument would probably take a generation to build. In a chamber hewn from rock deep within the mountain would rest the simple oaken coffin, bedecked only with an unpretentious laurel wreath—from the rostrum in the Forum Romanum. A side chamber would house the heraldry and insignia of the Reich, watched by an eternal guard. The Reich jewels, including the golden Scythian crown of Kerch, would be taken from the Meistersinger Church of Nuremberg to be carried before the dead Führer.

Bulletins, descriptions, speeches. In between the announcer reeled off the endless groups and organizations marching through the Goldene Aue and now approaching the Kyffhäuser from all sides, even though it had been declared a restricted zone on the Führer's death. There were no refugees, no panic. The war was forgotten. A world in mourning found itself united at the side of the greatest German.

The hours dragged by. Höllriegl's mood brightened as he realized that many Hitler Youth units had arrived to bid farewell to the Führer. Hitler Youth from the Northland; Hitler Youth from Brunswick, the city of Henry the Lion; Hitler Youth from the Ostmark, from the Middle Rhein, from Hesse, from the Saar-Palatinate. And thousands of members of the GYE (German Youth East), the young German settlers in the East. And the exhilarating parade of the Hitler Youth squadrons! Höllriegl's eyes moistened as always at the strains of their proud song: "Arise, unfurl our flags in the crisp morning air!" It all refuted the rumors that part—some even said most—of the Reich's youth had gone over the the Werewolf. A shiver of delight ran down his spine whenever the radio mentioned his fellow countrymen.

". . . SS Upper Sector Danube, led by Upper Sector Commander Schmöllerl. The Ostmark Detachment of the SS Special Task Force and the Ostmark Detachment of the SS Corps Death's Head. The marchers of the historic SA group Danube who received their final orders for the journey during drill exercises in Pöchlarn, the fabled Bechelaren of the *Nibelungenlied.*

"The Salzburg, Innsbruck and Laibach garrisons of the Reich Athletic League SS. The Strength-Through-Joy Sport Superintendents from Vienna. A delegation from the revolutionary city of Graz, at its head the mayor, SS Brigadier Sepp Schoissengeyer. . . ."

The parade continued kaleidescopically for hours. "Fraternities of the National Socialist German Student Union and their alumni: Young Boys, Boys, and Old Boys in full regalia. Now the political leaders: the executors of the party. And here come the SS Regiment 'The Führer' and the SS Regiment 'Germany.' SS General Killinger at the head of his men. Roars of 'Heil' (reverberating over the air) greet the Death's Head Reinforcements charged with Special Duties in the SHC's. The Prefect for the Eastern Territories, General of the Military-SS von Bessemer. A group of Great Skalds, the poetry prizewinners: in the forefront we recognize our great national bard, that valiant silverhaired warrior of the pen, Hans Henning Weinhold ("Heil! Heil!") and this year's winner of the Joseph Goebbels' Memorial Prize, Utz Saemund Griper. Next the Brown Sisters of the NS National Social Service from Wonnegau. The Lord Mayor of Worms, Horst Bagge. The giants of the Berlin Guard Regiment "Old Fritz"—a trumpet major at least seven feet tall in an old Prussian uniform is carrying the lead Glockenspiel. A delegation of the Society of Reich Workmen. Men and women of the Reich Civil Defense Unit in radiation-proof uniforms and gas masks with CDU Führer Ingomar Wunderlich at their head. The House of German Law from Munich, represented by a delegation under the leadership of Supreme Court President Dr. Manfred Sitte. The President of the District Court in Celle, Dr. Juergen Schoiswohl. The crew of the spaceship 'Mooneater.' (Again a surge of "Heils.") The Rector of the High School for Physical Education in Leipzig, Dr.-Dr. Giso von Jahn-Hegel. The German Gymnastic Front, represented by. . . ."

Höllriegl wanted to borrow some oatmeal from his neighbor, a retired needlework teacher named Luitgard Perchta Eberlein, a dedicated party member since 1931. He was out of it and the stores had closed at noon the day before. The old maid was devoted to him, bless her. (She'd love it if I slipped it to her, he said to himself. But he wanted none of that with her. Therefore control, self-control!) Once when he had been constipated for a long time—the condition alternated with his diarrhea—she had even given him an enema. That time things had almost gone too far. He must control himself!

". . . the flags, banners, and battle standards of the Movement are all hung in black. Be stern, comrades, be brave; do not let your emotions show. You have tears in your eyes, men! The banners wave brightly in the morning wind—our Führer sees them no longer! And each of you men must vow: Do with us what you want, oh Hitler, up there among the stars. We thank you even for this bitter hour! We belong to you for all time, as always. Our only aim —Eternal Germany . . ."

". . . when you ask these Hitler Youths what held the deepest meaning in their march to the Kyffhäuser, you get the same answer again and again: 'Our banners which we bring to the Führer. We are proud, enormously proud, to be allowed to carry these holy flags on the way into eternity for you, Adolf Hitler!' And sometimes when the wind whistles through the flags, it is as if your hand gripped them . . . from where the blast furnaces burn and chimneys smoke, from shores where the waves spend themselves on the sand, from heath and forest, from the great cities and smallest villages, they throng the roads toward Heydrich. Not death nor privation, not bomb nor blockade, not the Yellow Devil himself can stop this march, this proof of the unity and valor of our . . . Nordic man awakens anew as from a thousand-year sleep. With fresh eyes he looks at a world beginning to change with the death of the Führer and Reich's founder. The Nordic giant realizes that he is caught in a delusion . . . amidst the whirlwind war cries, the roaring surge of threatening prophecies and dark intentions, in a world full of murder and avarice, this Kyffhäuser mountain, the mountain of Friedrich Barbarossa, becomes a refuge of peace and meditation. At the same time it is a fortress, the rock on which . . ."

Höllriegl knocked on his neighbor's door. He was still numb, as if lightning had struck him. The old maid opened up hesitantly, trembling like an aspen leaf. Did he too already know? she asked. Know what?

"The Führer—it wasn't natural."

"The Führer—*what?*"

"The Führer"—her voice sank to a hoarse whisper—". . . didn't die a natural death."

The scene in the underground mine flashed before Höllriegl's eyes. "Listen to what I tell you, and pass it on. . . ." Old Fräulein Eberlein was close to fainting. Höllriegl had to support her back into her tiny sitting room. There of course she had her little "brown corner" with its pictures, emblems, slogans ("the Party thinks for you") and a bronze-tinted plaster bust of Hitler draped in black crepe. A shrine like many found in other homes: even the exemplary Kummernuss had one, and Damaschke in his janitor's quarters.

"Köpfler," she whispered. "The Werewolf . . ." Where did she get the story? "One person tells another. The whole city knows it." She quickly gave him the oatmeal and some zwieback and pushed him out the door. "I'd like to crawl into a hole," she moaned. "I am dying of fright."

He heard her lock herself in with both keys and throw the latch, sobbing loudly. What absolute nonsense! She should be reported. She? Had *he* denounced Unseld and Diebold? Or the Underground with them? Or Gundlfinger? Or Axel?

He couldn't think straight. His head spun as if he were drunk. This paralyzing feeling of a stiff neck! And now a major announcement on the radio: the foreign delegations. Impossible to concentrate. His "other head" came, and went again. Again he half listened as he fixed his cereal. "Listen to what I tell you, and pass it on." That tormented, unforgettable voice!

Roaring shouts of "Siegheil." ". . . and at their head the leader of the Italian Social Republic: Italo Vinciguerra. (Endless calls of "Siegheil!" and "Evviva!") Behind him the delegation of the Great Fascist Council under the leadership of war hero Ercole Farinacci. (Shouts of "Evviva!" and the strains of *"Giovinezza."*) The Secretary General of the Fascist Party, Marcello Prati, with seven Federal Secretaries . . . A delegation of the Fascist Militia led by Commander in Chief Count Giorgio della Rovere. (*Siegheil! Siegheil!*) Balilla Leader 'Carlino' Granvella with his aide-de-camp Ugo Sangiorgio. The chairman of the Fascist Press Assembly, Commodore Lorenzo Malfoto. The Honorary President of the Fascio Berlin, Dr. Juergen von Asenwimmer. . . ."

He had tried and tried to put the terrible thought from his mind. To no avail. Others, many others, had had the same thought. The Führer was . . . (A swelling crest of "Heil.")

". . . behind the aged Caudillo, who is wearing his historic general's uniform of 1936, comes a delegation of the Great Council of the Phalanx of Traditionalist Spain under the leadership of Secretary General of the Party, Ramón Cristóbal Nuñez de Larra y Ortiz. A delegation of Castilian bluebloods under the leadership of the Marquès de las Casas and the Cardinal Archbishop of Burgos, Gaspar de Jabirù. A delegation of the Order of the Knights of Santiago . . . And here come the Perónista cohorts, their bronzed and weathered faces defiant, their raised right arms greeting the dead Führer of the German peoples. Leading them is (thunderous cries of "Heil Perón! Heil Perón! Heil Perón!") . . . followed by the vanguard of the historic Organization Tacuara and the men of the Death's Head Auxiliary Odessa, the Organization of Former SS Members of the Provinces of Buenos Aires, Santa Fé, and

Tucumán. In their midst the national heroes Rudel, Galland, and Mengele. The rear is brought up by the dread Piranha SS of Guaiana."

Calls of "Siegheil!" reached a crescendo, overwhelming the announcer. But the raucous Wild West battle cry of the North Americans cut rhythmically through: Com-mér-cial! Com-mér-cial! Com-mér-cial! The delegation from the United Vassal States of America. The announcer, whose voice fought slowly through the din, described them flourishing their ten-gallon hats as they drove their bullet-proof limousines at snail's pace through the crowds.

". . . we recognize the representative of the Ku Klux Triumvirate, Senator William Washington Wagonner, called 'Double-U, Double-U, Double-U,' who has come across the big water in place of ailing Führer General Fazlollah. We greet the nine-man team of the 'Invisible Empire' league in their white mantles and white hoods, the state secretaries Roy 'Tarzan' Stuvengen, Bart M. Prefabber, Georgie Hank Squire, Rail Tycoon Jay Gould Hogg, Mackie Macbeth Hueffer, and Harry S. Gnome. We greet the Führer of the glorious Minutemen . . ." (at that moment the roar of "Siegheil!" and "Heil!" grew to such volume that the small radio threatened to explode.) ". . . Ted Akimbo; the Führer of the All-American NS Organization, John Adolf MacKinley; the Führer of the Aryan Crusade Movement, TV producer Lewis 'Hi Fi' Colorado; the Führer of 'We the People,' Dr. Sheldon Pryce; the Führer of the All-American League for Racial Enterprise, Franklin 'Bayard' Skindiver; the Chairman of the Union of Gentile American Businessmen of the South, Virgil O'Peewee; the President of the Hash, Dash, and Cash bank group, Gene Fatso Donohue; the Führer of the National Indignation Convention (NIC), Lloyd F. Kindelberger; the Führer of the Young Men's Aryan Association (YMAA) and of the All-American Hitler Youth, Irwin Jimmy Guiffre; the Führer of the glorious American Legion, Clarence A. Bugaboo; the Führer of the All-American Commercial Church, Father Rhyne; the spokesman of the All-American Holy Trade Association, the Reverend Hiram C. Susskind, also known as the 'Loudspeaker of the Almighty'; the Führer of the Knights of the New Order, Hughie Popcorn Stelle, and the President of the All-America Chamber of Commerce, Harold P. Updegruff. We also send greetings to the brotherhood of the 'Holy Killers' led by General William Salem Schwob; the fearless cosmonauts S. Ranger Nitribit, Dwight Hal Shuster, and S. A. Yevdokimov; the President of the National Blood and Soil Corporation, Duncan Hee Highfalutin. We welcome a delegation of the brave Knights of Columbus in their colorful costumes, capes, swords, and feathered hats, led by the Governor of Wisconsin, E. Neville Stronghold; the vice-president of the McCarthy Freedom Forum, John Ford O'Maille; then Jim Buck Clewes (a surge of "Siegheil!" and "Heil!") at the head of the feared rednecks; the President of the National Broadcasting System 'The Voice of America,' Gus 'Boaster' Andrews; the Chairman of the House Committee of the Investigation of Un-American Activities, Judge T. Himmler Parnell . . ."

Höllriegl lowered the volume and tried to force himself to read Schultze-Rüssing or Schubert's *Why believe in God?* or Schneidmädl's *Explanations to Bormann's Major Theses.* Impossible. He couldn't concentrate. Serious study was love's labor lost. When he read in Rüssing a detailed description of impalement, his thoughts wandered to Ulla. . . .

". . . a delegation of the Nordiska Radet under the leadership of the aged Vidkun Quisling ("Siegheil! Siegheil! Siegheil! Siegheil!") A delegation from the Anglo-Saxon protectorate under the leadership of Reich Protector Freiherr von Börlitz and the party leader, SS Obergruppenführer Sir Oswald Adolf Mosley. Worthy veterans follow: a delegation from the Breton Free State led by Marcel Déat, members of the Great Council of Burgundy, at their head Chancellor Léon Degrelle, Reich Commissar General Vlassow with a delegation from the Leagues of the Caucasus, Transcaucasus, and Little Russia. The former Governor-General Dr. Hans Frank (endless Heils.) Members of the Iron Guard and the Rumanian state youth. A crossed arrow delegation from Atlinik (as Budapest was sometimes called now) and Horthy-Varos. Hlinka guardsmen from Slovakia in their historic uniforms—and now the Boers! ("Siegheil, siegheil, siegheil.") First a delegation of the Council of Elders of the Afrikaaner Republic, the Orange Free State and Transvaal. Behind them march detachments of the Boer SA from the free states. We can hear the battle cry of the Boers, 'Baaskap', even in our sound-proof cabin. . . . now the Count of Jerusalem passes by, a handsome old man in his picturesque dress, accompanied by Knights from the land of the German Order (formerly Palestine). . . ."

Shortly before four—Höllriegl had spent tormented and nervous hours cursing his inactivity and waiting for Senkpiehl to arrive—the majestic, thrilling tone of the lures sounded from the radio. It was the signal that the great mountain entombment, and thus the high point of the funeral service, had been reached.

". . . the brown columns and black cadres have been drawn up. They resembled endless army trains as they marched through the streets to the Kyffhäuser. Sorrow dampens their steps. Slowly blocks of marchers cover the meadows and hillsides."

The announcer's voice sounded deep and full of pain. (It struck Höllriegl that the brown-shirted SA had been mentioned first—that had to be intentional. A concession to the Bundschuh? It was well known that many in the SS were sympathetic to the Werewolf . . .)

"Dusk descends on the multitude. The woods send their greeting—black, sorrowful, solemn. Searchlights illuminate the black-draped flags and the wide square into whose center the tiger tank carrying the mortal remains of the Führer and Reich founder . . . the gigantic fronts of two tribunals, filled with funeral guests from all over the world, radiate in magical floodlight. Pylon-fires burn slowly at the sides of the tribunal.

"Shortly before the arrival of Ivo Köpfler, the man to whom the immortal founder of the world empire handed the torch to be borne to a new morrow of victory and salvation, all lights will be extinguished. Only the flags and standards will remain faintly illuminated. The anticipation of hundreds of thousands has reached its peak.

"Now a command. Once more the batallions of the movement dress ranks. They are the advance guard of that great German People's Army filled with sorrow, but also with pride in the new leadership, which has lined up in spirit here. (Again a fanfare of lures.) Ivo Adolf Köpfler and the entire Führer Corps of the world empire have taken up their posts at the door of the western tribunal. They await the dead man—for that which was mortal in Adolf Hitler. His immortal spirit, however, imbues and steels all who are called upon to defend his holy inheritance and secure it for all future times.

"The mighty, scar-bedecked tiger tank, which took part in the victorious march of German armies to the east and has been painted black for this its last journey, has rolled up—on it rests the simple oaken casket containing the dead Führer of all the Germans. The tank is alone, the vehicles of the retinue have remained behind. Deep, awe-struck silence lies across the wide square. The great removal into the mountains has begun.

"Ivo Adolf Köpfler steps forward—he is bareheaded. And now, accompanied by a distant choir, begins this indescribable passage, this solemn passage of gratitude which the German people owe the dead Reich founder. Only Köpfler's aides, Reich Minister and Gauleiter Uwe Heckroth and Reichsorganisationsleiter Dr. Markward, walk behind this man—great in his humility in the face of death.

"Amid the sound of the lures and the funeral fanfares, Ivo Köpfler walks to the black altar of steel on which Adolf Hitler's corpse rests. The silence of thousands upon thousands is around him.

"Köpfler stands before the catafalque. With raised right hand he honors the greatest dead in German history—and with him all the heroes who in their devotion to Adolf Hitler and the German people, have given their lives. Köpfler's voice sounds through the darkness: 'My Führer, I report to you the whole German people gathered here for the last roll call!' At the same moment these words are heard in the most distant corners of the earth.

"The command 'Helmets off for prayer!' rings out. The helmets, the caps of hundreds of thousands—this great, wonderful German people's army—are off, the historic standards of the political Movement dip to honor the dead. In the silence of these seconds and minutes it is easy to hear the tread of history.

"Now the Junkers of Dankwarderode and Crössingen have begun to sing. They sing 'Holy Germany.' They sing for all those who have gathered here. A muffled roll of drums. Ivo Köpfler stands immobile before Adolf Hitler's coffin, a picture of collected power. A voice calls out; it is young and radiant and rises like an eagle into the sky. 'In you, immortal Führer, we honor the dead of our Movement.' A Wehrmacht band plays into the sudden silence the 'Argonnerwald March' and the 'Song of the Good Comrade.' " (Music fades in.)

"And now Ivo Adolf Köpfler and his adjutants return. 'Flags in equal step, march!' Now the mighty square formed by the standards advances amid the martial strains of the 'Badenweiler March,' filling the square with pulsating life. The storm flags close rank and pour past the tribunal in a victorious train, high above the ramparts on which the black and brown cohorts" (this time the SS was mentioned first.) "stand like walls. The flood of flying red flags disappears in the passageways the blocks of marchers have left open. But some of the flags remain behind, and these are now grouping themselves into eight small ribbons that radiate out from the square with Adolf Hitler's bier.

"All at once the searchlight beams have flamed again into the evening sky, bundles of light beams rise up, strive together, unite, and build above the silent multitude a cathedral of fluid blue light.

"Majestically this cathedral of lights—this German cathedral of lights—arches over us all. What an unforgettable display! Almost too beautiful, too powerful, for the mind to grasp. The Wehrmacht has placed thousands of searchlights around the Schlachtenberg, which now shoot their rays high into the ether of night. These glittering fasces are built into a wall of light around the dark circle of the Kyffhäuser Mountains. And the mass of light, which in the infinity up there forms the initials *A* and *H,* has built the gigantic cupola of this German cathedral. . . ."

Höllriegl had listened with an expression that grew progressively more pious. His chin dropped in sheer devotion, his mouth gaped. His face turned childish, soft and blurred, he dissolved as if under the impact of music. He strained to listen and not lose a word, but did not understand everything the announcer said. He was cold, his thoughts were feverish and giddy, wandering and lost. Accursed fate that forced him to inactivity on a day such as this! (On top of everything else, this unmanly, unseemly illness.) Waiting, waiting. This exhausting waiting! He went to the window and for a long time looked into the flaming splendor of the sky. A picture of enormous beauty and power—that was it! He could not distinguish the Führer's initials, the light blinded him too much. A stinging pain in the eyeballs made him close his lids. God knows he didn't feel well, he was sick. Where was Senkpiehl? Why in heaven's name didn't he at least call? It was almost five—high time! Once again he dialed the number, his hands trembling. No one answered. Senkpiehl was out, of course, perhaps already on his way here. Probably he could only get through the crowds and guards at a snail's pace, if at all. But they'd have to let a doctor on duty pass.

A vigorous voice boomed from the loudspeaker. The speeches had begun. ". . . in this hour of reflection, when we take our leave of Adolf the Great, when the existence of the Reich and the Western world is at stake, when mean hordes from the depths of Asia, bloodthirsty subhumans such as history has never witnessed, have set out to rob the German people of the fruits of the greatest victory of all time, to enslave and destroy it, we wish to give this pledge of allegiance to the new Führer." A cascade of Heils and an endless chorus of "Death to Japan" ". . . A thousand years of German history . . ." The voice was drowned in an incredible uproar from which, gradually, a sharply scanning chorus emerged: "Heil Köpfler! Heil Köpf-ler! Heil Köpf-ler! Heil Köpf-ler! Heil Köpf-ler! . . ."

And Ulla? Where was she? The scar still burned on his forehead. She had beaten him like a dog—she was magnificent! Whipped him! But he would kneel before her again, whine, even bring her a whip. . . .

". . . to turn the tide. The archenemy of the white race has tried" (again and again: "Europe Awake, Down with Japan!") ". . . the yellow devils have tried to overrun our continent; they have not hesitated to unleash the terror of atomic war. We have struck back, struck back terribly" (an uproar of Siegheil and the beating of drums) "and silenced them. The responsibility before history does not rest with us who with unparalleled patience watched the criminal activity of the Soka Gakkai . . ." (a chorus of "Gakkai perish") ". . . and his imperialist warmongers. They alone bear . . ."

Was Ulla still in Germany? He had to find her. Now, at once. But how? Impossible to get through the mob. On foot? Or could he do it after all? To fight through all obstacles, as the German people had to fight.

". . . our place in the sun . . . subhumans, beasts, the revolt of the apocalyptic animal . . . a clique of criminals such as never existed in the long and bloody history of mankind . . . ejected from hell . . . a world conspiracy . . . and the aristocracy of blood . . . the holiness . . . the mission of the heroic, Aryan, helio-Germanic race . . . the blond, light, heavenly . . . racially beautiful people . . . in our castles and breeding monasteries . . . our master religion . . . they have made a Jew out of Frauja . . . Adolf Hitler was the reincarnation of the Saviour . . . and again a savior has arisen: in Ivo Köpfler. . . ." (a storm of Siegheils and drums).

What a scandal that he couldn't concentrate on this great and holy hour! Ulla! Ulla's body! This body was German, was German reality, bursting with strength: solid, sinewy . . .

". . . has the purpose of strengthening the striking power of our people and its Wehrmacht spiritually and materially. Our fanaticism in the destruction of those who dare resist it must be as great. We promise you that, Adolf Hitler. There are among us some grumblers, fault-finders, men of little faith and other malcontents who have not yet understood, or do not want to understand, that a tough, dangerous time demands tough men, men of steel and iron, men with a dog's sharp teeth, men with atomic power and laser pistols in their hands. This new, tough, dangerous time is symbolized on this continent by the new Führer" (an uproar of Siegheils that lasted for several minutes) ". . . by the new Führer Ivo Adolf Köpfler and by no one else . . . by Ivo Köpfler, the man who received from the hands of the immortal founder of the world empire the testament . . ."

Ulla! Her breasts, her thighs, her lap, her smell! The fine blond hairs on her arms! To be beaten by her! To be beaten once more! To be allowed to embrace her, as he had that time . . .

Finally, at about half past six, the doorbell rang. Senkpiehl, harassed, bewildered, was at the door. The usually so calm and lofty man seemed enormously excited. "I kept ringing," he called out as he rushed into the room. "Hurry up, man, if you want to come along—but I can't recommend it. I have to go to Berga. I got my orders by radio: Kilometer sign fifty-two. That's where my column is. Do you know everything already?"

While Höllriegl got ready, Senkpiehl began to talk like a waterfall, at first nervous and stumbling, later with self-possession and his own brand of irony.

It had begun with a strange incident that had plunged people into a kind of frenzy. ("Mass hysteria, you know.") On the new serpentine highway which led around the Schlachtberg to the summit, two young girls had suddenly torn through the double chain of guards. "It's a mystery how they did it." They had thrown themselves in front of the tank with the Führer's coffin. Their bodies were literally ground into pulp, and a fire company later had to clean chains, fan, and rolling gear. The sacrificial death of the two girls had an incredible impact on the audience—unexpectedly joyous, liberating, almost a kind of exultation. For the girls had shouted with joy as they threw themselves in front of the tank; then the breaking of the bones, a soft, characteristic noise which only those up close could hear. Fewer guards had been posted on the open mountain road, so the mob did not have much trouble reaching the armored bier. The tank was surrounded and some climbed quickly on top. There were even a few who danced and shouted, smeared the girls' blood on themselves and tore off each other's clothes. This riotous mood, an ugly enthusiasm, had nothing hostile about it at first. But when the NSKK and SS men turned brutal, began to beat and finally to shoot, the whole thing turned into a horrible free-for-all. The aroused mob (many were in uniform), tore the NSKK men from their motorcycles, held up cars driving behind the tank, and dragged out those inside. Several regrettable deaths resulted. A loudspeaker truck was cleaned out and a man in SA uniform began to speak through a megaphone. What he yelled into the darkness was gruesome but sounded so familiar that the crowd kept right on with what it was doing. Köpfler had bestially murdered the Führer, the man shouted. It was known now that Hitler's personal physician, a fanatic Werewolf, had given the Führer a series of shots that produced rigor mortis. When Hitler awoke, he already lay in the massive sealed casket. But since the coffin had an air vent, the Führer had probably lived for a little while longer. ("Perhaps he's still alive, dying an excruciatingly painful death," Senkpiehl said.) Rumor had it that Köpfler's accomplices, who held the death watch, heard a scratching, scraping, and rattling, and they delighted in it. The Führer's so-called last will and testament too was a forgery from beginning to end and a simple one to boot; it was put on tape by a voice double. (Diebold had described the murder with almost the same words; the underground scene arose before Höllriegl's inner eye in all its details.)

"Köpfler," Senkpiehl continued, apparently forgetting that time was short, "had two aims. First, to take personal revenge on the Führer, specifically for what he, Köpfler, had gone through in the death cell in Munich way back when. The Forest Devil's chief characteristics are cowardice and thirst for revenge. Second, he wanted to put himself and his creatures into power with his cold putsch, which he succeeded almost a hundred percent in doing. For with the exception of a very few men who hold minor Cabinet posts, the new Reich government is made up of Werewolf people, in other words, of Köpfler's stooges—Hassenteufel, for example, is a leading NATMAT theoretician. Of course he did have one or two defections. Firbas is the biggest. Köpfler always thought he was devoted to him, but just before the final blow against the very sick Führer—in case you don't know it, Hitler suffered from advanced arteriosclerosis: the people call it senility—it came out that Firbas was in close touch with the Bundschuh. Since he lost power, Firbas has disappeared as if the earth had swallowed him. Perhaps he's already been liquidated. Köpfler has had bad luck with the SS Reichsführers, first Diebold, then Firbas. And Landsittel? He's a man from the eastern self-protective service, a fanatic SS man and Asgard propagandist. And what do you think? This Landsittel goes over to the Bundschuh even before the collapse of the eastern wall. Today we know all that. But what the supersly Köpfler didn't know, didn't even suspect, was that right after Hitler's death, i.e., his slow suffocation, half the world would rebel against the new order. The Japs had more sensitive antennas—I believe they just waited for the signal. And it wouldn't surprise me a bit if they knew of Köpfler's murderous intentions at a time when he himself wasn't too clear about them. They can read thoughts a thousand kilometers away. And then that fatal incident with the plane. There's no doubt that ploy was thought up in the Air Ministry, which takes its orders from the War Minister, whose name happens to be Köpfler. Moreover, the whole thing was done in such an amateurish fashion that even the yellow chicks had to smile. Or have you ever heard of an A-bomb exploding when the plane that carries it is hit? That's something you can only make the Germans believe. In any case we no longer live in the good old days. Köpfler must have imagined his seizure of power a little differently. The thing with the Führer was a perfect murder, only a shade too perfect. Then the Luftwaffe revolt—all that came so fast. What else do we want? This war is lost, even if we burn up ten armies. And you can't do anything smarter than save your own skin. For me, that's what I'll do, or try to do. Let's go now!"

Höllriegl was staggered. The usually so careful, detached Senkpiehl had lost his composure completely. He had never seen him so agitated. If Senkpiehl talked this way to an official and faithful party member, then something must have happened which could never be set right again. Something desperate, incurable. The word "senility" hit Höllriegl hard. Yes, the Führer had grown old, that was true. But age gives wisdom. For him the Führer had always been the incarnation of Aryan wisdom . . . (And Senkpiehl wore a party insignia—so that's what the party had come to.)

Utterly confused, he followed the doctor down the stairs. A sudden thought: Perhaps Senkpiehl was in touch with the Underground. When they were already out on the street, he realized he had forgotten Kummernuss' pistol. He ran back up the steps. He had lowered the loudspeaker volume before leaving. Now, when he couldn't find the gun right away, he turned up the radio. At once he was awash in a sound of bells. There were many bells alternating, deep and dark, high and light. Their ringing filled the room.

". . . the bells of the Berlin Memorial Church have rung in the great memorial service; other bells of the Reich capital have followed suit, the voice of the Potsdam Garrison Church is especially clear, as is that of the Dorotheenstädter Church; then we have faded in the bells of the cathedrals of Cologne, Ulm, and Speyer, the Pummerin from Vienna, the bells of St. Peter, the bells of Notre Dame, Rouen, and Chartres, the bells of Prague, St. Petersburg, and Kiev, the bells of the Uspenski cathedral in the Kremlin and St. Basil's cathedral, and now the iron tongues and clappers of the country churches in the Führer's home and ancestral *Gau,* the bells of Braunau and Leonding, the bells of Gross-Wolfgers and Döllersheim. They have all joined in, as if from tower to tower the solemn call were spreading out across the cities, across the whole German land and the wide, wide world, so that all men of good will could hear the message which the new Führer of the Germanic World Empire and protector of all allied peoples and nations has just proclaimed." (Where in hell had he hidden that pistol?)

". . . mighty and victorious . . . of all Aryan men, no matter what language . . . that now after a thousand years of desire and battle . . . to the German Urals."

There it was—he had tossed it into a corner of his closet. And the ammunition. Before he left the room he kicked the radio so it rolled tinkling off the table. It cried out plaintively once more, then the bells and the pathos-filled voice broke off.

Senkpiehl smiled ironically when Höllriegl showed him the gun. He pointed behind him. A rifle and a submachine gun lay on the back seat. As Höllriegl determined with practiced eye and grip, it was a 7.62-mm repeating carbine and an older-model submachine gun, probably a nine. A box of infantry ammunition also lay in the back.

The depressing thing was that they drove through virtually empty streets. Where thousands had thronged an hour or so ago, the roads now looked as if they had just been swept. Nevertheless, they drove slowly; Heydrich was under total blackout, which provided a grotesque contrast to the illuminated heavens of the mountain entombment. From the towers of Heydrich's three churches, bells boomed and moaned, and their sounds mixed with those of the bells that rang out from the radio poles. As the ringing grew weaker they could hear from time to time a suspicious sound—a dry chattering. Everything was somehow unreal. Höllriegl felt as if he drove down a toboggan run at breakneck speed.

Senkpiehl looked strenuously ahead of him and continued his story: "The reinforced SS began to shoot wildly into the mob, which first had crowded around the Führer's tank. A real battle erupted. Most of those attacked were battle-hardened SA men, with a sprinkling of Hitler Youth. They quickly drew their own guns and, barricaded behind cars and motorcycles, fired back at the SS, who had no other protection save darkness. You must realize, Höllriegl, that the hatred built up over the years played its role—SA jealousy of SS privilege. Plebeians against the elite. There were some quite ugly scenes. I was told that wounded SS men had their throats cut or their skulls smashed with boots. Luckily no one had lasers; otherwise casualties would have been much higher on both sides. Finally the Wehrmacht moved in with two fire companies and ended it. At first they had just watched from helicopters without doing anything. They drove the two sides apart with water cannon and a little nerve gas and at the same time hosed down the streets, so that the Führer could be driven to his Valhalla without leaving bloody tracks behind. Streets clear for the brown battalions, hahaha! Did you know that starting tonight Germany has two new slogans? 'Bundschuh, awake, Werewolf perish'; and 'Werewolf awake, Bundschuh perish.' The yellow devils are going to love it."

Senkpiehl laughed shrilly again and pushed down the gas pedal. They had now reached the main northwest road. Strange, the highway signs had been turned around: the Kesselring-Hildesheim-Hanover sign now pointed in the direction of Eisleben. The *tak-tak-tak* had grown louder, the bells fading in the distance. Suddenly Senkpiehl unfastened the party insignia from his buttonhole and threw it out the window.

The car had a secret-police radio which never stopped beeping and groaning, though you couldn't understand a word it said. At the intersection of Ritter-von-Epp Street and Guderian Avenue, shots rang out from all sides; at the same time it seemed as if a handful of peas had been thrown against the roof of the car. Instinctively, both men slid from their seats. Senkpiehl slammed on the brakes and tore the car around. At that moment, Höllriegl felt a cuttingly cold wind on his left temple. The windshield and the rear window had burst. The car staggered on for a few feet then, and with a gentle bounce, hit the side of a tall brick wall. Bullets encircled them; they seemed to come from above and from all sides. The chatter turned into furious fire bursts—automatic fire. Splinters sprayed from the wall, an invisible finger drew lines of destruction into the masonry.

Slowly they crept out. Höllriegl took the rifle, Senkpiehl the submachine gun; they said nothing. It was pretty dark, the sky was light only above the Kyffhäuser region. Now and again a light rocket spurted up high and poured a cluster of bluish light across the firmament.

Höllriegl groped along the wall, crawling flat as a bedbug. His eyes adapted quickly to the darkness—he didn't have cat-eyes for nothing. He approached one of those primitive tin latrines for men one still finds on occasion in provincial villages. He crawled up to it—a good shelter. It stank of oil and urine. Senkpiehl—he called out his name softly—had not followed him; apparently he had looked for cover somewhere else.

In the beam of his flashlight he examined the carbine. The magazine was full. More ammunition lay in Senkpiehl's car, but he couldn't get back there now. Then he still had that thing of Kummernuss'. He loaded the pistol. Another six shots. A crazy feeling came over him—he felt his manly strength and power.

But only for a moment. Already bullets drummed against the tin wall. It had to be a roof sniper. There was a method in the shooting—who fired on whom? A broad crack gaped between the floor and the latrine wall, through which the wind whistled. Now shots whipped across the square. If he kept crawling about so comfortably, he'd get shot in the balls. He straightened up a little and played the light against the wall. The usual graffiti: "Looking for lecherous couple," he read. "Am twenty-five years old, mine is . . ." Drawing and measurements followed. Exaggerated, surely. He'd have to get out of here. The square was covered. "The pussy of E. . . ." The rest was illegible. His hands had become oily from crawling about. He himself stank like a latrine.

It was pretty far from here to his house. Again his stomach was in ferment, but not as badly as earlier in the day. He dropped his pants and relieved himself. Then he crawled out into the open, dragging the rifle behind him. If he could only find Senkpiehl. There was the car, about thirty steps away. The radiator had rammed into the wall, but he could probably start it all right. He called out softly: "Senkpiehl?"

The methodical firing had stopped, only an isolated shot rang out now and then. The air was filled with brick dust, an icy wind had sprung up. Suddenly a heavy missile howled through the area, but thank God it was far away. The impact, a blaring crash, made the earth tremble, and the blast fanned Höllriegl's coat and trouser legs.

A few meters more and he'd be there. But an obstacle lay against the wall, a dark something. It was a man bent together like a bow. Höllriegl didn't have to look very hard—Senkpiehl. Once again the peas dusted the wall: The snipers were hard on him. On, on. But Senkpiehl should give up his submachine gun. Höllriegl tore at it, tried to pull it out from under Senkpiehl's body; it didn't budge.

The car smelled of gasoline. Perhaps the tank leaked. Höllriegl crouched into a knee bend and pushed the starter. The car jerked once or twice in reverse, then it was all right again. As Höllriegl sat down at the wheel, he noticed it was sticky all over. Senkpiehl must have been shot right away. That was for the "senility" crack. And now on through!

He had more luck than sense (as usual). He made it. Shots rang out behind him and again they hammered against the car's metal skin. It didn't bother him. He turned into the avenue almost mechanically. If he had wanted to go home, he would have had to drive in the direction of the old town. Somehow he felt free and unwoundable. This feeling was something quite new! Until now he had felt at best secure—but free? The party thinks for you! Surely that was wonderful. But who was the party? And where was it? And did a safe world exist? Hadn't he finished off all that today when he smashed the radio? No differently than Senkpiehl, who had thrown away his party button? No, he didn't want to have anything in common with Senkpiehl. How good it was to be dependent on yourself! How good, too, to care for someone else. Axel! Axel! Once and never again. He felt silly when he thought of the boy. Axel, dear Axel, it was not meant to be. . . . When he reached the last Heydrich house, the waving howl of sirens began. Was it radiation alarm? Doesn't matter either.

And suddenly he realized where he wanted to go. To the Eyckes! To Ulla!

MISERERE

The night was alive. He saw a large, blacked-out transport roll down the Heydrich-Kelbra highway toward the northeast. (Here too the road signs pointed in the wrong direction.) One truck drove close behind another. The reddening night sky reflected the dull glow of gray, net-covered steel helmets. Then the armor rumbled past; Höllriegl distinguished heavy and light tanks and big gun carriages. Not a shot was to be heard out here, or else the racket drowned every sound.

Dark, shapeless masses moved beside him and behind him along the road and across the field. They marched in large and small units, the night was full of them. Obviously troops on their way back from the burial services.

There was a decent dirt road to Rottleberode he could take, provided it was still open. It ran parallel to the rail embankment and crossed the track before reaching town. Once on the other side, he would have to drive back a few kilometers to get to the von Eycke estate. A small detour, but every delay infuriated him today.

Desire for Ulla—he lusted after her more than ever! He was deaf to rational argument, tactics, and what-have-you; he didn't give a damn about any of it now! Today he felt her equal. Whether she wanted him or not, whether she would even recognize him, all that didn't matter. With shame he thought of his adventure at the Eyckes'. Back then—was it only a week ago?—he had been truly afraid of her. He remembered that he wanted to turn around. How despicable! Dowsing too was despicable; he had behaved like a servant, and dowsing made him one. A degrading profession, at least in Ulla's eyes. Shameful! That woman had to be impressed with mastery, strength, race, will to victory (perhaps with money as well). He grew uncomfortable when he remembered that just a few hours ago he had wanted Ulla to whip him. Anselma too was that kind, only more artful and perverse—he seemed to be the type such women went for, to humiliate, exploit, and abuse. Shameful, shameful! He'd make an end to all that, once and for all! You couldn't crawl before Ulla, but had to take a whip. That Amazon had to be forced to her knees with raw and brutal power. And today he'd do it. If she refused herself . . .

The troops slid past him like phantoms; they hurried along as fast as the soaked ground and poor lighting permitted. Occasionally he was held up behind a group with sadly wobbling standards or flags rolled up and packed in their casings. A couple of times he was checked with a flashlight, but Senkpiehl's Sanitation Corps car passed everywhere. Finally Höllriegl couldn't stand not knowing what had happened. He stopped, pretending to have lost his way, and asked some soldiers if this was the road to Kelbra. Yes, it was. And with that he became involved in a short but instructive conversation. It was a troop in tiger-striped battle dress—a Wehrmacht patrol or Waffen-SS. "What's up?" Höllriegl asked right out. And after a little verbal fencing he learned the following:

The so-called armistice had been a fraud. For several hours an attack of unbelievable power had been under way against the Reich. The threat against the Harz and Kyffhäuser was especially great because of the large numbers of people gathered there. "The entire Reich has been put under red alert, but the radiation alarm was sounded only fifteen minutes ago." The man, a troop leader or something like that, pointed to his pocket radio. "The truth was hushed up until now—and rightly so. Only coded bulletins were put on the air. But now the whole nation, man, woman and child, has been called upon to fight to the last."

Just before 6 P.M. a large ICBM had scored a direct hit on missile-defense headquarters at Bitburg/Eifel and effectively put the whole missile-command structure in western Germany out of action. Other enemy rockets had destroyed underground missile silos in the Reich and the Western protectorates. So far they had all carried conventional warheads.

"The concentric pattern of hits clearly indicates that the attack is getting closer to the Middle German area. Our problem is simple enough: Our thirty-minute early warning system on which we counted so much didn't work, whether because of technical failure or enemy attack, I don't know. In any case, our antimissile defenses failed. Moreover, it looks as if the new Jap missiles have an undisruptable guidance system, perhaps inertia navigation." The man lit a cigarette. "And what's more, we've found a satellite that probably has nuclear weapons on board." He said all this very quietly. "Interception attempts are under way constantly. Late reports say we've sent a 'spy' after the suspicious spaceship—perhaps he's already destroyed it. The satellite is certainly unmanned. By the way, our Ausra attacks against East Asia are continuing. The Japs are going to spit blood soon."

"And our miracle weapon?" Höllriegl suddenly remembered what Gundlfinger had said.

The man looked him over carefully. "We can't count on it. Who knows if it will ever be finished. The war should not have started for another year at the earliest—that's the whole mess."

He spoke as cold-bloodedly as if he were talking about quite ordinary things. As long as the Reich had such men, it wasn't finished. On the contrary: It would annihilate every foe, even the strongest. And if the world were full of devils . . .

"We can expect more nuclear explosions too—the breathing spell is over." Höllriegl gave the man a pack of cigarettes; he nodded and put them in his pocket. "In case we get through here all right, we'll grab radiation suits in Heldrungen and go on down into the deep bunker. This stuff here is a joke."

"Lot of shooting in Heydrich. I live there."

"Where isn't there a lot of shooting?" The troop leader did not seem particularly disturbed. "The Bundschuh is active. But we'll clean up that bunch of shits in short order. You're Ostmarker, aren't you? Be careful. Those guys have it in for Ostmarkers." He pointed to the hole in the windshield and grinned. "You were damned lucky, Mr. Ostmarker. And watch it if you want to go to Kelbra—things are tough down there. Heil Köpfler."

Höllriegl suppressed his customary "Heitla" and drove on. He would quickly learn more. He passed a man signaling with a darkened lantern. The stranger limped up to the car and asked

Höllriegl to take him along. Höllriegl did; he wanted company. His fellow traveler turned out to be a simple SA squad leader, but he wore the Coburg insignia on his uniform coat. The man was about seventy, the type of old fighter from the days of the great beerhall battles. He reminded Höllriegl of Damaschke. The SA man worked in a Kelbra brewery as an overseer of foreign and SHC laborers. After an early departure from the Kyffhäuser the Coburger had stumbled over a wire and sprained an ankle or torn a ligament; he was very glad to get home so comfortably. As they drove along, Höllriegl tried to find out everything his companion knew. Yes, he had heard about the fight with the SS. "Bad business, that. SS and Werewolf are one and the same now." But then they rode on in silence; the man wasn't very talkative.

The clouds above Kelbra turned dark red. They could hear gunfire and occasional explosions, some quite big ones, even above the engine noises. Once again searchlights fingered the sky. Jets roared high over their heads.

"The Führer's entombment," the man said sarcastically. But Höllriegl couldn't be sure just where his companion stood politically. The remark had been intended quite generally. Nevertheless his sympathies clearly lay with the old days (mothballs!). Höllriegl liked him; he was a working man from the region and in general he got along well with such people. They were the ones who always sat around his office; he understood them at once.

"Do you know the Eyckes?" Höllriegl asked innocently, but his nerves vibrated as he did.

The man only knew them on sight, but he'd heard a lot about Ulla. And he had often seen Frau von Eycke on TV. Her riding had made her a star attraction. ". . . fantastic woman." Höllriegl grew hot, his heart hammered. He had not known that Ulla participated in the TV series "The German Home." He had to admit (to his disgrace) that he had never watched that very popular program, although he knew that the amber witch was sometimes interviewed by TV reporters. Again jealousy and hopelessness gnawed at him. The Whole Reich saw Ulla; all the men desired her!

The car inched along. Again and again soldiers flooded across the road, trying to reach Heydrich or their garrisons at Heldrungen. And then they all wanted to get back home, but fast. "Have you heard yet?" From the shreds of conversation which Höllriegl picked up during their frequent stops, and from the sparse comments of his companion (he must have known more than he was willing to say), he pieced together a picture of incalculable national catastrophe.

Germany was in the midst of a civil war of unparalleled brutality and a fury of self-destruction. Only a very few knew it, but for days—ever since that historic session of the Reich Council which Höllriegl had witnessed in Berlin—bitter fighting had raged in many areas. Höllriegl remembered Anselma's words that had made such an impression on him: that the time of the jungle was at hand, the time of the jackknife—"and behind us the wall." Man against man, woman against woman. Not even the conflict with the eastern world power, which had so quickly entered a decisive stage, was able to end this suicidal activity and mobilize Germans to joint resistance, surely strong evidence for the depth of hate and passion. The great split ran right through the party, the people, even, as some said, right through families. It had all the characteristics of an apocalyptic catastrophe. No one was able to understand all the ramifications of the disaster, let alone control or halt it. Nor would anyone in this fateful hour be able to weld the German people into an effective striking force. Only one thing had become terrifyingly clear to many, including Höllriegl: The evil now in the open had been in the making for a long time, and there had been signs of it in the past—which no one had bothered to notice or to interpret. Now there was nothing for it but to drift.

And to all that you had to add the dismal fact that the new men, all their reassurances notwithstanding, had been unable to destroy the foreign enemy in a surprise attack or even to hurt and frighten him enough to hold him back from using nuclear weapons. Instead, what no one had thought possible had actually taken place—nuclear explosions of terrifying power in the middle of the old Reich, on German soil, and no doubt more would follow. Chaos ruled, the battle of all against all, and it had spread like wildfire around the earth: in the two Americas, in Africa, in parts of Asia, in the polar areas, even in Japanese-occupied Australia. Wherever the New Order had built its bastions, the global power struggle of the two giants had mushroomed into a host of individual conflicts so many-faceted and confused no one could any longer grasp their full impact. Höllriegl felt that the subhumans had everywhere broken their chains, like Loki, Fenris-wolf, and the Midgard serpent in the legend of the gods. It was simply a battle between light and darkness. Adolf Hitler's world empire shuddered in its foundations—and with it that of the Soka Gakkai.

The murdered Führer's policies were now hotly contested. (It was certain that Hitler had met a violent end, there was dispute only about how he had been killed.) Even some of Hitler's most fanatic supporters harshly condemned his recent foreign policy. They charged that the Führer should have used—or at least reached some accommodation with—the Soka Gakkai movement, whose aims were more or less similar to his own. Instead the Reich had negotiated with the wrong people, the reactionary Tonno clique. There had been a great deal of talk about Shinto, the God empire, *Bushido,* samurai-spirit, and similar feudalistic claptrap. Diplomatic efforts to bring the two world blocs closer together ideologically had been clumsy, if not downright amateurish. Rosenberg and Ribbentrop were heavily attacked (people talked of champagne-salesman-policy against kamikaze) because of these and similar sins of omission, which all had their roots in the immediate postwar years. In short: The greatest victory in German history had been only half a victory. For obviously the government had failed to win the peace. Moreover, the Reich had only the haziest notions about the enemy's production potential and weapon technology. Intelligence had failed miserably.

Despite all that, the Führer's transition into a godhead made rapid progress. Thus the "German Christians" removed Frauja or Kristos from his role as mediator between God the Father and man, replacing him with Adolf Hitler. The messenger of World War I was thus enthroned above the clouds, and in churches and holy heaths of this powerful and widespread faith (strongly supported by party and state) Frauja statues were silently removed in favor of Hitler busts. It was the work of just a few hours. And chief apostle Dr. Nimmshin, chairman of the Reich Council of Brothers, another national and populist sect, whose members called themselves "Nordic Christians," had proclaimed in a solemn broadcast—Höllriegl had heard it a few days ago—that in keeping with his transcendental rank the Führer had been elevated into the Trinity on a level with the Son and the Spirit. In the "framework of an inner illumination," as Dr. Nimmshin had put it, he learned that Adolf Hitler had taken charge of all military affairs in eternity; it was now the Führer's highest duty to maintain "close contact with the heavenly legions."

The Bundschuh meeting in Stolberg had not been an empty threat, it had indeed taken place, even though original plans to hold a mass rally were abandoned. The flood of refugees and the huge movement toward the Kyffhäuser had made the scheme impractical. Nevertheless the hard core of the tightly organized peasant groups had participated undisturbed. For Firbas had simply placed the rally under state police and gendarme protection.

Originally the leadership of *Der Arme Konrad* had planned to encircle the funeral ceremonies at Kyffhäuser, move in shock troops, and grab Köpfler and his whole brood. The project was dropped at the last minute: So many SS, Werewolf, and Gestapo had been called up that the Bundschuh would have bled to death in the attempt. In addition, the Wehrmacht remained a huge question mark. Several Luftwaffe units had openly rebelled against Köpfler, but missile and armored forces stuck to a wait-and-see attitude. Perhaps the entire SA opposed the Forest Devil.

Höllriegl learned (and his heart stopped) that Unseld and Diebold, reappeared from the Underground, had spoken in front of the Thomas-Münzer Statue in Stolberg. An audience of thousands cheered them frantically as they demanded the heads of the usurpers. Effigies of Köpfler and the next-most-hated man, SS Brigadeführer Sausele, were hanged in public. This symbolic execution was attended not only by the "faceless leadership" of the Bundschuh and—hard to believe—by heavily armed units of the Asgard Ring, but also by high officials and delegations of the Reich Food Office, the German Labor Front, and other party groups who called themselves loyalist or Hitlerites to indicate they favored the older, more moderate, party line. Participation of the quickly formed Emergency Committee for Atomic Refugees was widely noted.

Firbas too had shown his strength: State police and gendarmes had either gone over to the Bundschuh outright or protected its activities. SS barracks, order castles, Reich breeding institutes, and similar Werewolf establishments were fired upon all over the countryside. In general, Werewolf and SS had all but disappeared from the flatlands and withdrawn either to their mountain hideouts or into the large cities. The purely agrarian regions of the Reich, especially in the east, were firmly in Bundschuh hands. And these were the areas with most of the refugees from the west, men who had fled from the death radiation of Lemgo. Refugees from the Ostrau coal mines—where the second big bomb had exploded (Gundlfinger had told Höllriegl about its devastating neutron radiation)—turned instinctively to the north, to Lower Silesia, or westward to the Sudetenland. They didn't dare go farther east—that part of the country was supposed to teem with yellow guerillas and SHC partisans. The atomic bomb that had fallen on the Allgäu later proved "harmless." However, it had tremendous incendiary power—a high-thermal bomb. No one knew if other nuclear weapons had hit Reich territory. The wild confusion on the airwaves didn't help clarify the situation.

For the SS, holed up in the cities, had kept control of all networks, which, as instruments of Köpfler propaganda, continued to broadcast hauntingly normal programs and the usual pro-government news. With unparalleled impudence Hitler was deified and Köpfler sanctified as his confidant and closest collaborator, the faithful paladin and trustee of the world empire's founder, now generally only called Adolf the Great. Nothing pointed to the split that ran like a trench through the middle of the Reich. (Only, coded messages increased rapidly.) The main propaganda thrust was naturally directed against the outside enemy, and even though the successful Ausra and Thor strikes were played up strongly, which was probably legitimate enough, the awful pressure of events had forced the regime to tell the truth: first, that the Reich had not succeeded in annihilating the enemy in his own country in just a few hours (half the world would have had to be destroyed in one fell swoop); second, that a major atomic attack by an apparently unweakened and merciless foe was close at hand (radiation warnings and radiation alerts succeeded one another); and third, that the enemy had won a toehold "in several areas of the European protectorates of the Reich" and that heavy ground fire had not disrupted delivery of airborne supplies.

Officially the current stand of the fighting was described as "limited atomic war." The expression "total atomic war" was never used in the news (official Wehrmacht reports in the old sense were no longer issued), although—as events proved to anyone willing to listen—both sides had employed strategic nuclear weapons with very high TNT equivalents and had done it with a clear and single aim: extermination of the opponent and destruction of his vital base. Massive use of tactical atomic weapons, not to mention laser, poisonous substances, gas, and bacteriological warfare was imminent.

Here and there *Der Arme Konrad* had succeeded in attacking and capturing power plants and local radio and TV stations, and a few stations of the rebellious Luftwaffe attacked Köpfler and the Werewolf without pause, accusing him of leading the Reich into an abyss. (If Köpfler had scored a massive success in the war against the Japs, such accusations would have stopped, but in this situation . . .)

And to complete the chaos, enemy troops in Europe used captured radio stations to broadcast news of fresh disasters, which confused the man in the street still more. Japanese parachute troops of the kamikaze class and American irregulars had not only maintained their bridgeheads but expanded and fortified them; as was known, the anti-German local population had given the enemy strong support. Several bridgeheads existed in southern Russia, Finland, Ireland, northern Italy, and on the Iberian Peninsula. All these areas were important outposts of the German heartland. Had the enemy already landed on the territory of the old Reich? Only rumors circulated. Rumor too had taken over news of the enemy's supply lines. The Japs had reportedly succeeded in building two air lifts which branched out in Europe: one from Honshu across the pole to Russia and Finland, the other, much longer, with bases in Australia and Mexico—thus circumventing the UVSA—to Madeira and Ireland.

Bitter fighting raged across the whole territory of the United Vassal States of America. Here too the official party was rent into factions; thus the very militant Minutemen (they were patterned on the Werewolf) had strengthened their dominant position almost everywhere and ostracized the Ku Klux Klan (whose historic services were of course acknowledged) as a "romantic remnant" from the era of "shit democracy"—the Jewish-Freemason-Plutocratic old Washington republic of bitter memory. In some cases major battles had erupted between the opposing forces, with citizen's militia and whole army groups joining in. Passionate religious fighting had flared up from coast to coast, accompanied by crucifixions, burnings at the stake, tortures, and other manifestations of a fanaticized populace. Two sects, who had escaped the general unification after 1945, suddenly entered the political scene, The Brethren of the Holy Order and The Witch Hunters of Salem. The Brethren, with strong backing from the Minutemen, preached a radical asceticism that included submission to "holy reducing cures"—public self-chastisement. Their bitterest opponents, the Witch Hunters (who lately had begun calling themselves The Blessed Gross Profiteers) told mass meetings that the end of the world had come and that therefore people should enjoy themselves without inhibitions; it was clear that here—on a religious plane—the playboy and striptease instincts of a decadent and lost era had resurfaced.

German forces stationed in the UVSA, mostly Waffen SS, SD, Death's Head units, and the German American Corps (manned by German-blooded Americans), were faced with the painful choice of supporting either the MM or the KKK. Actually, units of the overseas SS were the only reliable troops. They fought the foreign enemy with iron determination despite heavy losses.

On the other hand, several of the former Southern states were supposedly under control of the rebellious Free Corps (simply called "Niggers"). The Niggers had reintroduced the old federal constitution in all their territories, revived parliaments, and similar talkfests, and formed a government of colored subhumans and other apelings in a town they called Lincoln Center. Höllriegl refused to believe that. It was too absurd, especially since other sources reported that the South had prevented resurrection of mob rule and thus avoided an immense catastrophe for the master race. In fact, the Minutemen were supposed to be exercising absolute power in the South. It was obvious that under such circumstances the KKK delegation to the Führer's funeral could not return home.

The situation in Central and South America and especially in Australia, the "Magna Iaponica," were so confused it made little sense to worry about any of them. You could only base your guesses on conflicting radio reports from fleet units of the New Order operating in South American waters. One thing was clear, however: Unparalleled political chaos shook the continent (proclamation of the monarchy in Brazil had been no joke) and that, as in the UVSA, the battle of everybody against everybody else had begun.

Höllriegl listened to all this without any particular dismay. It was only confirmation of what he already knew, even though he had not believed it—and damn it, he still didn't believe! The washing-machine idiot in Sauckelruh, and a day later Professor Gundlfinger, had said much the same thing. Some people just had a sixth sense. One thing was sure, though: Two weeks ago such conversation between strangers, even among friends, had been unthinkable—those were still the days of the safe and sane world of Adolf Hitler. But it didn't exist anymore, and it would never exist again.

The Coburger had warmed up; suddenly he turned very talkative. But nothing emotional. Only when he talked of the party's battle days did he become sentimental. He had known and talked to the great men at the beginning of their careers. "I always did my job, I was never an ass kisser." You could tell that by looking at this simple, admirable brewery worker.

The little man was supposed to be able to climb up the ladder in the party and government bureaucracy, but the laws to that effect were now a dead letter. In earlier times it might have been possible now and again (Köpfler, to cite an example). But now Höllriegl knew young men, the best selection, real Führer material, who despite political schooling and self-sacrificing work with the Hitler Youth just could not get on in the world—simply because they were the sons of little people. Some bent their backs, others, the golden boys, bought the most beautiful castles and women. Eycke too, that repulsive popinjay. Where did he get his money? As Höllriegl had learned—he had gone after the story with real flair—Erik Meinolf von Eycke came from a good but poor house. A Hanoverian von Eycke had once served in the German Legion after the battle at Belle-Alliance, where he had attained the rank of colonel and was rewarded with a prosperous little estate. Then came hard times for the family. Herr von Eycke's papa speculated in real estate on the side, i.e., he swindled his fellow soldiers and casino colleagues from his Worms days until one of them had enough. As a result young von Eycke was expelled from his noble dueling fraternity and had to break off his law studies. Whereupon the family bet on the New Order, on Germany's awakening. With success. Erik Meinolf joined the SS and was assigned to the legal division. That was the big chance for the young law student without a degree. The party career of the Economics Inspector for the Upper Section Fulda-Werra had been a steep climb—and a lot of money had stuck to him on the way up. And Ulla? No one really knew where the amber witch came from. Somewhere in the Baltic, that much was certain; the rest was blurred. Her maiden name was Mlakar, Ulrike Mlakar, undoubtedly of humble origin. The wildest jokes and stories were told about her within the party, but could one believe such vulgarity? It was said that at ten she was already so beautiful and well developed that a Baron Wrangell, a rather elderly gentleman, had taken her to live with him on an estate somewhere in Estonia in order to marry her after she turned fourteen. But one night, allegedly after a considerable amount of intercourse, the man had died of a heart attack, and thirteen-year-old Ulrike was suddenly out on the street—as a sorrowing "widow." Another, nastier version, claimed that a swindler had deflowered the child. Or that the ten-year-old had seduced him. However that may have been, Ulla Frigg von Eycke had had no money either. (Anselma, some years younger than her brother, did not count here. She had married young, lived for many years abroad, and even now was independent. An outsider!) Perhaps, as rumor had it, Ulla had ridden beds into the ground during her camp career. Today the Eyckes owned palaces, a stud farm, luxury apartments in Fulda and Hanover, a car park like a plutocrat. Herr von Eycke maintained a racing stable, was considered a flying ace, and naturally piloted his own plane. Ulla was a star rider and TV favorite. The Guardian of the Breed, the idol of the nation. And he, Albin Totila Höllriegl, an unknown follower of the Führer, loved this idol with every fiber of his heart.

He listened distractedly to what the Coburger told him, for his mind was awash in a welter of thoughts that always collected at the same searing point: Ulla. A weird light had now spread across the countryside. Kelbra lay ahead of them—and Kelbra was on fire. Biting smoke poured through the hole in the windshield, the wind drove showers of sparks down the road ahead of them. The machine-gun chatter had ended abruptly, and the large convoy of army trucks must have turned off the road somewhere; the earth seemed to have swallowed the returning soldiers.

Höllriegl stopped the car. A crackling tension lay in the air. The walls of Kelbra lay white under the low, shining sky; there seemed something lurking behind them—what did they hide? In the silence one could hear a dog howling.

It would have been madness to drive through the town. The Coburger knew of a dirt road, a passable detour. Naturally, Höllriegl would take the man home. On such a night some contact with another human being was more valuable than anything else. They changed seats.

The red-glowing rails stretched into the distance. Something dark lay across the track at the point they crossed. An overturned trolley. Next to it, strangely flat, a human body. They got out to look at the man—a trainman, judging from the uniform. Nothing to be done . . . the second dead man Höllriegl had encountered that night. As they straightened up, quick shots crashed out behind them, and the stones at their feet splintered. They threw themselves to the ground and crawled back to the car, a hissing and whistling above their heads. That situation too seemed familiar.

Once across the rail embankment, they dived into the darkness of the fields. The Coburger drove very slowly. The ground was soft, and the path led up and down. Höllriegl had his rifle at the ready, but nothing moved outside. Flaming islands appeared here and there among the clouds on the horizon—perhaps a reflection of burning villages.

They parted behind the brewery. The Coburger told Höllriegl which road to take and then disappeared, limping into the night. He lived in a row of houses whose high-gabled roofs looked as if they had been taken out of a child's construction set. No one around. A nightmare. But flight would have been pointless. Where could the people go? At least the Coburger would find his family.

A Red Cross flag had lain in the back of the car, and now Höllriegl made use of the stop to mount it on the hood. Again he drove slowly; the strange terrain had its pitfalls, and the light from the sky was uncertain. Moreover the damnable eye trouble which had come upon him so suddenly in Sauckelruh bothered him again, as always after dark. Of course he had to drive without lights.

His companion had advised him to drive along the shelter of the embankment and to leave Kelbra behind on his right. Outside town he should cross the rail line again somewhere and see if he could make time on the highway to Berga. Fighting raged in Kelbra. Höllriegl distinguished the cough of machine guns, sniper fire, and the heavy explosions of big guns. Now and again the wind carried a shrill rattling across the embankment: scout cars. And he heard the crash of hand grenades. A bitter house-to-house battle must be under way. Here and there snipers had dug in on the embankment, and he saw some machine-gun nests. It was the SS. They paid no attention to him.

Abruptly the path dipped. The sound truck of an SS storm troop news battalion screamed propaganda slogans through the clash of battle. Höllriegl had to drive slowly around the truck because of the sharply descending road and even stop occasionally; as a result he was able to pick up a few key phrases.

". . . forced to battle on all fronts against a bloodthirsty opponent who is determined to destroy the Western world and eradicate the Aryan-Germanic . . . a laughable minority of former people's comrades has made the most treacherous attack of all times upon the Reich government put into power by the Führer's last will and testament . . . the political chaos in our ranks . . . not enough that these blackguards have not hesitated to accuse Adolf Hitler's most trusted paladin and rightful successor, our Führer and highest war lord, Ivo Adolf Köpfler, of a most heinous crime . . . judges himself. A betrayal without parallel in the history of our people . . . this rabble has blinded the proud German peasantry and made small groups do its bidding. It has been proved that they conspired with the archenemy of the Western world, the yellow devils. Moreover it has been proved . . ."

After a while Höllriegl had put Kelbra far behind him, but the noise of battle did not abate. There were only very short pauses—the silence was all the more oppressive. Apparently Berga, the next town, was under artillery fire. No doubt about it, the entire Kyffhäuser was now a battle ground. The air vibrated with the hollow roar of night fighters and reconnaissance planes, searchlights groped like giant fingers along the gray vault of heaven. Höllriegl saw how the antiaircraft guns posted all around the Goldene Aue found the range with tracer ammunition. Ground-to-air rockets drilled holes in the sky with bone-jarring roars, and finally a regular barrage opened up. Two, three planes fell burning through the dreadfully lit-up clouds, enormous torches whose flickering light tossed thin, waving shadows across the track. It was enough to make you vomit. Höllriegl thought of the rebellious Luftwaffe—

perhaps they were flying their first massive attack mission against Wehrmacht and SS at Stolberg. Despite everything that had happened, he felt like a neutral observer attending maneuvers.

He discovered a rail crossing, but no sooner had he passed over the torn-up tracks than shots sprayed at him. He stepped on the gas. Over there the road, white and apparently empty of men, ran to Berga and Rottleberode—his highway. He steered in that direction, repeatedly honking his horn. He reached the road amid a hail of bullets. Lucky again—not a shot had hit its mark. With headlights on (nothing mattered now anyway), he sped ahead. Every kilometer was precious.

The estate of the Eyckes lay between Berga and Rottleberode. What was the situation there now? he wondered. His desire for Ulla was gone—an impossibility, even if Ulla were still there. Madness! How could he have believed it! His brain was no longer capable of thinking normally. Anyway—Ulla must have fled a long time ago. With the children. He'd never see her again, and that was a good thing. It was a good thing. . . .

The street, an avenue, lost itself in the flaming distance. Ribbon-straight. Not a man to be seen, the night hid everything. Trees danced up to him like pale skeletons in the light cones. Sometimes he saw wrecked cars lying on the road. Atom refugees? The Kyffhäuser region was sealed. They must be refugees from the area. Again he thought how pointless flight really was.

Suddenly he thought of that Saturday eight days ago—an endless time back. The same highway. A deceptive Indian-summer day. The lackey with the white hair. The mess in Ulla's room. The flesh-colored panties. The riding boots. Ulla's smell. The bidet. The Führer's picture. The Andrew cross. The dangerous radiation of her flesh. Then she herself, Ulrike Mlakar. The wet splotches under the armpits. The smell of her riding pants. The whipping. The scar.

"Nonsense, nonsense," he said aloud and meant his present trip. It was a dangerous and stupid thing to do. The only sensible course was to turn back immediately and try to get through to Heydrich.

At high speed he almost drove the car into a barricade. Höllriegl braked so hard he was slammed against the wheel and everything rolled around wildly in the back of the car. Instinctively he switched off his headlights. In the pale sheen of the distant fires, wrecked cars lay piled on top of each other, a mountain of bent, torn metal. Debris lay all about.

He jumped out of the car and crawled in the ditch up to the barricade. Splintered trees and instead of the road, a hole. Dead men, arms spread wide apart, lay at the edge of the crater or had slipped into it, a shred of leg hung from a branch. Wehrmacht soldiers, young kids. Milksop faces under steel helmets too big for them. The weak beam of his flashlight hushed across the bodies, which resembled cockchafer larvae in black, loamy earth. It was all madness. German against German.

Those damned tears! And that ghastly dizziness and chill—he'd been suffering from it for days. Of course, today he had hardly eaten a thing, was overtired, then the diarrhea. All of a sudden he felt properly sick; he wanted to vomit. He spat out some acid bile and took a deep breath. But the air stank of lubricating oil, gasoline, and burned flesh and cloth.

As far as he could see, the street was littered with wrecked armored cars. Apparently a troop convoy had been hit; perhaps it was part of that large fleet of trucks he had seen near Heydrich on the road to Kelbra. That was the end of the journey. He could only continue on foot.

Back to Heydrich, then! But for what? What did he have to do there? His home, his sane and safe world, Ingrid, his piano? He laughed and wondered that he laughed. Berga burned ahead of him, Kelbra behind him. Who knew what Heydrich might look like!

Go underground, disappear into the night—that was the answer. Wait for morning in some hole in the ground. A medic was always needed. If necessary, he'd say that he was Senkpiehl; he had his orders: kilometer marker such and such. It didn't matter whom he met: SS, Werewolf, SA, or Bundschuh, they'd always need a medic, a straggler. But at once he had his doubts. Had his car not been fired on several times? The Red Cross was no longer respected.

Lost in thought, he walked upright down the middle of the road back to the car. Without a gun, he'd be finished even as a medic. He still had Kummernuss' pistol. He took out the carbine and some ammunition, the zwieback (that good Fräulein Eberlein!), and Senkpiehl's papers, the car registration, his orders—just in case.

The car stank bitingly of gasoline and oil. A wreck, nothing more. "It would never have made it to Heydrich," Höllriegl said to himself and whistled softly through his teeth. That settled it.

He cut sideways into the bushes—literally, because he had to walk down steep, heavily overgrown slopes, across a dry ditch and through underbrush. In the twilight of the muddy fields he wandered slowly in the direction of the rail embankment, always careful to take cover, his carbine at the ready. The night could teem with monsters.

It was not rumor but fact that wherever the Bundschuh had taken over, it had abolished serfdom. An unnecessary and thoughtless measure that betrayed the idea of the master race. Unnecessary because it was an open secret that many serfs who worked in factories or homes had already fled (Burjak!); and thoughtless, because armed serfs—the Bundschuh itself was supposed to have armed some of them—would kill everyone who had once been a master and wouldn't care less if the master were a German-blooded farmer and Bundschuh supporter or a golden peacock or God knows what. But even worse was the fact that the Bundschuh, in the process of repealing forced labor for subhumans (Führer decree of September 11, 1945, respectively the Third Amendment to the Serfdom Law of May 8, 1946—naturally Höllriegl knew all the relative articles by heart, that was part of an official's general education) had opened all the SHC's in their territory regardless whether Stralag or Strafalags were involved. In the Stralags criminals and loafers of German and related blood were reeducated into useful citizens through forced labor, whereas the Strafalags were the real SHC's. Thus public opinion saw the Bundschuh's cardinal sin in equating men of German blood with subhumans. It may well have been true, therefore, that the Bundschuh leadership had wanted to proceed more slowly on this but that *Der Arme Konrad* had gone too far to permit any holding back.

With that in mind, Höllriegl had to guard at all times against attacks by escaped SHC prisoners. He had heard reliable reports on just what such attacks entailed. Thus the Coburger had told him that serfs set free by the Bundschuh took a devilish joy in crucifying their own prisoners by nailing them onto swastikas. Impaling was another major "amusement." For example, an SHC trusty, a Pole, had terrorized Lower Franconia for days. He was called "the Impaler" with good reason: He had had hundreds, perhaps thousands, impaled. The bodies were cut into pieces and planted in so-called "corpse forests" which even horrified callous SD men rich in experience in the wartime Jewish extermination camps. And the Coburger had reported that imprisoned SS men had been pinched with glowing pliers until they obeyed orders to eat the meat off their dying comrades. All this pounded through Höllriegl's head in the form of blurred images as he worked his way through the countryside in a wide sweep around Berga. He kept thinking of his meeting with the human animals. God have mercy on anyone who fell into the hands of such monsters.

And suddenly he remembered a chilling rumor, a rumor he had dismissed until now as mad invention: Ever since the atrocities had become public knowledge, no one bothered taking prisoners. For in any hopeless situation the valiant German had a duty and obligation as a man to wipe out his clan and save the last bullet for himself. Moreover, the authorities had distributed specially designed hand grenades for just this purpose. The Coburger had shown him one: No bigger than an egg, they were easy to hide in your pants pocket. Even the classic cyanide capsule tucked in one's cheek was widely used. But the reason Höllriegl thought about these things with such dread was this: He had been assured that no wounded were left behind; they were shot in the neck to save them a worse fate. But where there were no wounded, who needed a medic . . . ?

He tightened his hold on the carbine. He at least would sell his life as dearly as possible.

Dawn neared as Höllriegl reached the Eycke estate. This time he came from the east, across fallow ground and wintry fields —burning Brega had pointed the way. From high ground he saw that Rossla and Rottleberode too were on fire; above Nordhausen (now called Kesselring) and the black hills of the Goldene Aue, the sheen of flames mingled with the budding dawn. Nevertheless it didn't turn much lighter.

He had been fired on just once—when he wanted to mount to a small, stone bridge across the Zorge. Here and there he had sensed more than seen stragglers or smaller troops in the dark countryside, perhaps on their way home from Kyffhäuser, or reconnaissance units. He had spent much time stretched out in hiding places, freezing, sweating his guts out and hungry—he preferred not eating to the recurrent, griping pains in his belly—and often he had thrown himself flat on the ground to avoid heavy shells. Once he had experienced a melinite explosion that whirled him through the air like a rag doll. He'd lost his carbine in that one. By sheer accident he found it again. He'd had just about enough.

Suddenly—it seemed to come from the Eycke's park—he heard shots and a distant shouting. He couldn't see the mansion from where he was, it must be a good two kilometers away; the entrance was on the highway side and he was at least that far from the road to Rottleberode. Only now did he notice the burning smell, and as he focused his tired and sandy eyes, he realized that what he had taken for fog was really a whitish smoke which hung on the trees and bushes in clammy swaths.

Shrill screams, a long agony to hear. He froze. That was without doubt a woman's voice. He began to tremble violently. He raced wildly to the garden wall. His pulse flew. How did one get into the park? The wall was made of natural stone; it was high, broken in places and reinforced with barbed wire on top, a double strand. No chance of getting across here. He had a choice of running to the trellised gate. There was no path along the wall, only bushes, rubble, streams, nothing but obstacles. Again the distant yells—tumult and barking and shooting. Höllriegl began to run faster, as fast as he could over this lousy terrain, ran upright although he made a fine target in the dawn light. It didn't matter! Up and down, slopes, scrubs, swampy troughs. He cursed through his teeth, his breath whistled. It stabbed his lungs and the sweat ran down his face. His time as a cross-country runner was long gone. He was pumped out. When he was in the SA he had always done well as a long-distance runner. Funny that now he should think of the medal he had once helped his unit to win.

At several points the wall showed signs of heavy damage—artillery shells? But it took time to find a spot where he could climb across the debris. He did it in great haste and cut himself on a bundle of barbed wire. He stopped to catch his breath. Shame and dishonor—he was finished.

The park seemed as overgrown as the land outside the wall. He noticed that the second row of barbed wire ran over insulators—a devil's trap, well camouflaged. Damned careful Germans, these Eyckes. But the electric power was cut.

At least an overgrown path led along the walls on the inside so that he could move ahead more quickly. The wood to his left seemed impenetrable; now and again paths branched off, but who knew where they led. He had to hug the wall. The manor house couldn't be far. And again he began to run.

The dogs howled nearby. Höllriegl heard voices and hoarse laughter between the frantic screams that broke off suddenly as if choked. The smell of fire became horrible.

He stopped, the blood pounding in his ears. Once again he checked his carbine. He knew the rifle; he had fired it last June during maneuvers and had had to take it apart as well. Automatic, gas-pressure loader—pretty much the latest thing in conventional arms. Everything checked. Only his hands trembled ridiculously. Mechanically he fingered his coat pocket for the extra ammunition.

As he did, he heard a rustling in the bushes and felt someone jump him from behind and hold him in an iron grip while a very small figure, dwarf or child, who seemed to have risen out of the ground, grabbed for the carbine. For seconds his heart stopped beating. But then—he had been prepared for something like this for hours—cold-bloodedness and strength returned. Unconsciously, because he had practiced it so much, Höllriegl used karate, the "fight with empty hands." He had dropped the rifle.

He loosened the grasp of the man behind him with a powerful elbow blow. He heard a loud gasp and saw how the man dropped. (Later he thought that the blow, which might have landed in his opponent's solar plexus quite accidentally, had saved Höllriegl's life.) Suddenly something glittered before his eyes. A knife. He jumped aside and the thrust, aimed for his throat, sliced open his blouse near his shoulder. With well-placed karate chops he was able to keep the dwarf at a distance. He seemed extremely strong and with monkeylike agility kept stabbing at him without hitting him. Now he had a knife in both hands. Höllriegl kicked and beat him, and as the little man staggered back, leaving his face momentarily unprotected, Höllriegl landed an open-handed uppercut. The dwarf tumbled back into the bushes and darkness swallowed him immediately.

Breathing heavily, Höllriegl leaned against the wall, the gun again in his hands. Most careless to turn his back on the wood. He had been observed, perhaps even as he climbed over the wall. Who were these people? He turned the unconscious man over on his back. A dark, bearded face, broad, flattened nose, slanting eyes. Surely an escaped SHC prisoner. The attack had been aimed at the gun; they obviously lacked rifles and ammunition—a somewhat reassuring prospect. But then, not that reassuring, for knives kill silently. His dagger was home in Heydrich, he could have used it well for fighting at close quarters. He saw an object shine in the grass. A bread knife. He picked it up.

His imagination peopled the wood with macabre characters. The carbine at the ready, he hurried on. How lucky that not a shot had been fired. No one could have heard the fight, and he had finished off those two. The stab wound burned, the dagger must have glanced off the collar bone. His shirt stuck to his skin. He noticed that he had other injuries, cuts on his hands, and his lower right arm hurt. His coat was badly slashed.

But onward, onward!

The wood became less dense and turned into a weed-covered park landscape. Yellow walls looked through bare branches. That had to be the gatekeeper's house. (Höllriegl remembered how haunted the house had seemed, alone and abandoned.) Again the wooden shutters were closed—did murderers' eyes look through the slits? Under cover of high bushes he crawled past the evil place on all fours. He took a deep breath when he reached the edge of the wood and peered around.

The driveway lay ahead. He could see no one, but heard a hue and cry up in the forecourt. There seemed to be a party going on; shots rang out and then he saw in the distance many drunks swinging wine bottles and booty as trophies over their heads, dancing noisily around a fire, a kind of stake—obviously furniture from the manor house. The mansion too was on fire, and sheafs of sparks struck skyward. The smoky air could choke you.

He ducked from tree to tree and soon reached the last one. From there he could easily overlook the forecourt, at least when smoke didn't block the view. About a dozen people, mostly men, bivouacked, drinking and eating, on the lawn and the gravel paths. A few immobile bodies, half nude and twisted, lay on the steps of the terrace. The smoke blew away a little, and then he saw something that made the blood clot in his veins. Using a horse's cadaver as support and breastwork, two men were shooting alternately at a target, and each time they did, the audience erupted into roaring laughter.

The target was a woman in boots and riding pants. She sat, tied on to a chair, deep in the garage, bathed in the glare of car headlights. A beautiful target. Her head had fallen back, the shirt hung in shreds from her shoulders, leaving her breasts exposed. A small white body, the body of a boy, lay across her lap. A broad wound gaped at his throat, and his head hung down as if it had been cut off.

The two men stopped shooting and began to stagger about. One of the bystanders ran into the garage, fetched a can of gasoline, then a second, and placed them beside the woman.

In the next moment a stream of fire broke from Höllriegl's automatic rifle. Never before in his life had he been as calm as in that second which he would later recall as a dirty eternity. He murdered well and according to plan, his hands no longer trembling; his senses were suddenly enormously sharpened. The man in the garage threw his hands up theatrically and collapsed. The jolly staggering of the marksmen turned into a quivering heap which abruptly grew stiff. Then it was the turn of the audience at this shooting match, the drinkers and the dancers. Höllriegl saw with wild joy how they jumped up or stopped what they were doing, stood there with gaping snouts and stared. He saw the jerking bodies and their convulsions. He jumped out from his hiding place, pistol in hand. Now and again something moved. But bullets were precious. One of the men jerked and screamed so piteously that he had to look away and almost administered the *coup de grâce.*

He ran into the garage. Was Ulla dead or unconscious? Thank God, she breathed. Carefully he took the boy from her lap and laid him—it must be Manfred—on the ground. He began at once to loosen Ulla's bonds. He had to work for a ridiculously long time, the beasts had shackled Ulla with sadistic thoroughness. At the same time he examined her. She didn't seem to have been hit, the marksmen had been too drunk to fire accurately. But Ulla had been badly beaten or tortured, that was easy to see; her skin was covered with dark splotches, perhaps some bones were smashed too.

When he had cut through the last strap—thanks to the bread knife!—Ulla pitched forward. Face down, she lay in front of him; the blond mane, a shining wreath in the headlights of the car, covered her shoulders and half her back. Her trousers had been split above the seat, presumably the swine had done themselves well by her. With a look he grasped it all and for a heartbeat he stood overwhelmed. She was still beautiful.

Shots rang outside. Höllriegl heard their impact, metal groaned, and shrill noise penetrated the room. Quickly he dragged Ulla by the boots to the nearest car and bedded her on a coarse blanket. He entrenched himself as best he could, took out his extra ammunition, and loaded the carbine. There it was again: the clatter of bullets, plaster falling from the walls, glass breaking—one of the headlights was dashed to pieces. Höllriegl shot out the other one.

The garage now lay in dusky darkness. Outside, day began. Very convenient. Whoever stepped into his gun sight was as good as dead. Damn the smoke. That could become dangerous, and under its protection the attackers—how many of them were there?—could enter the garage and overpower him. The air too became more biting; it was hard to breathe.

He tried to look around and out, his brain working feverishly. The ceiling and walls seemed made of thick concrete, the floor of the garage sloped toward the back, where sluicelike gates led somewhere, perhaps to a bunker, a deep bunker. They might have exits at the other end which opened into the woods. He'd have to find out. He searched along the walls to see if a layout of the building hung there as the law required. Nothing. If he went any deeper into the garage and lost his way, the beasts would smoke him out and capture him. There was still the last bullet—no, he'd have to save two bullets. Ulla wouldn't fall into their hands again.

Three cars and a small truck stood in the garage. Ulla's green Opel was askew; someone had tried to drive it but hadn't known how. Ulla wore riding clothes, so she had not gone to the funeral—probably the Eyckes had had some inkling of what was to come. Where was Herr von Eycke? He would have had to take part in the funeral ceremonies. Or had he been warned in time to flee? But then he would have taken Ulla and the children.

Ulla's clothes meant that she too had planned to leave. With Manfred. But what had happened to Erda? Erda, the Scharführerin—presumably she was with the Hitler Youth somewhere. (Someone had told Höllriegl that Erda was a fanatic young maiden and wanted to surpass her parents in devotion to Führer and Reich.) Ulla and Manfred must have been alone at the manor house when the monsters came.

She moved weakly. A basin was within reach, and Höllriegl pulled it toward him with his rifle. The little bit of water in it was dirty but cold. He tore a strip from Ulla's shirt and cooled her brow with the wet rag, rubbed her throat and bosom. As he massaged her breasts he felt faint. A strange feeling. Desire? Happiness? Now he was the master.

She opened her lids and closed them again quickly. Then she groaned loudly, a shiver ran down her spine and her limbs began to tremble violently. Suddenly she clung to him, he felt her full, pliant body and the old desire flamed mightily. But only for a moment. He was ashamed of himself and patted her tenderly, stroked her like a child while bullets whistled over their hideout. A desperate situation.

"Ulla!"

Again she opened her lids, her thick lashes were dewy. Slanted slits. She looked at him, saw his face up close, and her eyes turned rigid with horror. Screaming, she drew back.

"Ulla!—Ulrike!—Frau von Eycke! I'm your friend. Listen: your friend! Don't be afraid! I'll save you, so stay quiet. . . ." And again he tried to stroke her, to hold her hands. She withdrew them but did not move away.

"Jugurtha," she whispered, her face twisted with fear.

What was that, what did she mean? Was she crazy? The horror she had experienced had disrupted her mind. She screamed: "Jugurtha!"

"I'm your friend, Ulla, be reasonable. You've been attacked . . . by——"

He saw figures move through the curtain of smoke. He was on the rifle and a burst of fire sealed the entrance. Flight! The situation was untenable. Again he searched along the walls. Withdraw into one of the sluices—you could defend yourself in them more easily. For how long? With burning, tearing eyes he mustered the firing zone. No one would get past him.

Höllriegl heard how Ulla crawled, groping, up to him, again she clung to him. "Will you hurt me, black Jugurtha?" she whispered in his ear. "Black Jugurtha, black Jugurtha." Her voice trembled, but she did not loosen the embrace. He leaned his head on hers and stroked her hair and cheeks while keeping the carbine in his right hand, ready to fire. His eyes remained fixed on the door.

What if he possessed her here? They both had to die, that much was clear, there was no way out. He had one magazine left and a few bullets in his pistol. Christ Almighty! (Two of the bullets must be kept.) Why shouldn't he slip it to her before they both were done in? She was crazy and wouldn't put up a fight.

Again he felt a desire that would not leave him fog his senses. And . . . revenge, revenge for the beating. Revenge is sweet, this one especially so. He whistled through his teeth. With his free hand he fingered her shoulders, the hips; his hands slid down: There were the torn riding pants, her buttocks were half nude, her skin was rough, roughed up; he felt the welts, she had been beaten.

She snuggled up more closely to him—it was fear, what else? By and by she would regain her wits and an inkling of what was happening. Oh God—if only she didn't remember!

Pity swept over him like a sudden warm wave. But it did not wash away the desire, only increased it. He pulled her up close to him. Her hair, her face! The mouth was swollen as if it had been bitten. Crusted blood everywhere. What was all this about Jugurtha? A password, a code? Perhaps the secret was there. He took her breasts in his hand, big, strong, well-formed and elastic, her Valkyrie breasts! And no different from other women. (A passing memory: a woman he had met in a sleeping car from Graz, an official with the Reich Ministry of Food, well-fed, almost fat and no longer young. She had had the same Valkyrie-like forms.) His amber witch. His Valkyrie! Now he had her where he wanted her; he could uncover her most beautiful secrets, as in a dream, especially that treasure box. Ulrike Mlakar alias Ulla Frigg von Eycke, the Guardian of the Breed, the TV idol of the nation—now a heap of misery. And he had trembled before this woman! She was no different from a thousand others, damn it. He kissed the buds of her breast, those large, brown, soft nipples with the beautiful rims around them—of which he had dreamed like any masturbating boy. She let him do everything with her, her eyes were closed, she sighed deeply with half-opened lips, her teeth became visible.

"Jugurtha, Jugurtha!"

Again that word. Somehow it seemed familiar, somewhere in the distant past he might have heard it, but when and where he had forgotten. Jugurtha . . . and suddenly he remembered old Tartaglia, his teacher, the Triestino with the belladonna eyes and the long, black moustache. And there it was . . . the wars . . . the wars with Jugurtha. Something to do with the Romans . . . but what could it mean?

If he wanted to slip it into Ulla, he'd have to do it quickly. Not here, down in the sluice. He raised himself up a little and felt more than he saw that something, a shadow, jumped at him. Almost at the same moment he squeezed the trigger and heard how the head of the attacker slammed against the cooler.

The sluice!

For a moment he had seen his own face in the car window, smoke-blackened, oily, with white eyeballs—a horrible mask. For a lover he wasn't exactly a paragon of beauty.

He would have to cover about ten meters to get to the entry of the sluice at the back of the garage. Open terrain. He either ran a race against death or—but in her condition Ulla would be unable to run. Moreover she was so confused that she would not be able to understand his flight plan. But there was no time to lose, and then suddenly he had a glorious idea. "Ulla," he said softly, "the enemy is over there . . . the Romans. They want to catch us and murder us. Will you flee with me? . . ."

She embraced him hard. Her embrace had something intimate about it—or so it seemed. Her eyes remained shut.

"Then come on. Hang on tight."

Pressed flat to the ground, he crawled out from behind the car, slowly pulling Ulla and the rifle behind him; he had pocketed the ammunition. A wild confusion barged through his head, everything turned about. Every breath he drew burned in his lung. Smoke poisoning.

He covered a few feet in this fashion, gasping heavily for air. Sometimes he came close to losing consciousness and his ears began to ring, but he fought down the fainting spell. Finally they reached the entrance to the cellar, one of those massive bunker doors of heat-resistant steel that could be opened by lifting two transverse levers. Höllriegl knew the mechanism very well. He moved the levers but the door did not open.

Hesitantly he rose in order to repeat the attempt, the lock appeared jammed or was broken—or did it have a secret mechanism? Damn it! At that moment so glaring a brightness filled the garage that Höllriegl stumbled against the wall. The unbearable light seemed to come from all the slits and pores of the masonry, and although he had instinctively closed his eyes and covered them with his hands, it grew lighter around him than the brightest desert sun. It was an utterly terrifying light, and if Höllriegl had been in control of his senses during those eight or ten heartbeats, he might have thought of the eternal fire of Muspilli.

The flash of light plunged everything else into the pitch-black darkness of night. Blinded, Höllriegl cowered near the wall and groped along it. He rubbed his eyes—where was he? Blind! Was he still alive? Green and yellow edges danced and turned before his eyes, faster and faster. He tried to get up, his hands grasped empty space. The darkness became peopled with green phantoms.

And now he heard a heavy rolling throb, a long echoing, continuing cracking and thunder, followed by a hollow booming and whistling. The floor shook under his feet, as if he stood on a rolling deck, an invisible fist pressed him against the wall, and the air pressure hammered at his eardrums. At the same time the room filled with a singeing heat, the jaws of hell seemed torn open here. He saw—for he could again see a little—that the cars rocked violently and rolled around helplessly. Amid a deafening clatter a wall arose outside the garage door. Clouds of dust pushed inside. All at once he was able to think again.

Either an air mine had exploded or a big artillery shell had scored a direct hit on the garage. Out of here! The dust choked him, but Höllriegl saw water drip through a crack in the wall—a pipe must have burst—and so he wetted a strip of linen and held it in front of nose and mouth. In the half-darkness he had to climb across overturned cars and other obstacles. Finally he made it up the spoil bank at the entrance after repeatedly sliding back. He was outside. But what he saw filled him with horror.

The Eycke mansion had ceased to exist. Smoking mountains of debris from which flames still burst forth hid what might have been left of the house. But the park, too, no longer existed—Höllriegl faced an utterly changed landscape. A burning, glowing desert spread out before him and stretched far into the distance. The mighty trees that had lined the avenue lay broken or uprooted on the ground or stuck as splintered, skeletal stumps in the smoking earth. A part of the forest burned brightly—from where he stood, Höllriegl could not see how far the fire had gone. But the most terrible of all was the sky. In the west, facing the morning sun and obliterating it, stood an orange wall of flame, dazzling in its brightness —but paradoxically already paler than it must have been, for he could look at it without being blinded. It was as if matter of some heavenly origin had melted. The rest of the sky looked strange: It seemed destroyed, like a disheveled bed, and it radiated a pale chemical green.

Höllriegl took it all in with one look and understood. This was not a bomb dropped from a plane, nor an artillery shell or a conventional rocket. It was The Bomb.

And at that moment he realized his own grave danger. It hit him like a blow. But he did not really tremble because he was afraid; rather it was the visceral reaction of his poor flayed nerves. He sat on the pile of rubbish and cried like a desperate child, without will and without a trace of shame. He didn't notice it. Then—all at once—he stopped, wiped his cheeks, and just as suddenly his ability to think returned, worked faultlessly, like a well-oiled machine.

He was not too far from the place where the bomb had gone off, that much was clear; perhaps it had been aimed at the Kyffhäuser. The wind—after that initial blast of fire he could at least tolerate the thermal radiation—blew sharply from the northwest, like a hot wind out of the steppes, a sandstorm that smelled of fire. Höllriegl knew very well (he had taken part in enough so-called planning games) that unprotected persons absorb a dose of more than 100 R in the first four hours after a radioactive impact. (Oh, his memory still worked very well!) Moreover, who knew what kind of a bomb had been dropped? If it contained an extra mantle of heavy material (he remembered: U 238), then the radiation would be much higher due to a multiplication of the atomic chain reaction. (He had had to answer such questions often enough in special courses; his memory repeated what he had learned like an automat responding to a coin.) In that case it would not take four hours, but only an hour. He remembered hearing that the Japs used dirty bombs.

He didn't have any more time to ponder the issue. Flee, run, save his naked skin. He slid down the mountain of debris, threw away his coat, and began to run—terror followed the "planning games."

He didn't get very far, for the burning wood was an impenetrable barrier. The avenue! He thought (and at the same time realized the hopelessness) of reaching the highway from Rottleberode to Berga and Kelbra as fast as he could—if it was still intact—and then fleeing toward the east. He knew he was running a race with death —with a death that had already grabbed him by the collar and penetrated all the pores of his body.

While he searched in wild haste for a way through the burning chaos, his roaring brain spat out sentences stored away many years ago . . . basic protection, that means permanent protection against the effects . . . against the effects of conventional explosive . . . against the impact of pressure waves . . . against the effect of bacteriological and chemical warfare . . . against napalm . . . as a rule people in locally affected areas will seek shelter in bunkers. . . . Wait a minute, there must be such a bunker around here too, with all Eycke comforts . . . radiation-proof . . . with supplies for many weeks, toilets, masks, radiation suits . . .

The sluice! Ulla! He had forgotten her—completely forgotten her! He had deserted the amber witch. He was a brute, a mean dirty swine, a jerk, a scoundrel, a coward! He just wanted to save his own dirty life; he didn't give a damn about anything else. A miserable coward, that's what he was, and nothing more.

Höllriegl turned around at once. He still trembled and again tears ran down his cheeks. How shameful—and salvation had been so close! If he could only have opened the sluice door, they would now be in safety—but probably only those who knew how to handle the secret lock could enter the bunker—a safe with a password, reserved for Herr von Eycke and his brood; that was like him.

The feeling of extreme depression increased as he climbed back over the heap of debris—when you came right down to it nothing mattered anyway, it came the way it had to come. How awful that one was at the mercy of the unknown—unprotected, almost naked.

Ulla cowered in a corner, hands clasping her knees, brooding. She seemed to be thinking very hard. He stroked her hair. She looked up at him and he thought that the fear had gone from her eyes. Anyway she seemed fresher and clearer.

"We'll have to go, Ulla, quickly!"

He pulled her up, helped her to get on her feet. As he did, he noticed a crumpled piece of paper fall to the floor. Ulla bent down quickly to pick it up. For a few seconds she stood there irresolute, rolling the paper in her hand. Then she looked at him and pressed it into his hand.

"Salvation, black Jugurtha," she said. Her voice sounded normal, strong and pleasant. Was she crazy or wasn't she?

"Come on, Ulla, come on. We've got to get out of here quickly. The Romans . . ." Höllriegl interrupted himself. Was there any point in continuing this childish game? He embraced her in order to make her walking easier. At every step he felt her breast bounce, and, strangely, this touch gave him strength and confidence. He was her protector. It was good to have a human being around you.

He had to pull her, she didn't really want to go. When they were outside she looked about surprised—and curious. Without terror. She remained silent, untouched. Did she understand? Didn't she understand? They'd have to get out of here quickly.

With gentle force he pulled her along. The scrap of paper——perhaps it was important. They sat down on the hot ground amid the flickering flames. When Ulla leaned her head trustingly against his shoulder and the warm wind blew strands of her hair into his face a shiver ran down his spine. The horrid present disappeared. They were the first or the last people.

Hastily he read over the slip of paper; it was dirty and full of blood splotches. A long row of numbers, obviously scribbled in a child's hand. But a grown-up had written the rune and the corresponding German letter above each number. A game? Dumbfounded he read: Jugurtha. The word was written twice above the row of numbers, a third time only with the first five letters, the row ended then. A coded message—one only had to know the key word and the right combination of numbers. Or was it an explanation of the sketch below? The solution read: Junkers Gurnemanz Thale. The first few letters of each word again produced "Jugurtha."

Höllriegl read aloud and looked questioningly at Ulla. She only nodded and pressed closer to him. Her half-open lips were close to his mouth. He kissed her face, first her eyes, then her mouth. He felt the swollen lips, the smoothness of her teeth, the cool wetness of her gums. Her breath was fetid.

"Thale": That was a village in the Harz; perhaps she was supposed to meet someone there. "Gurnemanz": Did that mean Herr von Eycke? "Junker" was clearer. Eycke was a pilot and might well have flown a JU. Or was it a reference to a certain type of machine, the kind of luggage they should take along and the equipment? (Höllriegl remembered fleetingly what Gundlfinger had told him.) On the plan, for it was obviously a plan of escape, a place had been marked with an *X*, northwest of Thale in the direction of Quedlinburg. The meeting place.

"Ulla—what does Gurnemanz mean?" He searched her face and noted with dismay that her eyes had again become dull and apathetic. "Black Jugurtha," she whispered, and a trembling ran through her limbs, "will you hurt me?" The *idée fixe*. He stroked her and spoke kindly to her. So she was insane after all. Hopelessly. Where was his coat? He found it and placed it around her naked shoulders, carefully wrapped her body up in it.

Thale. That wasn't too far away. He knew the road, had driven down it several times. Through Rottleberode, Stolberg, Guntersberge—just a little way with the car. But on foot in this chaos? With a sick person? Anyway, it was a goal, a definite goal.

Well, on to Thale! On to face the radiation, run right into its arms, in fact—it was madness, death; no matter. And if the way led into hell!

The burning sky had faded, a pale sun floated like an artificial satellite in the low-flying, lava-colored clouds. The orange wall of fire had crumpled away—in its stead a spotted pink had spread over the western horizon. It was the pink in the Führer's picture in Höllriegl's home.

He could not sleep. With burning, tear-filled eyes he stared into the darkness. And although he was as tired as if every bone in his body had been broken one by one, his nerves throbbed. It smelled musty and sourish—his roughed-up senses registered menstruation, infant care, pumping of mother milk. Horrible! Ulla lay next to him on the cot, curled up like an embryo. His hand groped over her face. She snored softly, her mouth open.

He had had her twice today. One time in a hole in the ground behind Rottleberode. During a short rest she had pushed herself on him shamelessly, and had chewed biscuits while they were doing it. And she always relieved herself in front of him. The second time was here in the *Zuchtkloster,* the breeding monastery. Then she had resisted savagely when he wanted to take her, and he had nearly choked her. The first time wasn't worth much—a half-unconscious woman who has dropped all her inhibitions doesn't count, not even when her name is Frau von Eycke. The second time . . . it wasn't terribly exciting, just arduous. The paradise he had longed for did not exist. That too didn't have a great deal of value. And yet, slowly, gradually, step by step (they were tiny chicken-steps) she began to resemble herself again. Now and then he even encountered a whiff of her old stable-boy manners—that made him happy. It was the only happiness he had.

He had first remarked on this during their long, long wandering. Suddenly she had become very talkative, sporadically and mostly incoherently—but at least she did talk. Much could be gleaned from the confused images which darkened her reason. Presumably Manfred had brought her the coded message. Herr von Eycke must have written it. Gurnemanz? Höllriegl gathered from her partly confused, partly coherent speech that Gurnemanz was the castellan's nickname—the man who had told him to come and dowse the Eycke mansion. Apparently this "Gurnemanz" had been charged with preparing the family's escape and to make sure that everybody—the twins included—met at a certain place, in this case near Thale. Höllriegl remembered having heard that the SS had a well-camouflaged and heavily fortified air base in that region, in the flat woodlands along the Bode. Could the base still be operational despite the battle around Stolberg? The Eyckes' escape probably would have succeeded had the Japs been the only enemy.

Again he thought of Gundlfinger. How striking that Herr von Eycke or whoever had written the cryptogram had used signs which an expert could recognize at once as belonging to the so-called younger Nordic runic alphabet, not to the common Germanic "Futhark," which any *Pimpf* could read. (Only the "z" in Gurnemanz was taken from the Futhark; it was the same sign as the young Nordic *m.*) Did that mean that the flight—"Junkers"—would go to the north? Or was it purposely misleading and the Nordic runes meant the equator instead? On the other hand, Thale and Thule were similar-sounding names, and Thule, the island nation of the ancients, lay way up in the north, just as did Thule in Greenland. . . . Idle speculation.

What an end for Manfred . . . Höllriegl had seen how he died.

The escaped subhumans had grabbed and slaughtered him like a calf, presumably in front of his mother. There was undeniable evidence that Ulla had been tortured and raped several times, again presumably in the presence of her still-living son. A merciful fate had cloaked those scenes in Ulla's consciousness with an impenetrable curtain of forgetfulness, and Höllriegl was careful not even to lift a corner of the veil, although he sensed that this would reawaken the former Ulla, Frau Frigg von Eycke, the fanatic Nazi who headed the women's concentration camp "Dora" . . . Reawaken her old glory and horror.

Where was Erda? Had she received a similar message and now too was on her way to Thale? Ulla appeared to have forgotten that she had children. Her mental state forced her to live only for the moment, instinctively, without memory—somehow like a point in time. (Had he not said the same thing about Anselma?) She even forgot things that happened just a few minutes ago.

Höllriegl and Ulla had wandered through soulless, depopulated crater landscapes—where wild dogs seemed to be the sole living creatures. They had met people only once, a dispersed radiation-tracking unit of the Wehrmacht, whose members had no idea of what they were doing, or were supposed to be doing. The soldiers rode motorcycles and gave them a ride for part of the way.

They could have obtained radiation suits in Rottleberode if Rottleberode still existed. But it didn't, neither did Stolberg—a ghost town; in the distance its remnants looked like charred bones. Höllriegl decided to avoid the place; you never knew who or what you might meet amid the ruins. As a result, no warehouses and no radiation suits (for us, Höllriegl thought, it's too late anyway). Nor did air-raid or ABC defense units exist anymore. Nothing existed. The Wehrmacht men said that some people must still be alive in many of the bunkers because a radiation alarm was sounded the night before and the all clear had never been given. Debris had not buried every bunker exit, but people were still afraid to come out. All local alarm centers had been knocked out, the atomic-surveillance system, so carefully drilled to meet the reality of war, had broken down (something the programmers for the "Landgrave, Get Tough" project could not have imagined in their worst nightmares); the airwaves were described as utterly chaotic. The troop's Geiger counters showed that the Harz and Goldene Aue areas were most heavily contaminated.

They were running into death's arms, indeed had already been embraced mightily by him. It made no difference. Höllriegl wanted to take Ulla to Thale and then go someplace to die—he still had enough ammunition. Both could stay alive for a few days if need be, the troop leader had given them some food (radiation protected), a lined coat for Ulla, and a field blouse.

They had marched through endless deserts—past charred trees and forests and villages and farmhouses still on fire. The black rags that hung from some branches reminded Höllriegl of the mourning flags for the Führer. Ash fluttered constantly in the air—a fine, gray rain driven by soft breezes. But what made the going hardest of all were the great sand drifts that clogged all the roads and paths north of Rottleberode and forced them into time-consuming detours. Nor could they move any faster through the woods because fallen trees had wreaked great havoc there.

Toward evening they had stumbled upon an undamaged shelter: the "Luginsland" breeding monastery—abandoned, inhabited only by a lost kitten. Typical of the many Reich Institutes for Reproduction (*Zuklos,* they were called) built across the country after the war, usually near schooling castles and camps, it resembled a pleasant farmhouse. Inside were vast dormitories with rows of cupboards, recreation halls, and single bedrooms for progenerative purposes. Each one of them had the prerequisite hip bath and shower. (Incidentally, some of the monasteries had done away with use of selected SS men as studs. They resorted to artificial insemination instead and thus took all the sensual element out of pairing. As a result, single rooms fell into disuse.) Other facilities included an operating room for emergency cases, special housing for maternity service, doctors, baby nurses and teachers, and an experimental station. The complex was built in the shape of a square, and each tract had high-gabled roofs made of imitation shingles. A sign above the courtyard gate repeated in wrought-iron Gothic script the Führer's slogan: THE HIGHEST PURPOSE OF THE PEOPLE'S STATE IS THE MAINTENANCE OF THOSE PRIMEVAL RACIAL ELEMENTS WHICH CREATE THE BEAUTY AND DIGNITY OF A HIGHER HUMANITY.

Höllriegl had stumbled on the cat playing in the gymnasium. He found no one else. He had even gone down into the well-equipped pressure bunker, but it was empty; protective helmets, radiation suits, and food were gone. Either the maidens had marched in full regalia to the Kyffhäuser or they had been evacuated in time. The Harz was a battle area.

The abandoned *Zuklo* stood at the foot of a broad, sparsely wooded mountain, one reason why the bomb's fire burst had done little damage. Air pressure and whirlwind too seemed to have passed rather harmlessly across the depression. Only the windows on the west side were smashed and the doors torn open. In the so-called rest and relaxation room he found that the wind had blown books and papers about—*Clan, Motherhood, Love* (his heartbeat stopped abruptly as Höllriegl recognized a certain issue among them) lay strewn on the floor, as did musical scores: "What is Erika Playing on the Accordion?" and Köpfler's favorite march: "We Wolves Howl at Night." Nothing pointed to the Last Judgment outside—straw flowers and fir twigs were everywhere, fortune-telling wheels, housewifely slogans, framed rough wood carvings, schedules for roll calls, bed making, singing lessons, examinations, body care. And everywhere he found the customary "Brown Corner." On the wall menstruation and pairing calendars for every dormitory. Pale asters, scarcely withered, were stuck in empty shell cases that stood on tables and on the floor. Nothing but still lifes —and you could have eaten off the floors. Everything was nice and demure and betrayed the orderly hand of the German woman.

This idyll annoyed Höllriegl more than he could say. It seemed to him as if he had come from a moonscape straight into a friendly, earthly world with delectable evening shadows and a twinkling night. The contrast was staggering. The destruction he had witnessed now seemed to him the normal, accustomed condition, even a measure of things. Peace and security were unnatural, deceptive, a result of accident. Next to him lay a pistol—that was real. The hours crawled slowly past while he pondered and thought. There was a kind of harmony between the total destruction outside and the domesticity in here. As the borders blurred he saw the similarities. Were the contrasts really that harsh? The Germans had the accursed talent of combining such opposites. They had invented something the world had not known before: orderly chaos.

The past day, which he had called the "Last Judgment," had opened his eyes—finally. Anselma was right: There was nothing. Nothing existed that had any value. The Führer was dead, and with that Höllriegl's world had lost all meaning. Life had no meaning, and yet how much less had death. Nothing was meaningful, everything was worthless—right down to the absolute zero. It was like his profession, that hocus-pocus profession, the existence of earth radiation which one had to "believe," the party—only now did he see it sharply and clearly—was nothing but an enormous dung heap, all of it wasn't worth much. This war too, carelessly and criminally begun (how right Senkpiehl had been!), did not have any value, had been utter madness from the first moment, a completely senseless, instinctive battle of all against all, that was obvious. A war of life against itself. Down to the knife, no—two knives, like that subhuman who had attacked him. And a hero's death? That was no more than slaughter, the way Manfred had been slaughtered. Or like those carp bodies which, though cut to pieces, still jumped high . . . fight with your back to the wall! And die! That's what Anselma must have meant.

And the higher world, his belief in a holy salvation embodied on earth in the person of the Führer? It was all deceit. His fingers crunched together in shame when he thought of the feeble-minded nonsense he had dispensed way back then—way back then? It had been just a few days ago. How much Anselma must have pitied him!

And Axel? And Ulla? Axel was a beautiful idiot, no more, no less—and only pure and good because he was an idiot. And Ulla was a dirty little woman just like his Ingrid who did the ladies' hair. Perhaps—back in primeval times—Ulla's conquest would have made him the proudest of mortals—back then when he still believed in heroism, the Valkyrie, and similar idiocies. While she was doing it she behaved no differently from the other girls he had slept with. Only a weak shiver, a memory of long ago had remained. Oh, if she would again whip him!

He fingered her, felt up her body, while she slept deeply. Desire and disgust, disgust and desire. This life was one great shit and vomit.

He fell asleep over her body. In his dreams a Geiger counter ticked.

ENTERPRISE BIFRÖST

It was noon, the sun stood somewhere below the arctic horizon. The man whose name was now Jugurtha came out of the canteen.

He froze pitifully, froze steadily. He had even been cold in the overheated dining room where one's eyes glazed as in a fever. Nerves, surely. He felt awful, and he hoped the fresh air would rid him of his headache. He had crept out even though no one took the slightest notice of him. Nevertheless he suspected that someone was concerned about him, not hostile, oh, no—cold, impartial, as if he were a thing, not a being.

But that must be a product of his ruined nerves. He stamped his boots hard as he walked in order to make some noise. This island far in the arctic was so still. The mushy ice splashed under his feet and his breath smoked. He was tolerated here, that was all. For how long? He kicked an empty can as he walked past. It rattled. No wind, dead silence, only the hoarse screeching of sea gulls above the bay over there. The sea was gray and mirror-smooth, a gloomy cesspool.

You would get sick here if you weren't already. Not day, not night, the water gleamed in melancholy—it didn't really look like water, but like lubricating oil or some residue. Everything seemed so strangely distant, even at close range: the three tanks, the pile of old fuel barrels, the generator house, the fur-clad guards—great big lads who suddenly appeared in front of you out of the fog—finally the barbed wire with the high-power tension lines. There was nothing else. The horizon glowed weakly in the south, like white gold, and the low hill that hid the air base gleamed metallically. The tower skeleton with its radar equipment was hard to recognize.

Every inmate of the camp (AL Ju 33) could move freely within the enclosure. But you rarely saw anyone outdoors. Most of them lay in the barracks on their plank beds, read or napped. Waited. Waited for interrogations, examinations, inoculations. If you were allowed to fly on, you changed barracks. Whoever transferred to the camp near the airfield had made it.

How long had he been here? He didn't know—there was no way of telling time. At the beginning he had oriented himself by the meals, but he had missed some of them and then everything had become confused. Sometimes he saw searchlights flame on the other side of the mountain peak—ramp illumination. That was a short-lived joy each time, however, for strict blackout measures were in force on the island. Right afterward jets roared; a transport departed. Jugurtha could not see the takeoff from where he stood, but he waited nevertheless. He saw the lights of the heavy plane blink a few times. The searchlights dimmed and the noise ebbed. Night, night and fog.

He stomped around the enclosure for the umpteenth time. The guards resembled black statues. Why the many guards and the barbed wire? What were all the blackjacks, flamethrowers, laser guns, bloodhounds, and smoke-screen apparatus for? He thought —feared—he knew. This final selection did not always proceed smoothly; everybody wanted to get into the lifeboat, but the doctors and the officials of the Chief Race Office had the last word: only the political elite, the strongest, racially simon-pure Germans with healthy genes would have a chance for survival. Age, potency, martial spirit, rank, and ideological outlook were also taken into account. (In principle he favored this type of selection, in the past he had undergone similar examinations, perhaps not quite as ruthless.) The island resembled a fortress. Collar patches identified the guards as members of the Death's Head units "Viking" and "Vidkun Quisling." Best Nordic material. They even had provost marshals up here—what an old-fashioned institution. The people spoke broken German but were under orders to keep quiet. Somewhere he had heard that only the camp leadership, doctors included, were German SS.

Another question: Why the silly cover names? Whoever arrived in the AL had to scratch out his previous life and start anew. All right. But you just didn't put your whole life aside simply by changing your name. It continued—in a thousand things, especially in memory. Did these cover names have any practical significance, or was the change of name purely symbolic? Was it one of the many vexations, an arbitrary complication? The Eyckes had registered him, Höllriegl, right after his arrival simply as: *Jugurtha; profession: therapist and editor.* (Wisely he had stated that himself.) All his papers, draft card, party card, racial credentials, identity card, etc., were made out to Höllriegl; therefore the authorities here must know his real name, for his documents were at headquarters. If he were "admitted," would he get new papers made out to Jugurtha? (Jugurtha was more than silly!) Somehow the game with the cover names reminded him of the runic writing with which the author of that fateful message had encoded its meaning still more. Life in the Thousand Year Reich of the Germans was full of such cryptic touches.

Everyone in the camp was tight-lipped. People waited their turn, and there wasn't much anyone could say about that, but even so, caution did seem in order. The two men with whom he shared a room, for example—what a taciturn pair. One of them was a stud master from Trakehnen, he had read that on the room list (name: *Bütefisch*), the other a typical peacock (name: *Wolfskehl*), a Labor Führer and at the same time a wheel in the German Labor Front. They only talked to him about the most necessary things, but confided more in one another and played checkers or chess together. They also exchanged meaningful glances behind the Ostmarker's back—he had seen them do it in his shaving mirror. In such exalted society an ordinary official was a simple piece of shit.

The canteen was just as monosyllabic, stiff, and above all, anonymous, but nevertheless ranks had formed quickly. A pink, bullnecked type with a brush haircut who introduced himself simply as "German Synthetic Fibers" had sat at his table at first. A short time later this sparkling leader of the economy was moved to a different and—presumably—better table. The silence in the dining hall was only broken when an SS man entered, stood at attention, slammed his heels together, and whipped up his right arm. The one-dish ration had to be fetched at the kitchen window, and today the Eyckes had been in line not far from where he stood. As usual the *Obersturmbannführer* had stared arrogantly and snobbishly into space—the "*Ostubaf*" had a habit of staring through him as if he were glass. Höllriegl didn't know what Eycke called himself now. In any case Ulla's name was Sigga. He had met her twice secretly, and these hasty meetings, no more than a touching, really, had re-awakened in him that feeling of imminent danger. Sigga looked worn, but her disease seemed an added attraction; one could believe that she had just arisen from an endless embrace. At table no one turned a hair when she entered although the men covertly let their eyes wander. It disgusted Jugurtha each time—this enormous atmosphere of sexuality that enveloped her. In addition to the Eyckes, four or five other couples waited to fly on, all of them young people. There were no children about; presumably they lived in another camp. AL Ju 33 didn't have serfs either; labor volunteers and Norse maidens took care of the service.

Jugurtha had come to the barrier that blocked the road to the air base. Two guards armed with lasers walked up and down in front of it, the delicate optical-looking instruments gleamed black. He thought guards were an exaggerated measure; placards warned against touching the fence. In a few days he would be passed through—or not. It was all right with him if he wasn't.

Slowly the thought had taken root in his brain that Eycke planned to kill him. The pompous little man had agreed only reluctantly to take him along in his twin-engined plane, and because of him, he knew, the couple often fought bitterly. The "*Ostubaf*" had tried to get rid of him several times, after all he was an unwanted guest even if he had saved Ulla's life. And this troublesome guest was now here—Frau von Eycke's stubbornness had won all down the line. She loved him, if the desire to have him touch and possess her could be called love. He couldn't kid himself. He was simply younger and stronger, a better lover. This Eycke with his bird's head? Enough to make you vomit.

He would have to fight for his life and for Ulla, alias Sigga. That really wasn't much fun. But then it didn't matter if he died here, in Germany, or God knows where. And he'd have to die soon—and Sigga too. Both had been exposed to massive doses of radioactivity, and the disease had already made its presence known. He felt how radiation was eating into his inner organs. If he had just a little bit of luck at the examination, he could hide his condition for a while at least. But the symptoms were there: disrupted vision, the flow of involuntary tears, the diarrhea, the "other head." Wasn't it an irony that he, the radiologist and healer, had to die from radiation, which that real devil of creation—man—had unleashed?

Perhaps Eycke planned to denounce him to the camp doctors. If that happened, he'd have to talk, unfortunately. Then the radiation-damaged Sigga wouldn't be allowed to go "over there," to Niflheim, as people called it here. (Anyway Sigga had hereditary defects; she had had several miscarriages.) Eycke, he was sure, would not let her go at any price, the man remained enslaved despite everything. The children had to be written off—not a trace had been found of Erda—all the more important then to save their own skins, Herr von Eycke and Sigga's. Precious skins.

Sigga's mental state had improved rapidly, except for the gaps in her memory. To the extent that her body deteriorated (something only he noticed), her spirit came alive. In some things she was again the domineering, cold Ulla. When she had come to his barracks for the second time (after hasty, unconsummated love play) she had whispered him a warning: Her husband was ready for anything. Here people dissolved into nothing—and such disappearances were not investigated; no one had time for it, and the authorities were glad to cross people off their lists. Too many atomic refugees waited in the camps.

"You mean, I should kill your husband?"

"Jugurtha may not do anything. Sigga will do it."

"With what? Do you have a gun?"

"I have a laser . . . Meduso Six."

"What? Where did you get it?"

She laughed dirtily. "From . . . Knud, Scharführer Knud. A forfeit, a toy. I let him touch me here for it." She took his hand and showed him.

What a woman. A Meduso Six—a ruby laser! He'd have to try and coax that gun out of her.

"No, you mustn't get involved in such things. Men have to take care of it among themselves."

"Silly boy. I have a very personal account to settle with Erik. He's accused me of polluting his escutcheon. He, me! He'll regret it. Don't get involved in our affairs."

Eycke had thrown Sigga's past in her face, her lower-class ancestry—probably in connection with him, Höllriegl, who came from common people as well. Both of them were bastards and belonged together. But according to the aristocratic code of honor, this wrong could only be washed away in blood. Very careless of von Eycke, to hurt Sigga so much. She had become the old Ulla again and would act accordingly.

No! He'd have to do it first; it wasn't manly to leave such business to a woman. Ever since he left the canteen, he had thought about how it could be done. Dueling code? Two shots each—as they used to do it long ago? This Eycke was a dangerous chap and surely a much better shot. And in this darkness a bullet from an unexpected quarter could hit him easily. Or draw lots, yield? But he didn't want to yield, not like that, the other man ought to yield. To be sure . . . perhaps it would be better to die from a bullet than from radiation.

And then there was that one weak, fantastic hope. A silver stripe on the horizon, like the sun that never rose. Senkpiehl and Kummernuss had talked about it months ago. A kind of secret miracle cure, supposedly well tested, that could neutralize or at least arrest the aftereffects of radioactive exposure. It was said that initial successes had been achieved in the SHC laboratories after a series of failures. Some real cures were supposed to have been effected. A triumph of German research.

But suppose it had been a lie? Still, one time Eycke too had hinted at such a possibility. Right after their first landing—was it in Aalborg?—Höllriegl had talked openly to the icy and flabbergasted husband about the deadly danger Ulla faced. For hours she had been exposed to the strongest radiation—what should be done? (Höllriegl had not mentioned his own exposure.) Then Herr von Eycke opened his mouth suddenly to make this memorable comment: "Over there we'll pull her through, once Bifröst is behind us." The sentence seemed to have slipped out unintentionally, to judge from the furious expression on his face. Good. And Sigga had heard from a general staff doctor who ate with her in the canteen that one could be cured "in Niflheim." Apparently she knew more about her condition than she let on.

Jugurtha strolled past the empty barrels again. It's him or me, he thought. Not that he really hated Eycke, he had no reason to. But it was true that he couldn't stand him. And incidentally Eycke wouldn't have the slightest scruple about shooting him down like a dog. . . . Where and how should it take place? When Eycke walked home from the canteen? The Eyckes lived at the other end of the camp in the barracks for married people. It was quite a way, and the *Herr Obersturmbannführer* might end that walk sooner than he would wish to. The barrels would make a good hiding place. But the shot, and for all he knew he might need two, would be heard in the whole camp. Laser! Laser only hissed—like a welding tool. Pity—Herr von Eycke wouldn't look very pretty afterward; laser dead did not look very pretty. His charred remains could be strewn solemnly on the sea. He must get the weapon from Sigga and get it at once.

He walked into the sparsely lit room and saw an envelope lying on his seat. The peacock snored on his plank bed. The afternoon nap. The Trakehner stallion played a game of chess with himself.

Stenciled text, summons from headquarters: "Report to the camp doctor tomorrow . . . empty stomach . . . bring early-morning urine. . . ."

Here he wasn't even Jugurtha, that creature of Sigga's imagination, but just a number. They had determined his racial blood group, centrifuged his urine and analyzed it, taken finger, sole, and ankle prints, done an electrocardiogram, drawn stomach fluid, examined his ass and his cock, he—Albin Totila Höllriegl alias Jugurtha—had been auscultated, percussed, weighed, measured, sero-chemically examined, his reflexes tested, the back of his eyes checked out. . . . What else, what else? He had been assigned Number 18.

And for the longest time now a milksop with glasses and a doctor's coat, pantaloons, and high boots had circled and fingered his skull. Three bright lights were turned directly on his face—as if he were getting the third degree. It was stinking hot in the room. He was cold—low blood pressure, low body temperature. To the side in the shadows three men in uniform (naturally SS) sat around a horseshoe-shaped table, their jackets, sword belts, and hats hung on the clothes rack. They stared holes into the air, while the doctor dictated the results of his examination to a secretary in a softly bleating voice. Everything went off in very businesslike fashion. In the background other naked men waited their turn.

". . . dinaric or predominantly dinaric . . . blood type with dark-eastern influence . . . skull index eighty-four point twenty-one . . . face index one hundred point eighty-one . . . clearly steep occipital . . . side view . . . colon . . . so-called shako head . . . nose and chin strongly developed . . . comma . . . suspicion of acromegaly . . . occipital protuberance, easy to feel . . . facial cut . . . colon . . . forehead bent back flatly . . . comma . . . but gives high impression . . . nose protrudes strongly . . . septum visible from side . . . firmly drawn mouth . . . comma . . . typical for Ostmark sound formation . . . lower jaw angle blunt . . . front view . . . colon . . . forehead protuberance clearly visible . . . hair color dark brown . . . comma . . . iris gray-blue . . ."

The instruments clinked, the rattle of the typewriter made one sleepy, the three men looked off into space and stretched themselves with creaking joints. The doctor felt his teeth. Tooth status. What was it all for? Goddamn stupid. And so serious. Quite aside from the fact that all the data they collected here was written down in his passport. Or weren't documents to be returned? In his case that didn't matter anymore.

For ever since last night he owned the properly validated papers of the Herr Inspektor for Economic Affairs in the Upper Section Fulda-Werra, Erik Meinolf von Eycke (God have mercy on him), only they were made out in a different name. Eycke had really looked horrible. They—he, Sigga, and Knud—had not strewn what was mortal of the *Obersturmbannführer* (his soul might now embrace Walvater Wotan) on the sea but poured it into a bucket, a kitchen garbage barrel.

If one could believe Sigga's report, they had had another fight that afternoon. As usual Eycke had planted himself in front of her, hands in his pockets, legs spread apart, and had raked her over the coals. Always the same thing. Befouling his honor, his name, the escutcheon of the von Eycke. She jumped into bed with everyone, even with servants, and now with an Ostmark quack. She was the TV whore of the nation and so on. Sigga had replied in kind. Something he did with his hands, had always done, and which is popularly called "pocket billiards," roused her to white heat. Now he played "pocket billiards" copiously, and this time it was especially disgusting to her. Thus in the end she had killed him not so much because of his abuse, but because this childish, unconsciously onanistic little game had tipped the scale. Moreover Eycke had done it with such impossible arrogance. One would have to understand.

Knud, the white-blond, taciturn, and simpleminded Nordic thane who worked in the headquarters archive had the job of fetching the Eycke documents and stamping the proper visas into them. Certain highly placed persons were allowed to keep their old papers and did not have to assume new names, unless they wished to do so. Eycke had chosen one voluntarily, an especially ancient one, but he would keep it only for the length of his stay in Niflheim (he had insisted on that): Hadmar Götz von der Leyen. The necessary changes had already been made. The former Ulla Frigg von Eycke was now called "Sigga von der Leyen," her Nordic honor name was "Gutrune." Herr von Eycke had not asked her consent, but taken it for granted. That was only one, even if one of the smallest, of the many recent little jabs and grievances. The roots of dissension, however, were older and deeper. They were linked to Ulla's TV career.

The doctor stopped bleating. Number 18 was allowed to dress and was sent on to the next place. Of course the whole thing was monumentally stupid, but would there have been any point in arousing suspicion? Whatever the outcome of the examination —he would travel with the notarized papers of Herr von der Leyen. Knud had promised to get him and Sigga on their way "over there" today, by which Knud meant the air base. The question arose as to just how Sigga would reward Knud's services. All right, he'd have to live with that too.

For the time being he was still Jugurtha, at least with her, while his old, real name gradually lost all validity. That had been such a long time ago—back when he still dowsed earth and body radiation. Left ellipses, right ellipses. That Höllriegl was canceled, burned out—like Odin's breath. Like everything else. All that was far away, gone and done.

A thin man with a weathered warhorse face and rounded back now sat across from him. Civilian. In his buttonhole he wore the insignia of the NS lawyers' guild and the League of the German East. Sharp, inquisitorial look. Apparently these bright lights were standard equipment around here. A tape recorder was switched on.

"Do you know the approximate circulation of the German Labor Front's press?" . . . "What share of the total does *Arbeitertum* have?" . . . "How do you punish serfs found stealing?" . . . "At what age can the chancery court declare a young German of age?" . . . "What is the greatest crime in your eyes?" . . . "Who is the author of the *Sachsenspiegel?*"

All very harmless, general-education-type material. (Or was the ease of the questions a trap?) Perhaps Knud would come soon —he had entry to every room—and give him the prearranged signal; he was supposed to do that if a favorable opportunity for flight developed earlier. Where was Knud? With Sigga? He stole a glance at his watch.

"The name of the *Gauleiter* of South-Hanover Brunswick is . . ." "Of Central Memel?" . . . "Of Weser-Ems?" . . . "When was the peace of Westphalia signed?" . . . "Tell me something about your field, dowsing." . . . "Who was German water-polo champion last year?" . . . "Who won the Tschammer Cup last year?"

The questions jumped from one subject to another. Intelligence test. Some of it was intricate because it seemed so simple—and he didn't have a clue about physical fitness or championships. When Knud gave the sign, he'd have to get out of here, no matter what. The smartest thing would be to cite his trots and scram instead of going to the toilet. But if they guarded him, what then? The walls must have ears around here and the doors eyes. (He remembered those awful slits in Anselma's flat.) The tape moved silently, he watched the busily turning reel.

"How do you control the *Schweinehund* in you?" . . . "Since when have all SS Führers been forced to take achievement tests?" . . . "Who solved the Jewish question in Lublin?" . . . "What offices belong to the agenda of the Reich Finance Minister?" . . . "Sing the first verse of '*Schleswig-Holstein* Sea-Surrounded.' " . . . "What is the position of racial thought in painting?" . . . "What are the first two of Bormann's theses?" . . . "How do you view the future of the Werewolf movement?" . . . "What was the designation of the Sixth Reich Party Congress?" . . . "When did it take place?" . . . "Express your thoughts on the subject 'Think Western, act German.' " . . . "In what year was the first unmanned German satellite shot into orbit?" . . . "The first manned satellite?"

The questions pelted down on him. Only rarely was he now able to reply at once, but next to very difficult questions there were also ridiculously easy ones. They must be trying to confuse him. Some questions were obviously traps—then it was vital to stutter or talk around it (in that he had a fair amount of practice). More and more this bleak chatter turned into a full-blown interrogation, with the pace stepped up all the time. If he didn't find an answer right away, the next question was thrown at him. Although he was cold, he began to perspire freely. He felt faint. Goddamned nerves. But Knud would and would not come.

"What is the significance of the sign NN?" . . . "Describe some of the torture methods used in Bolshevik camps." . . . "Do you know the aims of Enterprise Bifröst?"

Bifröst—the rainbow bridge of the ancients that connected Himinbjörg with the earthly world! (But Muspell's sons waited to destroy it.) Bifröst was also the great air lift, one of the great air lifts the master race used to reach secret, impenetrable areas—at least that's what he had been told under the seal of utter confidence. (Was it Sigga?) He knew nothing about any "aims," except one—survival. The master race, he said, had to survive no matter what so that its task, domination of the world, could continue.

Abruptly he faced another man; the thin one had disappeared like a shadow. He had not noticed the exchange, the lamps blinded him. His new interrogator was a pale, beardless, and bony fellow whose bald head stuck out of a neck girdle. He wore a Wehrmacht uniform, but collar and shoulder patch showed neither rank nor unit. His voice sounded hoarse, the sentences were pushed out almost harshly.

"How many armored divisions did Army Group A have at the beginning of the French campaign?" . . . "Army Group B?" . . . "Do you know the Morse Code? The Morse signal for *U* is . . . ?" . . . "For semicolon?" . . . "How do you understand the term 'tank-unfavorable terrain'?" . . . "How high can the Me-Fafnir climb—its climbing time up to six thousand meters?" . . . "Nine thousand meters?" . . . "Cite the name of a nerve-damaging gas." . . . "Lung?" . . . "Blood?" . . . "What do you know about the use of helicopters in jungle warfare?" . . . "When do you build an igloo and when a snow hole?" . . . "Is the strategic thinking of the world empire influenced more by long- or short-term planning?" . . . "Which of our weapons systems fly at supersonic speed?" . . . "On what day was the Narvik Task Force relieved? And how?"

While he was answering, the door opened and Knud—a broadly grinning Knud—entered. Finally! He handed the Wehrmacht examiner a piece of paper. The tape recorder was switched off.

"You'll follow this man to headquarters, the questioning will be interrupted. Your new number is"—the examiner looked at this list and wrote in name and number—"thirty-two. You'll wait until called."

Number 18, now 32, marched out, that is, he followed close on Knud's heels. In the corridors other examinees sat stiffly on benches or leaned against the walls—there weren't very many of them, nor did he see many official personnel. Soon they found themselves in the doctors' quarters; everything was white and clean, the pale-blue light reflected in the shellac.

Knud stopped in front of a door marked "X-Ray Station," and saluted amiably. As Jugurtha opened the door he saw Sigga walk toward him. She was obviously ready for the trip and carried a small suitcase. "Here are your things," she whispered, "Knud got them." With these words she tossed him a thickly wadded fur-lined coat with Greenland collar and a fur cap with ear muffs. He dressed silently. "And Knud?" he asked, his face turned away. "Knud will come later sometime," she said softly. "He's got to stay—until the camp is blown up." (Oh, Höllriegl thought, he's expendable then.)

A wave of childish joy almost made him drunk. Both of them now looked like North Pole explorers. He smiled happily at Sigga and embraced her. But she withdrew. "Hurry up, Knud's waiting."

His coat pocket was stuffed with documents. Outside in the corridor he glanced through them quickly. Not only were all his old papers in hand, crumpled, dirty, and blood-splattered (even Senkpiehl's car papers), but the new ones too. Knud was a genius.

"My name is Ritter Götz von der Leyen with the iron fist," he laughed, in high spirits, although he still felt quite horrible physically (he had forgotten that for a moment.) "And you are my wife!"

He embraced her again; this time "Gutrune" let him. He had not been in such a good mood since his meeting with Axel. And "over there in Niflheim" they'd be cured—he clung to that belief. He whistled through his teeth, while they walked toward the camp exit. Knud carried the suitcase, the two of them trotted behind arm in arm.

It worked marvelously. The guards looked through their papers quickly and passed them on. How strange! On the one hand nothing but hurdles and pitfalls, on the other a carelessness so monumental as to arouse instant suspicion. (In point of fact: The whole thing did have a foreboding air about it.) And yet he suddenly felt free of the enormous nightmare, the compendium of all the offices through which he had ever been forced to pass. He took a gulp of the sharp, icy air. Behind that door something different, quite strange, began—and he desired it with every fiber of his heart. It was freedom, the freedom of the animal.

At the door to the waiting shed, Knud, smiling sunnily as always, turned to go. His smart good-bye was impersonal; it might just as well have been said to an inspecting general. Sigga's good-bye, too, was meaningless. (Good, good, good!) Herr Höllriegl alias Hadmar Götz von der Leyen returned the greeting with military precision, for he was happy now; he'd almost burst out with his accustomed "Heitla"—a greeting that belonged to days long gone.

Nor did the feeling of freedom fade when he and Sigga had to march between a row of SS men who had occupied the corridor, every one of them a monument to the New Order. A nerve-racking running of the gauntlet. With sudden displeasure he saw the wide-open wolf's jaw on many collar patches. The laser guns gleamed in the blue light.

The waiting room, swampily lit by air-raid lamps, was jammed. Those inside looked like black lumps. They cowered or stretched out on benches or on the floor next to their meager luggage. All were silent, seemingly lost in thought or asleep. Who knew how long they had been there! (Again he praised that miracle-man, Knud, who had managed their unexpectedly swift departure.) The nervous tension in here was thick enough to touch, and it communicated to everyone waiting to make the great leap into the unknown. At least it struck Jugurtha that way because his sensitivity allowed him to experience things much more intensively than others. And on top of everything the news blackout that had lasted for days now—who could take all that without snapping? Knud had told Sigga that the radio had broadcast regular reports on the military situation until very recently, then nothing. Loudspeakers yawned at you everywhere, but not even local announcements were made on them. (There's nothing more deadly than a silent loudspeaker!) Communications within the camp were now handled via written messages.

They found a hole in the crowd. Jugurtha leaned against the wall and Sigga sat down at his feet on top of their folded coats. An animal warmth in here. He felt her head against his legs and involuntarily he flexed his muscles so that she would feel how hard his thighs were. Tenderly he ran his hands through her mane; she raised her hand and for a time they took delight in the play of their entwined fingers, but this was not the place to give their desire free reign. When would he possess Sigga again? No one stood in his way, the proud Amazon was his alone. And suddenly he dreamed so vividly of her embrace that he felt physical pain.

No one had come in after them; they seemed to be the last passengers for today's flight. After a while the door to the airfield flung open with a bang, and several men of the ground crew cordoned off the exit. A shiver ran through the waiting men and women; everyone had been aroused with a start; the clumps of people began to move. Quickly, they all made ready to leave. A Luftwaffe helper, a Norse judging from her accent, read names from a list, her dark lantern illuminated the scene. Everyone thronged to the exit, Jugurtha and Sigga too were swept into the whirlpool. A senseless, needless scramble erupted, the smoldering, feverish nervousness that had weighed on them for so many days found some relief in curses and blows. The voice of the Luftwaffe helper drowned.

But already the SS had poured into the hall. The SS with their laser. Wedge-shaped, the troop worked its way to the exit, brutally shoving aside those who waited. Minutes passed before the uproar subsided. Silence fell on the gathering, people were ashamed and dismayed. The elite of the master race had faltered; now they all fell back into their old apathy. One—was it the "German Synthetic Fibers" man?—screamed: "You all ought to be shot." But this cry of rage aroused no echo.

The roll call continued under the threat of laser muzzles (their charming little mouths). Slowly—it took time. Those called up had trouble pushing their way through the exit with their baggage. Then the business with the documents. Finally, when "Götz and Sigga von der Leyen" were called out, the room was half empty. For the second time today their documents were examined, this time closely; then they stood outside in the winter night.

A soft snow fell. On the darkened airfield, enlivened only by lonely signal lights, one could see the outlines of two great planes. One seemed ready to start, the engine had begun to cough. Jugurtha and Sigga, holding each other in a close embrace, were told to walk to the second plane, which waited silently and shadow-like in the darkness. They ran across the wide tarmac, a cutting wind whipped snowflakes and ice kernels into their faces. The mighty wheels of the gray giant rested on the runway, which was made of punched steel ribs. A red cross on a white background was painted on the wings and stern. The gangways were down; behind the doors metal walls shimmered in the pale light.

Again they all assembled. The barriers between them seemed about to fall, hesitantly people began to look each other over; it was clear they wanted to start talking. But instead only their teeth chattered and they hopped on one leg, then the other. The ground crew still blocked the gangway.

As if in response to a cue, the lights of the runway flamed up, formed a long glistening street, and under the high whine of the jets the first giant turned gracefully on its axis, and ran trippingly, a dully shining griffin, down the runway into the night. You could hear it stop as if it were collecting strength before taking off. At that moment they were allowed to board, and Jugurtha and Sigga were busy entering their "ship." While they were mounting the steps, Jugurtha had one of his romantic imaginings: He felt himself a Viking and Sigga his Viking bride.

The Viking ship, however, turned out to be an old-model troop transport. Narrow, uncomfortable seats that hung on metal straps ran along both inside walls. The seats swung gently; you sat with your back to the wall. It was damned cold, the portholes blinked in silver. Jugurtha saw that several of the refugees had made themselves comfortable on the floor under the seats, and so he stretched out too, and Sigga did the same. He found a thick coat as a cover.

Sigga's suitcase and fur hat served as pillows. Snuggled as close together as the wadded fur coats allowed, they lay there and found their situation tolerable despite their enormous fatigue. A broad passage had to be kept clear down the middle of the plane.

The long, gloomy tube filled with people; life preservers were distributed, vitamin tablets, and small first-aid kits. Hot coffee was served. The radio played brisk music. It began to rumble in the plane's bowels. The ground crew made another body count and compared papers with the passenger list—and then the escape almost failed.

As a married couple, Jugurtha and Sigga had a common passport, but without any notation in it about inoculations. Now the camp inmates had all been given shots against all kinds of diseases, including examinations for scurvy and other deficiency illnesses. (No one could avoid the inoculations, but Knud's "abbreviated procedure" had helped.) In any case they didn't have the certificates. Anxious minutes. If they were turned back and booked on a later transport, the authorities would uncover the whole swindle, even —horrible thought—the business with Eycke.

Again they were lucky; the starting signal saved them. The official merely ordered them to report to the medical center once they arrived. (They'd have to do that anyway, but with great caution —who knew if they wouldn't simply be put to sleep if their radiation dose was too high.) And as far as the missing scurvy examination was concerned . . . the official gave them an extra ration of Vitamin C tablets and wished them a good trip. Jugurtha wiped the sweat from his brow.

The jets screamed and whistled. The giant bird trembled a little and began to roll down the runway. The searchlights of the air base glittered through the ice-covered portholes, their rays wandered across the dark cabin wall, faster and faster. Most of those on the plane had ignored orders to fasten seat belts. Jugurtha and Sigga pressed their bodies closer together, she bedded her head on his right arm and let him caress her. Her face lifted toward his kisses; no one saw it or would have cared about it. As the whining singsong of the engines grew into a powerful roar, their lips found each other. Both yearned for a passionate embrace.

Imperceptibly the craft rose from the runway, only the floor of the cabin pressed against their bodies, the plane rose quickly and steeply. They felt the up and down of flight as an extra pleasure.

Jugurtha had the feeling that something marvelous would happen, not right away, but soon. Had he not won this splendid woman for himself? Nothing, therefore, was impossible. The nearness of her opulent, lustful flesh and the extraordinary sensations he felt made him tremble. He opened Sigga's coat underneath the blanket and searched for her skin. She herself unbuttoned her blouse and her hands, too, became greedy. A giddy delight.

For a time he had played with the idea of humiliating her and then sending her packing. He had wanted to possess her in the vilest way possible and show her that he held her in contempt as a tramp. A just revenge for the whip. (The scar was still visible.)

But he could no longer do that. Sigga had no memory of that disgusting and lamentable scene, nor did she have any idea who he was or had been, what he had wanted then or that the recollection tortured him. Occasionally she thought of her children—it was a game of hide and seek, a rustling of phantoms, a game of tag—but wholly without longing or suffering. Manfred and Erda were strangers to her. (The exemplary mother she had always been made out to be was strictly a product of the women's magazines—Sigga was nothing but a terrifying lover, a devouring bed companion.) Everything that concerned her marriage seemed to have disappeared with Eycke's death.

She was, or had become, a different person; probably the disease was at work in her and changed her. And this other Ulla—oh, how dead the old name sounded already!—belonged to him skin and hair, her beautiful hair and her beautiful skin. (He tugged at her pubic hairs.) He loved her deeply and completely, down to her least secretions.

What chained them together? he wondered. Was it that dreadful march through the atomic desert? Was it a chemical change going on in both their veins ever since then? For the first time he realized that "blood" was not just a party slogan, was not abstract, but real and able to decide over life and death. Not even as a hospital attendant in Greece and on Crete, where he had often seen real slaughterhouses, had he felt the reality of blood as strongly or as sweetly. Blood—beautiful, warm, circulating blood—yes, that was it; it tied his life to hers.

In the dusky blue light of the cabin the travelers with their chalk-white, yellowed faces—wafer faces—resembled the dead. Some seemed to sleep, a few stupidly chewed their candies. No one knew when the flight would end or where it led. The motors groaned and moaned.

Jugurtha and Sigga did not talk; words would have destroyed their intimate sensuality: darkness, delirium, forgetfulness, salvation! It was so dark they couldn't see into each other's eyes. They were touching sensation. For Jugurtha the world disappeared. He did not think of his own and Sigga's disease or of their uncertain future, he thought of nothing at all. He was drunk with joy over his beautiful booty and filled with remorse when he remembered how disappointing the first few times with her had been for him, that he had thought of her only as a sperm depository. Now he embraced her passionately. How could he have felt that way? He would have to make it up to her.

Bliss to have her . . . as blissful as what she just did with her hands.

They'd never part again. (Abruptly he whispered in her ear: "Now and forever, Sigga.") They'd live together no matter where. He'd be a swine if he didn't work for her. But at what? He heard suppressed groaning and felt her limbs quiver; she couldn't get enough today, invented new refinements: Her hands were full of surprises. How lovely if they'd have a child. A child? A home, and if it were in an icy desert at the edge of the world. But what absolute nonsense! Sigga was too old—she was well over forty, perhaps fifty—and she had had several miscarriages. Moreover her nerves were shot. And the radiation! That was the beginning and the end. They had to get well, under all circumstances get well! Everything else would come later.

Soon they were exhausted. With satiety the painful fatigue returned that had lain in their bones for days. Sigga turned away from him, his face sank into her mane. Body on body, they fell asleep.

In the timelessness that surrounded everything up here, it didn't matter how long they had lain together. They awoke almost simultaneously as it dawned in the cabin. They sat up and looked at each other lost in dreams. The sun! It was day. They threw off the blankets and pressed their faces against the portholes above them. The washy, uniformly milky brightness outside hid all details, but obviously the plane was flying in a southerly direction. The polar night was behind them. Joyfully he kissed her on both cheeks.

But they quickly found out that they had no cause to rejoice. Unknown fighters had sighted the plane over the ocean and pursued it for some time. The captain had asked for a fighter escort but hadn't received it and as a result had been forced to go down to a very low altitude. For about an hour now they had flown at reduced speed, protected by a seemingly endless blanket of fog from reconnaissance planes still believed in the area.

The man who told them what happened, an extremely good-looking chap of at the most thirty-five (Höllriegl immediately suspected a rival), knew much more. In fact, it was amazing and almost suspicious how open and frank he was. Perhaps the party's power began to wane or cease altogether after a certain point was passed, and its ears need not be feared as much. Moreover the man held a key job and thus could afford much bolder language. As they started talking to him—he devoured Sigga with his burning eyes (Werewolf eyes!) and she too hung on his every word in the most unseemly manner—they learned he was not part of the refugee exodus, but had business in the Far North: He was an engineer and heating specialist sent on an inspection tour of the caloric plants of the polar region. For the time being—he shrugged his shoulders—he would have to keep away from Europe. Of course he could talk openly. He had a dashing, all-too-masculine way of speaking, adopted, Jugurtha suspected, only to make an impression on Sigga. She did look especially beautiful this morning, with decay written all over her face.

This is what he told them: The Reich was completely encircled or rather, crowded into a relatively narrow area. The destructive atomic blows against heavily settled regions had, as far as he knew, ceased and for good reason. The Japs had applied very sophisticated tactics and techniques of softening up and penetrating so that no movable or fixed fronts existed anymore, but only an indefinite, continual slaughter. To overstate the case a little, every square meter of German soil was a battleground. Under the pressure of this desperate situation, the civil war in the Reich seemed to have abated as everyone prepared for the final battle against enemy forces which were smashing forward on all fronts. The Japs used their most brutal butcher elite—kamikaze parachutists and guerrillas. At present the Reich resembled a medieval barricade of wagons, completely surrounded and attacked from all sides while heavy fighting raged inside the enclosure, man against man. The means of battle signaled a return to the Middle Ages; people fought with daggers and jackknives, even the good old technique of biting an opponent's throat had come into vogue. Whoever could, saved himself through the still-existing airlifts or disappeared during the day to lead the life of a rat. (Jugurtha thought of Gundlfinger, of the Underground, of Axel.) No really planned defenses existed any longer. The engineer had heard just prior to his departure that a Japanese military governor resided in Stuttgart, but this might well be someone's nightmare. The most awful thing, however, was the fact that the yellow apelings had landed great masses of settlers in evacuated Reich protectorates, especially in the east. These were people from the depths of Asia who appeared much better able to resist radioactivity than the white race. With all that, strangely enough, the Reich was still carrying on atomic attacks. As if nothing had happened at home, it sent one superintercontinental missile after the other hurtling in the direction of the Far East, where in fact most civilized territories had been turned into deserts. As a result, something like a modern repetition of the great barbarian invasions began to take place as the surviving Asian masses pushed west. It was nothing short of miraculous that underground or mobile missile-launching pads still functioned on Reich territory or elsewhere in Europe and that missile-firing U-boats cruised the oceans. The battle morale of the master race simply couldn't be broken, and this alone gave the defenders a big boost. They were determined to bring about a Ragnarok such as the world had never witnessed. People were ready to fight to their last breath, and women and children would not be allowed to fall into the hands of the Asiatic beasts.

The eyes of the man who had told them all this gleamed fanatically; no doubt he was a seasoned Werewolf. And the Werewolves would fight to the bitter end—with words, from a safe distance. Truly a handsome man, only his bitten fingernails, which Jugurtha wanted very badly to point out to Sigga, disturbed the overall impression.

Other passengers came over to talk to them. Sigga was the magnet; questions and answers rained down, everyone pretended to have heard this or that. The curse had been broken and they all became downright gabby.

The German people seemed to return to the blackest superstitions of their history. Wildest rumors circulated and were believed. Thus it was said that the body of the Dalai Lama, which had disappeared under such mysterious circumstances from a Cologne clinic, lay in the coffin in the Kyffhäuser crypt; to be more specific, the body in the coffin was indeed the Führer, but his face had taken on the Dalai Lama's features—and similar nonsense. It was alleged, for instance, that Köpfler had appeared to many Germans in different places simultaneously and done it in broad daylight. The apparition carried its head under its arm. Those on board the plane discussed this nonsense in all seriousness until the knowing engineer, who had listened with an ironic smile on his lips, intervened with the question: "Gentlemen, where do you think Köpfler is at the moment?"

No one had a clue. Embarrassed and furtive looks. Then a sympathetic, still young, bald-headed soldier pulled himself together and said with the requisite steely look: "Of course, with his men." To which the engineer replied, grinning: "Yes, but with his men along the Rio das Mortes."

"Where did you say?"

"On the River of the Dead in Mato Grosso."

"Oh!" Understanding and embittered grins all around.

As far as one could see and hear, this transport seemed made up of leading business executives and a few secretaries, with just five Nordic, arrogantly sexy women. Apparently all were bachelors or grass widowers—the wives must long since have been sent into safety along the arctic Riviera. In general the JU 33 camp seemed to have been the jumping-off point into a second life for most of the business tycoons of the Reich; obviously, therefore, it had been the goal of the Inspector for Economic Affairs von Eycke. (Whatever happened to his plane?)

All the big firms were represented: Thyssen, the Reich Bank, Opel, Hoesch, Telefunken, VW, IG-Farben, Ruhr Coal, Taunus, Henkell, Brüninghaus, DDG (German Thinking Machines), and so on. Friendships were made quickly now that the great silence was over. The men became high-spirited, behaved like sparkling jokesters, the ladies giggled dutifully, cognac was handed round—almost every one of the men produced hip flasks. As usual Sigga had a tremendous success. Jugurtha noted with growing concern that the color had slowly drained from her face. It had become clay-colored, the circles under her eyes stood out in dark purple, the flesh underneath the cheekbone had caved in. He saw that she kept herself upright only with difficulty, and he stayed close to her. He had to do that because a few of the more drunken ones had tried to get fresh, and Sigga let herself go too much for his taste. Now she was only a frail ghost, someone seriously ill, her weakened organism was on the verge of capitulating. And because she looked as she did, no one recognized her as a former German TV idol.

After initial resistance, the other women had accepted Sigga into their group without reservation. They talked, were intimate, went in pairs to the washroom, and when one of the pilots stepped out of the control room, they offered themselves up as if they were on a serving dish. Everyone agreed that Sigga was the uncrowned queen of the flight, and the nicest secretary—her name was Doris Völlenkle ("That's my real name, but I'm usually called Heidrun and I work for the German Wurlitzer Company")—served unbidden as Sigga's lady's maid. And it was Doris who took Herr von der Leyen to one side and whispered that she didn't want to make any fuss, but his wife had just fainted in the toilet.

As Jugurtha ran down the cabin to the front, the radio came on playing marches. At once all conversation stopped; Jugurtha noticed the astonished expressions on some faces and then he was inside the narrow, hot toilet where it smelled of vomit and disinfectant. The low cabin vibrated in the thunder of the jets. Sigga lay or sat there, head leaning against the toilet bowl, her face wax-yellow. She had obviously vomited bile. Jugurtha patted her cheeks hard and washed her, then looked for something strong in the first-aid kit, found ammonium carbonate and held the salts under her nose. Gradually she began to move as if asleep. A knock on the door. "It's me, Doris. How is your wife?" "Much better."

"We're going to make an emergency landing."

Sigga opened her eyes, looked about her, looked at him. "Black Jugurtha," she murmured. Then she swallowed spasmodically a few times and spat out. He held her head while she did. Sigga's face had a frightened but at the same time annoyed and strangely inquisitive expression, as if she were thinking strenuously. "What is it, where am I?" she asked. "Where is Manfred?" Everything spun around. "Oh, yes, Manfred is gone," she said and spat again. She tried to sit up but sank back at once. He explained the situation to her but she seemed uninterested. Doris knocked, came in, and together they brought Sigga back to her seat. He laid her down carefully, pillowing her head and covering her with a blanket. As he felt her pulse he noticed that her whole body trembled. A nervous attack?

No one had noticed the little incident; they were all more concerned with themselves. Only the engineer bent over and asked politely: "Is your wife sick? Airsick?" In reply Jugurtha asked what was up and received an alarming answer. The captain had announced they couldn't land at their destination because of unusually thick fog and that he was looking for an emergency landing place. "Radio contact with a ground station is impossible now. The enemy is too close, which is why we dare not risk a blind landing," the engineer explained. What did he mean, the enemy was too close? Well, this part of the sky had been under close surveillance recently and the enemy—whoever that was—had tried to locate transports before and shoot them down. As they had learned after the fact, the enemy had spotted several flights already and they had escaped with some difficulty. This time the stupid fog made everything that much harder. "A little while ago a fighter without markings fired on us, despite the Red Cross. No one noticed it and the fighter suddenly turned and disappeared into the fog." Where had he learned all this? He ducked the question. "I was told." In any case the captain didn't dare make radio contact with the ground.

"Why do they let these transports fly without cover?"

An ironic grin. "The Reich needs fighters elsewhere."

Jugurtha thought about the Luftwaffe mutiny.

"Where are we going to land?"

"Only the gods know that. Supposedly there's a little less fog farther south."

The martial music stopped in the middle of a bar and a rough voice came over the loudspeaker. "We'll try to land in a few minutes. Please observe emergency-landing regulations."

The few minutes turned out to be damned long ones. Jugurtha removed all pointed objects from his clothing and rummaged through Ulla's things. He found the small laser Meduso in her coat pocket and put the filigree thing together with her other effects. Then he sat down on the swinging seat and fastened his seat belt. Ulla lay at his feet, her eyes closed, but she breathed regularly and some color had returned to her face.

Through the porthole he could see a bright spot way down on the horizon—the sun. The fog had grown thinner, dispersed gradually into tattered formations. The plane flew in great curves and gradually regained some altitude, the position of the sun changed steadily, the wings lifted and sank. Now the sea of fog lay far below them. It had the deceptive thickness of a wavy, white plain across which the shadow of the giant bird moved swiftly. The slanting rays of the sun fell from a blackened sky.

Now the roar of the jets changed its tone. They descended quickly, the sea of fog literally tumbled up at them. Gray gloom again entered the cabin, the plane bumped through the sky as if it were jumping across a street pocked with potholes. No, they still floated high in the air, had punched through the cloud cover and raced toward a point, a distant, black pinhead in the midst of a sunless continent of snow and ice which spread out monotonously and endlessly in all directions. The only color, a little shout of joy in the white desert, was a Red Cross flag on a pole surrounded by a few lost-looking sheds. They couldn't make out the runway—did one really exist? Nevertheless the plane touched down gently and safely. When they had rolled to a stop, someone called out: "Heil for our crew!"

They all shouted with joy. Everyone loosened seat belts, shook many hands, embraced the pilots, and handed them around for kissing. In the confusion a beery bass attempted to sing the "Horst Wessel Song," but no one joined in. Sigga lay there and moved her lips silently.

ON THE ASPHODEL MEADOW

Yet the whole thing was a full-fledged catastrophe. They were about three hundred kilometers southeast of their destination, another transit camp which was the mirror image over here in Canada of Ju 33 (Enterprise Bifröst rested on several such pillars). It would have taken another long flight before they reached journey's end: The underground shelters and bases north of the Arctic Circle, somewhere in the mountains on the border of Alaska. But at least every regular camp had decent lodging, doctors, and medical help, motor sleds, helicopters, and, most important, powerful defenses. A wide circle of such fortified camps made up the forefield of the great arctic redoubt itself. But an advanced outpost in the wasteland such as this one had nothing.

The fuel dump had the transmission signal Y 771 and was located in a water-rich tundra area of the Canadian Northwest's barren lands, 64 degrees and 23 minutes northern latitude and 96 degrees 25 minutes western longitude. Several quonset huts and igloos stood around the wooden station house with its radio transmitter, and a long-abandoned meetinghouse of the Society of Friends. The runway stretched out behind the camp far into the landscape.

The Red Cross flag (a camouflage) fluttered from the radio tower. They had not used the radio for days now; it would only have attracted hostile reconnaissance troops. A German couple and a Dane were living there. The men were geologists; the German, who had served in a signal company during the war and was a trained wireless operator, handled the weather service. A few Eskimos lived in the igloos.

The pilots waited and waited for the thick shroud of fog to lift. But it began to snow instead, and the geologists said it might take weeks until the first winter storms changed the weather. And there they sat in the mess. The crew was under strict orders to fly the plane right back; they had already overstayed their time limit by a day. They could not possibly go on, fog covered the whole area. So on the third morning the crew decided to start back and fetch help from somewhere. Because of the protecting fog, temperatures were not all that low, but the Icelanders left a large quantity of heatable polar suits behind anyway. Half the passengers flew back with the plane.

They had decided by lot. For the von der Leyens it would have meant waiting at the outpost until help came. Sigga was obviously ill, she apparently was not able to recover from that last attack, and Herr von Leyen suffered from all sorts of things, so that two younger men offered to remain in their stead. But Sigga didn't want to do that at any price, and Jugurtha was horrified at the thought of having to return to the polar night of Ju 33. At least here there was a hint of a difference between night and day; moreover, they were closer to their goal. No, they wouldn't go back. Sigga was taken to the finest and best-heated room in the former meeting-house, which she shared with Doris and another secretary; Doris, the trusty soul, had volunteered to remain behind. All the other passengers were herded into the barracks and snow huts; only the engineer, whose name no one knew, moved into the main station house as if that were a matter of course.

Eventually there was a plan, worked out by the geologists, not to wait for relief but to abandon Y 771 and make the dash to the AL Ju 12 camp on dog sleds and skis. Perhaps that would be the best way of deceiving the enemy should he be operating somewhere in this district. They could not hope to hold the fuel dump over the long haul anyway, for the enemy's reconnaissance had become increasingly troublesome. After blowing up the station and destroying the runway, they would have to sneak away.

Not far from there were some Indian and Eskimo families living side by side in apparent harmony, together with their reindeer, dogs, and totem poles, in an abandoned Apemen camp (AMC).

The camp had been shut down after the construction of airfields, police bases, and strategic highways was discontinued in this part of the Northwest Territory. At night they could sometimes hear the howling of dogs. The geologists planned to get their sleds, equipment, and manpower from there.

Jugurtha soon learned at the station that the ancient blood enmity between Eskimos and Indians, which had lasted until the turn of the century, threatened to flare up again. The reason was a curious one. Wherever the Germans held sway on this continent, especially in the Reich protectorates, the Indian race received preferential treatment over other primitive peoples. Of course they were not put on the same level as the white race and certainly not on par with the Helio-Germanic master race, but were treated according to the so-called Hiwi statutes. As an admirer of the author Karl May and his Indian hero Winnetou, Adolf Hitler considered the redskins heroic men worthy of bearing arms, and he had supposedly issued a secret edict according them unusual rights which aroused much resentment, especially among the Eskimo tribes. The latter were considered descendants of immigrant Mongol peoples and were treated as common colored aliens of an inferior race.

And Jugurtha found out something else, this time not from the German geologist but from one of his own fellow passengers, a white-maned, soldierly gentleman who wore the Golden Party Insignia in his lapel. Although born in Germany, the man had studied mining and metallurgy in Graz and Leoben and had become technical director of the Hermann Göring Works in Styria. Moreover, he loved his adopted homeland, the Ostmark. They had hit it off right away until, during a discussion of the arctic fortress, Jugurtha had praised the marvelous underground heating plants and other technical achievements and, in passing, mentioned the engineer and the Führer role he had begun to play. Abruptly Höllriegl's friend clammed up. Jugurtha sparred with the man a little, then asked outright why he didn't like the engineer. Oh, it was nothing, the director replied. If the engineer wanted to play a Führer role, he had no objections (much to Jugurtha's sorrow, Sigga held the same view), but the engineer pretended to be something he wasn't. Far from being an engineering technician or inspector, he was a nuclear physicist and despite his youth one of the best. He had taken an active part in development of the antiparticle bomb right from the beginning. Now he was under orders to continue working on the superbomb, together with a team of international antimatter researchers. They were to work on a lonely isle in the midst of the ice region where the Werewolf and SS had built laboratories and giant workshops. He was part of the so-called Frauja project. The explosive power was said to be so great that it couldn't be calculated in conventional megatonnage, only in the Giga row (10^9). The scientists were under orders to detonate the bomb even if its development came too late for strategic use, for unfortunately the miracle weapon was still a long way from completion.

Jugurtha was dismayed. "How can you talk so openly about this kind of state secret to a stranger?"

"Yes, it's a top-secret Reich matter, all right, but at the same time it's an open secret. Many know about it—quite a few in our group, by the way. Köpfler and his people were smart enough to spread the news among the elite but not let out enough hard facts to rob the bomb of its mystery. Hassenteufel, the new propaganda chief, is supposed to have thought up that approach. And, in fact, hope that this last arrow in the quiver would work kept many in line who otherwise would long ago have deserted or killed themselves.

The word "Frauja" had brought Jugurtha up short. Frauja, that was the odious Saviour of the Christians. What did he have to do with the superbomb? The name had been chosen on purpose. A paradox. Jesus wanted to save the world but do it in a typically underhand way, through word-of-mouth propaganda, and he did nothing but enormous damage; whereas the Frauja bomb was true salvation, utter destruction, the salvation of death, of nonexistence, of nothing. Detonation of an antiparticle bomb probably meant the end of all life—men, animals, and plants would be exterminated at one blow; only a dead planet would remain. It was said that the island, whose exact location no one knew, was called Suicide Island, or had once been called that (strange coincidence), and there was reason to assume that it didn't lie in the Arctic at all but near Antarctic, somewhere behind the Kerguelen Islands and the mainland, beyond the drift-ice limits.

"Possibly," the director said and lowered his voice to a whisper, "the first antimatter experiments will be carried out in Canada, and that's why the engineer is here. You must know that the Reich leadership is determined to hold Canada's northwest and Alaska at all cost. I've looked at it on the map. The line Uranium City–Yellowknife–Port Radium–Aklavik will be defended to the last man, the Mackenzie District is a holy place for the Reich. But the belt of atomic mines supposed to protect these important strongpoints and territories could prove too weak, just as the Ural wall did. In my view, a rigid defense should be abandoned in favor of an aggressive, flexible, and mobile one. The endless ice deserts of Canada's north are an especially ideal experimental field for big and superbig weapons."

"And we?" Jugurtha asked, feeling such pressure on the back of his neck and head that he could follow the words of the director only with difficulty.

"We, my dear friend, find ourselves in a strategically quite unimportant zone, flooded, as we have heard, with guerrillas. I'm convinced that this whole area, all the way up to the Arctic Ocean, will soon be evacuated without even a fight. I wouldn't give you a penny for that camp we're going to try and reach. We must get out of here quickly, otherwise we'll miss the crossing. The season and the fog are favorable. Remove all traces, leave nothing behind. We ought to get going tomorrow morning."

So that's how it was. Jugurtha noticed that the old gentleman wore his party insignia with a black border. In answer to his questioning look the director said quietly: "For our Führer." It was obvious: As a refugee the man was forced to howl with the Werewolves, but had the backbone to wear mourning openly for Adolf Hitler. Officially the period of state mourning had never ended, but in practice black for the Führer was viewed as a sign of allegiance to the past, if not as a political challenge. Or perhaps this was no longer so. Jugurtha still heard the deprecating words with which the engineer had referred to Köpfler's alleged flight. And a Führer picture still hung—or had been hung again—in the radio room of the geologists' station.

Was the Reich really leaderless? Once again Jugurtha wandered around the little station in the endless waste of the snowscape, feeling restless. Even in the nights out here he would sometimes be so nervous that he had to stomp around outside, growled at by dogs and challenged by guards. But he could not stand the snoring of the ex-tycoons. The Eskimos seemed busy people, the ground around their huts was neatly shoveled, and the whistle-clean runway was evidence of their diligence. Jugurtha enjoyed them, and wherever he saw their fur-covered, flat, dark-skinned faces gleaming like wet copper, he greeted them covertly with his eyes. And the slit black eyes glinted back in friendship. Only the smell of blubber was enough to make you vomit; his stomach nerves had started to act up at every little trifle.

Was the Reich without a Führer? The founder of the world empire was dead; his murderer and successor had disappeared. Who was in charge? Somebody had to give orders, even if he was a murderer. Nothing existed without orders. Clear-cut fronts had formed in Germany despite all the chaos. The future had risen against the past, a future that had begun to emerge everywhere after the Führer's death. The past was finished—forever. The fate of the Reich lay with those powers who could determine its future, one way or the other. But this future was no longer NSDAP, SA, and SS. It was either Werewolf or *Der Arme Konrad.*

And, of course, only if something like a Germanic future could still be envisaged within the great storm from Asia. The fury of this storm shook the ash tree of the world to its marrow; the leaves blew from the rotting branches. On that dark autumn day on which Adolf Hitler's death was made public, the wind had blown the last leaves from the trees. Jugurtha remembered it very well.

He tried to talk about these things with Sigga, who, when she was not in bed and asleep, sat near the window, huddled in blankets, and stared out into the distance. In vain. Sigga remained apathetic despite the supposedly bracing and stimulating shots the geologist's wife, a former medical student, gave her. Moreover, Sigga again began with her confused chatter. It often seemed as if she were talking in her sleep. Sometimes the Romans rose in her imagination, and "black Jugurtha" and the war—and the person to whom she spoke was always "my dear boy;" at least that was Doris' report. Only when the engineer entered the room (he came a lot) and talked to her in his sparse, definitive, half-ironic and half-gay way, did she wake from her dozing, become lively, even flirtatious. Pure torture, having to watch that. Jealousy and disappointment. First Knud, then this one here. Again she was slipping from his grasp.

The engineer—or physicist—had taken charge. You had to admit that his directives were brilliantly thought out and realistic.

He was a born planner and organizer, a Führer by nature. He and the two geologists (who knew the region) developed an exact plan of escape, every detail of the expedition was determined in advance, every risk carefully weighed, and preparations were begun at once. So and so many sleds and dogs, so and so many tools, heatable parkas, weapons, just this quantity of fuel. So and so many attendants. They'd be Indian Hiwis, not Eskimos. Matter of honor. Indians were closer to the master race. Although there was no need for secrecy or for a cover name, the engineer (perhaps from habit) gave their flight a secret designation—"Enterprise Winnetou." A few mothballs left over even here. A "police" force was selected. Of course Herr von der Leyen was a member.

It was Tuesday. They would start out either Thursday or Friday morning, depending on the weather. The runway and the radio station would be destroyed first, the rest later. The air pressure would knock the igloos down, no matter. Sooner or later the Eskimos would have moved into the SHC anyway.

A large, comfortable motor sled was prepared for the sick—in addition to Sigga a young industrialist whose nerves had given out during the Rhineland bomb night—and another for the leadership of the caravan. Food was tight—the first problem. The geologist promised to find more supplies in the labor camp. A careful calorie count was worked out and strict rationing put into effect.

The outlook was murky, as murky as the weather. Jugurtha pondered the situation. How would this adventure end, and what kind of life awaited them in the ice holes of Niflheim? His optimism melted—he'd just had enough of everything. (Once again.) For all practical purposes the Reich was leaderless, abandoned, it fell apart, rattled under the choking grip of Asiatic hordes. And the fate of the world, not only of the Reich, lay in the hands of a few adventurers and scientists whose political thinking had been formed by the Werewolf. Researchers, organizers, managers, ingenious leaders, but also born murderers and self-murderers. If they gained their goal, domination of the world, the planet would die. If they didn't, the planet would die anyway. With that outlook, was there any point to surviving? Any point for him? In case Sigga recovered (which was unlikely), he'd lose her. She'd latch on to a stronger, more brutal, man, like a bitch in heat. Oh, they were tied to one another, but the ties were limited, love on recall; it would last as long as they were both ill. A blood relationship by a special kind of decomposition of the blood. Not companionship, not belonging together, but a galloping cancer of the blood. The companion, the wife of his dreams, was a chimera. He didn't love an Amazon, a Valkyrie, but a slut, a fatally ill, mad slut.

And if despite all the putrifaction life continued, what would it be like? The new society wouldn't be made up of individuals but of machines, of the mindlessly commanding and the brainlessly obeying. Unfortunately the trend had already begun. The high ideals for which he had once fought as a simple soldier in Hitler's brown army were betrayed, falsified and trodden in the dirt every day. People made fun of them. Romanticism. Old rags. It stank of mothballs here. A quite different type of human being (human being?) pushed to the top. The coming wielders of power would replace the German temperament with a radio-controlled think tank. Giant ants with the minds of supermen.

Despite the fatigue that sat in his bones and ate at them, he walked one round after another. Planes roared somewhere far in the invisible sky, high above the blanket of fog. It reminded him of that steady droning back home in the German skies. And suddenly he thought of Heydrich, gyromancy, his home, of Ingrid, and of playing the piano. For the first time he felt utterly abandoned amid foreign stars.

A strategy session in the station—the Führer portrait, on which someone had hung a black rag, looked down on the small assembly. The engineer spoke to the armed men of the expedition.

The geologists had dismantled and partly packed the radio station, for its most valuable parts were to be taken to the other camp. Just a few hours ago, coded messages had come which explained that AL Ju 12 knew of the situation in Y 771 (presumably the Icelanders had radioed all the necessary information on their return flight); they would try to send help halfway—the geologists had asked for it most urgently. Then the connection had broken.

As far as they could make out, the situation in the United Vassal States had all but collapsed. American fascism, which had split in two under the blows of the yellow conquerors and the rebellion in their own country, was close to extinction. In the engineer's scornful words, "The firm in Duluth is bankrupt, the other in Corpus Christi has started insolvency proceedings. . . ." The German

Protection Corps and the German-blooded cadres had to bear the brunt of the war against the Asiatic invaders as well as against the rebels. The latter, too, waged a two-front war: on the one hand against the fascists and the Reich forces, on the other against the Japs who, according to unconfirmed reports, held bases in the Middle West. A few Banzai missiles with atomic warheads fired from Hawaii and other Japanese Pacific isles had made the UVSA ripe for invasion; but German missile bases in America had replied in kind. A comedy played out at the edge of the American tragedy was the fact that the so-called Lincoln Free Corps often had to fight shoulder to shoulder with Minutemen and Ku Kluxers against the Japs. When the apelings disappeared—and they had a mysterious way of simply letting the earth swallow them up from one minute to the next—the allies of convenience opened up on each other once again. "Things are so deep in the mire, so hopeless down there, I don't even want to waste my time on them. For us up here in the north quite different things are important," the engineer said. Every inch a general, he bent over a large physical map of Canada (a political map was not available), on which he entered points and lines. Everyone carefully followed his discourse.

"The problem is this: How will our units escape safely to the north? What will Schimming do? (Major General von Schimming, former Panzer general, now chief of the Wehrmacht High Command for North America.) Undoubtedly he will try to pull his troops out of the mess and lead them into the arctic fortress. Of course we don't know if the North American Luftwaffe Headquarters in Smithers still exists or is combat ready. If it is and enough planes are available, then everything should go smoothly. As far as I know, a great withdrawal maneuver is now underway. Gentlemen mark that well—it is of the utmost importance for us all. For if Schimming leaves the American muck in its own mess and moves the whole protective corps out of the UVSA, then he'll doubtless pull back to the Rockies, especially since he has some excellent Alpine troops from the Ostmark—and not risk marching across the open terrain in central Canada. It'd be sheer madness if he did. The broad belt of forests which would offer some protection is impassable in winter. Besides, it stops eventually. The timberline is at about fifty-nine degrees. So! Schimming will try to push north from the Rockies as fast as he can, and the enemy will scratch together what forces he has here in Canada to block Schimming's retreat. That means a vacuum will be created up here. . . ."

The business bosses drew an audible sigh of relief. "Enterprise Winnetou" sounded like a nice little joy ride. Later they'd be able to recount this life and death adventure in their clubs.

". . . the Japs are supposed to have tried pushing a bolt straight through the mountains, starting out from several coastal bases" —he gave a questioning look at the German geologist, who pointed to an area on the map—"here in Columbia and here near Wrangell, that's already in Alaska. I don't quite believe it because our coast guards are right on top of things in just those areas. In any case, the enemy we must deal with here in the lake region will re-group his forces toward the west and push in that direction."

"Who is the enemy here?" one of the listeners asked.

"We can't tell you that exactly," the weather man answered in the engineer's stead. "But they certainly aren't Japs. We've intercepted many English and French radio messages, many more French than English. That would indicate French Canadians, partisans, who are slowly moving up north. Slowly, because they're awaiting rein-forcements and air support. And of course they sense that the Polar Circle is one great belt of atomic mines. A week ago they were pretty far in the southeast, between Lake Dubawnt—here—and Baker Lake—here. That was a week ago. How fast they have moved and how strong they are, that is, how many joined up en route, we cannot judge, we——"

"Gentlemen," the engineer interrupted, "I believe Enterprise Winnetou will begin under favorable auspices. In all probability we won't even see the enemy except perhaps some reconnaissance and scout troops. Of course things are on thin ice. We'll have to march very quickly, but we should make the three hundred kilometers to a safe harbor easily. Kircheiss and Laale (he meant the German geologist and his silent Danish colleague) are reliable guides through the mine belt. And if we come into contact with the enemy and things go wrong—so, well, you know what to do then. . . ."

They all did. Pour gasoline over the sleds and set them on fire. Fight to the last bullet. That means: the last bullets . . . women first, then yourself. The unwritten law of this war.

The engineer knew what he was doing. What a man! As long as

the Reich had such fellows . . . Jugurtha recalled that he had used that phrase a little too often lately. Old hat. Perhaps he should vary it: As long as the Reich has such hirelings . . . ridiculous and miserable! He was just jealous, envious, ugly, a weakling. Above all a weakling. All right. He was sick through and through. (The engineer would have said "So!") He'd have to prove all the more that he could do his share. There were things one could bear only by grinding one's teeth together. For example eye cramps, brain pressure, hallucinations, the leaden feeling in the bones, the continual freezing, loss of hair. Days without bowel movements, his old disorder. And then suddenly diarrhea. Since—what was the name of that idiotic village in the Harz?—well, since then he had suffered from serious disruption of vision; it had all started there and grown worse from day to day. Despite snow goggles (which he had taken to wearing even in darkened rooms) everything, for example artificial light, dug into his pupils with painfully sharp contours. Moreover his eyes began to play tricks. Walking about the countryside, it seemed for several minutes as if the area around him filled with black air and the blanket of snow came alive, slowly undulating in white and gray waves toward him as if the ground moved under a breath of air, a tepid breeze. Stupid hallucination. The heated suit was surely to blame. It afforded good protection against the cold, but the warm air befuddled his senses. If he turned off the battery, he began to freeze at once like a puppy.

The heat suit was a personal insult because there were so few. Heatable parkas (even the hood could be warmed) and mukluks had been given only to elderly people and women. And to him. Because he was "known" to be ill? Or because he was the husband of the much-desired Frau Sigga von der Leyen and a weakling on top of it? Preferential treatment. And he had accepted. Shame on shame!

Jugurtha tested his weapons while the other residents of the barracks lay on their plank beds, talked shop, or slept. All except the sick were armed, but only members of the "police" corps were given carbines. He stole a glance at his personal secret weapon, the ruby laser 6—Knud's "forfeit," the devil take him, and his, Jugurtha's present from Sigga. A curiosity, nothing more. He could only fire the weapon once. He knew how to handle the release; everything else was theory. For this was a so-called chemical or gas laser, which radiated an infrared bolt (timing: one fifty billionth of a second) of gigantic intensity. The Meduso had one disadvantage, however: Because it combined the laser effect with a very complicated chemical, or rather, atomic transformation, it could fire only a single superstrong bolt of uniform wavelength before the gas filling had to be reloaded for the next shot. The Meduso did have a mechanism attached that reloaded automatically ten times. But how did you start it? Jugurtha had learned how to handle laser in his defense courses but had completely forgotten how it was done. Nor did he dare ask anyone for instructions. Non-members of the SS were enjoined from carrying laser. (The weapon chiefs of the SS awarded lasers every year to young SS men in what had become a very special ceremony, and lately the custom had arisen in old SS families for dying fathers to hand on their lasers to their firstborn sons.) So Jugurtha possessed Thor's hammer, but only a single bolt would flash from it.

Then he still had that shooting iron of dear old Kummernuss—where might he be now? Two bullets were still lodged in the gun and he had a full clip of ammunition left over. And he had laid his hands on another museum piece, a 98 K, the gallant "soldier's bride" of World War II that had proved its worth from Murmansk to Tobruk. The most popular carbine the Wehrmacht had ever used, it had apparently wandered north after the war. For obviously no one wanted to junk so heroic a relic, which the skalds had celebrated as a symbol of victory.

Only the leaders of the expedition, the engineer and the geologists, had modern firearms of highest destructive force. Again the engineer proved himself a most admirable leader. His elegant, cold-blooded way of handling laser and other new weapons, his strict firing discipline (there was no slovenly shooting despite high firing speed) were all exemplary; it could almost make you forget that he had stroked Sigga's hair all too intimately and called her "Blondie" . . . damn it!

The caravan of sleds moved across the tundra. Jugurtha, guardian of the supply sled and at the same time supply master, sat behind a dwarf of an Indian driver. The motor sled with the two sick persons in it spurted through the snow, the Red Cross flag fluttering in the wind. Then came the long rear guard. Sleepily

Jugurtha observed the slowly-moving landscape. Despite the heated parka and the bear rug he had wrapped around himself, he was freezing to the marrow of his bones.

The land was an endless white map almost without points of reference. Allegedly they drove along a road or kept near one, but he couldn't recognize any differences in the structure of the ground. Once they came upon a brightly colored plank with the sign "North American Trading and Transportation Company" on it. Jugurtha jumped from the sled and investigated. The plank probably came from a truck and was laced with holes—fresh bullet holes. The others hadn't noticed his find. So he forgot it too and continued to doze.

The weather had begun to clear yesterday. Had blowing up Y 771 torn a hole in the cloud cover? In any case the gray, deep sea of fog had begun to move and seemed looser. Murky light, languishing between day and night, expanded, making distances clearer, contours sharper. Kircheiss, Laale, and the engineer conferred and prodded the Hiwis to greater speed.

A wind had blown out of the northwest yesterday evening: the temperature sank quickly to about 15 below zero centigrade. Jugurtha and four others had been put on guard duty, a bitter joy, while the others with the redskins built a night bivouac in a broad depression. His skin burned in the icy air, his limbs were numb with cold. If this wind continued and drove away the warming fog, they'd have even lower temperatures. They'd been lucky so far.

The bivouac was made of a combination of tarpaulins, reindeer skins, and small holes dug into the snow. The entrance to each tunnel was protected by a piece of canvas held in place by skis driven deep into the snow. It was like a foxhole. The Indians, quick lads with broad shoulders and thickset bodies, clay-colored faces deeply furrowed and tanned, proved themselves true masters in building such bivouacs quickly. They were supposed to be more comfortable than igloos.

The Indians were Tlingits, Kircheiss said, immigrants from Alaska. At first they had looked for work along the upper Yukon, then the nickel mines on Rankin Inlet were the big magnet; but once these came under German administration and wage earners were replaced by forced laborers—Alaskan Russians and Siberians—the Tlingits formed small settlements. They lived there now, sprinkled across the giant plain, and eked out an existence trapping fur animals, doing odd jobs, and working in the fur trade. The redskins Kircheiss had hired were descendants of the widely dispersed Wolf race, more specifically the tribe of the Porpoise, which was also their totem animal. The tribe, once feared for its cruelty throughout the Northwest territory—Schultz-Rüssing had mentioned them in his textbook—now lived in relative harmony with the Eskimos, which meant that whenever they could, the redskins beat up the Eskimos and let it go at that. The Porpoise Indians venerated their big Chief Adolf Hitler (they called him simply "Big Hit") and had been, as Kircheiss assured his listeners, big buyers of winter-relief insignias.

The evening had passed in a gloomy mood; no one spoke. They had canned fish, marmalade, bread, and a little condensed milk—scanty rations. People moved close to one another inside the sleeping bags in order to taste the animal warmth; a cutting wind whistled through the air holes in the blanket. Sigga lay between Jugurtha and the engineer; with her pointed yellow nose and dark eye holes she resembled a dead demon. But somehow she remained beautiful. Jugurtha, who did not close an eye but feigned sleep, felt more than saw how she let the man paw her in secret with his nail-bitten hands. It disgusted him. Finally the blubber candle, which was supposed to burn in every bivouac, had burned down. Deep black night was everywhere, and despite the snoring around him he gradually lost consciousness.

Again they were on their way. Sigga had vomited after breakfast, so he had a pretty good idea just how far the one-sided night games had gone. After their love scene in the plane she had thrown up too. In her condition she could no longer tolerate such excitement. She was finished.

Jugurtha noticed it for the first time shortly after lunch (a swallow of hot tea and a piece of bread with margarine each, just as in the morning, and a Vitamin C tablet). The gentle little waves which at times (those cursed optical illusions) he saw roll toward him under a black sky were not waves of snow, nor did they roll, but were millions of flowers with great pale blossoms, a kind of edelweiss. They swayed under a breeze, lifting and sinking their heads. This flower-filled meadow reached to the horizon, and Jugurtha recalled a similar sight the spring they had marched through Greece.

Only up here in the north everything was much more sinister, forceful, threatening. For now the flowers grew man-high, even as high as bushes and trees, they bent apart before him, formed streets or valleys and then closed behind. They were thickets, not meadows. Snowy labyrinths. And Jugurtha wondered how the Indian dog drivers retained their sanity.

After a while he became confused and took off his snow goggles. The vision had vanished, everything was once again white and uniform and motionless. They glided across the snow, the driver hunched calmly in front of him, the huskies keeping time with their heads as they pulled the sled. He saw their sinewy legs move fast, saw when they turned their bushy neck-frills, their dark faces, as if they were blackened by smoke, the clever, bright lights of their eyes and the steaming breath that burst from their jaws. Far behind them the motor sled with the sick on it rattled peacefully. The thickets had been walls of snow, akin to women's bodies, as beautiful and as curved, or sloping shores of ice-covered rivers they had crossed. Perhaps true meadows (not illusory, deceitful ones) did exist here, but then only during the short summer; Kircheiss had said the tundra burst into bloom then—and that the sky above it was full of arctic mosquitoes, giant swarms, whole clouds of them, that hung brown and immobile like curtains in the air. Kircheiss had used just those words.

Ah, here they were again, the visions! Was he feverish, or did he dream with eyes open? The air turned black with mosquitoes, swarming close to him. He heard their deep humming. And the waving, surging meadow again, only this time the image seemed much more graphic, smoldering. He could now take the flowers into his hands, while at first they had seemed small and cabbage-like. They felt lifeless, like edelweiss made of felt. But later they grew higher, more luxurious, swayed in the wind like opulent women's bodies. When he bent aside the pale blooms he saw emerald and blue shimmer below. Were these abysses filled with a strange and extinct vegetation—or were they ice flowers—was it ice? Yes, of course, it was ice. For when the thin snow spurted under the runners, the glassy ground beneath appeared. The sleds ahead of him had made the track shiny, and you could see frozen moss and grass through the ice. They drove across a thick, bright-green mirror. The runners crunched and sang on the ice, the Indian clicked his tongue or shouted roughly when the dogs slipped, stopped, growled, and shook themselves. And not the fake flowers had been lifeless but his own fingers were—up to the elbows. The fur mittens weren't worth a damn.

The wilderness was veined with rivers, sprinkled with small lakes and water holes. Jugurtha had seen it on the geologists' map. Their journey across the ice meant that they had either left or lost the overland highway—the only one in the district—and that they had to orient themselves by radio and compass. He knew that the pilots at the head of the convoy had heard coded position reports on their transistor radios, now sent out regularly from AL Ju 12. That camp was their polar star.

Yesterday evening they heard a report that AL Ju 12 had sent out an SS rescue corps in a southeasterly direction. A village called Kuharuk, once inhabited by Eskimos and Dukhobors (the English name was Ten Little Fingers), had been selected as the rendezvous: Laale and Kircheiss knew it well. According to their calculations, they should link up in the morning hours of the third day; that would be tomorrow.

The meadow had dissolved into vapor, again he saw nothing through his green eyeglasses but the endless snow desert. Only the deep humming of the mosquitoes had remained, even increased. A ringing in his ears; from force of habit he held his nose and squeezed his breath against his nostrils in order to balance the pressure—nevertheless the humming became louder. What was up? Suddenly the caravan stopped, they heard the deafening "Whoa" of the Indians. He saw the engineer and the geologists run back along the row of sleds, wave their arms wildly and shout something. Hastily and stiffly the grotesquely bundled figures tumbled out of the sleds. His Hiwi too had jumped down and run away as fast as a weasel. Before Jugurtha could understand what they had called to him, he knew: planes.

Quickly he rolled out of his bear rug and jumped down, almost colliding with the Dane. "Take cover," somebody yelled, "everybody take cover." Instinctively he ducked in the snow, but the ground around him was as flat as a board and did not afford the slightest protection. The motor sled! Sigga! With two giant bounds he was there. She slept or was unconscious. He had to lift her like some dead weight from her bed. The sled driver and the second sick person (he seemed to have improved; Jugurtha had even seen him on skis) helped hide her rigid body underneath the chassis. They too crawled under it and now they lay breathless below the warm, steaming motor.

They pressed their bodies flat on the ground as the plane flew toward them with a drilling roar. Close over their heads. Low-flying planes. Despite the noise they heard the dry chatter of machine guns and the thud of bullets into the sled's metal plates. Little snow fountains shot into the air on their right and left, ice was pulverized, metal splintered. They had barely caught their breath before the next plane roared over them. Again hammer blows rattled with lightning speed against the groaning metal, and the traces of machine-gun fire chased tiny wind spouts across the snow. In between a dull cracking. Again and again. Endless. Jugurtha concluded from the flight pattern that only a few planes were involved. But the attack lasted an eternity.

Perhaps it was just a matter of minutes. Long and anxious minutes. When they dared to come out, it had grown noticeably darker; night was near. The attackers appeared to have withdrawn. They heard loud groaning and moaning, an occasional scream of intense agony, flames crackling, but the worst on the nerves was the incessant howling of the dogs. What they saw resembled a slaughterhouse: The dying rolled whining in the snow, the wounded crawled slowly on all fours among the burning sleds; outside in the phosphorescent snow lay black dolls with rigid, strangely disjointed movements. It smelled of fire and shit and blood. The quickly-falling night threw her gray sheet over the gruesome sight.

The three of them lifted Sigga back into the sled, which had suffered quite a bit of damage. She looked around her with wild eyes and did not seem to grasp anything. The Indian Hiwi was busy with his motor, nothing else interested him. Jugurtha saw Doris and the other girl, Thusnelda or whatever her name was, come up. Doris limped heavily, a piece of shrapnel had grazed her, "nothing serious," and she had bound up her own wound. Jugurtha asked the girl, still shaky from her experience, to take care of Sigga. Unfortunately the first-aid kit was ruined.

Was the supply sled still intact? There it was, blown on its side, broken, a charred skeleton. Only a single dog was still alive and miraculously unhurt, the cadavers of the four others were stuck in their harnesses. While Jugurtha and the young industrialist searched for supplies—they only managed to find a few cans—the poor devil jumped up on them and licked their mittens, whining piteously.

The enemy had either fired incendiary ammunition or dropped canisters of gasoline (it didn't look like napalm). One of the wounded, who asked Jugurtha for a cigarette, told him he had seen a stream of fire break from the attacking planes, but that must have been his imagination. They learned later that the so-called rear guard, about twenty-five sleds and their passengers, who had driven behind the Red Cross sled, had suffered the worst damage. (The remnants of the last few sleds still lay strewn across the ice of the little river.) The load of carbines had been hit several times, the boxes of munition had caught fire and blown up, fortunately not all at once, but one after another.

Suddenly shots rang out. Jugurtha ducked quickly and pulled out his pistol. The industrialist was unarmed. Jugurtha's carbine must lie nearby in the snow; he had thrown it away when he brought Sigga to safety. The firing grew more intense, they could hear the tac-tac-tac of a machine gun. There was no point lying here and freezing fast to the ground. He had to get in touch with the leaders—where in hell were the engineer, Kircheiss, and Laale? Were they still alive? Bullets whirled around his head as he looked for the rifle and found it. Traces of machine-gun fire from the low-flying planes ran through the snow, the butt of his rifle too was damaged. For the present the industrialist could stay with the Red Cross sled and defend the women with that old 98 K.

In the twilight of the arctic night, Jugurtha jumped or crawled forward. The fires had begun to die away, snowflakes fell from a glowering, low sky, a sign that it was warmer than it had been in the morning. Rifle fire faded only to flare up now and again after short pauses. It seemed to come from all sides, but out here in the steppes sound could be deceptive. Some of the shots might well come from his own people.

From time to time someone called to him: a seriously wounded man, whose fur was drenched in blood, would plead for the *coup de grâce;* he did not pay any attention. Only once was he taken aback. A body hung out from one of the wrecked sleds. The bullet must have hit the man as he jumped out, his face was turned skyward. He knew that jovial smile, still winning out even as a grimace. It belonged to the Styrian steel director. Look, dying could be cheerful too.

The engineer and the geologists—they were still alive. He recognized their voices as he came closer. They had obviously managed to restore some order out of the chaos, at least at the front of the column. Everywhere people hunched behind the sleds or what was left of them, rifles at the ready. It was quite impressive. He talked to someone who seemed familiar—oh yes, they'd been on guard duty together yesterday and he'd never stopped telling jokes, Köpfler jokes, and some very unappetizing ones at that. The man said that Kircheiss was trying to put together the FM unit stowed away in the lead sled. They wanted to send out SOS messages and contact the AL Ju 12 troop, which had radio equipment, to ask for transport planes and helicopters from the camp and so on. If that could succeed . . . ?

"How is it down your way?" the engineer asked. He seemed intentionally to have overheard Jugurtha's Ostmarkian "Heitla."

"Rotten," Jugurtha said. "From rotten to hell." The engineer's snotty tone annoyed him. "We've hardly any supplies left."

"Go back and bring everyone who can still hold a rifle back up here. We'll have to form a hedgehog. Leave the wounded where they are—we can't help them anyway, and they're just extra eaters. And weapons, whatever you can scratch together and what's left of the food. Every bullet is precious, and every can. Those over there . . ."

The *Oberbaurat* made an indefinite gesture and took up his binoculars. The conversation took place under cover of the lead sled, a heavy, bull-like, tracked vehicle generally used for snow removal or pulling a snow blower. It had suffered almost no damage. Jugurtha looked around the corner. In the dusky dark he saw shots light up all around—streaks, chains. Slugs slammed in everywhere.

"They have mortars, too. Unfortunately. And an awful lot of people. Our chances right now are a hundred to nothing. A really big crock of shit. And when day comes, we'll have those horseflies back. There were only two of them, old crates, but they did a good job for themselves."

Kircheiss came in view. He took the gaps between the sleds in bold leaps. For the rest he stayed close to the ground.

"The radio works, chief. I've been trying to establish contact with the troop for quite a while—nothing. I heard nothing. The devil knows what's up." Yes, the devil knew what was up.

"Keep at it, Kircheiss!" And as Kircheiss chased away again in his panther leaps—Laale had motioned to him from the distance—the engineer shouted after him: "We've got to get through, *we've got to!*" And again turning back to Jugurtha: "The goddamn Nanooks got us into that bloody mess—bunch of pigs! Nothing but traitors. They all ought to be shot or hanged. Nevertheless I still like Nanook's ass better than an American face." (But Jugurtha thought: You idiot, why did you take the Indians and not the Eskimos?)

A mighty roar from the other side, a shell howled toward them. You could hear it fall on the ground far out, it sounded like a heap of wet laundry. No detonation, though. "They're finding the range," the engineer said, more to himself than to Jugurtha. Both had thrown themselves to the ground. "Medium caliber, I'd guess—did you hear anything? It's not an impact fuse, it's a delayed one. Stay on the ground."

Half a minute later the grenade exploded, its steel splinters whipping all the way to where they were lying.

They crouched on the ground, expecting another explosion at any moment.

"How is your wife?" the engineer asked.

"Bad enough." Jugurtha shook with anger. The swine was to blame for Sigga's poor condition today—Blondie indeed!

"She suffers from atomic decay, rot in the bone marrow. I read it back at the camp in her dossier. I took an interest in Frau von Eycke right away"—he said Sigga's real name with ironic emphasis—". . . Leyen, be a man and finish it. There's no point, man; do you want the Nanooks and their saw knives to do it? Landgrave, Get Tough. That's a party order."

What that shit didn't know! Frau von Eycke. He stuck his nose into everything, didn't he, not just antiparticles. Party orders—the hell with all party orders.

"Don't do a sloppy job, Leyen. Have a lot of fun!"

Jugurtha felt drugged. As he crawled back, he saw that despite the fusillade, efforts were underway to build a kind of redoubt out of the wrecked sledges, a four-cornered bulwark. It was supposed to be a rough-hewn fortress but looked more like a mousetrap. A better name for Enterprise Winnetou: Enterprise Mousetrap—or Shithouse.

"Have a lot of fun," he muttered. He crawled past the eternally smiling director and past the dying man who had asked him for deliverance (and who still moved). And finally he reached the supply sled with the whining dog. The animal greeted him with a long-drawn-out howl and tore at its strap.

Doris and Thusnelda were hunched trembling and half frozen behind the hospital sled. The shooting was especially bad here. They had lost their protector. The young man lay face down in the snow, the carbine under his body. He was careless and had been hit right after Jugurtha left. The Hiwi too was gone—he fled after he had tried and failed to restart the motor. Jugurtha ordered the girls to go up front and take some supplies with them . . . they could surely be of some use in the camp. He'd follow with Sigga. The girls were so frightened they obeyed without objection. Jugurtha saw Doris' despairing look.

Party orders! Have a lot of fun! For a long time he looked into Sigga's marble face. He imprinted her petrified features deeply in his mind. Of course it would be the best thing . . . she wouldn't feel much. He couldn't leave her behind, nor drag her to the camp. And what would happen there? The engineer would do it. Jugurtha's legs were suddenly numb, his hands trembled and his intestines growled. Weakling, Weakling. Quick, before you collapse!

He freed her head and bent it slowly forward. Then he spread her mane across her face so her neck was bare. With thumb and forefinger of his left hand he groped along her neck looking for the uppermost neck vertebra and thought: C-One and C-Two. The scene in that bedroom stood before his mind's eye, when he had knelt on the couch, the hair of the pendulum in his fingers . . . his amber witch!

Party orders. Have a lot of fun.

With his right hand he put the pistol against the exact spot where the neck stopped and the back of the head began. At that moment the trembling in his hands was so strong that Sigga's head bounced back and forth in his arms. (If only she would not awake from her deep sleep!) As he had learned to do in the SS, he slanted the barrel up and pressed the trigger. Once again. Then he blacked out.

The cold revived him. His whole body shook. Under an irresistible urge to look his victim in the face, he swung himself up on the sled. But he didn't dare do it. He felt sick enough to vomit and he fought against passing out. Coward! Weakling! He put his hand under the blanket and felt the warmth that still remained there in the sled's cot. How long had she been dead? Four, five minutes? More? For her they might just as well have been four, five, six million million years. Mechanically he thought: From her point of view she had never been alive.

Everything was senseless—and nonsense—life was an asshole. The pistol lay in the glowing snow, he put it in his pocket, looked down for a long time at his hands, turned them over and over. He tried to bend his fingers while he thought of something quite different. His fingers were so numb that he had trouble squeezing them into the fur mittens. Now it seemed as if the shots were coming much closer; or did his ears deceive him? He lifted his head and stared out into the night. The dead lay like coffins in front of the wrecked sled, but farther away . . . there he saw dark, longish objects which now and again moved. They crawled. They crawled toward him.

He slid over to the industrialist and pulled at his carbine. The dead man refused to give it up, just as Senkpiehl had refused to give up his weapon.

The animal! He freed the dog, but at once was sorry. For the dog howled with joy, danced like crazy around him, jumped up and licked his face. Shut up, you beast! Far away the enemy's dogs answered. It seemed as if the night itself barked. In order to quiet the animal Höllriegl—there's no point calling him Jugurtha any longer—held his snout shut for a while. The dog understood and, sniffing, followed his liberator who, like him, walked on all fours and therefore must be one of his own kind.

There were the cans they had been able to save. Höllriegl let them lie there, and smiled coldly. Having finished his business here, he'd quickly have to take care of another. He hurried on, crawling or jumping from cover to cover.

God knows, what an asshole of the world! His life was shit, the Führer was shit, everything was one great big crock of shit. Again he felt sick and nervously flatulent. If only he could vomit, vomit everything out of himself.

But he couldn't even do that, unfortunately. He had to swallow it all down. He noticed that he was dragging something behind him. The dog halters. He passed his friend, the steel-company director —the straps would have fitted him beautifully. *Pour le mérite* first class. A sympathetic gentleman, an adopted Ostmarker. Heitla.

The Hiwis had really worked hard; you had to give them that. A real Wild West fort, just like the movies. A fortress of debris. "A Mighty Fortress is Our God." Where was he—our God? And who was he? Bullets whistled through the night, shots came from front and back, apparently no clear fronts had been drawn. We're here in the fortress, they're out there in the snow. The enemy had dug in all around them and was firing from all barrels—he must have an awful lot of ammunition. It was more like a prize shoot. In this critical zone Höllriegl shoved himself forward centimeters at a time; the dog stayed close to him. (How comforting a dog's wet snout can be.) From where he was it was obvious that the engineer's fortress was completely encircled.

He waved and shouted in order to prevent his own people from shooting at him. "Kircheiss!" he screamed as loudly as he could, and "Laale!" They were the only names he knew. When he was just a few steps from the barricade—someone had hoisted a Reich battle flag—he saw a flash of lightning far out on the plain. He heard a dull explosion and almost simultaneously the impact. The pressure wave felt like a hot wall. Things whirled around him, and something big and heavy fell vertically from the sky into the snow right ahead of him. The dog had snuggled up close and whined. He suddenly felt easier in his belly—he had shit in his pants. Funny, he thought, there's no question of digestion in the heroic epics, the ancient Germanic heroes had no intestines. But now he'd have to go ahead.

He made use of the pause to climb over the wall of sledges, the dog behind him. A joyful barking. Well, there he was.

The refugees climbed from their holes like moles. Someone said that a reconnaissance troop was being put together to go out front; they'd asked for him. Höllriegl shirked it as well as he could, he'd had everything up to here. He saw the engineer select people, mostly Hiwis, judging from their clothes and bearing. Laale was among them, he seemed to interpret, and then Kircheiss and the two women joined the group. At that moment the engineer, who stood on the chain of the motor sled, offered a perfectly marvelous target.

Höllriegl sat down comfortably behind a sled and took the laser out of his holster. Laser kills silently, only hisses, an underhand weapon. All you had to do was push the button when the target was in the range finder. This time Höllriegl didn't tremble; he had the steadiest hands in the world, nor did the flow of tears bother him as he aimed the laser and looked through the lens. The engineer appeared quite enlarged in the crosswires; in this situation not exactly an advantage for him. Nevertheless: an admirable man and a light of science. So! Höllriegl manipulated the mechanism and saw the engineer shrink as he charred. Greetings from Blondie!

He heard the women scream, everyone was screaming, almost like a chorus. He tore out his pistol and put it against his temple, handle turned up, thumb on the trigger. With his left hand he pressed the mouth, it was icy and painful, against the skin of his head. It clicked, clicked, clicked. Damn, the gun was empty. Where had he put that magazine?

Feverishly he searched his pockets, a great fury seized him, he wished he could beat his own head in with the gun. The dog had returned and danced around him, eyes shining with delight.

He saw Kircheiss and the Hiwis run toward him. Somebody must have seen him. It was too late to load. They wouldn't get him. *Not they!*

He jumped over the barricades and down to the ground, the dog with him. Then he ran out into the white-waving fields, toward the welcome bullets.